That Other Realm of Freedom

That Other Realm of Freedom

Barry Nonweiler

GAY
MEN'S
PRESS

First published 1983 by Gay Men's Press, P O Box 247,
London N15 6RW, England.

World copyright © Barry Nonweiler 1983

British Library Cataloguing in Publication Data

Nonweiler, Barry
  That other realm of freedom
  I. Title
  823'.914 F   PP6064.0/

  ISBN 0 907040 19 5

Cover art Sue Dray
Typeset by MC Typeset, 34 New Road, Chatham, Kent
Printed by Book Plan (Billing & Sons Ltd), Worcester

For Tim and Dick and David and Caryl and Verena,
some token of my affection and esteem.

The attention and criticism of several people has been
important to me in writing this book, but I would
particularly like to thank Philip Derbyshire, Richard Dipple
and John Keidan for their support and their suggestions.

Through heroisms and deaths and sacrifices,
Always for the poor and despised, always for the outcast
and oppressed,
Through kinship with nature, and the free handling of all
forms and customs,
Through the treasured teaching of inspired ones – never lost
and never wholly given to the world, but always emerging–
Through love, faithful love and comradeship, at last
emancipating the soul into that other realm (of freedom and
joy) into which it is permitted no mortal to enter –
Thus to realise the indissoluble compact, to reveal the form
of humanity,
To you, dear comrade, I transmit this charge . . .

Edward Carpenter

The Elder Soldier in the Brotherhood to the Younger.

PROLOGUE

It seemed he could see so far. He had wanted to climb to the top of the hill, setting off at a run up the endless slope of waving grass that rose where the white sands ended, the wind sliding all over him, exultation rising at the stirred boyishness of his legs – only to find at last that the summit still lay far off, seemed in fact no nearer at all. Instead the standing-stone was there only a few paces away, rearing up sudden and dark from the pale grass bent double beneath the wind. Slowly, quietly, as though he were in the presence of a living creature, he had taken a few steps towards it. From far below on the sea-shore it looked like a pointer: but here, close to, a monument of the past, it seemed oppressive, meaningless, casting a vast cold shadow that reached out to engulf him, its surface harsh and scarred. Panting, Simon had turned his back and leant uncomfortably against its unyielding lumpy substance, slowly lifting his eyes from the barren ground.

Beneath him the beach along which he had run was almost lost to view; only a thin cream ribbon marked the edge of the wide sweep of the bay, which flickered green and purple beneath the tall summer sky while the wind herded slow arcs of wave across it, one after another. Further out the land seemed to lose all certainty, entering the sea hesitantly in a school of little islands grey and hazy in the distance, tiny uninhabited unconnected points, fading at last into the blur of the endless ocean, rolling out towards the horizon – beyond which, invisible and unimaginably far, lay a new world.

Perhaps this would be the last holiday with his family in the islands he would ever have. The day after tomorrow they were going back to Glasgow. It was the beginning of his second year at university, and he was going to move in with his cousin Annie and her boyfriend Philip who had more or less taken him under their wing several months ago.

The wind gently washed him with the fresh smell of the sea. He held his face out to it as to a kiss, giving himself all up to a regret. He was shedding years of dreams like a skin he had grown out of; he was alone again with the mountains and the islands. For so long freedom, independence, self-definition had seemed to lie only here where the secluded earth itself was continually vanishing into mists, drifts of empty loneliness that slid down over its hunched shoulders. Finding himself in a strange valley, looking up into the inscrutable vacancy, he never knew what magnificent peaks might rise above, what far views might lie ahead; all merged into a grey susurration of hopes and fantasies. He had wanted to leave and live here, free from the solid reality of other human beings who so often terrified him, and with whom he never used to feel at ease let alone at home. And above all, forgetful of those endless little lusts for members of the rugby team or television stars which seemed to stalk by night through his imagination like comic-book Red Indians, with bare torsos and single-minded purpose and complete unreality. They somehow seemed to fall from him here, lost in the thrill of the responsiveness to the land of his moods.

But now everything was changed. The love of the land seemed an adolescent phase of which he felt almost ashamed. From the moment of his first spending time with Philip and Annie they had opened up to him a strange new world of literature and politics. A tough haunted world: Dostoyevsky and Kafka, Japanese poetry, protest against the Vietnam war. A world of human achievements on the one hand and human sufferings on the other of which he had been quite unaware. Readily he had longed to assimilate the achievements as sincerely and yet vaguely as he longed to relieve the suffering and injustice.

Simon felt akin to Annie for her fragility and reticence: and vice versa. Yet it was she who had shown him also how to be free from care as only those can be who live in it as their element. And the fondness that passed continually between her and Philip stood in a revelatory contrast to the tenseness and tiredness of his parents' relationship – which was kept together as much as anything, he often felt, only by an endless succession of brothers and sisters, from all of whom as the eldest he felt cut off. Philip the schoolteacher, solid and bearded, his shadowy brows continually clenched in thought, exuded a sense of rightful possession of all life had to offer that left Simon breathlessly admiring.

At school Simon Palmer had felt trapped, alienated, confused. He had been bright and hard-working because it was a way to cope. He had taken refuge in second-rate poetry and novels but it had been impossible for him to imagine a real world outside. The city he lived in, to which the family had moved from the south of England some twelve years ago, had been only an ill-defined intimidating backdrop to his daily incarceration, through which he would pass quickly, uncomprehending and isolated. But the affection and respect of Philip and Annie, which at first had come only as a surprise, had slowly convinced him that there was a place for him among other human beings after all. Now, in their company, undreamed of for him, in warm moist pubs and the dingy rented rooms of friends, the city unfolded itself in nights of drunkenness and laughter and friendship.

He slid down the stone and sat on the hard ground, feeling for the first time a moment of chill as the sun slipped behind a cloud, closing down the brilliance of the sea. Somehow for months on end, dazed perhaps by the novelty of it all, not just the growth of friendships but the whole context of strange new thought about the world, he had been able to shut his sexuality safely away in some dark west wing of his being. It had always been so private in any case, quite unrelated to the reality of his day-to-day existence, a secret garden where the unknown weakling took doomed fruitless exercise. There was no one to know of it but himself, and when he ignored it, it seemed that it had just gone away.

It had no connection to reality. When for example in his last year at school, he had noted the relaxation of legal penalties against homosexuals in England with approval, it was only out of a vague liberal idealism which he had acquired mainly from reading poetry, not because he felt it relevant to him, or to anyone he knew, for that matter.

Along the horizon the gentle summer sky was beginning to cloud over. He drew his knees towards him, clasping them, and laid his chin upon them.

He had become involved with Philip and Annie through a student drama production – of a French farce. It was not long afterwards that whenever they found themselves alone, Philip began to regale Simon with tales of his past sexual exploits. There was little pretence that the tales were historically accurate – grotesque, exuberantly inventive fantasies of cunning and prowess that they were, a hunter's tales, constructed out of what might be, not even what might have been. And this seemed in accord with their immediate purpose, which Simon sensed was Philip's clinical trial of Simon's reactions, timid and blank as he must for the most part have seemed to him. And his reaction – a discovery to himself – was to find the stories quite simply irrelevant: it was as though he were listening to an account of the sexual behaviour of some remote animal species, hippopotamuses or giraffes or some such. And yet, if put to it, he could not have explained satisfactorily even to himself why he felt like this.

Gradually, during the course of the year, he had got to know Calum, a quiet gently-spoken person who was doing some of the same courses. Mutually suspicious at first, out of a sense of politely suppressed intellectual rivalry, hesitantly they had grown to become closer and closer friends, until by the beginning of the summer they saw one another at least every other day, and frequently spent the night at one another's family houses. Simon felt at times an excited closeness to Calum that he never felt with Philip and Annie, the fact of whose couplehood seemed to mark them off irrevocably as belonging to a world which Simon supposed he would never himself enter.

Then, quite suddenly, Calum found himself a girlfriend.

Simon shivered in the oncoming grey weather, restlessly shifting his position, trying to make himself comfortable against the standing-stone.

At first, nothing much changed. For a few days they seemed to see one another as often as ever before, as indeed it never occurred to Simon they should not, and the only difference was that Debbie became a frequent topic of their conversation. And then Calum disappeared. Simon waited for a while, puzzled as much as anything; then he began to phone, only to find that Calum was never at home. At what seemed long last, though perhaps it was not much after a week, Calum turned up one afternoon to visit, with Debbie. They stayed for a few hours, and then to Simon's surprise they left. Slowly, very slowly, following a succession of similarly brief and periodic visits, Simon began to adjust to what had really happened, and to realise that it demanded a total reassessment of his position in life.

Just what this might involve was brought forcefully home to him one mild evening, as he waited with Calum and Debbie for a bus, after the three of them had caught up with an afternoon showing of *Help!* The words of the theme-song running monotonously through his head, Simon watched a puppy-eyed young man in a corduroy jacket emerge out of the distance and with a ripple of chubby ringed fingers greet Calum briefly as he passed. Simon was sure he had never seen the man before, and yet he felt a strange sense of recognition, almost like a persistent physical noise inside him, which seemed to compel him to track the man with his gaze, even turning his head to follow his progress beyond Calum's shoulder, feeling his pulse quicken with some enormous but unidentified anticipation. And at that point the stranger himself, already a few steps on, quite suddenly turned and looked back over his shoulder as though he had been called, his eyes at once homing in on Simon's momentarily with a look Simon found almost impossible to read, as if of exchanged secret reassurance. Then he moved on his way, leaving behind a faint but suddenly unmistakable trace of perfume, which struck Simon, in the dazedness that at once came over him, like some overheard muttered wickedness.

"Who was that?" said Debbie to Calum, almost aggressively.

"Oh that's Paul," Calum answered her, with the tone of referring to something sadly familiar. "He played the piano for the revue we did last year. He plays the piano very well."

"He looks like a poof," said Debbie, burying her hands in her pockets and looking disgusted.

"He is a poof," said Calum, picking up the final word by its tip and dropping it as if it were an offensive object. "He's Dennis's – boyfriend. Dennis used to make the tea at rehearsals."

"Well, if he's a poof, what did you say hallo to him for?" Debbie shook her long red hair from her angular face, and turned to look challengingly at Calum.

"Well, you can't deny that they exist," said Calum, with cold discomfort. "It's a fact of life, and I don't see that people should be ostracised for something that's not their fault. It happens to make my skin creep, and I don't want to know anything about it, but they can't help being queer. I suppose we should feel sorry for them."

"Sorry for them!" said Debbie, panting with outrage, her eyes blazing. "It's – it's unnatural."

"It's natural for them. They're just like that." Calum's voice had become quiet and reasonable, but aloof.

"Well, I think it's disgusting," said Debbie weakly, after a moment, her eyes pacing from side to side in the hunt for a defence of her argument. Suddenly they sprang questioningly on Simon. She said, "What do you think about them, Simon?"

He felt himself blushing helplessly, drastically, as if he were catching fire in front of her, his mouth and lips going completely dry, his heart pounding so fast his chest literally ached. He opened his mouth to speak, and finding that no sound came, closed it again like a startled goldfish, hoping that nothing strange had been noticed. Finally he said in a hoarse strained voice, "Well, I don't really think there's anything wrong in it." He was terrified at his own audacity, and had to actually struggle to stop his muscles from wincing, as if in anticipation of not just Debbie, but the very air itself perhaps landing a physical blow upon him.

This was the first moment in his life he had actually confronted the fact that among the friends he had come to trust he was secretly and irremediably one of "them"; that his very existence, without his doing any more, was a source of horror if not loathing to every other human being he knew. It was a realisation that had little, if anything, in common with the crises of private self-disgust and self-castigation that had punctuated his schoolday dreams; and with the force of an earthquake it promptly shattered every social institution to which he had been looking for security.

Fortunately just as he finished speaking the bus appeared round the corner. As it drew up, Debbie stepped quickly and determinedly onto the platform, leaving Calum and Simon lagging behind. Turning back to look down at them, she said scornfully, "You're a couple of nice boys, I must say." The nearness of Calum's physical presence, as they stepped onto the platform after her, filled Simon with as much fear as if it had been white-hot metal.

And that night, for the first time, he woke alone in the darkness to find that he had had a sexual dream about Calum. He lay for a while and shook with fear, unable to move, as if he had woken from a nightmare and dared not turn his head to find there really was a murderer there, feeling the cold gelatinous liquid inch its way inexorably down his thighs like the pollutant slime of some symbolical snake. The thought had never crossed his conscious mind, but what was more it was a long time since he had had a sexual dream about anyone. Yet there only a few moments ago, the naked white body, visible in every detail, had seemed to lie beside him, to take him in its concerned arms and run its firm warm hands curiously and tenderly about his back and waist, pressing its soft pink mouth against his own. And quite suddenly a sense of terrific imminence had woken him, both too early and too late. He was alone.

Catching his breath, feeling his pulse slow down, he rolled over and climbed out of bed, if nothing else to escape the accusing wetness of the sheets. In a daze he walked from his room to the landing, and stood there for a moment, listening. The house might have been empty, there was not even the sound of sleep: nothing. Suddenly feeling faint, as if his physical powers had been drawn from him by a spell in a nightmare, he leant himself heavily on the banisters, dropping his head and looking down into the dark empty stairwell, as if into the utter aloneness into which he had been cast at the very beginning of his life, never to escape. Wasn't that what lay in store for queers?

He knew something had to be done, and there was precisely nothing that could be done.

All this had happened just a few days before he came with the family to the Hebrides, as so often before. For a few weeks everything seemed held in abeyance. He willingly lost himself once again in the demanding presence of the landscape, or found consolation in the sparse natural growth that was at once so defiant and so tender amid its harsh environment. Finally, he was sure, everything would be well after all. The weather had been unusually kind; today's outrunners were almost the first dark clouds they had seen. There was enduring shelter here in the simplicity of his past. And already the city seemed to call to him with only the open face of companionship, to which he looked forward without awareness of fear.

Drifting past on the hollow sound of the wind, there came a human voice calling "Help!" Although he heard quite distinctly, he could not at once convince himself he had understood. It was hard, even threatening, to believe that anyone in real life should find themselves in a situation where all they could do was shout "Help!" He sat dead still, watching the huge cloud shadows glide slowly over the wrinkled sea towards him, and waited intensely, waited to see if the voice would come again, would confirm its reality. There was nothing but the soothing lamentation of the wind; and again, cutting through it, the word "Help!", infinitely sorry for itself, distrust of everything rushing in, nothing left it but hope.

He stood up and looked pointlessly about him. It was his mother's voice. There was nothing of course to be seen. He was alone. "Help!"

she called again, from endlessly far away, barely recognisable because inconceivable, and then a long string of names, as if it were every name this voice could think of, "Kenneth! Simon!", and so on, through every member of the family, until at last falling over and over into a faintness despairing of its own comprehensibility: "Help! Help! Help!"

He began to walk in the first direction there was, slowly and calmly because to do otherwise would have been acquiescing in unreality. But already he found himself running headlong down the steep straight slope of the hill, the wind flapping and shrieking in his face, his legs picked up and hurled on by the earth itself. Then the daylight went away behind the suddenly forbidding ridge of the hill, and he was stumbling out of breath over the dunes, the solid earth crumbling away beneath him, his feet tied up with loose sand. The wind rustled mournfully through the scarcely living reeds protruding from the sand, which stretched on and on, up and down; and over it in the distance, other tiny figures were visible inching slowly, very slowly. It became so difficult to move: as if in a nightmare, one's greatest efforts got one nowhere, and somewhere in this spider's web the voice calling "Somebody help!". The dunes reached out to block Simon's path, he tried to dodge them, only to find himself cupped at the bottom of yet another. Throwing himself forward, he grabbed at the reeds with his hands, pulling himself up, feeling the sharp sapless quills stabbing his skin; until he found himself suddenly where the dunes rolled over and lay still, and the knuckles of another hill buried themselves in the bone-white sand, gripping the seashore. A little way ahead of him, the dark figure of his father was climbing out of the white sand, as if in slow motion.

His mother lay stretched out on the grass at the bottom of a small slip of broken rocks and scree. One leg stuck out at an odd angle from her body, and a tiny trickle of blood ran down past her eye from a small cut on her forehead. To Simon, as he approached, she looked so graceless and inappropriate, the clothed body that was normally bent busily over the sink or the stove or the sewing lying there like a stranded whale on the mountainside, a small smashed instamatic camera a little way from its hand.

"Kenneth, I've broken my leg," Simon heard her say to his father, in an unlikely voice that still seemed not hers, that might have been produced by a ventriloquist's dummy.

"Don't jump to conclusions, my love," said his father, lowering himself awkwardly and reluctantly to the grass. Simon wondered if he was pale from shock, or from anger at his own helplessness – or from anger at having to treat his wife as a responsibility?

Simon came across the grass and stood at her feet, looking down at her. Her eyes turned towards him, tiny and fearful and pathetic in the great heap of flesh that lay motionless where it had fallen. "I'm sorry Simon," she said. It seemed such a strange thing to say that he just stood there gawping at her, not answering. Amid the bloodless expanse of her face her lower lip began to quiver, and a tear rolled out of her eye and down her cheek. "I'm sorry I spoilt your holiday for you."

He wanted to say something reassuring, something that would make her feel she did not need to apologise for herself, as she did so often, as she had shown him how to, but all he found to say was "Are you sure your leg's broken?", though he could see as well as anybody that it must be. He just hoped he could deceive her for a moment, dangling there at her feet, feeling terrified at being caught out in his own uselessness.

"Yes, I heard it snap as I fell," she said, like a small child patiently pleading to be believed. Simon's father laid his hand stiffly on hers, almost as if he was giving her a bullet to bite on, and her fingers scrabbled round it, tender, desperate, like water round a log. "What will you do, Kenneth? I'm sorry, I was stupid. I should have been more careful, I thought it was safe."

"Don't talk about it, love," said his father along a short sigh, staring horrorstruck into the ground, moving his jaws ruminatingly in bewilderment, his shoulders slumped as if put upon. "One of us will go and phone for the ambulance."

One of Simon's brothers came up beside him, and stood there looking at his mother. Silhouetted against the sky, they seemed to Simon for a moment to tower above her helpless figure like hunters over a seal.

His mother went on anxiously recriminating herself, her throat becoming tense with the effort of her sincerity, her restless eyes looking as if they wanted to leap from her head to plead for her. Simon did not want to listen. "I'm going to hold you all up. I knew I'd do something like this one day. You'll have to go back to Glasgow without me."

"Of course we won't do anything of the sort, love," said his father, running his free hand across his face and through his hair. It could have been a gesture of exasperation, and in the heat of the moment Simon suddenly filled with suspicion and resentment towards him, supposing that the only reason his father wanted to get back to Glasgow on time was to resume one of his endless affairs with becharmed young women.

"Simon!" His father lifted his head, his eyes veiled slits, and spoke to him sharply. "Will you run down the road to the village and telephone?"

The words were a challenge. Simon hated and feared making telephone calls to strangers with a childish fear. The alien disembodied voice coming at him from the plastic filled him with a nightmare panic he had still not overcome. Already he felt his tongue go dry with terror, even as at the same time he began to blush and shuffle with embarrassment, saying nothing, trying to think of a conceivably reasonable excuse for such apparent fastidiousness in the staring face of emergency. For the first time his mother, trying to shift her position, gave a quiet groan, a flake of sound melting at once into silence, undeniable.

"Oh good God, Simon!" his father shouted, ignoring the groan, flinging his gaze down in misery and anger, punching the earth with a big fist. "You're the eldest son of the family, for heaven's sake! You're nearly eighteen. I'm just about fed up making concessions to this stupid behaviour." His head swung up and leant back imperiously, his eyes roved up and down Simon in sheer contempt, the sea wind lifting his hair like a mane. "When are you going to act like a man?"

"Oh, don't go off at the boy now, Kenneth," said his mother quietly, and pathetically, straining at least to turn her head towards her husband and failing. Simon felt himself as it were visibly retrogressing, shrinking away, reduced finally to an object of debate. "Go in the car, Kenneth. It will be quicker. Please. Leave Simon here."

His father leant awkwardly over, swaying clumsily, and dabbed a kiss on his mother's lips. Then he rose up, up to his full height, towering over Simon, and lunged past him, the rough tweed of his jacket brushing against Simon's face. "You can stay here and be a nursemaid," he said under his breath as he passed, not even looking at Simon, striding on down the hill with that laboured gait of one who goes everywhere by car.

Another of Simon's brothers and his sisters had joined the first, and the four of them stood apart, talking quietly with one another, occasionally looking across at Simon, waiting to see what he would do.

Simon crossed the few steps of windswept space and knelt by his mother's silent motionless form. He dared not touch her, he felt useless and unusable. Her eyes turned slowly towards him, half-apologetic, half lost in bewildered terror. He thought, Somehow you always taught me that men had a right to feel helpless, that we had a right to expect someone out there to look after us.

He fumbled for something to say as frozen fingers might fumble to do up a button. "Does it hurt?" he asked.

His brothers and sisters, watching from a distance, turned towards one another and exchanged inaudible comments.

"It's not too bad now." Her voice struggled up from some remote place besieged by fear. She looked away forlornly into the sky, grey now, with a touch of damp chill coming in on the wind.

Most of all I learnt from you something you never intended, he thought. I watched you and I learned how to suffer. I was never interested in learning from my father how to act.

Silence came. He hunched his shoulders and shivered. At last he said warily, "How did it happen?"

"I don't know. I was just trying to finish up the film in the camera you gave me. I was feeling so pleased with myself, and I was being very careful. Really I was being very careful. And then I just slipped. I don't know how it happened."

A horror of human vulnerability crept all over Simon. "I think the camera's broken now," he said.

"Oh Simon, I'm afraid." His mother whimpered, like a trampled puppy, and suddenly her hand grabbed his hard, and clutched it as though someone were trying to steal it from her. "They'll have to put me out to set it, I know. I'm afraid. I'm afraid of never coming round again. Don't laugh at me."

The universe seemed a hostile place to Simon, threatening and deceiving on every side. There was no safety after all; even as one felt most secure, everything gave way suddenly and inexplicably beneath one. The world shattered at the very point of manipulation. His hand lay stiff and inert in his mother's, seemed to him as useless as a twig thrown to someone drowning in a quicksand, and he had to jog his memory to remember what he had just heard her say. "Oh I don't think that kind of thing happens these days," he said with little conviction.

His mother shivered. "I'm very cold," she said softly, an excuse not a plea.

Clumsily, Simon took his jacket off, getting his arm stuck in the sleeve as he did so. He laid it over her and it dwindled into futility, a tiny flimsy rag lost in the exposed spaces of his mother's wounded body. Helplessness overwhelmed him. It seemed impossible for one human being ever to reach another, we were all walled off once and for all in our own inaccessibility. Compassion, thrown out again and again, fell short each time.

One of his brothers came up the hill with a tartan rug they had used to picnic on, and wrapped his mother in it. "You'll be alright now," he said. "Dad will soon be back." He picked off Simon's jacket by the cuff of one sleeve and handed it back to Simon in silence. "Shall I go and see if there's any tea left in the thermos?" he said to their mother.

"Oh yes, please," she said, her eyes wet with tears. "My mouth's all dry."

Simon stood to put his jacket on, the strengthening wind flapping its hanging sleeves, and saw his father in the distance coming back along the sand, erect, purposeful, sure.

"Daddy's coming," he said with some relief.

He thought, Once you said you would lose any of us sooner than him. You used to tell me, as I lay in bed in my pyjamas, precociously questioning after bedtime prayers, how you had been a poor brick-layer's daughter who was carried off for love by a handsome bank-manager's son, with great prospects as an academic. You used to make

16

marriage seem a mystery, a goal, an experience the unlocking of which alone initiated one into the life of a complete human being: unmarried, one remained somehow incomplete.

"Simon, sit by me again," came his mother's voice from beneath him, a strange naked voice, unashamedly defenceless. "Sit by me and hold my hand."

He sat and offered his hand diffidently, rather as one might offer something in response to a request in a foreign language one was not sure one had understood. The scarcely warm and yet electric flesh of his mother's hand closed round it, the fingers slipping in and out, searching for reassurance and seemingly finding it. He felt his own hand become soft and steady with reassurance. Amazement at the reality of the contact dazed him.

His father loomed up, a tall black shadow against the sky, and at once he pulled his hand away and scampered aside like a timid animal to make way for him. His father knelt and held out a solid hand of real comfort with such unhesitating confidence, seeming to radiate capability as he spoke. "The doctor will be here in a few minutes, my love, and the ambulance is following him." Simon felt again his limbs, his tongue dangling from him in feeble uselessness. His father's purposeful efficiency seemed so remote, unattainable. He wondered why he had been cursed with his own terrified passive fecklessness.

"Why did this happen to me?" he heard his mother say earnestly, tearfully, as if she really thought there was a relevant answer. "I knew something like this would happen to me one day." The wind whistled through the following silence.

"Accidents happen, love," said his father with a distant certainty.

Looking up, Simon saw the doctor coming along the beach, a squat aged figure in tweeds with a resilient gait, one hand holding his fisherman's hat against the wind. Behind him a long knotted string of men from the nearest village were moving sinuously in uneven bunches, as an undertow of shyness drew some back while a surge of curiosity swept others forward. Slowly, slowly, they advanced up the dunes, coming together at last in a wide arc behind the doctor, shambling persistently through the pale sands. Loudly panting the doctor stepped onto the grass and came up the hill, calling out a brisk greeting into the wind as he did so. Simon backed away and leant half-hidden against a boulder, watching timidly. The islanders came to a stop round the bottom of the slope and stood motionless in silent groups, old and young together, their eyes intent, staring at the woman with the English accent laid out on the slab of the grass, and at her strange awkward family dangling around her in their city pallor and feebleness, as they might stare at the life-and-death struggles of fish or insects. Bent over Simon's mother, the doctor manipulated her leg as if it belonged to a lifeless puppet. Again and again Simon's eyes rose and lingered on the wall of watching men now closing them off. Their skin was browned and weathered like the rocks; within their coarse jerseys, still smelling of the sheep, their bodies seemed massive and perdurable, contoured by the memory and possibility of tremendous energy like the mountains; their occasionally murmured Gaelic like sounds on the wind. To Simon it seemed that like the standing-stones on their land, like their fishing-boats at sea, these human beings were a part of this earth. But he and his family did not belong on it, not here or anywhere. Weak, pale, effete, wrapped up in clothes expensive rather than efficient, nervously prattling; for all their education and their prospects, it seemed the earth would like to shake them off its very back. No help was to be expected.

His life was at most the subject of a murmured aside from the impassive gaze of human history, whose concerns were rightly elsewhere.

And now the cordon of watchers had opened, and the ambulance attendant had passed through, and he and the doctor had lain his mother on the stretcher and were carrying her, a heavy bundle of fear that had abandoned even dignity, down the slope towards the long sweep of the beach and the distant road to the town. Simon stirred, and began to lag self-effacingly behind the small family procession moving past the still dark line of islanders. The first chill drops of rain came tumbling from the wind and broke against his forehead, and began slowly to turn the smooth white of the long sands to a troubled grey.

Part One: COMING OUT

CHAPTER ONE

Calum and Debbie were the first to arrive for the house-warming, squeezing through the front door locked arm in arm, sitting together in one armchair, glowing through the thin coating of autumn drizzle that lay over their hair and faces. The room had not even been tidied, the tea-things were still in the sink, and as they came in, Annie rose as at the press of a switch and began bobbing up and down, bundling her Victorian novels into shelves and Philip's uncorrected exercise-books into piles, fending off all protests that she need not bother with the strained flippancies of someone excusing a compulsion. After a while Philip rose from setting the guests at ease amid his cloud of pipe-smoke, and under cover of making a cup of tea at the same time washed the dishes.

Simon sat apart, silently staring into the fire with a look of melodramatic resignation, because he could conceive of no other that was appropriate.

He had scarcely lifted a finger to help with the housework for the past month. He had closed himself off from the world to contemplate a life of unsought isolation and ignominy. For that was the only image that presented itself. Oscar Wilde alone in jail. Blackmailed spies in exile.

How, he thought, could he have time to notice or care if mere squalor overgrew his environment? And yet however graceless his posing, the nagging fact of the matter remained.

"Simon, the kettle's boiling," said Debbie playfully.

"What?"

"The kettle's boiling. Seeing as Philip's doing the dishes, you could make the tea."

"Oh. Alright."

He rose slowly and wearily from his chair, cast a pitying glimpse down the length of his frail body, then shuffled across to the kettle. As he passed Calum and Debbie, they smiled and gave one another a quick kiss, which cut through Simon's play-acting like a shock of pain.

As soon as the tea was ready, Annie sat on the floor by the fire and wrapped herself round a mug of it as if it were a teddy-bear, radiating comfort, leaning her head on one side and effortlessly entertaining everyone by demolishing her own anxieties with her wit. After several unsuccessful attempts at interpolating a schoolteacher's anecdotes, Philip jumped up in a burst of businesslike energy and offered to go to the off-licence.

"Come on, Simon," he said, in a tone of no-nonsense invitation, "a walk will do you good."

Simon shrugged, and got up to do as he was told. He drifted silently down the stairs of the close and into the street, behind Philip's brisk and purposeful step. He felt the night air attack his skin with a bullying chill, a threat of the relentlessness to come. A light rain fell steadily from a sky muddy with orange lamplight. Closing off the horizon on every side, tenements reared up over him, characterless and rotting beneath their mourning of corrosive soot. They seemed to stand motionless and passive above the empty wet pavements as around mass graves. Philip slowed his echoing footsteps until he drew back on a level with Simon. An expectant silence hovered threateningly over them.

Philip drew a loud breath. "Well," he said, with a characteristic mixture of the stern and the playful, "and what's been the matter with you for the past few weeks?"

Simon longed to be able to break his silence. He felt the longing twist his body within his clothes, as if there were something within it wishing to burst out; but the fear was greater. Already he could feel his mouth filling with saliva, the blood draining from his face. To be alone all one's life was terrible, but to be exposed on all sides as an object of horror and contempt as well would be worse. He recoiled from the possibility of the conversation as from the edge of a dreadful cliff over which he had briefly looked. Trying to compose himself he said quietly, with a slight tremor in his voice, "There's nothing wrong. It's just the move was a little strange, that's all."

Philip did not reply, and at once Simon tingled with guilt, feeling as if he were a small child about to be found out in a cover-up. He could even feel the tears waiting to rush out. They walked on slowly in silence, their breath hovering in a mist about them.

"Alright," said Philip suddenly, firmly announcing a new strategy, "have you decided that you're impotent or queer?"

The panic terror of being accused was submerged almost at once in a wave of relief. The spell had been broken, the word had been uttered – and by someone else. In a tiny pleading voice he said, "Yes, I'm queer," uncertain even as he spoke whether he was going to be able to make it to the last word. As soon as he realised he had said it, he felt almost concussed, his vision span, and he dragged his feet. But he waited intently for the words of reassurance that Philip's tone had seemed to promise.

"What makes you think that?" said Philip, with friendly dismissal, like a doctor addressing a favourite hypochondriac. "So you were brought up at a segregated school, you knew very few girls, you've had the odd crush on another boy, that's not very surprising, is it? But it's hardly any need to jump to conclusions."

Slowly something strange and unexpected happened inside Simon.

A sense of terrific indignation began to form in him. At first not least because he seemed not to be believed. "But remember that time with Sally MacDougall," he said anxiously, recalling an incident from a party before the summer that Philip was witness to. "I didn't feel anything at all. Nothing. Really."

Philip shrugged, and began to pack a pipe. "Well, that wasn't really a very good way to start, was it?" His voice had now a sympathetic condescension. "Overwhelmed by a very drunk and mildly curious mountain of flesh."

Simon's indignation was becoming clearer. It was a struggle for his integrity. Quite to his amazement, he found himself rising defiantly to the defence of what only just now he himself had been thinking of as a disability. "But I've always felt that way," he interrupted protestingly, "even from when I was very young." Only the other day, in the midst of self-pitying introspection, he had realised with a shock the significance of the intense and even then distinctive excitement he had felt when playing chasing games with his best friend at primary school. He remembered the soft little brushes of yearning that moved up from the pit of his stomach, and seemed to dissolve all over his body like a warm bath, when they caught one another in a corner of the playground. Even now the memory flooded him with a lingering wistfulness. Who had the right to deny the reality of that tenderness?

"Childhood sexuality doesn't really have much to do with what happens to us later on," said Philip. He had assumed the tone of a kindly mentor. "At first, there always seems to be an unleapable gap between sexual fantasy and the reality of experience. It's hard – for everyone – but of course, once you have leapt, you always make it to the other side. Which is worth making a note of. Along with the fact that everyone's always disappointed at first when they get there."

He sucked audibly on his pipe, and along his sigh of satisfaction Simon felt the calm aromatic smoke settling over him. "Come on. We mustn't be breakable," Philip resumed softly, "like your mother was. Life is too treacherous for us to be able to afford to be breakable."

The lights of the off-licence were visible on the corner ahead. The discussion was about to come to an end, and as if he had suddenly gone to leave a room and found the door locked from the outside, a cold utter uncomprehending panic fell suddenly over Simon, as he realised he was being left helpless and alone after all.

"Anyway," said Philip, and Simon's ears pricked up, "if you think you're queer, why don't you go ahead and find out. There's plenty of people facing in the same direction."

Where? The word almost came to Simon's lips, but the great incoming tide of desolation caught it and swept it away. He ceased to struggle and was carried silently far out. It was as if Philip had seen him drowning from the shore and had shouted to him "Swim!" He was sinking into such impenetrable aloneness, an aloneness peopled only by ghosts from the distant past, like Michelangelo and Tchaikovsky, or from distant cultures, like the Zuni Indians he had read about furtively in someone's psychology textbook. He was the only queer he knew. Perhaps he was the only queer in Glasgow. But no; a memory stirred, of Paul who had passed them on the street waiting for the bus and looked back. Tenderly, surely? Romance suddenly surrounded this isolated figure, and yet Simon had no clear memory even of his features.

In the off-licence there was a small queue. Philip went to stand in it, but Simon lagged behind. He pushed himself aside into a corner by the door, separated off from the world by his apparently irremediable unhappiness.

A rickety wrinkled-faced man in a worn overcoat and cloth cap limped unsteadily from the head of the queue, clutching a small wrapped bottle of whisky, and reeled against Simon in his vague effort to grasp the door-handle. "Sorry, son," he said slowly, gasping for the breath from dying lungs. "Dud nae see you there." He leant a roughened nicotine-stained hand against the jamb, and stood for a moment with his head bowed, panting. "Tha's me laid off the day," he said dreamily, staring into the floor. "Off to the brew on Monday. Thus's me celebratin', eh?" He raised his eyes with difficulty, as if they were great weights, and tried to indicate to Simon through their glaze that he had just made a joke. Simon smiled tentatively. "Y' havin' a guid time yerself, son? Saturday nigh's a great time, eh? Saturday nigh²,
 . . ." Suddenly his body seemed convulsed, his shoulders were thrown up and down, his face went pale. After a moment Simon realised he was trying to hold back an attack of coughing. Dismayed, he watched the man pull his free hand from the jamb, swaying as he did so, and fumble shakily with the whisky bottle, peeling back the brown paper, unscrewing the top and raising it awkwardly to his mouth. The panic of struggle left his eyes, he lowered and resealed the bottle, wheezing shallow but regular breaths. " 'S a hard life, son," he murmured nodding, staring full at Simon for a moment in perplexity, and at last focusing his gaze not on Simon as he was, but on something he could represent. He said solemnly, "But people should be happy, son. Tha's what matters. People should be happy." He turned cumbersomely away, as if no response could be needed, and went out. Through the glass of the door Simon watched him take a few ponderous steps. Then he tottered, and clutched the rim of a wastepaper bin attached to a lamp-post, his eyes closed, shaken by a paroxysm of coughing, filling the cold darkness with the incensed rattle of phlegm and the desperate whoop of starved lungs.

Irremediable unhappiness. Simon watched it: as he might the life-and-death struggles of fish or insects.

What had he to offer the man? What could he say?

Philip came back from the counter silently. Simon took one of the brown paper bags from him and they left. Once outside in the darkness he wanted to resume their conversation, but he caught sight of the rickety man swerving slowly away in the opposite direction, and it was as if he dwindled in his own sight, shrivelled up, blasted by his ineffectuality. His eyes followed the man with a look of helpless pity.

At the party he found himself leaning against the wall, watching it all laid out in front of him. In the soft light dancing couples passed endlessly to and fro.

Against the opposite wall stood Calum, who tolerated fools badly but was still engaged in conversation with Norman, the dumpy and yet gangly little man with the oversized glasses whom Simon had managed to avoid some ten minutes ago. Norman, thought Simon, nodding a little drunkenly to himself, was pretentious, flannelling, and effete. Just then Norman caught his eye and smiled broadly, a benign but timid grin, making him look even sillier than usual. Simon pretended not to have noticed.

Debbie, brow knitted, was moving her hands and face in a typical mixture of angular aggression and anxious clumsiness, engaged in earnest conversation with Vanessa, the nextdoor neighbour. Vanessa was a primary school teacher, a little older than Philip or Annie, a figure at once very solid and very delicate, with a charismatic honesty and a seemingly endless fund of interest in other people. She was divorced, but seemed now never to lack for several younger lovers in tow. She was listening to Debbie with a knowing look, her statuesque face still and kindly. As if feeling Simon's gaze, she turned to give him that puzzling characteristic glance of hers, that seemed to understand more of him than he understood himself.

There was another fellow student, Dave, the Edinburgh public school boy, crouched in a corner, his eyes visibly bloodshot, with a characteristic look of pained perplexity. He was being talked at animatedly by a very purposeful-looking Pansy, dressed tonight in a black lamé mini-skirt with her hair streaming down her back. On her this style of dress managed to look at once a knowing but light-hearted joke and an act of carefully judged calculation.

Annie was dancing, her athletic and graceful body momentarily set free from its habitual polite inhibitions, her face liquid and glowing, rising effortlessly on her long legs again and again into the space she seemed to make vast above and around her.

Philip strode past Simon to get himself some wine from the table, choosing and seizing the bottle with what seemed to Simon a certainty that was almost ostentatious. Even in such passing actions it was as if Philip confidently expected to be able always to take what he wanted from the world, to Simon an expectation simply unimaginable, giving Philip again and again the fascination of an incomprehensible being. Only the more so because – unlike for example his father, who had struck him with something of the same aura of ownership – Philip seemed not only acknowledging of Simon's existence, but prepared to foster it. Seeing Simon now, he came over to him and stood for a while, his jaw moving as if he was chewing the sentence he was planning into shape before he uttered it.

"Look at Annie," he said, smiling at first, and then screwing up his face in puzzled amazement; and in the words Annie too seemed marked off from the rest of the world as Philip's experience above all. Breathlessly he went on, "Sometimes I honestly think she's going to take off. You must have to feel basically ill-at-ease in the world to be able to escape from it as convincingly as that. My feet are planted so firmly and stably on this earth, I hold no hopes of merging with the air."

It seemed a haunting observation, which Simon for a moment felt vaguely loth to have heard. As Philip moved off, his thoughts realighted on his own unease like a favourite perch.

He was drinking beer with whisky chasers and later he got very drunk.

Someone had put the light off, and the room was lit only by the red flickering of the fire. He sat apart in a vast armchair that stretched unoccupied on either side of him and loomed up behind like a high wall. He was cocooned in a warm self-pity, the rest of the world closed off beyond heavy lush drapes of sorrow. Somewhere out there in the party a woman began to sing, a dark swirling voice. Leaning back, he sought his reflection in its troubled sound as it flowed past him:

> I once loved a lad, and I loved him sae weel,
> I hated all others that spoke of him ill,
> But now he's rewarded me for my pains weel,
> For he's gone to be wad til another.

He lifted his head to look, and saw in the orange glow that it was the black-haired woman called Granya who, he realised for the first time, had been hanging around with his friends for several weeks now. She seemed an irrepressible fount of gentle concern, he thought, lapping around them all like the sea round rocks.

The song stopped, and someone else began to play the guitar softly, a mere whisper of plucked notes amid the play of the flames. And suddenly Debbie had come up beside him, and was sitting on the arm of the chair, leaning over and placing a hand lightly on his shoulder.

"What's the matter, Simon?" she said gently.

He lay with his head against the back of the chair, staring blankly ahead, as if he were ill, the corners of his mouth turned down. "I can't tell you," he said after a while, furrowing his brow, not daring to look at her, and to his surprise somehow hoping that she would guess. "It would be more than my life is worth to tell you, of all people." That should have given the hint. At least she might tell Calum.

"Come on, tell me," said Debbie insinuatingly, shaking his shoulder a little, looking at him with an earnest kindness. "This is what friends are for."

"I'm lonely, I'm left out," he almost snapped, feeling a lump in his throat, drunken tears threatening behind his eyes. "And – and I'm attracted to other men, and you think that's horrible and unnatural, like everybody else. And I don't know what I'm going to do." He hid his face behind his hand, stroking his forehead with his fingers.

"No, Simon, no, it's alright, it's alright," said Debbie, slipping off the arm of the chair and kneeling at his feet, pulling his hands from his face. "No, Calum has made me think differently about that now. It's not the end. Cheer up." He looked at her. She looked like a nurse trying to tell an incurably ill patient that they would be up and about in no time. She patted his hand, and after another murmured "Cheer up," she rose and walked slowly, as one does from the scene of tragedy, across the room to Calum.

Simon followed her with his drunken gaze, and saw her sit beside Calum and whisper in his ear. From across the room they stared at him with a look of helpless pity.

Out of the first heavings of nausea in his stomach, indignation surfaced once again, reaching up like an arm brandishing a sword, holding out the promise of better times waiting to be won. I have to stand up and fight for my life, he thought ponderously, the words veering at him out of a growing giddiness. Pity's not what I need, no more than the man in the off-licence. And if I have to do it alone – I'll do it alone.

Granya had come up to him. Resourcefully she said hallo. He felt her concern streaming down over him like a warm shower. But for the moment he had no need of it.

CHAPTER TWO

The English department's junior student common-room: black leatherette chairs, striking cold to the touch; unpainted wooden shutters closed against the bleak outside; a small bar-heater glowing pathetically and ineffectually in a dark corner. A saucepan half-full of congealed baked beans, dried orange sludge down its side, lounging beside an untidy pile of unwashed plates, on the shelf of a dumb-waiter perpetually jammed half open, channelling an icy draught into the middle of the room. On the walls, a faded poster for a production of *Huis Clos*, and a picture of Che Guevara. On the chairs, tense and hunched up, habitual student residents: Dave, Pansy, Granya, Simon. Sitting in silence, sipping from mugs of instant coffee, but looking as if sipping from skulls.

Dave heaved a deep sigh, which vanished into the sullen silence as if it had never been. He placed his mug solemnly on the floor. No one looked up. A look of dismay and uncertainty crossed his acne-scarred face. "I suppose I should go to my French lecture," he said, sitting perfectly still, listening for the encouragement to stay he did not expect to hear. He sighed again quietly, as if to himself, and rose slowly, fussily gathering his coat, his bag, and his umbrella, the anxious Scottish public school boy's symbol of independent respectable manhood. Pansy's tiny eyes surveyed him with resentment, then returned to the floor. Dave glanced back at her with timid discomfort, and moved towards the door. "See you all at Calum and Debbie's engagement party, if not before," he said flatly, as if presuming the remark could be of no interest to anyone. Simon lifted his eyes to acknowledge his departure and found Dave looking at him with confused entreaty, before he shrugged his eyebrows and left the room, shutting the door gently behind him, as though on a room of sleepers.

Pansy scowled and grunted, wriggling as if setting herself straight inside her clothes.

The door reopened tentatively, and Norman peered round, mawkish behind his enormous spectacles. Nobody was in the mood for Norman. Pansy glared at him, and he grinned sheepishly and withdrew his head in silence. The door closed again,

Granya sighed. "Well, I'm going to wash the dishes," she said with martyred breeziness, and stood up smartly. She moved and spoke with a kind of pleasant rough-hewn spontaneity, in contrast to the generally nervous and hesitant manner of Dave and Simon, or the tense planned manner of Pansy. "I'll take the mugs through, too," she added, "if you've finished with them. I don't expect anybody to give me a hand."

Granya and Pansy exchanged a meaningful look that Simon did not try to read. Pansy was Granya's confidante. Simon handed his empty mug to Granya as she stood over him with an apparent expression of blank efficiency, and then burrowed in his bag for the play he was supposed to have read for the day before, hearing the door close sharply as he leant awkwardly head-first over the edge of the chair.

When he re-emerged with the book, he found that Pansy had drawn her chair up beside him, and was looking steadily at him with a teacherly frown.

"We're going to have a little talk, Simon," she said with not completely convincing sternness, in her rather prim and South-Side-respectable accent. "You can put your book away again." Today she had her long hair done up in earphones, her eyes heavily kohled and her mouth in a red oxbow, like a figure from *Dr Finlay's Casebook*. Sometimes she tied it in bunches, or even pigtails, on either side of her round, almost podgy pink face, with its seemingly inbuilt winning smile, so that she looked like a little girl out of Mabel Lucie-Attwell. This effect was often heightened by her continual enthusiastic consumption of chocolate and ice-cream (one of her favourite topics of conversation) and by the regular appearance of two or three handsome middle-aged men to take her to dinner or the cinema. Emerging from a neurotic guilt-ridden family, she had snatched the world in a firm and cynical grasp. Thoroughly hedonistic and quietly knowing, impeccably demure and tough as old boots.

Simon squirmed at her words, guessing what she was going to say. The headache that seemed to have been almost constantly present for the last month or so slammed shut with a bang, closing him off. "I have to get this read," he whined weakly, looking at the floor.

"I'm sure you know very well what I'm going to talk about," Pansy went on, with a kind of businesslike swiftness, still staring straight at him. "And I wouldn't be putting myself to the effort, if I didn't think that basically you were a very nice person."

"I don't know very well," said Simon unconvincingly, almost petulantly, rubbing his brow with his hand.

"Honestly Simon," said Pansy, with outraged reproach, "how can you look at her in that state? When I think of how she's been to you, when I think what she's worth, and when I look at how you treat her, I'm – I'm scunnered." The word was flung in Simon's face with almost chauvinistic vulgarity.

Simon tried to focus his thoughts. "Do you mean Granya?" he managed to say in a sincere effort to suggest that he did not consider it his concern. No, he was not unaware, as Pansy well knew; but he was bound and gagged by his own reality, which she did not know. Or so he supposed. Those who had been told to their faces refused to speak about it: as for others like Pansy and Granya, it was not that he had not given hints, it was just that they had gone either totally disregarded or simply disbelieved. Even now, descending over him like an icy fog, it seemed as if he alone belonged to a dislocated darker reality, beyond the reach of others. Sitting next to him, Pansy might have been calling to him into the wind from a distant cloud-covered mountain.

"You know fine well I mean Granya," snapped Pansy scornfully. "Sometimes you get away with far too much with that raffish charm of yours, but this is a time when playing the little urchin isn't going to help." She picked up her handbag, settled it neatly on her lap, opened it, and took out a Mars bar. She bit into it aggressively, wrenching it dripping with toffee from her mouth, and proceeded to chew purposefully. "And I know perfectly well what you think about yourself," she said challengingly, between chews, fixing him with a look of angry ridicule, wielding the Mars bar as if it were a potential weapon.

So often Simon felt as if he had been slipping slowly into a crevasse of fear that had opened quite suddenly beneath him when he realised the truth about himself. While he scrabbled desperately on its steep walls, his friends passed by along the top, seemingly uncaring; or rather, if they heard his cries, looking everywhere but where they came from. For a moment it seemed as if Pansy was at least looking in his direction, and he looked back hopefully, though he was too dazed to say anything.

She went on munching noisily, pausing to speak between mouthfuls. "Don't think I haven't noticed all your pointed remarks about having Paul McCartney's picture on your wall. Or staying in on Saturday evenings to see Micky Dolenz on television?" Her voice came heavy with mockery, like her breath with the smell of chocolate.

Crouched alone again already on his chair, Simon winced at the sound of the names of his fantasies on her lips, as if they were real and she had somehow hurt them, savaged them. They were so vulnerable, his only sexual partners, painstakingly given body by his imagination again and again, from the blurred fixed features of a photograph, from the tantalising glimpse of a passing television film, here and then gone. A little spreading blot of tenderness, suddenly wiped out by a headache.

Pansy engulfed the last wedge of the Mars bar, returned her bag to the floor, and vigorously brushed the crumbs of chocolate from her blouse. "Don't you think it's about time you started living in the real world," she said, studying her clothes in the draining light for any further specks, "instead of in a lot of adolescent daydreams?"

Simon felt baited like a captive bear. With a kind of tired pain and anger, he heard himself saying, "It's not dreaming, it's true," but he seemed to feel no real concern for his defence any longer. All he wanted was peace, somewhere, somehow. Or the gentle companionship of one of his fantasy lovers.

In the momentary silence Granya could be heard singing indefatigably in the kitchen as she washed the dishes, the muffled lapping of a repeated eddy of melody:

> O dig me a grave, and dig it sae deep,
> And I'll lie me doun for to tak a lang sleep . . .

"It's a matter of mere decency," Pansy began again, hard, toneless. "If someone offers you something, the least you can do is try to respond. There are a lot of people who would have every reason to be very grateful to be offered what you are. And so, what are you going to do? Tell me."

Simon glanced at her sheepishly. She looked intransigent, her chin in the air. "But I can't respond," he said helplessly, with a shock as of someone forced to confront again the fact that they are lost in uncharted territory. It was totally uncharted territory through which he must make his own path, where even if others had passed, they had left no record. There was nothing to trust to but the lone determination to find the way.

Pansy heaved a loud sigh, and drummed her fingers on the leather of the chair. "This," she said, "is going to hurt me more than it hurts you." Even Simon heard the banality of the script, but nonetheless it took him by surprise when there came not the expected little slap, but a hearty thwack that brought water running to his eyes and left his cheek tingling.

He cried out, "I can't help it. I just don't feel anything." And it was true, he suddenly realised, truer than he meant: he felt nothing, not even for Paul McCartney or Micky Dolenz. He felt he must be incapable of ever having a sexual response again.

"Have you ever made the attempt? How do you know?" said Pansy, in a scoffing voice that made him seem ridiculous even to himself. "Come here." She spoke like a mother to a child who is consistently complaining that their shoe-lace won't tie right. He turned towards her obediently, all resistance gone, and her face, unnaturally pasty in the lurid glare of the fluorescent light, loomed towards him nearer and nearer, until it blurred and he could smell the sweet unaccustomed smell of her make-up. When he opened his mouth a little awkwardly to let her kiss him, it was no longer out of mere obedience to her, but a kind of nervous reaction to what he knew he was meant to be in the world. It was a strange wet sensation; for one who had been taught as a child not to drink from another's glass, a little shocking to feel the hygienic secrecy of one's mouth invaded by another; but in itself neither pleasant nor unpleasant.

The door opened and Granya came in. As usual she flung the door open on to the room as brightly as if she were opening a window to a sunny morning.

It was a reflex of politeness that made Simon draw away from the kiss at once; and only when he turned to look at Granya did it occur to him what she must think. Even then he felt such a distance from the situation, as if he were the accidental observer of some puppet of himself being manipulated in a show by and for others. It's nothing really to do with me, he thought. It's not my fault. It's not even real, any of it.

And Granya seemed scarcely to pause at all, only a certain jerkiness interrupted her entry into the room, as though a film had been accidentally slowed for a moment. Perhaps the habitual light in her face seemed for an instant almost imperceptibly misted over, as if small clouds had gathered at the corners of her eyes and the corners of her mouth. As even Simon had noticed before, she hid her moment of pain behind a veil, a veil so effective and yet so thin that one scarcely noticed any interruption in the glow of that decent kindness with which she always broached the world.

"Well," she said softly, "that's the kitchen all clean and tidy for Monday. That should get our week off to a happy start." For a second she looked thoughtful. "Time to go home," she said briskly, like an encouragement; but then paused, and avoiding looking at Pansy and Simon, went to the corner and began to tidy the pile of records and magazines.

"I'll do that," said Pansy, who seemed quite unruffled.

Granya smiled, looking in Pansy's direction, but not quite in her eyes. There was a spent light-bulb lying by the magazines, where it had lain for the past few days. She picked it up. "Don't mind me," she said buoyantly, moving purposefully back towards the door. "I just suddenly feel in the mood for breaking something." She went out quietly, delicately, hidden behind a public mask of bemused self-mockery.

"Very well, Simon," said Pansy sharply, turning back towards him. "Remember, I expect to see you making an effort." Her gaze bored motionlessly into him.

"I'll do my best," he said, barely audibly, secretly beginning to stretch out in the relief that the interview was ended, as over a much needed bed.

There was the sound of the back door opening, followed by the tinkle of broken glass.

Pansy sighed and closed her kohled eyes for a moment. "You could start right now," she said, "by offering to walk with Granya to her bus, when she comes back in. I should think that's the least you could do."

Simon nodded, closing his eyes. "Yes, alright, alright," he said. "I'll be back in a minute. I'm just going to have a pee."

He passed Granya in the hall without speaking to her. Safely alone in the toilet, he stopped to stare at his pale anxious face in the mirror, as if to reassure himself that he was actually there, amid this hopeless uncertainty about everything. If he was to find a way out, it could only be in some assertion of himself, however beleaguered and indistinct that self was. Looking steadily into his own eyes, he seemed to remember, as if from a long long time ago, that he did have the ability to see and judge for himself. The fact of his sexuality – well, that was clear enough. But it was naked; without role, expectation or precedent to clothe it. It was vulnerable and exposed in this harsh climate.

When he came back into the common-room, Granya already had her coat on, a bright red shining PVC. From her chair Pansy fixed him with a pointed look. "Shall I walk you to your bus stop, Granya?" he said flatly, acquiescing like a child in what others wanted to make of him, for the sake of longed-for peace.

It was not far to the bus stop. Neither of them said a word. Both walked with bent heads and hands in pockets.

It was a cold foggy night. A sooty vapour swirled in the pools of orange lamplight like paint dissolving in water.

As relief at the interview's ending staled, Simon found himself muddy and turbulent with the confusion that Pansy had stirred. Looking around him, he felt as if he was sinking in dirty waters.

A moment of anger bobbed against him. He wanted to be on his own, to be himself. "How long does the bus usually take to come?" he said petulantly as they reached the stop, hunching his shoulders. He stared, lonely, into the distance. But there was nothing coming.

"Not long," said Granya quietly. He was staring ahead over the shoulders of a middle-aged couple, so that he could not see her face, but her voice sounded resentful at last, he thought.

He was a naughty boy, whom no one wanted to feel sorry for.

He eased his head round warily to see what she was doing. Her eyes started up, like a hungry pet that latches onto the hint of movement, and filled again at once with their brimming warmth, as blood wells up again in a cut that has only been dabbed.

"Pansy and I had a little talk while you were in the toilet. I'm sorry if my misunderstanding made you feel awkward," she said, laying out her words gently and carefully, as she often did, as though they were something pleasing continually on offer to the other. She smiled in the misty orange light, her smile filling her whole face, every crease, every corner, transforming it as utterly as a change of season a landscape. Except that in Granya's face it seemed always spring, with the perpetual promise of summer.

Simon shivered. What should he say to that? He felt his brow coming down over his eyes like a blanket pulled over his ears. He stared ahead from under it, frightened and resentful. "It didn't worry me," he said in a clipped voice, rounding his shoulders, as if seeking some warmth for himself from himself. He felt isolated.

The light seemed to waver in Granya's eyes. "Anyway, thank you for seeing me to the bus stop," she said, uncharacteristically quietly, the words almost dwindling away. Silence obscured them from one another like the thick fog. Then Granya's voice came, rich and musical, like the chords heralding some central desolate aria. "Oh Simon," she said, and paused. "Couldn't you at least pretend?"

And she began to sob.

But he had been moving far from her, moving as fast as he could go, deep into the wastes of himself; unpeopled, without way, without landmark. Yet he heard her cry of pain still; he had not outrun it after all, he heard it. He saw her tears as one might watch someone drowning when one could not swim, unable to help though one wanted to, knowing one might one day drown oneself.

He stood there motionless, staring at her distantly with a look of helpless pity.

After a moment he realised that the middle-aged couple in front of him had turned silently to look. Their eyes were fixed on him coldly with an expression of impatient expectation.

Once again, as with Pansy, a great weariness came over him, he could struggle no more. He gave himself up into the hands of his manipulators. They pulled his strings, and though his heart was of wood, he produced a lifelike imitation of their actions, which they watched and applauded.

Stiffly, awkwardly, he put his arm round Granya. At once she felt hot and liquid in his arms, quite unlike a human body, unlike anything he might have expected. She subsided against him like a great weight that had suddenly become weightless. Her face seemed to float up towards his, as if by some natural physical force, and in obedience to what he had seen performed elsewhere, he made to kiss her, uncertainly, clumsily. Her tongue seemed to hunt his, to chase it about his mouth. Locked together in the closed space of their two mouths, there was no escape for it. He wanted to take a breath, but he could not. It seemed as if the kiss would go on for ever, as if she would never tire of it.

At last she let go, and he gasped for air, but almost at once she was kissing him again, relaxed now, her tongue lolling against his like some wet basking sea-creature. He felt empty, a hollow puppet; empty not just of thoughts and feelings, but even of vital functions. Granya's tongue lay in a vacuum, unsensed, uncontaminated. He just began to wish she would finish. Everything had gone out of the world, and there was just this gentle rasping in his mouth, and a sense of a shell containing a void.

She did stop after what seemed an age, and leant her head against his shoulder, breathing heavily and saying nothing at all, which seemed strange to Simon, though he could find nothing to say himself.

A tall dark shape appeared in the fog. Noise and great bright lights lurched suddenly towards them, like a whale rising out of the sea by a small boat. "Here's your bus," he said quickly, his heart suddenly leaping with the anticipation of escape.

She pulled away, pecked him on the lips, and stepped with unexpected suddenness onto the bus platform. Then she turned slowly, and her face was radiant, he could hardly look at it. "I'll see you tomorrow," she said, seeming to make the air shimmer with her smile, "my love."

The bus began to move. She grasped the pole, and hung there watching him for the few moments before he was out of sight.

Slowly he began to walk. The fog was thickening. There was no one to be seen. Only odd dismembered fragments of trees and houses marked the way. The fact that home was there somewhere was almost a matter of belief.

The next day was a Friday; and he did not go into University.

On Monday he was surprised to find himself in the common-room before Granya, a fact so unusual as to be uncomfortable. When at last she came in, he thought at first she had had an accident. But no, her mouth was cratered all over with cold sores, distorted, submerged. Her skin seemed grey, her eyes without light, guttering with disappointment, flickering as she saw him into a feeble dark flame of resignation. She said nothing.

35

CHAPTER THREE

Change begins to come, he came to think, once one is ready to see that it comes through experiment; from whose failures as much as successes one can learn and gain.

A year and half another year had slipped by. And nothing had happened to Simon. That last inexorable winter had drawn to its end. With the hesitant approaches of spring, a watery sun nudging now and again through shambling clouds, his confusion had begun at last to flake from him like an old skin. He felt himself emerging anew; vulnerable, but whole.

But it was as if having left behind an impenetrable dark forest, he found himself in an open waste, free to move forward, but still with no path to tell him where to go.

"Wee Simon," said Annie fondly, as they walked one afternoon through the park's already shrivelled daffodils, a cloud of reluctant acceptance crossing the brilliance of her face. "I don't really feel there's anything *we* can do." She smiled wistfully, offering honesty as a gift for what it was worth.

He made friends with Granya. All around them people were pairing off – Pansy and Dave among the latest – and an alliance, however uneasy, provided both of them with a certain relief. He lived like a kind of parasite off her comfort, and she found in him at least a sponge into which to pour her brimming affection. But for both of them the spring became one of vague frustrated restlessness. In the summer Granya went off to the Highlands to work in a home for handicapped children, and became engaged to a fellow volunteer. Simon's summer, half of it spent working as a kitchen porter in Dunoon, petered out in a swamp of dreams.

There followed a long numb self-absorbed winter.

Now, quite unexpectedly, spring had crept up on him again. As he passed the river on his way home, the green branches of trees seemed to him to stir in beckoning gestures, but there was nowhere to go. The darkness drew back from the days, like curtains sweeping back from a bright expectant stage, but the stage was empty.

It was a sunny Saturday. A few days ago he had met Pansy and Dave in the street. He had not seen either of them for ages. His relations with them had become more and more remote after they entered the mystic state of couplehood, forming yet another ratification of his hopeless exclusion. The very sight of them revived his sense of aloneness as a discord in the social order. But they had been fond and talkative, and invited him to a party to warm the flat they had just moved into with a couple of friends, one of whom, they added laughingly, was an engineering student. He had smiled uncertainly, and said he might come.

Now, as it was, Philip and Annie had gone off to visit Annie's parents, and he was on his own. He went across the close to see if Vanessa was in. She answered the door in her street-clothes, lush with dusky pinks and maroons. "Och Simon," she said, her voice spilling out in its characteristic warm gush. "I was just on my way out. Off to have dinner with one of my boyfriends and all that, you know. And are you feeling lonely over there?"

"Oh, just at a loose end, I suppose," he said, uncertain whether he was glad this option had been closed or not. "Actually, I know of a party to go to. I'm just not sure whether I want to go."

"Oh yes, you should, you should," she said softly, with that air she sometimes had of blessing the rightness of a decision, so that it seemed already made.

"Well, perhaps I will then," he said, feeling encouraged. "Enjoy your dinner."

"Leave the door, I'll be setting off in just a minute." She kissed him lightly on the cheek, leaving a lingering tangy perfume like jasmine and lemons. "Have a good party. You never know what might happen, you know."

Smiling, he went back across the close and into his room. As the light began to fade, he swallowed the last of his misgivings and set off.

Outside a thin film of mist hung in the still air, making the world unreachable beyond a veil. It took Simon a long time to track down the unknown address. The street turned out to be a short cul-de-sac, at least half of it demolished. A couple of solitary moth-eaten tenements reared up into the gathered darkness, surrounded by a lunar emptiness, where not even a blade of grass was visible in the glare of the marooned street-lights. It had become chilly. As soon as he entered the party he realised he might as well not have bothered. Drunken bodies hung along the walls of the dim draughty hall like the corpses in a mortuary. Among the blank inflamed faces there was not one he knew. He was aware of vaguely aggressive male stares rolling slowly in his direction, fixing on his fragile appearance as if it were a social affront.

Gritting his teeth, he decided at least to look for Pansy and Dave and pushed into the indifferent crowd, which yielded surlily only just enough to let him inch through. Propped against the draining-board in the kitchen he found a fairly remote acquaintance, who told him Pansy and Dave had retreated to their room before the flood of invading engineering students. Simon was reluctant to turn round and go home at once, so he hung where he was for a moment, squeezing out a little conversation in slow drips.

"Do you hear of Calum at all these days?" said the acquaintance after a while.

Calum had gone off some time ago to do six months in Paris for his French course. "No," said Simon, "I don't." They had begun to grow apart from as long ago as Calum's engagement.

"Somebody told me he and Debbie had broken up," the acquaintance said casually, and was silent.

Simon shrugged. Such things belonged to a world he was excluded from. He looked at his watch. Time was deceptive, it was already late. He mumbled some excuse, and made his way back through the hall towards the front door.

"Hallo. I didn't expect to see you here." It was an unrecognised voice, from almost under his nose.

Confused, he hesitated, wondering if it was really himself who had been spoken to or someone else; and only then realised that he was looking more or less straight at Norman. He would probably not have noticed him at all if he had not spoken. Norman after all hardly entered his consciousness, except as a subject of minor scorn or mockery among closer friends.

But now Simon stood gaping blankly and silently into Norman's wide untidy face, with its resilient welcome hovering awkwardly behind an enforced timidity. He took in those features that looked as if they had been thrown haphazardly at the pale paste of the cheeks, the black wiry hair that looked as if the effect of repeated combings was only to make it ramble the more: and felt a sudden remorse breaking into an uncertain warmth.

"Oh, hallo," he said, a little flatly. "I'm sorry. I didn't notice you."

"That's alright," said Norman, his tense facial muscles subsiding and yet looking none the less ungainly. "I noticed you as soon as you came in. But I thought you hadn't noticed me."

A sense of fragility seemed to fill the very air between them. Simon felt that if he so much as moved or spoke either he himself or Norman might break into pieces. It was as if they had both shrunk together to pinhead fairy-tale midgets, and the other men surrounded them like unseeing uncaring giants, threatening to crush them underfoot at any moment. And in that context, Norman's mincing voice, his great flopping hands, his ill-fitting teddy-bear-like overcoat, his ingratiating smile, all of which until now had seemed to Simon merely tasteless and absurd, quite suddenly took on another significance as well.

He had to break the enchanted silence, and yet his throat hurt with the effort, as though he were struggling not to weep. "It's not a very nice party, is it?" he said.

Norman grinned nervously, showing a range of craggy rabbit-like teeth; and seemed to go on grinning until Simon began to wonder if he was going to reply. At last he said, "No, it isn't. I was just standing here trying to merge into the woodwork."

"Perhaps you'd been successful, which was why I didn't notice you," said Simon, beginning now to feel a certain ease, even a certain improbable power.

Norman looked confused, his eyes hovering behind his thick glasses like startled goldfish, uncertain whether to yield to the temptation that Simon's words were a friendly gesture, or whether to shield himself from further mockery. "I noticed you straight away," he said finally, "I always notice you." He had resorted to an ingenuous honesty like someone parading their weaponlessness in the hope that they would not then be attacked.

"Oh really?" said Simon, genuinely surprised. For a moment he did not know who was most in control of whose emotions. "I know I see you so often, but I've never talked to you. I suppose it's rather rude of me."

"I was always a bit afraid of you," said Norman disarmingly.

A group of three large men, loosely supporting one another, swayed past mumbling raucously and lurched out of the door, leaving it wide open behind them. The chill night air poured in over Simon and Norman, making them both shiver. Simon pushed the door to timorously.

Looking round at Norman huddled in his ridiculously fluffy jumper, Simon noticed that he was even smaller than himself. In fact, his head and hands were disproportionately large, and gave the momentary impression that his whole body was likely to fall apart at any moment.

"It's a bit draughty here," Simon said, just for something to say. In fact he was beginning to feel exposed, almost afraid to be found consorting with someone so ridiculous.

"What I notice about you most is your hands," Norman said in an enthusiastic rush, fixing Simon with a clumsily earnest look. "It's the intent way you use them when you talk. As if you were trying to catch hold of the words as they flitted by through the air. Did you know?"

"No," said Simon, bewildered, immediately conscious of the position of his hands.

"Whereas I just wave my hands about while I talk," Norman went on, his voice getting quite excitedly loud, "as if I were having a conversation in semaphore." His fat fingers flailed the air in support of his words, making him look a bit like Mickey Mouse as the sorcerer's apprentice.

Perhaps Norman was not so silly after all, thought Simon.

A man stumbled past them on his way out, leant against the door-jamb, and vomited onto the carpet. Then he jerked open the door and went out. The little purple and orange puddle steamed in the cold air.

"Let's move further in," said Simon. The crowd was thinning. They moved further along the wall towards the kitchen.

After a moment Pansy appeared as if from nowhere with a mop and pail, a look on her face at once longsuffering and efficient. She caught Simon out of the corner of her eye as she passed, and stopped at once to greet him. But when she saw Norman beside him, she merely gave what seemed an amused knowing look, and went on her way to clean up the vomit. Simon felt uncomfortable. The scent of disinfectant drifted past, and hovered unwelcomingly in the smoky air.

"You're queer, aren't you?" said Norman brightly, smiling his preposterous smile.

This was the very first time anybody had actually asked Simon. He felt himself blushing feverishly in spite of himself. Defencelessness and gratitude scrambled for the upper hand. There had been something almost admiring in Norman's tone, like a young schoolboy talking to a prefect sports hero.

"Yes I am," said Simon baldly, his voice shaking a little in spite of himself. But he could think of nothing more to say.

"Oh, that's nice," said Norman, beaming like a neighbour over a baby, making his face look even more than usual like a pantomime dame's. "I think you're very brave to say so. I'm not any more, but everybody thinks I am."

Simon had never thought so. It had never crossed his mind. He did not know what to do with any of these compliments or these confidences. He stood there awkwardly, as if holding an expensive present which was one of the last things he wanted, and trying to think of something convincingly nice to say about it.

"Oh really," he began – but having got that far he found there was nowhere else to go. "I suppose – I suppose it must be rather worrying, everyone thinking you are, when you're not."

"Well, I always think it makes me seem rather interesting," said Norman gravely. An intentness seemed to screw up his features as though he were straining, absorbed in the processes of himself and unseen by the world. "I wrote a poem about it once. Of course, I don't write poetry any more. Do you? You see, I'm sure I'm an interesting person, but I don't take myself seriously enough, and so nobody else takes me seriously." He looked at Simon questioningly, his eyes bobbing ingenuously behind his glasses like beachballs abandoned on a swimming-pool in the rain.

Pity began to seep into Simon, for all his embarrassed unease and half-amusement. Someone so preposterous must be very vulnerable. "Oh, I'm sure people take you seriously," he blurted out clumsily, doubting every word of it, but unable to bear saying anything else.

Norman's face flopped out into a relieved smile. "I knew we'd get on well together," he said, quite sentimentally. "That's why I've always wanted to talk to you." Tentatively, like a child with a stranger's dog they both want and fear to touch, he patted Simon's arm lightly with his loose gangly fingers. Simon tensed.

There was an awkward silence. Simon surveyed the battlefield of the hall. Amid the piles of empty cans and bottles, a few red-faced men still stood, swaying silent and morose; others were already crumpled on the floor in stupor. He slid down the wall and sat on the floor. After a moment Norman followed him. Simon did not really want to go home, but he wanted the conversation to become more distant. With an effort, he began to talk about plays he thought they must both have seen.

The conversation petered out only slowly. It was getting very late. At any moment the cold spring dawn would come seeping under the curtains. All that was left of the party now were a few stragglers too tired to leave, who perhaps, like Simon, had been seeking exhaustion as a compensation for something longed-for they had never expected to find.

"I can give you a lift home, if you like," said Norman, a little tentatively. "I've got the loan of my parents' car."

Simon yawned and sat still, staring at the pattern on the carpet. "Ok," he said, stretching himself slowly and painfully. "I didn't know you could drive. *I* can't." He stood up unsteadily, and they moved towards the door.

"I think everyone should be able to drive," said Norman, in the timidly pompous voice he seemed to reserve for the Important Opinions of Norman. "It's one of my things."

Outside the birds had already begun to sing. A cool breeze carried the scent of hawthorn from nearby trees. The sombre terraces were changing from black to grey.

"I always start to wake up again with the dawn," said Simon anxiously, shivering and yawning, suddenly wishing he was free of Norman, even free of consciousness.

"Let's go for a drive in the country." Norman literally hopped in the air, like an awkward child imitating a sparrow. "Come on, let's." He scampered towards the car, and stood looking questioningly at Simon.

The idea was preposterous, and yet exciting for that reason as much as anything. Simon stared doubtfully at Norman, trying again and again to come to some judgment of him, but failing. A shaft of yellow light hit the windows of the house opposite, and all about Simon the world seemed suddenly to leap into beckoning animation. The grimy tenements glowed orange like some dream-transformation of themselves, and a deep luminescent blue began to fade into turquoise endlessly above them. "Alright let's," he said softly, awed by the unexpected affirmation of the moment.

And the roads were empty, they could drive so fast, it was as if they could fly. The Campsie Fells reared up ahead, all yellow grass and deep shadows in the low sun, stretched like a sleeping lion barring escape from the city, growing more and more massive as the car moved to meet them. They rose like an insurmountable wall up whose side the car seemed to rush, swallowing the thin ribbon of road ahead which led on and on for them alone, throwing the city down behind them till it became only one brownish smudge among the receding layers of the lowland landscape, glimpsed laid out like an abstract painting in the early morning pallor as they turned the corner to climb the final ridge.

They stopped, and got out of the car.

But from that point there was no view. Only the vacant moorland stretched as far as the eye could see, undulating half-heartedly, covered in a low sickly grass: empty of trees, of rocks, even of sheep. Empty. The wind whistled quietly, bending the odd yellowish stalk that rose a little above the rest. It struck cold and damp.

They had nothing to say to one another.

In silence Simon wandered into the wind, slowly, aimlessly, down the blank sweep of the incline in front of them, until he reached a tiny sluggish burn, a trickle of brown water seeming to seep rather than flow between a few clumps of straggly rushes. He stood still, staring at it, his shoulders hunched, his hands clenched in his pockets, feeling his ears begin to ache with the cold, his eyes to water in the wind. Life seemed a constant upward struggle, from which there emerged the momentary illusion of winning through, only to affirm the reality of disappointment once again. Human beings were only the helpless victims of history's repetitiousness.

A sigh stirred in his stomach and seemed to put its arm around his shoulders and nod to him in agreement. No, there was nothing to be done.

Norman had followed and was standing beside him. He looked fearful and restless, gazing at the ground in front of his feet, but again and again glancing at Simon from the corner of an eye.

Suddenly he drew in a big breath, like someone preparing for a dive, and turning to Simon with a deep blush, he said, quite quickly and clearly, "I'm terrified to ask, but I'm still going to. I want to kiss you." A nervous grin split his face, and his big front teeth spilled out of it, like the white breaking through as a boiling egg cracks. He stood rigid, looking Simon straight in the eye.

At once Simon knew he was not at all surprised; but perhaps he had not expected it just then. And he knew that, although he did not particularly want to kiss Norman, he was going to say yes. After all, he no longer disliked Norman, if he ever really had; and yet he did not really like him either.

And then all at once, the dawn wind rustling in his ears, lifting his hair, he realised that this was a critical moment in his life. He felt a surge of tremendous excitement. "Of course, of course you can kiss me," he said.

Norman stood teetering on tiptoe, his short arms groped stiffly round Simon's shoulders, his face reached up towards Simon's, nearer and nearer, until its increasingly strange proportions seemed to fragment like a cubist painting, just as Simon closed his eyes. Their mouths collided awkwardly, their tongues fumbled against one another, like passengers thrown together by the lurching of some broken-down bus that was taking ages to get nowhere.

The moment it happened, it was so ordinary, it was so boring.

When they came to a stop, as if coming out of a daydream, Simon found himself caught trying hard to concentrate on whether he had an erection; which he presumed was what he should have, though he certainly did not feel sure that he did.

Time seemed to have slowed almost to a standstill. Norman was just hovering there, smiling beatifically. At last he blushed and said coyly, "Let's go back to your place."

So they drove home, hardly exchanging a word. Only occasionally Norman turned to smile at Simon.

Suddenly Glasgow was closing in around them. They were being hemmed in by uniform soot-blackened walls, overlooked by dead characterless windows, halted at unused intersections.

"I thought you said you weren't queer any more," said Simon at last, half-curious, half-apprehensive. They were stuck at a red traffic-light, in the midst of a deserted street.

"No, I'm not any more," said Norman, with an air of momentous self-definition. "But I can't help wanting to go to bed with you. I hope you don't mind."

Simon felt a certain puzzling relief. "No, no, I — I want to go to bed with you too," he said flatly, as if he were listening to himself reading a line from a play.

"That's nice." Norman's voice cooed distantly, as if commenting on the happy end of a romantic film. "Is this your first time?"

He felt defensive, almost ashamed. "Well yes, sort of," he said, looking away.

"That's nice."

The lights changed and they moved on.

Simon entered the house on tiptoe, though he knew perfectly well there was no one there to wake. His heart pounded, sweat trickled down his sides, he half-expected someone to appear from behind every door, even the cupboards. He found himself speaking in a whisper. "This way." Norman giggled nervously, and took a loose hold of Simon's fingers, as if they were something he was not quite sure he was allowed to take. To Simon the two of them seemed like conspiratorial children, both doing for the sake of disobedience something neither especially wanted to do.

They were in Simon's room. His single bed stared at them, accusing them mockingly with its inadequacy. Simon was afraid to pull back the covers, as though they might snap at him. Everything was submerged in fear.

Suddenly Norman leapt at him, like a tiny kitten pouncing on a large ball. Simon tensed apprehensively. All at once he felt himself overbalancing clumsily onto the bed, with Norman puffing and panting beside him, his stubby fingers falling over one another to undo Simon's jeans, without any success. Simon felt a loss of dignity like a sharp pain. "Just a minute," he said stiltedly, realising as he did so that Norman's shoulder was thrust in front of his mouth,

Norman slid off the bed, and swaying to his feet, began hurriedly to take off his own clothes, throwing them unfolded about the room. As it emerged before Simon's harassed gaze, this podgy white body, dotted with red pimples, and sparsely scattered with long black hairs, seemed only an abstract absurdity in the context of his own room, whose solitude Simon knew so well.

Norman said, "I should go first. After all, it's up to me to take you through your first time." And there he stood grinning, looking in his nakedness, Simon thought, for all the world like a potato-man, a few spindly limbs stuck into a great white peeled potato, from which projected a clumsy carrot-like penis, like an irregularity that ought to have been smoothed off.

Simon felt his heart sinking. Was the human body really, after all, like the stick arms, the red bums, the spotty backs that he'd had to confront with a certain reticence amid a fug of smelly feet and farts in the gym changing-room? His own prick seemed to have shrivelled away, like a curled dead leaf. He pressed himself timidly against the wall, feeling the inches of bed between him and Norman like a moat. A helpless pause stretched endlessly before him.

But it must be that Norman had not even noticed this, that he was thinking, experiencing something quite other, something quite unrelated to Simon. Because there he was launching his disproportionate body onto the bed like some misshapen bean-bag thrown in a school pillow-fight, so enthusiastically that Simon believed he glimpsed for a moment the flabby pink buttocks still quivering with the effort. A hot wet mouth engulfed him, like the unrestrainable unwanted blandishments of a visitor's dog, and his clothes were jerked and yanked awkwardly from him; till he knew himself exposed. His thin pale body recoiled like a maggot unexpectedly laid bare by a bite in an apple.

With a shock of amazement he caught sight of his own erect penis. He did not know whether he had ever seen it as belonging to the rest of his body before. Let alone as a part of the world beyond him.

But Norman allowed no time for reflection. With a kind of handless urgency, like an ant struggling with a giant crumb, his arms manhandled the load of Simon's tense body on top of his own, shifting it this way and that. Or so it seemed, though from his smiles and strange distant grunts, it must have had some other ineffable significance for Norman, which distressingly, without explanation, eluded Simon. He found himself incessantly distracted from whatever pleasure it was he knew he should be feeling, by the intrusive unfamiliar smell of pubic sweat, or the repeated hot slobbering sensations of kisses threatening to stifle him (which both seemed somehow distantly unhygienic) and by the numbing panic-stricken rapidity of his own pulse-rate.

It began to seem to him they lay there for ages, tumbling against one another like two logs caught in a river, becoming sweatier and sweatier; until at last there began to descend a certain calming familiarity.

And it was just then that Norman suddenly pulled away. Their skins came unstuck with a noise like a mocking raspberry that Simon had never heard before. Breathing stertoriously, Norman laid Simon back on the bed and awkwardly leant over him, beaming apparently vacantly from under his hopelessly deranged hair. A thin cobweb-like thread of semen joined him to Simon's belly. He seemed to dangle there from it, like one of those fuzzy toy spiders with big felt eyes and pipe-cleaner legs that bob about in the back of other people's cars.

"You're a really sweet person," he said, unexpectedly loudly and clearly, words sounding strange in the silence that had been broken only by panting. "You see, you're not alone. Are you happy now?"

Politeness overwhelmed Simon, for all that he was stark naked. "Yes," he said quickly, and closed his eyes from scrutiny. I suppose I would be if it was someone I really fancied, he thought; I'd be bound to be.

Norman sighed with childlike emphasis, and slumped down on his stomach beside Simon, who opened his eyes warily. They lay still for a moment. The smell of sweat seemed to have become almost attractive. Tentatively, Simon lifted himself a little, and then hesitantly knelt astride Norman's prostrate body, staring at the hump of his buttocks. He touched it gingerly.

"Actually, I don't enjoy being entered," said Norman's muffled voice, rather tonelessly. "But you can have a go, if you really want to."

Simon stared down. He had no idea what to do. He had never even had a passing fantasy of having intercourse with anyone, yet he felt dimly, with a kind of tired routine, that he ought to want to assert his maleness. He made a few stiff lunging movements and then stopped, feeling gauche. His heart began to pound again so that his skin tingled uncomfortably.

Norman rolled over onto his back, and smiled condescendingly. Gracelessly he pulled Simon down on top of him, and thrust his damp body to and fro, like a walking seal. Gradually the motion seemed to take control of Simon, as though it were the motion of a vehicle taking him passively somewhere by some route he did not know. Quite suddenly an immanence seemed to fill the whole world, to flood his body with heat, and for a moment he felt embarrassedly as if he were a child about to wet the bed. And then it had happened without him having a chance to stop it. He felt flat, puzzled, wet.

Norman heaved himself from under him, and swung his legs onto the floor. "I'm glad you enjoyed it," he said, glancing back complacently over his shoulder. "Have you got a tissue or something? You've made rather a mess of me."

Simon lay still on the bed, beached by a retreating tide of fervour of which he had scarcely been aware, shrivelling up. "I don't know," he said hazily. Silence came. Sleep stirred in the distance.

He opened his eyes. Norman was dabbing at himself with a tea-towel. He smiled sheepishly and held it up. "I found this in the kitchen," he said feebly. He looked quickly about him, and placed it carefully on Simon's writing desk. Then he began to gather his scattered clothes, and put them on, tottering clumsily on one leg as he wrestled with his jeans.

Simon sat up suddenly. An overwhelming realisation had come over him. He was changed. I've had sex with someone, he thought, I've actually had sex. He got off the bed and stood up, fully naked. For a moment he no longer looked to himself like an advertisement for famine-relief.

"Let's have some coffee," he said brightly.

He stepped across to the window and drew back one of the curtains. A thin wash of high cloud had covered the sun. Time stretched across the sky, blank and uncertain.

CHAPTER FOUR

He was still awake. A whitish half-light was beginning to ooze under the curtains and into the room. A blackbird began to sing.

Another year had gone by. Another brief spring had come at last; reluctantly and hesitantly another brief summer was beginning.

He lay stretched out, trapped between the grey slabs of the dusk and the dawn advancing to meet him, sleepless again, burning with memories. Every restless shift of position caused yet another one to flare.

He had gone to bed with Norman several times during the course of last spring. It was never very different from the first time, and it never quite lost its strangeness.

After a while he even let other people know they were sleeping together. Everyone seemed either indifferent or mildly amused.

The birds began to sing more loudly, inappropriately. His body ached with the longing for sleep.

When the summer came, Norman went off to stay with friends in Edinburgh, and Simon went south to take a summer job in a department store, arranged for him by an uncle.

When they met again in the autumn, they found there was nothing between them but an antagonistic awkwardness.

And when he was alone, Simon found himself feeling actually resentful. He persuaded himself that however disappointing and unremarkable sex with Norman had been, at least it was better than nothing. As for Norman, he had consciously dangled a carrot before Simon, only to whisk it away again the moment he got his teeth into it.

He pulled the covers over his ears, over his eyes: but the light and singing remained.

One evening, at some student party or other, he had found himself getting self-dramatisingly drunk on a mixture of Carlsberg Specials and whisky. The real world had blurred beyond a haze of martyrdom and tragedy, and he had stridden purposefully into the midst of a crowded room, and with planned suddenness, thrown a glass of beer in Norman's face, or rather, in its general direction, uttering a string of bitter reproaches, that neither could his audience make out, nor he later remember. He left Norman being dabbed down by the timid woman who was being taken, at least, for his girlfriend, and went to spend the next hour locked in the bathroom, vomiting.

When he awoke the next afternoon, feeling as if the parts of his brain and stomach had been shaken loose inside his body, he was purged of all thought of Norman.

Instead, there stretched before him the niggling discomfort of a life of utter sexual emptiness, from which even the sorrow of an unrequited love would have been some relief.

Now the sun was here – now and again, at any rate – and the days had grown long, stretched tight, lingering palely beside the river; where he would walk after he had been swotting for his finals, longing and dreaming. If only he could meet someone whom he even had reason to believe might be gay, someone he could just fantasise about! The stale smell of the polluted water, where it gathered dark brown in the twilight under the roaring weirs, hung in his nostrils like the smell of sexual arousal, weaving itself around the distant shadowy figures of young men in shirt sleeves walking arm in arm with women beneath the flickering trees.

He turned over, plumped the pillow, and drew his legs up to his chin, cradling himself.

His body seemed to be emotions made matter. Where the sheet rubbed him, they were tender.

I must get at least an hour or two's sleep, he thought, screwing up his eyes, or I shan't be able to cope with tomorrow. Philip and Annie were going camping on Inchmurran for a few days. He had hesitated to join them, afraid of being found out in his uselessness, but as it was, he and Vanessa had decided to go out with them tomorrow just for the day.

His one enduring happiness was the companionship of Philip and Annie, a bond which had deepened in a way unexpected and unimaginable for all of them. When Simon had moved in, there was no doubt that the arrangement had seemed to Philip and Annie just one more passing state. They happened to have room in their flat, and they felt fond and pitying towards Simon. The way in which their lives now interwove, the subtle fluctuating interplay of support, not one of them would have guessed then.

The future must hold other such surprises, thought Simon, his eyes jerking open once again, other such joys, other such reassurances. It must.

To the uncomprehending outside world, it must have looked as if Philip alone bore all the weight, as if he alone led the way. Some people even spread the rumour that he was bisexual.

"It used to be a great surprise to me," said Philip once – and when he spoke, his voice would always seem to rise up, slow and dark, from the solid darkness of his beard, wreathed in the incense and mist of the pipe-smoke slipping from his nostrils and lips – "that I find myself as close to some men as I do. But now it's a greater mystery that I find myself totally physically unresponsive to them."

He took to calling Simon "love", though at first it was very strange

48

for him, and the word came out only with a great and awkward effort; but after only a short while, it could never have been more natural nor more sincere.

The presence and the persistence of Simon changed Philip. He would never now respond to someone's coming-out as he had responded to Simon's. And this in turn gave Simon a sense of his own reality, a witness that his sexuality had some existence and effect within the world.

His eyes had fallen shut again, and for a moment a wave of well-being seemed to rock him like cradling arms.

And Philip was always there as a source of wisdom, a kind of ultimate authority, for whose calm help and judgement Simon turned no less often than Annie, trusting and admiring.

Because of the three of them it was Philip alone who dared to have confidence in his own perceptions of the world.

Which were wrung from him at such pressure, unremittingly. It seemed that Philip could look at nothing without understanding it. At night he would sit, pale and exhausted, the skin of his brow stretched tight, trapped in the moment seen as the point where the past was becoming predictably the future; seeking oblivion in vast greedily swallowed quantities of Guinness.

For Annie Simon was a reassurance that there were people who felt even more vulnerable and insecure in the world than herself, whose very presence seemed even more tenuous. While it was the awareness of her vulnerability that made Simon feel so close, and her ability to transcend it in gentle self-mockery or in the abandonment of dance that brought him some of the happiest moments he knew.

Many people found the three of them quite threatening.

"To some people it seems almost like incest," said Vanessa once.

Vanessa was one of the few who had no reticence towards any of them. They had grown closer and closer to her in the course of their increasingly frequent visits to the Kist o' Whistles, which was not the nearest pub, but was certainly the most congenial. It was impossible not to notice Vanessa, no matter who you were nor how you might least have expected her: a heavy figure, who yet moved as if balanced precariously, very dark of hair and skin, dressed in blocks of bright colour, with a face that changed like a lake with the weather, one day flashing and shimmering, the next still and silent. A lake where one played, or where one rested, where one went to seek oneself, even to look at one's hazy reflection.

When she was happy, the laughter welled from her, and all were invited, or even drawn to share in it and its purity; when she was sad, she was no more afraid to break amidst other people than she was to put the pieces back together again, however clumsily, quite by herself. Her great shoulders would rise slowly with sobs before you, like a harpooned whale surfacing and diving, surfacing and diving. It was as if the final agony had come. And yet each time she re-emerged whole and new: carefree and yet serious, controlling and yet responsive, tough and yet vulnerable.

Whatever she felt, she said; and the effect was devastating: as it was planned to be.

One evening, while the sky still glimmered palely as if the sun's setting was uncertain, Vanessa had sat drinking with him on the step of the closed pub door. The hawthorn trees across the street were creamy-white with a froth of blossom, and from the murmuring river came the strange smell associated for him with wandering alone in the park.

"I'm fed up with people saying to me, 'But he looks so feminine,'" she said protectively. "So what! What does 'feminine' mean anyway!"

He smiled, uneasily. He did not know people said that. "I try to look what I am," he said, the realisation creeping over him at that moment.

"Oh yes," she said, her voice a soft ripple of enthusiasm, "I like your quiet honesty. You've taught me quite a lot."

"I thought it was you who taught me about honesty."

"It's never as straightforward as that. Relationships of any kind are always a balance of give and take. The more that's given and taken, the harder to keep the balance."

She was silent, sitting there, glowing in the gathering darkness. The noise of the pub was a distant confused murmur behind them.

"And I admire your strength," she said quietly.

Moved, surprised, he said, "My strength?"

"Your standing up for what you think is right. And your persistence in pursuit of what you need." She touched him lightly on the knee, looking into his eyes in the half-light. "But yes, it's a long pursuit. And so much of it is spent on finding out that wasn't what we needed after all."

Conversations like this would come back to him, like waves washing a shore, as he lay sleepless in the dawn. Philip, Annie, Vanessa: three people he loved. Loved?

Restlessly, he got out of bed, and walked quietly through the silent flat, which was bathed in a strange pearly luminescence. He stopped at the door of Philip and Annie's room, listening to the soft lulling sound of their breaths intermingling. He took a step forward; and through the half-open door, he saw them asleep in one another's arms.

He walked back and stood alone in his room for a long time. Sometimes he felt so deprived, he almost expected to just disappear.

But he must have slept at last, or at least fallen into fitful dreams. Because now all that seemed long, long ago. The four of them stood together in the patchy late morning sunlight, bobbing up and down on the launch that was cutting across the dappled loch, with a nipping breeze in their faces. Conversation had been reduced to the laughter of excitement and startled comments on the beauty of the landscape, shifting in and out of the sunlight all around them.

For a moment everything seemed very easy.

They had to walk across the island to find the place where Philip had decided to camp. Simon let the others go a little ahead and stopped for a while on the top of a rise, lying down on the sweet-smelling grass, touching it with his hands and lifting it to his face, gazing out at the glinting waters of the loch which surrounded him and cut him off, and beyond to the mountains rising higher and higher towards the north. He felt a sense of simplicity and completeness, as though he were at one with the quiet green island, where it seemed to him at that moment, if boats rarely touched, they were not missed.

At last he heard Vanessa calling to him, and reluctantly he got up and followed her.

Philip and Annie were already setting up the tent, and Vanessa was calling encouragement and approval as she busied herself making sandwiches. They seemed all shut off in a world of purposefulness and cooperation from which Simon felt at once a stranger. He sat apart in the sun for a while, basking with his eyes half-closed. Twice Vanessa came over to him with a sandwich, and seemed as she spoke to sing like a kettle about to boil.

Later Philip cooked everyone a meal, which because of the fuss over lighting the fire was a long process.

Afterwards, as the sun grew low, each of them wandered off separately to gather wood for the big fire they would need when it got dark. In the fading light, the fretwork of the alder branches seemed to close about Simon like the bars of a cage. Shuddering involuntarily, he filled his arms quickly with fallen wood, careless of whether it was properly dry or not, and began to grope his way back to the tent. Halfway there he heard the crack and rustle of another body, and moved gratefully in its direction. He stopped on the edge of a small leafy hollow, and saw through the trees Philip and Annie lying on the ground making love. He winced, and crept away quietly, pretending he was not really there.

He reached the tent alone, and sat down on the pebbles, waiting. Dusk was gathering fast. When the others came back, laughing together, they told him they had decided to go to the small pub on the other side of the island, which would be open as it was already into the holiday season. There certainly seemed to Simon nothing better to do.

By some kind of inevitable process, it seemed, as they walked back across the fields cool and damp and dim in the twilight, they fell into couples. They passed over the rise where Simon had lain earlier, and as he looked out from it now, he saw that the sun had left the loch and it had turned a flat grey, while the evening clouds were already beginning to slither down and nestle over the mountains, muffling up their shapes in surmise.

The moment they entered the tiny pub, Vanessa's singing and bubbling hit boiling point, and as though with the shriek of a whistle, she accosted a total stranger leaving the pub with laughter and flattery, till he passed through the door with a glazed look on his face. Then she swept to the bar and engulfed the bar-staff with chattering comfort and compliments, before leading the rest of them in a noisy circus-parade, in which Philip for one was already beginning to play his part, down the length of the pub to a table by the window which commanded the widest sweep of the other drinkers.

Simon turned away and looked out of the window at the darkness descending on the lapping waters. Soon the last boat would come out from Balloch and they would go back to Glasgow.

Vanessa was throwing her uproarious peals of laughter over them all like paper streamers. She had set the rate for drinking, and they were drinking fast. The table was already thick with empty glasses. Through the dingy light the thinly spread other customers kept glancing in the direction of their table and muttering to one another, half in amusement, half in shock; so whenever Vanessa floated off down the pub to the bar or the ladies', she would stop and descend on some group or other like a flight of coloured balloons.

Just before ten the boatman came up to their table to ask them if they were ready to take the boat back to Balloch, since he would not be doing the trip again. He smiled at Vanessa out of a young freckled face, and gave Simon sitting beside her a quick glance of dour incomprehension.

Simon felt a certain relief. Soon he would be alone in his own room again.

"Och, we're not going back to Glasgow tonight!" cried Vanessa with a wave of her arm, as if she were stating something preposterously obvious.

"But we've got no sleeping-bags, no tent, or anything," said Simon quietly, in shocked dismay. The dark waters of the loch, which he could just see beyond the others' heads, suddenly began to confirm the island not as a refuge, but as a trap. He looked to Annie for support; and found her locked in murmuring conversation with Philip, the two of them totally oblivious of what else was going on.

"Och, come on! Of course we're staying," Vanessa shouted. "We'll manage somewhere to sleep somehow."

"I doubt you'll be doing much sleeping, eh?" said the boatman to

Vanessa, again with a puzzled look at Simon. "Well I'm off anyway, hen." He turned up his green jacket collar raffishly under his red hair, pulled his brows down like the insistent closing-in of night, and flashed Vanessa in parting a vast distant flare of libido from amid the wondrous Milky Way of his freckles, just in case she did not know she was missing out on what real men were like.

The closing bell wailed mournfully across the pub. "Oh my goodness, is that the bell already? And we haven't got a carry-out," said Vanessa with, however, only a superficial concern, belied by a dogged confidence. "Philip, come with me, we'll have to fix that."

She rose, and moved noisily through the empty tables. Philip smiled and shrugged, slipped his arm from Annie's shoulders, and stood up. Simon and Annie followed suit, and the three of them fell into formation behind Vanessa. She strode on ahead like a ringmaster, Philip followed like a clown brightly painted with a grin, while Annie and Simon drifted behind, Simon thought, like absurd white-faced pierrots.

He went to have a pee, grateful to be alone and to be able to sigh to himself without drawing attention. By the time he came out, Vanessa was standing at the bar alone.

"Philip's gone on ahead with the carry-out," she said, taking him by the arm and ushering him towards the door. "He says they'll race us for the sleeping-bags."

Outside the raw cold was a shock. The mildness of the spring daylight was gone as if it could never have been nor could ever be again. Simon felt his shoulders hunch forward and round, as though they were trying to shield him from the freezing air.

"Oh my, it really is awfully cold," said Vanessa quietly, in dismay almost, suddenly humbled.

They trudged on in silence for a while, heads down, hands in pockets, their faces stinging already, their breath rising in a mist about them, through the shapeless forms of the trees veering at them suddenly out of nowhere on this side and that. Ahead of them they could hear Philip and Annie murmuring together somewhere, invisible in the moonless darkness. The treacherously pitted ground kept surging up unexpectedly beneath their feet, causing them to stumble. Simon felt as though this walk alone was already becoming some desperate expedition threatened with disaster.

"Let's sit down for a minute," said Vanessa, commandingly. "I'm afraid. We could get lost, you know."

"But it's so cold if you stay still," said Simon.

Vanessa sank down on the spot, like some great bird that had been shot. "I know, I know," she murmured, the words welling out of her like tears of compassion. "Here, sit down. If we hold onto one another.

we'll be a bit warmer."

Simon dropped beside her, and they put their arms around one another and hugged protectively for a while, so that they could feel the other trembling, out of fatigue and fear. "We've no need to be afraid, we can help each other," said Vanessa softly, urgently. She leant closer and kissed Simon gently on the mouth, a strange kiss, not like any he had felt before, so open, so various. He was caught without being able to plan a response, and he just lay back, and her kiss seemed to mould itself around his anxiety, like warm water round a wound.

She drew back and said, "Don't worry. I'm only *saying* something I want to say. It's just a way of saying."

Simon felt both soothed and ashamed, as though this were a confessional.

"I don't know the language," he said, and paused for a minute, filled with regret. "I mean, not even with men, I don't know it. I'm sorry."

"Oh, but you'll come to know it," said Vanessa, in a tone of prophecy peculiarly her own. "You'll come to know it. And don't be sorry, I'm glad you're here, just as you are." In the darkness her determined voice out of her invisibility was as certain as music. "Let's get up now. This damp will give me rheumatism in my arm, you know! And if we hurry, we might still beat them, and we could use Philip's sleeping-bag for a while."

Simon stood first, because he was the lighter, and bent and helped her up. As he put his tiny weight under her strong heavy body, a sense of his own incompetence overwhelmed him like a pain. He took her firm arm, and steadying themselves, they walked carefully on, linked together for warmth; guiding one another past the obstacles looming out of the dark, that frequently turned out not to be there at all.

They passed over the rise and came down to the tent at last. Everything was silent.

"Quick! Quick! In here!" said Vanessa, leaving go his arm and scampering to the tent in a sudden childlike burst of energy, plunging into it like a sea-lion diving for a fish. "Come on," she called from inside, "or you'll freeze."

Simon stood for a moment, guilty and perpelexed. After a while he noticed that he was shivering, his toes and fingers were bloodless and aching. Looking round he saw above the trees, the hills, all over the world, an endless colourless nothingness; and he remembered, like an injury forgotten in a moment of panic exertion, that he was alone.

"Come on," Vanessa called again, impatiently, uncomprehendingly.

He walked to the tent, his teeth chattering uncontrollably, and slowly made his muscles kneel and push him in through the flap, the touch of the chill ground on his legs sending a shock through him as though it were metal. In the sudden greater dark he could only just make out Vanessa, lying bundled on the ground, making exaggerated whimperings to distract her from the dull relentlessness of the temperature.

"We could die on a night like this," Simon said, with a flat difficulty, feeling his lips going numb and sluggish.

"Crawl into the sleeping-bag with me. Perhaps we'll make the Guinness Book of Records for the number of people in a sleeping-bag."

In the dark they clutched at one another, each as at a last branch that could save them from falling; but then it was as if they *were* falling, rocking and tumbling over the ground, their bodies launching out into the abyss of cold, their legs struggling for a hold in the warmth, the real warmth, of the sleeping-bag. At last they rolled to a stop, half-in and half-out. Vanessa gave a laugh, pulling him to her, so that he felt the vibration as well as the sound, and found himself laughing too as though by instinct, and she led the laughter like singing, now a lullaby, now an anthem of triumphant resistance.

"Your fingers are frozen," she said between laughs. "Put them here. It's the warmest place." And she laid his hand between her thighs.

"It's the warmest place," she said again, so simply and surely.

Simon stopped laughing. The draught was seeping in through his clothes like a realization. He laid his cheek against Vanessa's, but the soft flesh felt cold to the touch.

Vanessa whispered, sighed, "The cold's winning", like air hissing out of a puncture.

Outside they heard a persistent low murmuring and the sound of things falling or being thrown to the ground. They listened, and after a while they realised that it was Philip and Annie piling up firewood.

"They're going to make a fire," said Vanessa with a kind of childlike excitement. "Why didn't we think of that?"

"I don't know how to make one," said Simon quietly.

In fact the sticks were already crackling, and irregular flashes of yellow light were stabbing at the damp blackness inside the tent. Annie was singing softly, and the crack of two beer-cans being opened mingled with the sound of the fire.

"I'm going out to join them," said Vanessa, half-apologetically, tentatively. "Are you coming?"

"I'll stay here."

She said, "All right then", with that tone of hers of blessing the rightness of a decision, and struggled out of the sleeping-bag, laughing at her own slapstick awkwardness, lumbered across the ground like a seal making for the water, and burst out through the flaps with a cry of greeting.

Simon burrowed down, down into the sleeping-bag, and drew it over his mouth, over his ears, and waited expectantly to get warm. But after what seemed scarcely a moment, the little warmth went out like the pathetic flame of a candle in a draught. He felt the terrible hard earth beneath him draining all heat out of his body as though it were sucking him dry. He fell into a kind of faint torpor, through which he heard persistently the formless sounds of the others talking outside, as though they were something hacking raggedly at the silence; or half-woke in a shuddering fit, as though they were something undigested in his stomach leaping nauseously up his throat into the channels of his ears.

After a totally indeterminate time, he turned over with a start to find Vanessa surging in, letting a faint hint of grey slip through from outside as she did so. He could just see Philip and Annie lying together peacefully asleep in the other sleeping-bag. He had not heard them come in.

Vanessa said, "Can I have a turn in the sleeping-bag for a while?"

He pulled himself slowly out, and crawled past her in silence, as clumsy as a baby. Outside there was nothing but the fire, shamed into insignificance by the coming dawn, and a haphazard scattering of beer-cans.

It was still murderously cold. Simon sat over the fire and watched it dwindle. The energetic red flames stopped scampering up and down the branches, and let their tiny black worn-out corpses drop down into the graveyard of ashes below. It was going out.

A breeze off the loch set Simon shivering again. He supposed he should look for more firewood. He stood and wandered off along the line where the rickety alder trees came to a stop among the purple pebbles of the shore, stooping occasionally to pick up sloughed branches, which were all twisted and torn as though they had struggled not to be cast off from the community of sap. In a little while he was quite out of sight of the camp, alone among the black cagework of alder trunks and the smooth faceless dead pebbles, with the silence and the raw cold air constricting the life out of him. He gave up and stood still, letting the firewood drop to the ground from his limp hand, and after a moment lifted his eyes only, out towards the water and the mountains. But there was nothing there. Only a great foggy absence seemed to be rolling in ineluctably toward him, as if it would soon subsume him too into an utter blankness. Only the belief or memory of others could affirm there was anything other than the grey, even unhaunted vacancy that met the baffled eye.

CHAPTER FIVE

That summer of 1971 Simon sat for his finals and, despite his disinterest, did well enough to be given a grant to study for a further
degree. He was intensely relieved to remain a student. He felt it
sheltered him from the full rigours of a world that was continually
experienced as outside, because it offered not even an image of a place
for him within it.

Winter came early, as it always does in Glasgow. The dreadful bleak
dark crept up and sealed one in, closing down nature all around as
though it were a project indefinitely abandoned.

Philip and Annie decided to get married. Their wedding took place at
Hogmanay, in the midst of a spell of more than usually cruel weather.
Simon was best man. Afterwards, the newly-weds went to Edinburgh
for a few days.

Simon was left alone. He hated the long New Year holiday, when the
shops remained shut and the streets deserted for a whole two dismal
days. The morning the holiday was over, and the shops were open
again, he wanted to rush into the streets to walk in a crowd, to be
reassured of the continued dogged persistence of other human beings.
But he had stocked up with such pensioner-like meticulousness that
there was nothing he actually needed to buy, and he did not like going
out on an obvious pretext. In any case, it looked aggressively cold.

So he split his time up for this or that bit of reading or writing, till in
the late afternoon, stopping to stand by the fire for warmth, he found
himself feeling like a caged bird. What light there had been was already
leaving the sky, and panicking to catch it, he dispensed himself on the
pressing errand of buying an air-freshener for the toilet.

Outside he realised at once that snow was lying in ambush behind the
colourless sky. His lips winced away from the very air he drew between
them. Nevertheless, immediately his sense of time went pleasantly
loose; merely walking could slow time up and fill it almost richly, in
just asserting the prime dispensation of mobility.

But he had scarcely crossed the street when he made out the figure of
Calum coming towards him, bundled into an inadequate anorak, but
looking as if he braved the terror-campaign of the cold with the same
self-reliant placidity he had come to show elsewhere. Retrieving
himself from the split with Debbie, he seemed these days to give out a
sense of quiet optimistic patience in the face of a world he recognised as
outrageous. Despite the gulf that had opened between them, he and
Simon could still feel fond.

"Hallo, Simon," he said. "I was just coming to see if you would come for a drink with me."

Simon was touched that someone should have been seeking him out for all his solitariness. He asked, "Were you really?"

"I went to my parents' after Philip and Annie's wedding, and now I've got away, I wanted to see someone human."

Philip and Annie's wedding must have been upsetting to Calum. His several recent relationships with women were repeatedly breaking up, one after another, to which he made no public reference beyond the odd remark of mocking self-disparagement. "Are you going somewhere, though?" he asked Simon now.

"I was just going — shopping," said Simon, feeling he had been caught in the act of futility. "But it's not important."

"If we walk slowly, we could just be at the Sultan's Palace for opening time."

They walked together, heads buried in their collars and their frozen breath rising in clouds about them.

"Cold," said Simon.

"The winter doesn't last for ever, even if it tries to kid us on it's going to."

When they reached the Sultan's Palace, the door had already been opened, and there were even a couple of other customers, middle-aged regulars with puffed faces and looks of self-neglect, leaning on the bar and coughing over their pints. The air was a fug of tickling cigarette smoke and moist yeasty beer smell, striking only a little warmer than outside.

"What'll you have?" said Calum.

"Oh, just a half-pint."

"Lager? Or what?"

"Oh, whatever you're having."

He waited just behind Calum till the beer was pulled, feeling the middle-aged men stare at him as they might at a toad, something they regarded as verminous but too large to swat. He sat down at a table with Calum with some relief.

Slipping easily into an empty stomach, the beer instantaneously soothed both of them. The winter darkness had now closed in, but the early alcohol made the prospect of the evening seem endlessly exciting, and even the pub's yellow lights burned brighter. It even inured them to the draught they soon found around their feet. They were chatting easily, in excited spurts and quite happy in the silences between. Simon found himself calculating longer postponements of his tea the more he realised he was enjoying himself. He was uneasy about breaking with routine, but both the alcohol and the unexpected pleasure of company led him at last to fling aside the idea altogether. He and Calum ate a packet of peanuts each, and made expansive promises to one another about a Chinese meal later on. They began to find that time was racing. Coming back from fetching his third round, Simon looked at the clock, and was astonished to find it was nearing nine.

The evening suddenly threatened to lose its charm. It had gone, almost, and nothing really had happened. They both found themselves watching the door to see if anyone else they knew would come in.

At last the door was flung back with a bang and held wide open, letting the icy air stream in, while some very noisy arguing about who should go in first went on in the doorway; then a knot of four drunken men manhandled one another through and into the centre of the pub, where they split apart motivelessly, and drifted at different rates towards the bar. Simon noticed that one of them was wearing a cream-coloured safari jacket, which he rather envied.

It made its wearer look dashing. Or rather, he realised its wearer was thinking — or was it hoping? —it made him look dashing through the contrast of the cream with his deep black hair. Splendid glossy blackness, thought Simon too. But then, it was not just his hair, but his whole face which was dark, dominated by two pools of shadow under his cheekbones, which flickered in accord with his flickering confidence. And across his face two bars of black: one, his eyebrows, which did not in fact meet, standing guard like sentries in busbies over his retiring eyes, which were venturing uncertainly to twinkle; the other, a moustache, which was probably meant to look seductively macho, but bordered rather on being dapper. As he attempted to saunter to the bar through the drab Tuesday-night clientele, he seemed to imagine himself, in his somewhat drunken vainglory, a black swan sailing through a rabble of scruffy ducks.

The seconds in which Simon observed him struck him as longer than usual seconds. And then he realised that — whether because he was looking, or whether this had led him to look, he was unsure — the man had noticed him. He felt embarrassed and looked down, but he heard him say, "Hallo, Calum" as he went past.

"Do you know Frank?" Calum asked Simon.

"No," said Simon, noting the name.

"Oh, I thought you would have done."

Frank seemed to have joined the three he came in with; he had accepted a drink from one of them, but he broke away apparently abruptly, and moved, at first hesitant, and then decided, towards Calum and Simon.

"I'll join you. You don't mind," he said quickly, sitting down. "How are you anyway, Calum?"

"Oh, fine," said Calum, with a shrug. "You don't know Simon, do you?"

"We've never met," said Frank. Simon himself was too drunk to tell how drunk Frank was, and whether it was drunkenness or intention that gave his remark a supposedly meaningful solemnity.

"Simon Palmer — Frank Bryan. Simon's doing a higher degree too. In English."

"Oh, English," said Frank, nodding as if he understood all, but finding nothing to say.

"Are you doing a Ph.D?" asked Simon.

"Yes." He paused as if about to reveal something momentous. "On China."

"Oh. What in particular?"

Frank became very vague, and waved his hand, a large hand, expansively. "I haven't yet — settled. A history of the Kuomintang, the career of Liu Shao-Chi, women in China, youth in China, something like that. I'm just reading around and learning the language at the moment. I should be able to read the Peking papers soon."

"I tried to learn Chinese the other year," said Simon. "I only wanted to read T'ang poetry."

Frank took a drink of his beer, which left the fronds of his moustache dripping, giving a seal-like effect. Above this came a sudden boyishness in his eyes, and being very ostentatiously loud, he said something in Chinese.

Simon did not catch a word of it.

"Christ, you didn't learn very much," Frank said almost sulkily, as if a favourite game had been spoilt. He frowned into his beer.

"Very impressive," Calum muttered kindly.

Suddenly Frank shot to his feet in a great burst of animation. "I'll get us all another drink," he said, as enthusiastically as if he were offering to fly everyone to Paris.

"We've none of us finished," said Simon.

"Well, we'll need another one before closing-time, won't we? You'll let me get you one drink, for Christ's sake! What are you drinking?"

"A half-pint of lager."

"A half-pint! Not a pint? Oh well, Calum you'll have a pint." He turned away without waiting for an answer.

Calum nodded slowly. Simon realised his look was in transition from generally benign to merely glazed. He had been drinking heavily ever since working for a while as a barman after giving up on his degree.

"Once I start, I find it hard to stop," he explained to Simon, as he might have explained some reason for having to walk slowly.

Frank's black and cream flashed in on them, and he stood the drinks together proudly in the middle of the table, sitting down to admire the prospect of a job well done. His cheek-shadows were flashing too, as the muscles moved with his sensations of satisfaction and excitement.

He drew out a packet of French cigarettes with a confident gesture, but fumbled over lighting one. The heavy smell of the dark tobacco seemed to drift from his own darkness. Nobody said anything. Simon turned to contemplate his glass, and put out his hand to it, but did not lift it.

"Have a drink," said Frank. Simon looked up. In the initial careless calm of nicotine, Frank was looking at him with a look of ingenuous invitation. Simon took a drink and smiled hesitantly, uncertain as to what he was being invited. Though at once a frown, as of something urgent, forgotten, passed across Frank's face, and he laid down the cigarette impatiently, reached out for his glass and doggedly gulped down all that was left of his first pint.

Calum, who had noticed only the comparative silence, said, "Are you still doing some teaching, Frank?"

"Yes, I take one first-year tutorial a week. I think the kids like me, I think so. You see," he went on to Simon, "the history department wants to make use of me because I was their best Honours student. You know, after the results were out, Professor Shanks came up to me and he said, 'I must tell you, Mr Bryan, I must tell you how much I *enjoyed* reading your papers.'"

"You got a first, didn't you, Simon?" said Calum quietly, apparently only too used to Frank's self-congratulations and wanting to gently deflate him.

Frank would have obviously liked to take up this topic, the fact pleased him; but at this moment one of the people he had come in with arrived, pint in hand, and leaning unsteadily over him, began in a drunkenly aggrieved tone, "Listen, Frank, what you were saying earlier . . ."

Simon turned away from the conversation. He noticed Calum's eyes go up hopefully as the door opened, which made him suddenly aware that he was no longer doing the same. Had something exciting happened to him then? He looked at Frank out of the corner of his eye and assessed him, able to regard him just as someone unknown while he was not talking to him. Handsome (that seemed the right word), but in a bland way – someone who was, if timidly, attempting to look like a glossy advertisement for, indeed, French cigarettes. And as for his present motives, he would allow them, as with those of any acquaintance of a few minutes, to be merely completely mysterious, and most likely he was only wanting to bind himself to as many people as possible by favours and ingratiation in a moment of drunken insecurity.

"Shall we go for that Chinese meal after this?" said Calum, cutting through Simon's reverie.

"Oh – yes," Simon said slowly, jerked into realising he was reluctant, at any rate, for the present situation to end.

Frank's friend left him now, and Frank turned back with an apparently contemptuous smile. "Friends from my Honours year," he said, seeming to dismiss them. "They're going back to London tomorrow."

The three friends appeared to be having to hold one another up. They all had flushed, almost inflamed faces, and one had lost control to the point of starting to dribble. If Frank had drunk as much as they had, he held his liquor very well.

"A first?" he mused, nodding appraisingly, getting back to the favoured topic. "What subjects?"

Simon told him.

"Ah! We must have a talk, mustn't we? I think we'll find we have – some things in common. I mean, there aren't many of us around – firsts, that is. Hey, listen!" He took on the intransigent air of a small schoolboy gang-leader organising a game in the playground. "We'll finish these drinks quickly, and then we'll all go to the research students' club. I can get drinks from there up till ten past. Calum, what do you say? You're coming?"

They both looked anxiously at Calum, whose presence seemed necessary to both of them.

"I think my body could find a few more drinks very acceptable," he said, "even if I personally doubt the wisdom of my body's judgement."

"That's settled then. I've never seen you at the research club."

"I never go," Simon said, feeling it was made to sound like an admission. "Is that the old house in University Gardens?"

The closing-bell went, and at once one of the younger barmen strode across and opened the door to let in the cold. The change in temperature was so violent it felt like the first symptoms of an illness. Conversation all round them faltered.

Frank drained his second pint as if in a race. Simon's last half-pint was untouched. "Hurry up! Let's go! We'll have to run. Leave it if you don't want it. You can tell me what work you're doing on the way up."

Once outside all words dropped from their lips. The cold was so cruel that the body at once forgot about everything except enduring it. Frank seemed ridiculously badly protected in his light safari-jacket, which he nevertheless pulled more tightly around him as if that would do some good, hissing and growling inarticulately at the weather. Suddenly he went bounding off up the road, flinging back over his shoulder a clipped cry to "Come on!" Simon and Calum followed on at a quick walk, their lips and brows tight against the cold, their shoulders tense and hunched. The cream jacket flashed through the pools of lamplight ahead of them and vanished round the corner while they were still only halfway there.

Once they reached the house, they found no sign of Frank. Still cold, they stood for a moment uncertain, surrounded by doors in the large Victorian hall, which was unlit and unheated, until there could be made out the sound of solemnly sentimental music and the clink of a few glasses coming from somewhere above. As if suddenly remembering, Calum, who must have been here before, led the way upstairs, round a corner, and through just one more dark door. Frank was revealed, standing alone at a small bar-counter, looking harassed but competent as he tried to stack too many pints on to a tray. The barman was watching him as he might a precocious but charming child, whose outrageous requests he was at last becoming fed up with. The tables in the room were all empty, and not many of them appeared to have been occupied during the evening.

"Here, Calum," called Frank, rather imperiously. "Take this tray through to the lounge. I'll bring the carry-out." And somewhat to Simon's surprise, he reached through and picked up from the bar a bag easily containing some half-dozen cans. It seemed as if a very large amount of drinking indeed was planned.

The lounge was lit with dingy, forty-watt bulbs. In one corner two bespectacled Pakistanis were bent dignified and silent over a game of chess. Round another table cluttered with empty glasses sat three drab men, now staring glumly at their last pints in the growing awareness of total inebriation, but who looked as if they might well have spent the rest of the evening swapping dirty stories. One of them looked up and disinterestedly greeted Frank, who promptly directed Simon and Calum, wavering with the overladen tray, over to them. At the sight of so many unexpected new pints the three pulled themselves up in their chairs, and made to look as if they were hunting for a topic of conversation. Frank took hold of a pint and stretched himself out full-length in an easy chair, looking smugly pleased, either at being the bringer of such sudden plenty or at the prospect of tormenting the comparative strangers by having his party drink all the pints themselves.

"Well," he said, since no one else was saying anything. The pause was long enough to notice that even here it was cold. The music, some unnoticeable Mozart, came to an end with a mechanical flourish, and the record-player arm clicked back into place. Silence.

"Choose a record," said Frank to Simon, and watched him carefully as he went to make his selection from the small well-thumbed pile of cheap popular classics. He found a version of one of the Brandenburgs, and was about to put it on.

"What's that? What are you putting on?" snapped Frank, and had leapt over to Simon's side. He too bent bear-like over the records, and the nearness of their bodies brought a tension that caught them both by surprise. "Here," said Frank quietly, pulling back, subdued perhaps by that unexpected unease. "Put this on. We don't want Bach when we're having a few pints, for God's sake."

He put a copy of Mahler's Sixth into Simon's hands. Their eyes caught unintentionally, but before they winced apart, Frank seemed to dare a look of appeal, an appeal that came struggling from a very distant, very troubled place.

They both sat back down, purposely separate, and the Mahler started up its inexorable doomed pulsation, occasionally bursting like a fire-work into a bright explosion of hope that fell shimmering away into the only more strongly confirmed gloom. Simon distrusted Mahler, distrusted his apparent indifference to losing his balance. Frank however lounged back with a look imitative of rapturous absorption, and made a little sigh of approval. Calum merely raised his eyebrows and nodded, as if granting that Mahler might have a point; he appeared to Simon to be getting unusually drunk.

"Er, have you seen George around since Christmas, Frank?" said the stranger who had greeted Frank, nervously fingering his dwindling pint.

"No," said Frank, sitting up straight with a show of reluctance, "no, I haven't."

"I suppose he's gone home to Motherwell till the grants come in," the stranger went on, staring down at his glass. "That'll be it. That was some party he had, though, eh?"

"Yes, yes . . ."

The stranger now warmed to a topic he felt an expert in. "Christ man, you were paralytic. Not just peed, you were paralytic. That was some carry-out the four of you had. Er . . . how's the research coming along there, anyway?"

"Oh, I'm just . . . studying the criticisms' of Ch'u Ch'iu-pai."

"Oh yes. who was that again?"

"Ch'u Ch'iu-pai."

"Oh, aye."

Frank looked boyishly pleased to have baffled the dull stranger, who however indomitably started up again. "Is Alistair still going around with Eileen then?"

Everyone else's conversations always sound the same, thought Simon, and sipped the excessively gassy lager without much interest. The glass was dripping on his clean jeans. He began to wish he was sobering up at home, near a fire. Quite clearly, he thought morosely, Frank was as remote as any other acquaintance, and those apparent come-on glances could only be willing misunderstandings on his own part. He felt the length of the table between them, with its empty glasses and puddles of spilt beer, and he felt his own body hunched in on itself.

But when he looked up, Frank was looking at him, as if both afraid and concerned that Simon might be slipping away. "I don't know what Alistair's doing," he said to the stranger with aggressive disinterest, and turned towards Simon. "Mahler, you know – penetrates the recesses of loneliness!" He waggled a hand in a vague gesture, to grant that his remark was more ostentatious than precise, and took a deliberately greedy swig of his beer. "Wouldn't you agree?" He was addressing Simon directly.

"He seems to take a lot of risks," said Simon.

"Perhaps we should all take more risks." Frank certainly seemed to be trying to convey some secret mutual understanding, in a diffident and yet stagey fashion. He had already nearly finished his pint.

The two Pakistanis had finished their game of chess and were packing the pieces quietly into the box. One of the three strangers had fallen asleep and was beginning gradually to snore.

Frank emptied his glass and stood up in a continuous movement. "Come on," he said. "Calum! We've got a carry-out to drink. Where shall we go? You, where do you live?" He was reluctant to use Simon's name. "We'll go there! You'll invite us for a drink, for Christ's sake!"

It would seem a very strange disruption of his evening routine to have these people in his home, with so many cans, but he felt as if Frank was telling him almost sergeant-majorishly that to face a little strangeness would do him good. In any case, he thought, it would be impolite to turn away guests. Calum stood up and docilely padded after like a dog, a zombie to his own appetite for alcohol.

The stranger called tentatively, "Hey, what about these pints?"

"Drink them yourselves," said Frank offhandedly.

Across the stranger's face spread the relief of being able to postpone finding something other to do than drink.

Outside in the hall, once again the cold fell on them like a police clamp-down. They shivered and wanted to keep to themselves and say nothing. Going ahead down the unlit stairs, Frank said, "We'll just have a few drinks, and then I'll go home."

And outside it was snowing. It came gliding down from the black sky through the lamplight like slow tickertape, covering the earth in a deceptive gleam. It was as if the winter night were spitefully tearing off pieces of itself and throwing them down on human beings to make the world hostile to their continued survival.

Emboldened by his growing drunkenness, Frank did not even bother to do up his safari jacket, but marched on ahead, drawing his breath noisily through his teeth as he shuddered.

Calum, head down in his collar, observed meekly, "A lot of snow this winter."

When they reached the flat, Simon's fire had died down – he had not made it up before he left – and a damp chill hung in the room. Calum sat down quietly in the armchair, and the snow melted from his hair in little rivulets, which he did not bother to wipe away. Frank flopped down heavily on the floor with the carry-out bag, directly in front of the embers, and when he realised there was no heat coming from them he almost shouted, "My God, aren't you going to do something about that? Do you want us all to freeze to death?"

Simon hurried off like a dutiful unobtrusive host and fetched a scuttle of coal. He heaped the coal rather recklessly and poked at it violently to make it draw. A crack of red light appeared between the old grey ashes and the new black coal. It seemed for a while as if it might still go out, but slowly it spread upwards, and there was a hint of coming warmth.

Glowering to himself, Frank ripped the top off a can, and pulled two more out of the bag. Calum leant across and took one mechanically. Simon folded himself up silently in the corner of the fireplace, as if he supposed the more he behaved like a piece of furniture, the more his guests might feel at home. For a while Frank's eyes bored into the lone can sitting there on the carpet, until at last he snatched it up and thrust it under Simon's nose.

"Aren't you going to join us then?" he said.

Immediately Simon scuttled into the kitchen, saying, "I'm sorry. I'll get some glasses." He could only find two glasses in his hurry, and he brought a tea-cup for himself.

"Cups!" said Frank. "What's wrong with cans?"

Calum gently rationalised. "It's good drinking out of cans at this time of the evening, because it means you can't drink too fast."

Simon opened his can very warily, confidently expecting it to spray everywhere – which it did not – and poured himself a careful half-cup – which did, however, froth up and overflow. He sucked some in; it was watery of course and the overriding taste, after tin, was sugar. Frank watched his performance with a mixture of amusement and exasperation. Then, sounding both nervous and irritated, he started up a conversation with Calum.

Huddled there among the ashes, Simon drifted off into an habitual seclusion. At such close range there was no way his and Frank's eyes could touch as if by accident. This mere meeting of appealing eyes, this mere mutual acknowledgement of a hoped-for possibility, even though it was destined to be missed, was at least itself some kind of erotic stimulus, sufficient to revive the starving for a few days and give a momentary growing season to frozen hopes and dreams. Many people survive that way. And meanwhile, even in his turning his back on Simon in this group of three, Frank was affirming either his discomfort or his fear for the obviousness of the secret between them.

The fire had become a roaring column of yellow heat, so that the sides of their bodies that were turned towards it were uncomfortable. But against the wall of the other side of their bodies the terrible cold was solid, like a beleaguering army. The cold even seemed to make the light burn dimly, as if it could not last out.

Time passed. Simon began to feel simply bored, fed up with what was after all the routine hopelessness of the situation. He wanted to be left alone so that he could at least relish the pain of his solitude in a fitting manner. Soon it was long after midnight, and he even began to have moments of sleepiness, except that the cold woke him up.

Suddenly he realised there was silence. Calum had fallen asleep. Frank sat staring gloomily into the fire with three empty cans before him and a fourth still clutched in his hand.

"You, what's your name, Simon," he said, looking up from under his brows, as one might look up for a glimpse of the sky from a narrow street of tall dark buildings. "Your fire's dying down again."

Now there were just the two of them. Between them an awkward fearfulness struggled with a despairing resignation to indifference.

"I'll get some more coal."

"No, don't bother. Don't go all the way through there." He spoke now with the slow careful pace of one who is used to reaching the point where the speech is slurred, and has learnt tricks to hide it. "You're hell of a quiet. You just sit there placidly, letting it all go by you." He nodded to himself over this problematic situation. Simon shrugged and made noises imitative of seeking to find the right words and failing.

"How's one supposed to know what to make of you, then?" Frank went on. "You must lead a very quiet contented life, I suppose?"

Simon spoke, at last. "No. Well, it's not contented. Though I suppose it's quiet. I mean, doing research – I spend a lot of time alone so I try to keep to a sort of strict daily routine – you know, just of things I do by myself, at certain times of day – to make sure there's no time when one can start feeling sorry for oneself, lonely . . ." He tailed off, rather abashed at his confessional tone and at admitting to his weaknesses.

"You've got friends?"

"Oh yes. Some good ones. There's Philip and Annie, who live here . . ."

"So why do you feel lonely? What do you think you're looking for?"

"Oh well, I suppose – I suppose – it's not important but – well, I still want there to be someone – special, you know, someone who . . . " Whenever silence came, the recklessness of the conversation cropped up like a pain. This territory was already strange; he felt lost.

"Someone? Someone?" said Frank. "Are your friends married? Do you want to get married?"

"No, no, I don't want to get married."

"Well, for Christ's sake, we all feel lonely sometimes, we all feel lonely." Frank was staring down at his can. "Well that, at any rate, is something we have in common."

And he stretched out his hand to Simon, his open hand. Simon hesitated – after all, anyone can join hands only in drunken solidarity – but then he put his hand into Frank's and Frank grasped it. The firmness, the warmth, the silky surface of other flesh, forgotten, and now unexpected; indeed as if one human being touching another was the rarest thing in the world. They both looked down at their hands, lingering there together, the hands of two men. And then the clasp slipped apart.

Frank said subduedly, "It's a beginning."

But for Simon it was a *fait accompli*, the whole thing now seemed straightforward. The concept of recklessness was forgotten, no longer relevant, and he raised his eyes like a lost lamb to the shepherd. Frank's eyes had withdrawn under the shadows of his black eyebrows, worried, holding off, but Simon's naivety bypassing all details and racing on ahead was too winning, so that he allowed himself to be kissed. Simon felt him retreat, but he thought it was discretion, not fear; not fear here.

Simon's sense of relief jarring with his incredulity was too obsessive; he failed to notice Frank fighting hard to keep up a veneer of drunken worldly-wisdom over a sudden incapacitating diffidence.

"I'm – surprised," said Simon.

"I thought it had been obvious from the start," said Frank. "At least from the research club. Whenever I looked up you were gazing at me, and vice versa."

"Yes," said Simon, wondering if it had really been so. "But one never really believes – that it's actually true."

He ventured an arm round Frank. He felt less vague about his actions than his words and thought they could compensate. Frank stiffened and shuffled it off by pretending a burst of drunken restlessness, changing his sitting position and jerking his head towards Calum.

"Christ, I thought he'd never fall asleep."

Simon looked at Calum, who was sleeping quite silently with a look of content that suddenly made Simon realise how discontented he usually looked.

"He wouldn't have minded," he said.

Frank looked quite uncomprehending.

"I'll get him a cover," Simon said. And both realised that in the tension of the last few moments they had even ignored the cold.

"You'd better make the fire up."

Simon went and fetched coal. He pulled back a corner of the kitchen curtain and stared out. It was still snowing. As he came back to the closed door of his room, he was halted in his steps by the realisation of the strangeness on the other side of it, and he opened it slowly, so that his re-entry should be gradual. Frank was standing just where he had been sitting, with a look on his face as if he was debating over making a move. Simon put down the coal without saying anything. Frank moved suddenly, grabbed hold of him and kissed him; but quickly, like a formal Russian greeting, and awkwardly because of their different heights.

"Can I have a drink of water, Simon?" he asked quietly, using his name. "I've drunk a bit much."

"Yes, in the kitchen," said Simon, and then, daring to feel as if he could fondly chide someone for whom he now had some responsibility, "You *do* drink rather a lot."

But Frank looked at first hurt, even threatening actually to pout, and then darkly defensive. "I like a little drink," he said.

Simon poked at the fire and then tipped on some coal. Frank called sharply from the kitchen, "Do you want some water too?"

"Yes," said Simon, and went through to join him.

He handed a cup of water to Simon and said, trying to cover up timidness with a note of self-annoyance, "I think I'm too drunk to go home. Can I sleep – here tonight?"

Again in Simon's mind the whole thing seemed decided, this was the breakthrough he had been waiting for; and he murmured his assent, as though humbly submitting himself into the hands of providence. And yet he had to admit he was totally bewildered by the immediate situation, that he had really no idea how to approach the lover who had finally appeared.

They went back into the other room, not speaking. Simon pulled back the bedclothes and laid the eiderdown over Calum. Frank stood looking as if he were steeling himself to jump into a swimming-pool that might be cold. Simon stood looking down, waiting for a direction.

"Where's the toilet?" said Frank.

"At the end of the hall."

He went out. Simon stood where he was in almost a physical pain of perplexity. Frank came back in, avoiding Simon's look. "I'll put the light off," he said, doing so before he had finished speaking.

In the sudden darkness, barely broken by the red glow from the fire, he stumbled against the bed and swore. As his eyes adjusted, Simon, still standing, could just make him out as he pulled his clothes off quickly and leapt under the covers, hissing and shaking.

"The sheets are like ice, for God's sake," he complained.

Shivering as he did so, Simon undressed, avoiding the light of the fire. Misery seeped quickly in through the skin exposed to the cold air. It crossed his mind that this was not like the mutual slow awed unveiling of the naked body he had sometimes fantasised. The cold made him scamper across to the bed, and when he got into it, he found that Frank was taking up so much room that he had to balance on the edge, and the cold closed like a vice on the parts of him not covered by the bedclothes. He was enveloped in the aroma of beer on Frank's breath, which he found nostalgically exciting, and the breath was so close that he could feel not just its warmth but its moisture. Flailing about a bit because of his balancing on the edge, he managed to slide his arm round Frank's shoulders; but there at once seemed so much of his body, such a huge area of other's flesh, that he stopped his hand there, overwhelmed in confusion and inexperience.

Frank's arm, alienly bulky, slipped like a cushion under his neck. "Christ, you've hardly got any room. Why didn't you say?" he said, not very quietly. But he did not move. Instead, he seemed to become at that moment very still and quiet, so that Simon could hear the tiny gurglings of his stomach, and he came out in gooseflesh. Simon felt as if his hand on Frank's shoulder had got lost halfway up a mountain, and was refusing to move in panic, waiting to be rescued.

Frank said, "I'm going to be sick. Let me out." In a flurry of knees and elbows he surged up and over Simon, banging him on the nose, landing shoulder-first on the floor and picking himself up swearing, and thudded to the door, which he flung wide open and did not close, so that the temperature dropped at once. Simon heard him run along the hall, then pause and retch, and there was the splash of vomit on the boards; then he padded on into the toilet, and coughed there for a while. The dry foggy smell of the outside air crept up over the bed. Simon lay there and felt utterly isolated, a stranger lost in his own life.

Frank was coming running back, his alien silhouette appeared in the light of the doorway; and then the door shut, and he was clambering over Simon, a sudden weight on the bed, and in beside him without touching him. He was shivering so much he could not speak, and from his breath now came the sour reek of vomit, and his skin, when Simon touched it, was as cold to the touch as metal.

"Are you alright now?" Simon asked.

"I don't usually do that. I can usually hold it. I haven't done that for years."

"Never mind."

"Hey, you can't stay in bed with me. What if Calum wakes up first?"

"He wouldn't worry."

"What do you mean? You'll have to sleep on the floor or something."

Puzzled, Simon silently moved his hand and ran it through Frank's hair, which was oily and wiry, quite unlike his own. He ran a finger along his moustache, so that he could feel its individual hairs springing back from his touch. It was all too alien to be erotic; but it felt transiently tender.

"There's just one thing," said Frank. "Who's going to clean up the mess in the hall?"

"I'll do it," said Simon. Suddenly he felt glad of the familiarity of quietly submitting himself for a chore. He slipped out of the bed and quickly pulled on some clothes, and scuttled with a bowl of hot water into the hall. When confronted, the vomit filled him with an unexpected horror, only aided by the cold. But fortunately the cold became the more preoccupying and also made him do the job quickly.

However inadequately heated the room was, he came back into it with relief, to find Frank had fallen asleep, breathing noisily through his mouth. He stood in front of the fire, and physically could not face sleeping on the floor in the freezing draughts. So he resolved to be sure to be up the first, since it seemed to worry Frank tonight, and eased himself painstakingly into half of the bed and lay tense on his side, trying to take up as little room as possible. Under the circumstances he was scarcely likely to sleep well, and it seemed as if no real unconsciousness came at all, no respite. When inevitable wakefulness began to assert itself, it did so by pointing to physical discomforts, the aching in the limbs he had held tight, the bar of pain over the eyes that had not slept. The room was lit with the false white gleam that reflected from snow. Calum was grunting and tossing in his chair. Simon sat up quickly and got out of bed. Again the heat of the fire had died down completely.

He dressed and ran through to get coal. The noise of making up the fire woke Calum. He stretched. "Jesus! My head!" he said quietly, like a commonplace observation. "It really should know better than to ache like that. I'll have to give it an aspirin. Simon, have you got an aspirin? By the way, good morning, if a slightly cold one."

"I'll get you something. Yes, it's freezing." He fixed Calum an Alka-Seltzer, and went shivering back to the kitchen to make coffee, not yet daring to open the curtains to see how heavy the snow was. In its sleepless blurriness his mind did not yet reach beyond the immediate mechanical tasks in hand. Calum went out to the toilet, with a little self-remonstrating groan, and while the kettle boiled Simon ran through to poke the fire. Frank heaved over in bed and woke suddenly, his eyes not sleepy, but at once louring. "What? What? What's that? What is it? Where's Calum?" he said, fumbling wildly to find what was specific in his sense of alarm. The toilet flushed wheezily in answer. "How long's he been up?" Frank asked.

"I was up first," said Simon, almost apologetically, going through to attend to the boiling kettle. "Would you like some coffee?" Only a grunt in answer. He put everything onto a tray and took it through, as

Calum came back into the room.

"Good morning, Frank. My head's not behaving. How do you feel?"

Frank was struggling to pull on his trousers under the bedclothes. "What's the time?" he said, now swinging his trousered legs out and sitting on the edge of the bed to finish dressing. "Oh, I don't get hangovers. I feel fine." Belying his words he went to stand, and sank back again, momentarily couching his head on his hands.

"It's not much after nine," said Simon, distributing the coffee.

"You shouldn't have bothered to make coffee," said Calum, smelling it appreciatively. "I'll be going soon, and leave you in peace."

Frank pricked up his ears. "I'll come with you, then, I'll come with you."

Simon's mind was suddenly jolted from the breakfast routine into a panic-stricken helplessness, that made him stare downwards, since its very violence made it impolite to reveal. Yet as he raised his cup as steadily as he could, Frank threw him a dark glance, but it was so very quick that it could just as well have been challenging Simon to keep silent as pleading with him to do something. Amidst absurd slurpings as they all waited impatiently for their coffee to cool, Simon felt inarticulacy, squirm from it as he might, close on him like an iron-maiden. He realised that in the whole seemingly momentous course of events he had exchanged only a handful of bland sentences with Frank. He wished that the coffee might cool slowly (ridiculous considering the temperature), so that there might be even a little more time for some-thing, just something to happen. But Calum was already gulping his coffee, and he could feel his own cup becoming comfortably warm in his hand. Then he raised his own eyes quickly but definitely to Frank, as if from the depths of a quicksand; but Frank was staring stolidly into his coffee, looking noticeably pale.

Calum put down his cup and stood up. "Thanks a lot for the coffee, Simon, it was good. And for letting me fall into a drunken stupor in your armchair," he said.

"Yes, thanks, thanks," muttered Frank, at once standing too.

Simon sat still, finishing the last sips of his coffee, knowing that his immobility must hold them up for a few seconds, a minute, a possibility.

"How much snow was there?" said Calum.

Frank said, "Come on, we'd better be going."

Simon put down his cup. He went to the window and drew the curtains. Dreariness. A whole world gone black and white. The snow was piled thick and already going grey with soot on the crests of the drifts. The sky was so pale, almost merging with the snow, and the false white gleam drained all brown from the stone of the looming tenement walls and left them yellowish-grey, their windows black holes into empty frozen vaults.

The weather forced Simon's concession to its hopelessness, its blankness. In any case, in the night he had felt only doubtful, he had been incredulous. It was Frank who had led the way, it was up to him – and he had given up, without speaking.

"Well, that was an enjoyable evening," said Calum as he clambered into his coat, frowning self-mockingly at the difficulty it gave him.

"Yes, well, I'll see you out," said Simon, feeling careless enough now to try consciously to look tragic, but to the hungover Calum succeeding only in seeming to look fed up with his company.

The three of them trooped into the hall, each now wrapped in a secluded hurt silence. Calum opened the door first, and Frank stepped regularly after, turning only at the last, and fearfully, to look at Simon, who stood still on the bare boards of the hallway of his solitary cell, like a marooned sailor watching from the dunes as his ship pulls away.

"Well, thanks again," said Calum conciliatorily. "See you."

Frank muttered, "Goodbye, Simon."

"Goodbye, Frank," said Simon; he had intended it to sound deliberate and reproachful, but it ended up timorous and bewildered. Even as he walked the few yards of the hall, had he not been thinking that it could not end like this, that something would still intervene, like a last-minute reprieve? Had he really acquiesced, so readily, in the dictatorship of silence?

Frank looked back at Simon as a schoolboy might look at a fellow who is being punished for some blatant transgression which he in fact committed, when both are too afraid of authority to speak. Then he seemed to have a sudden sensation of mere distaste at the situation, and turned and strode away impatiently.

Simon looked at the cloud of his expelled breath drifting through the freezing air, and then he shut the door slowly so that Frank might hear the long wail of its hinges, followed by the short slam, like a gunshot through the temples.

He went straight to the fire, and sank down, cradling himself by its generous warmth. He thought that the great sorrow of his life had just happened. The whole day fragmented before him; it could just as well already be evening, or even the next morning. Or even the next week. The ocean of torment ahead seemed endless and monotonous, and in a daze he stepped into it at once.

It seemed ages since darkness had fallen when at last he heard Philip and Annie come home. He heard them go into the kitchen, murmuring and laughing. He hung back, sitting motionless in his armchair. Suddenly he felt ashamed to impose himself on them, failure that he was; and yet it was necessary that they should know how complete a tragedy had now befallen him.

Slowly he got up and went out. In the doorway of the kitchen he stopped and stood waiting.

Annie looked up from making a fire and stared at his wraithlike appearance with genuine surprise. "Hallo love, come in," she said questioningly.

"I won't bother you for long," he got in at once. "Did you have a nice time?" In a martyred tone, he added, "I'm sorry, I feel a little upset."

From the stove where he was making tea, Philip exchanged looks with Annie and smiled knowingly. They knew the game that was about to begin. But they were feeling very happy with one another after the wedding. There was enough support to go round.

Yet silently but mutually both at first ignored Simon's announcement of a problem. Annie drank cups of tea and crocheted squares and babbled, in her own combination of sweetness and pointedness, about her odd relations who had been at the wedding, and their days in Edinburgh; and Philip curled up amid clouds of pipe-smoke and tossed out scraps of plans for all their futures. The fire went well, and in a while they ended up in front of it playing scrabble.

When the game finished, Simon, who had been nervously watching the clock, said that he had better be going to bed, finishing pointedly, with a distant glance into the fire, "I'm feeling better now, thanks."

"Just have one more cup of tea before you go," said Annie.

"No, I'm alright, I've imposed my misery on you long enough. I'll go." But the routine was all rather wasted on Philip and Annie, who did not need to be ingratiated and knew it all too well, were even bored with it because of its strict limitations.

Philip cajoled affectionately, and with a note of a laugh in his voice meant to suggest that Simon would in fact be silly not to give way. "Come on, what's wrong, Simon?"

He yielded with relief. "Well, I'm upset because – because of *someone*, last night."

Philip rather shrunk away, perhaps because realistically he supposed there was no forseeable way out for Simon from his sexual inexperience. Annie, however, was ready to make the concession to triviality.

"Did you see someone you liked?" she asked, trying to make it sound as if she thought Simon's concern would seem quite justified.

"Well, no, I met someone." And he proceeded to pick his way through the story, like someone who believes in ghosts having to cross a graveyard to reach their desired goal. But at last he had to come to the end, to the final terrible parting. He fell away in silence in awe of his great sorrow. No condolence, he now realised after all, would have any effect whatsoever.

"But Simon, that's wonderful," said Annie. "What are you so upset for, when you've finally met someone?"

Simon did not understand. "But he went away."

"But he's bound to come back. Do you know where he lives?"

"He didn't tell me."

"Did you ask him?"

"Well, no."

"Well, most likely he'll come to see you then. And listen, you met him in the Sultan's Palace? Well, most likely he'll look for you again there. At the weekend, for instance, when most people go. So I tell you what, on Saturday night Philip and I'll come with you to the Sultan's Palace – it's not such a bad pub after all – and most likely he'll be there."

Such a practical approach was overwhelming. Simon had expected nothing more than consolation.

Philip asked, "There would have been the sense of there being something between you in the morning, even if you didn't talk?"

Simon was somewhat nonplussed by the general air of heterosexual optimism. "Yes, I think so," he said. That was true in a way.

"Tell us what he was like," asked Annie, curious to know.

Simon thought. He realised he had perceived very little about Frank at all. "He could drink an incredible amount," he said.

Annie looked puzzled, as if that was not what she had been expecting.

"He probably needed to build up a bit of courage," said Philip.

"Well, m'dear, it's only the beginning, you should be feeling glad," said Annie firmly, settling the final atmosphere. "Now let's have a last cup of tea." The tension broke. It was all over as quickly as that, and all changed.

They chatted and made jokes over the tea, and Simon relaxed sufficiently to sit back from the edge of the chair for the first time that evening. Then he decided to go to bed anyway, because the lack of sleep was beginning to tell on him.

It was much less cold than it had been. Peering from his window, it looked to him as if the surface of the snow was no longer even frozen, and the branch of a tree could be seen swaying in a gentle wind.

He turned on the radio. The end of a news bulletin passed his ears in an unregistered blur, though he caught something from far away about an improvement in the weather at long last. He switched it off again, and stood in the silence, which had lost all sternness, as under a warm shower. Then he began to undress.

He paused before the fire, and its warmth was kind and sufficient. The shape of the day had fused together again and it was time to sleep. He put off the light and lay down and wrapped himself up tight in the darkness, while the bed held him afloat, as if he were drifting somewhere he would be happy to reach. And outside there came a hesitant quiet patter of rain – the thaw! He placed his hand on his own warm naked shoulder and cradled himself. Quickly the patter grew more and more insistent, and soon there came the slither and thud of melting snow falling from the eaves.

CHAPTER SIX

He did come back after all.

Looking back now, it all seemed so very clear: and yet so very distant.

Yes, he thought, settling back in his seat beside the train window, glancing smilingly at Philip and Annie snuggled up opposite, he had gained great strength from the relationship with Frank. But not in the way he'd expected. It was as if in order to find one's strengths, one had first to understand one's weakness.

The train creaked and began to move. The weather had held, and they were off to do their observance to the spring on the shores of Loch Lomond. Simon closed his eyes, lulled by the sunshine falling on his face through the glass and the rhythmical movement of the train, feeling his mind slip back through all the levels of his recent experience, right back down to that moment in the dead of winter.

Yes, he did come back after all. On the Friday Philip and Annie had gone with Vanessa to spend the night with her parents in Milngavie. Simon sat reading; and late, about ten, there had been a timid knock on the door, so tentative that at first Simon was uncertain whether he had heard it at all. But it came again, a single quick tap, as if the knocker themself were hesitant whether they were knocking or not.

He had got up, unwilling to be disturbed, and slowly gone to open the door. There, so incredibly to Simon that he did not realise it at once, was Frank: but it was as if a different Frank. Pale, timorously polite, unsure of himself, unsure even how to manage his heavily built body, which had moved before with such swagger. He had missed the pub, he explained. Perhaps Simon had something to drink in the house? But was he alone?

Simon had only coffee. They sat stiffly on two hard kitchen chairs, staring into their mugs. They had nothing to say to one another.

In the silence it was possible to hear the ticking of Philip's alarm-clock from the other room.

Eventually Simon said in a hushed voice, "I didn't think you'd come back." He gazed up at Frank over the edge of his mug like a stray kitten at an approaching stranger.

Frank froze momentarily, mug raised. "Oh, I always intended to come back," he said, with a start of embarrassment, as if challenged about an act of rudeness. Warily he began again to move his mug to his mouth.

"But yesterday –" Simon began, and faltered in the strangeness of the place.

Frank swallowed noisily. "I thought to come back yesterday would have been a bit presumptuous," he said nervously, dipping his eyes, and then frowning. He was silent for a while, as if in pain, clutching his mug tightly. Simon waited, lost in fearfulness. A trickle of sweat ran out from under his arm and slid slowly and coldly down his side. Frank said, "I was wondering if I could stay here tonight." Almost in a whisper, looking straight across at him.

So everything was alright after all, Simon had thought. And it was, because later they had gone to bed.

They lay beside one another like ramrods. As though each was waiting for something from outside to take control of them. But it did not.

"Shall we go to sleep?" said Frank at last, after a few fumblings. And sleep did not come either. Simon stumbled through half-consciousness, reaching out for points of reference that were not there, menaced unexpectedly by violent dream-images that shocked him back into wakefulness. The comfortable warmth of two bodies, the suggestive scent of sweat – the most they had managed to share – seemed to change to an irritating heat and stench. And then suddenly Frank was throwing off the covers, getting out of bed, saying he could not sleep, turning on the table-lamp, sitting sighing restlessly over a book. At last he had gone home in the middle of the night, arranging hesitantly to meet Simon at eleven o'clock the next morning in a pub, where Simon would normally never have dreamt of being so early. By then Simon was too anxious to sleep.

Frank had kept the appointment. But the day was tense and aimless. They went to a film neither of them wanted to see; they had a Chinese meal neither of them felt much appetite for; they had, as Frank put it, a few drinks. That night they agreed to go home their separate ways. And Frank would visit Simon the following evening.

Much to Simon's relief, Philip and Annie had been in that next night. On his own he had already begun to feel the zigzagging thread of Frank's attention slipping from his grasp like a kite-rope. But with Philip and Annie Frank seemed to relax, becoming quite expansive, talking confidently about history and politics. To Simon it was as though this was yet another Frank. A sense of confusion had begun to threaten which he refused to acknowledge, even to believe in.

Philip and Annie liked Frank that night. "He's a very nice man indeed, m'dear," whispered Annie excitedly in the kitchen. "You're very lucky." Even Philip allowed a cautious smile. They were optimistic for Simon. The light was at the end of the tunnel.

So it had started. Rather perfunctorily, he thought now, drowsily watching the bright green of trees in new leaf flash past the windows again and again. Yes, it all seemed so brief and superficial in the memory, but how every minute must have dragged and grated past at the time, as if the fearfulness, the sensitivity of it would never be forgotten, would never be healed.

How endless had seemed what had followed that hesitant beginning. And yet objectively it had lasted a few short months. If only, he thought now again as he had thought often before, if only Frank had liked himself a bit more, it might all have been different. If only he had just accepted himself.

Poor lonely Frank! So much in need of love: so full of a hatred of being gay.

An endless time, an endless time. How to separate one night from another? They had taken a bus to the city, and were walking to their third pub — "One of those pubs," Frank said, "where poofs go, like you. Or so I've heard." Tonight he'd had four pints so far.

Frank's legs were long, and he walked quickly and stridingly as usual when he was beginning to feel his drink, so that Simon had to keep breaking into a scampering run to keep up with him. An erratic north wind kept flinging masterful drizzly gusts at them from behind corners, halting them in their steps, reaching through their coats with an icy grip, numbing their faces. The streets were damp and empty.

As they drew near the pub, Frank deliberately speeded up, so that he was standing in the dark doorway looking mockingly impatient as Simon came scuttling after. "Ladies first," he said, gesturing clownishly, shutting himself away behind a smile at his own gibe.

Simon hesitated, looking panic-stricken. This was one of the last places he wanted to go, with or without Frank. But to appease him, and to show him that for all his dismay he at least was not contemptuous of this place, he stepped forward and put his arm warily against the smoked-glass door, through which there penetrated only a dim yellow light.

"What's the matter? Don't you want to join your own kind?" said Frank snappily, determined not to have his scorn defused.

Simon leant against the heavy door, which swung open reluctantly, fanning out a smell of stale cigarette smoke, and stepped gingerly inside, trying to look confidently straight ahead, worried by his wind-swept hair. He could feel his skin prickling under curious and suspicious gazes lurking behind the veil of smoke. The pub was gloomy, all dark wood and dingy light. Then the door opened again, and with the cold draught came Frank, swinging his body loosely beside and above Simon. "Well, well, fancy finding you here!" he said, gathering Simon into a supercilious survey of the other customers. Then, seeming suddenly galvanised into purposefulness, he said shortly and seriously,

"It's your round. I want a pint and a whisky chaser. And you can manage one of your half-pints here, not another orange-juice."

Simon pushed forward and nervously ordered the beer, regarded rather aggressively by the barman. While he waited for it, he looked from the corner of his eye at a group by the corner of the bar. They were of indeterminate age and grotesquely dressed. The one nearest to Simon was wearing an overly tight-fitting white suit with wide lapels, and his hair was tinted and piled in a perm above his haggard face, dull sad eyes hidden in cavernous sockets among the deep lines.

"We all know what you want, hen," he was saying, in a voice whose mechanical vigour seemed out of phase with his appearance. "Bleeding piles once a month."

There was a shriek from a greying man in a pale blue cashmere sweater and yellow check trousers. "Do you hear that! Just because you're past the change of life," he said, and turning to a third, touching him on the arm, added, "They'll soon have to pull her down, because her internal structure's rotting." And then there were shrieks and hollow laughs all round.

The barman handed Simon his drinks with an inhospitable, almost a warning glare. Managing the glasses precariously, Simon turned and found Frank gone. At last he spotted him lounging at a table, apparently enjoying Simon's discomfiture.

Simon watched the progress of the whisky uneasily. He knew the stages of Frank's drunkenness only too well these days, and whisky was among the worst.

But true to his strenuous efforts at total elusiveness through sheer unpredictability, it was one of those rare moments of an almost humble sobriety that seemed to follow his first taste. "Christ, what are we doing coming here?" he said quietly. "This is like a freak-show contrived and put on by the freaks for one another."

Cautiously, Simon allowed himself to look a little further about the pub. To him now the faces of young and old seemed all alike engraved, above all, with bitterness. Aging men smoking quietly in dark corners like hunters' hides, boyish young men laying themselves out vacantly against the walls, big butch men leaning arrogantly back against the bar, the primped queens endlessly trying to put one another down, all seemed united in a great tiredness, and beyond that, a greater resentment. These might have been the faces of the starving.

When Simon looked back at the table, he saw the whisky almost finished. Raising his eyes with a start, he saw Frank at the point of change, uncertainty flickering in his face.

"Eyeing up the talent, are you?" he said distantly. Already he was retreating somewhere else. "Well, I doubt if any of them will find you particularly beautiful. Christ, you might at least have washed your hair to come here."

"I didn't know we were coming here," said Simon quickly, perplexedly.

But Frank had vanished behind Miss-Havisham-like veils of tragedy. "You don't know what it's like, you don't know what it's like," he said, a thin trickle of spittle inching out of his mouth as he left it gaping for a moment, "to have lost something truly beautiful."

Simon recognised the theme, and was overwhelmed by helplessness. His only resource was his persistence. He felt that if only he waited, love at last would sort everything out for them; that if only he bore everything Frank asked of him without a grudge, Frank at last, having spent all his bitterness, would be grateful and kind. And certainly, it was true, Frank had stayed with him.

"It's terrible. I should have married Su-Lin," Frank said in a voice of melodramatic outrage, throwing his head back against the wall and staring stormily into space. "Her father takes her back to Malaysia to marry some relative she hardly knows, and I end up here! You never saw her. You never saw something so beautiful. You don't know how much she was admired. How much I was envied." His voice seemed to posture like an overenthusiastic amateur actor.

Distressed, Simon looked across at him, a dutiful audience, although he had heard this story many times before. But he wanted to know what part he was to play in it this time, whether he was to be commiserator, or just a point of comparison, or what. He wanted to feel of service in order to screen himself from the scorn and injury he did not want to believe in.

Frank was still looking away, gesturing now with his hand in the smoky air. "The first time I saw her, she seemed to float along, she wasn't connected to this world. Her face never moved, she was so graceful, she was like a statue. And I said to myself, I have to know that woman." His speech was beginning to slip and slide. For a moment his expression became immobile, and then his eyes filled with tears, and yet remained stupidly vacant, so that he looked like a small child dutifully preparing to cry again over a long-healed hurt.

Simon suddenly became aware of people looking at the two of them, some of them mildly amused, some scoffing, some filled with distaste. He felt awkward and powerless. "Frank," he murmured, vaguely, half in quiet remonstration.

Frank turned sharply to look full at him, grasping his pint glass firmly, his eyes narrowing with spite. He guzzled his beer, and his moustache dripped lankly. "I know what you'd like to think," he said between his teeth, nodding slowly. "I know. But it was because I didn't touch her that she liked me. Because I handled her with respect. I wanted to have her because she was a thing of beauty – of true beauty –

and other people would envy me. Yes, and I know that she was pleased, she was flattered, to have such a handsome companion. Her sister called me that — 'your handsome companion, Su-Lin'. Because I am handsome. I know you have to admit that." He cast a glance of scornful challenge at Simon, and sipped his beer.

"Yes," said Simon, humbly glad to find some support to offer, "of course I think you're handsome, Frank."

"You think, you think!" muttered Frank hissingly, turning aside again, lifting a foot onto the leather bench-seat and crooking his knee. "I am. Among other things. So what am I doing ending up here?" He sighed, a sigh of exasperation closing in on itself, and was silent for a moment. Simon felt sure that people must be talking about them, but dared not look. "I suppose you feel put down by all this," Frank said, adopting a knowing expression.

"No," said Simon, "I understand." He wanted to believe that he did. The topic of Su-Lin recurred erratically, and it seemed impossible to sort fact from fantasy in much of what Frank said about it, as with most things. He chose to assume that the element of fantasy in this case made it less threatening, though nowadays he often found himself quite uncertain where the threats to him really lay.

Frank smiled dismissively at his response. "Never mind," he said wearily, "never mind. You'll make somebody a good wife one day." He turned back to face Simon, looking pleased with himself, and slid his hand across under the table, grasping Simon's knee and then inching his fingers along till he could touch his crotch. "If not me," he added, suddenly withdrawing the hand, and drumming now with his fingers on the table.

For a moment, Simon drooped in bewilderment.

"Look at me," Frank went on, grumbling and aggrieved, staring at the table, until his whole face seemed thrown into shadow by his brow. "Look at me. Christ! The best graduate of my year! I could be an important historian. And instead I end up wasting my time with these – side-issues. Why, why can't I make do with masturbating among the manuscripts?" And suddenly he had ceased to be theatrical or manipulative. He had become naked and desperate, his eyes no longer young but old; as if he were lying there unable to help himself, wounded in the battle of self against self.

"I don't think that would be the answer," said Simon gently, and in spite of his constant terror of rejection, he leaned across and reassuringly touched Frank's big hand where it lay motionless and exhausted. Frank did not pull it away.

After a few moments he said, "Christ, let's get out of here and go to that party you were talking about." He moved his hand away, seized his glass, and downed the rest of the beer in long gulps. Then he slid energetically along the bench and sprang to his feet. "Come on."

Simon followed uneasily along the windswept street, down the muddied steps to the subway station, into its dank dungeon-like smell. Silence immured both of them, they were prisoners side by side in solitary confinement. The train rattled out of the tunnel, small and pathetic and slow, like an asthmatic old man. Tossed around inside its dingy interior, Simon felt trapped.

He seemed to have to be always on the defensive. Every meeting with Frank seemed to leave him with yet more reproaches to answer to. Waiting for Frank, who was always some half an hour late, or sometimes did not turn up at the arranged time at all, he would sit embarrassedly alone in the pub of that night, pretending to read but in fact going over again and again a confused apologia for his very existence, a fantasy discourse that in reality he was never given time to deliver, even if he had mustered the resignation to do so in the first place.

The train lurched and creaked as it drew unevenly into a station, and he reached out to steady himself. There was always the belief that patience would finally be rewarded. A red-faced drunk dropped heavily into the seat opposite, and stared at first incredulously, and then contemptuously at Simon and Frank. The train swayed into motion again.

Simon had come to dread meeting people he knew with Frank, and so the prospect of tonight's party – which was being held by the friend of a friend, no one he knew personally at all – filled him with trepidation. Frank always seemed suddenly possessed of a violent desire to disown him in public. With his own friends he would do so by mocking Simon, while with Simon's friends he would become generally objectionable or actually abusive, and go on mocking them to Simon even when they were alone. Simon always found it much more straightforward to defend his friends than himself, but it left him disturbed by a conflict of loyalties he hardly understood, and certainly did not want.

When they arrived at the party, they did not seem particularly welcome. The little-known face that opened the door made no attempt to hide a suspicious discomfort. Perhaps, Simon thought with some alarm, their reputation had gone before them. People seemed to him to be looking at them over their shoulders, turning away sharply once they were noticed and looking busy with another conversation. He felt cut off.

Not so Frank apparently, who had already launched himself into the midst of the group in the lounge like an unknown dog rushing into the midst of a children's ball-game, unaware of or undaunted by their immediate suspicion and reluctance. Having turned into a display the opening of a cadged can, which sprayed everywhere, he began to scatter miscalculated charm about him like someone trying to force leaflets into the hands of a passing crowd, concentrating with a clumsy pointedness on the women who had obviously made an effort to be noticed, but who equally obviously were far from flattered by the mawkish attentions of a drunken Frank. Simon slipped quietly and ignominiously into a corner in embarrassment; only to realise that he had ended up next to Norman, whom he felt obliged to acknowledge quite warmly, in a flurried attempt to salvage his own dignity.

Norman smiled at him benignly, as if bestowing his blessing, one eye on Frank, not quite successfully hiding its misgivings. In his dismay, Simon found himself striking up a conversation with him in a desperate search for a touch of companionship. He hoped Frank would not notice them, or if he did, that he would not feel curious about Norman, or suspect anything that might provide further fuel for his ridicule.

But Frank could be seen leaving the room, looking rather petulant, head in air, obviously in search of more willing playmates. Despite himself, Simon felt relieved: but not for long. The hostess of the party, a woman of his own age, but in her dress, her manner, and her self-possession seeming much older, suddenly appeared at his side with a worried purposeful look on her face.

"I wonder if you could take care of your friend Frank," she said coldly. "He's being, well, a bit obstreperous. I'm afraid he's going to do some damage or something."

"Oh, he doesn't do that," said Simon breathlessly, filling with a shocked consternation.

"Well, that's alright," the hostess went on stiffly, her concern clearly unallayed. "Nevertheless, I'd really be happier if he went, Simon. Of course, you can stay if you like. But he wasn't invited, and – well . . ." She stared at him awkwardly, and then with a half-smile of politeness, turned and left the room in silence. Simon gave Norman a brief nervous glance, doing his best not even to see his response, and followed quickly after.

He found Frank in the hall, propped untidily against the door of the toilet, frowning solitarily at his boots. The door opened behind him, he stumbled out of the way, almost losing his balance, but covered this with a mock bow and muttered some complimentary badinage to the woman who came out. Her impatient embarrassed forward gaze and refusal to reply suggested this was not her first encounter with him. As she marched past Simon, she threw him a look half-puzzled, half-amused.

Simon went up to Frank, and stopped at a timorous distance, as if subconsciously planting himself beyond arm's reach. "I think we should go," he said cautiously.

"Oh, you do, do you? I don't want to go. I'm having a good time. Do you object to me having a good time?" Frank rocked perilously from side to side as he spoke.

"We've been asked to leave," said Simon into his boots, feeling reluctantly forced into telling the truth, even if that was not quite the truth, which he proceeded to stumble awkwardly into. "They're worried about you – about your being drunk."

Eventually, Simon ended up having to more or less drag Frank away. Of course, he could not have done so if Frank had not been willing to move, and merely enjoying a teasing game – a mood which continued once they were outside.

"I'm coming to sleep in your bed tonight," said Frank, ambling unperturbed through the cold wind a little ahead of Simon.

"That will be nice," said Simon, with a certain deep relief at the confirmation of his beliefs.

"Nice! Nice!" Frank spoke in a mincing tone, picking the word up by its tip and dangling it in front of an imaginary audience, like a schoolmaster trying to shame a schoolboy before his peers. "You have such a nice vocabulary, Simon. Such a nice way of putting things. Sometimes your background sticks out like a sore thumb." Frank's father was of working–class origins, but had become an army officer and married the daughter of an up-and-coming family in the clothing trade. Frank, however, liked to think of himself as working–class, despite loud pretensions to academia. "Yes, I know your type," he launched out. "When I was at school, we used to stand on the edge of the rugby ground and peer through the railings at the public school kids who played in the ground next door. We knew what they were, and you were one of them."

"I don't think I'll stay with you after all," he said suddenly, stopping still and trying to look proud, but looking more absurd, his eyelids drooping, his body swaying. "You'll have to make me." And he ran off down an alley just ahead.

Tears of exhaustion came to Simon's eyes, but he rejected them. He ran after and found Frank lurking just around the corner, with a boyishly mischievous look.

"I knew you'd come after me," he said, moving away at once as if for fear Simon might touch him. "The devoted dog following its master."

They arrived at Simon's place at last, cold and wet. It was deathly silent. The others were already asleep.

Frank cast his eyes slowly and balefully around the room, as though surveying the walls of a cell in which he was about to spend a long sentence. After a moment's stillness, he seemed suddenly to crumble onto a chair, and buried his head in his hands. Fearfully Simon went to him, and as tentatively as though it might have been red–hot, laid a hand on his shoulder. Frank reached for it fumblingly with one hand; and for a second nothing moved. Then he shook it off restlessly, and scowled up at Simon through his fingers like a caged animal. He leapt to his feet, his face once more animated by mischief. "Let's have some music," he said. "It's as silent as the grave." He went to the record-player and put on a record of Piaf, which he was always playing.

Exhausted, Simon made coffee, and they drank it in sullen silence, while the by-now-familiar record of Frank's choice surged on. At last it finished, and Simon turned down the bed.

Frank waited ostentatiously until Simon had got into bed before he undressed in front of the fire, grumbling as usual about the temperature, as if the weather were Simon's fault. And yet he stood naked for a moment by the fire, as though posing, until he could be sure Simon was looking at him.

"Quite a fine body, all things considered, wouldn't you say?" he said, staring into space above Simon's head, running his slightly nicotine-stained hands down his heavy torso to the point where his stomach was only just, surprisingly enough, beginning to run to beer-pot.

A strange dark confusion moved deep down within Simon's body, fear and desire contending somewhere in his abdomen. He said nothing, humbly receiving the exhibition of Frank's body, expecting no more, suppressing resentment.

Frank leant his head back and shook it from side to side, stroking the top of his shoulders with his thick black hair. "That's nice," he said purringly, "very sensual. I think I'll just stand here and do this. A lot better than your inept hands fumbling all over me."

Simon's tentative erection subsided, and a small pain suddenly lodged like a stone in his throat. He stifled a long sigh, pulling the covers tightly over him, trying not to touch his own flesh lest he awaken the ache of its frustrated arousal. To escape decisions he closed his eyelids, while his eyes struggled restlessly for resumed wakefulness; but he kept them shut, until at long last he heard Frank padding heavily about the room, the light went off, and hot and smelling of beer and cigarettes, his presence invaded the bed beside him.

"I'm going to sleep," he growled distantly, and turned over on his side, holding his body so that no part of it touched Simon's. Simon lay still, tense, waiting for the unconsciousness that would usher in another day, another resumption, another chance.

Yes, there had been so many nights like that, over and over, nothing really changing, thought Simon, opening his eyes as the train drew into a station. In a few moments they would be there. He blinked in the sunlight. The platform was studded with bright beds of tulips and daffodils. How remote now was that feeling that everything had come to a dead end when Frank first left. As the train began to pull out on the last stretch, he remembered with a wry smile how he sat alone in his room with the darkness gathering about him, staring out at the empty eventless March sky, waiting, waiting.

The front door opened and closed. He heard Annie going into the kitchen. He rustled the pages of a book on the table beside him to try and signal his presence. She came into his room.

"Hallo, m'dear. I didn't think you were in. What are you doing sitting in the dark?"

"Oh, I just – felt like it," he said softly.

"Is something wrong?" Annie struggled with the after–work weariness of her voice. "Just a minute and I'll put your light on. Then we'll have a wee pot of tea."

Light slammed into the room, relentlessly exposing its stark familiarity. He said nothing. Annie came tentatively towards the chair again, curious and concerned. "Well, do you want some tea?" she said quietly, impatient at least for a response.

"Yes, yes," he said, making a frail noble attempt at acknowledgment of the outside world, adding, as though it deserved to be regarded like himself only as a side–issue, "Frank went away last night."

Annie paused. A certain momentary relief crossed her face, and as her features settled into a look of concern, they seemed to do so almost dutifully. "You can't be sure it's for good just yet, m'dear," she said, kindly and wisely.

"Perhaps not," Simon said weakly, as a bereaved person responds to a well-meant lie.

"And anyway," said Annie, looking down, "there were problems. You must admit. Well, I'll just go and make a wee pot of tea and we can talk about it. Philip should be home soon. You just stay there." The sweetness of her words seemed for a moment the only real light and warmth there was.

And of course he had come back again. And again.

Simon had bumped into Frank about a fortnight after their first separation, although the interval had seemed much longer. He walked into him in a queue in the union coffee-bar. Frank went ashen, as if he had seen a ghost. Simon had his manner of civilised friendliness already prepared; no other manner was allowed within the dictates of his longsuffering loyalty.

Clearly Frank was surprised that Simon spoke with him at all; at first surprised, then rapidly grateful. Loneliness welled out of him, like blood from a wound. Within a few days the routine of their relationship had recommenced almost as if nothing had happened.

And Frank left for a second time some three weeks later. That was when things began to change.

It was late at night, about twelve, and Frank was very drunk after the habitual pub-crawl. Somewhere during the evening they had chanced on some woman friend of Su-Lin's, whom Frank, recognising, had tried clumsily and unctuously to charm, pointedly ignoring the presence of Simon: a presence whose significance the woman clearly understood only too well. Polite at first, she had become increasingly cold and silent, and finally, much to everyone's surprise, she had suddenly stood up and called him "a drunken calculating self-inflated hypocrite, who might at least have had the decency to introduce your boyfriend", before walking stiffly from the pub.

Shaken at first, Frank had slowly been putting his pride back together again by attempting to degrade Simon. By the time they got home to Simon's place, he had gathered a considerable momentum. He alternately stood before the fire or lounged in the armchair, haranguing Simon about his ineffectuality, while Simon pleaded patiently that he was tired and wanted to go to bed.

Frank muttered, "Where's that record?" He lurched over and rummaged untidily through Simon's records like a burglar.

"Quietly," said Simon. "The others are asleep. Let's just go to bed." He felt momentarily defeated.

"Just because you don't appreciate real music," said Frank, with an intransigent playfulness, his back to Simon, putting the record on the turntable. "I don't know why you've got this record. I'm not sick of it, anyway."

It was the Piaf, of course. Frank must have played it at least every other time he visited. Her voice suddenly electrified the room, inescapable, undeniable, and Frank sat back with a look of satisfaction, soaking up this self-pity and self-delusion raised to the level of an act of devotion, that could not be argued with.

His expression suddenly changed to a scornful leer. "So you want to go to bed do you?" he said ruminatively. "And I suppose you expect me to get into bed with you. Though you don't actually say so. But that's all your little brain revolves around, isn't it? The need for a husband." He paused, and his voice resumed increasingly harsh and loud, as if he were trying to shout down the record. "You don't know what intellect means. You could never be a real man, you could never have any effect on the world. Ok, so you want sex, do you? Well, I'll give you sex. Now. Yes, you've waited long enough. I'll show you how a real man gives sex, so that you have something at least to remember."

And he rose to his full height and advanced slowly towards Simon, swinging his hips like an actor in a B-western.

"Take down your trousers," he said portentously, looking down out of eyes narrowed to slits, one index finger playing with an end of his moustache.

Simon was alarmed and confused. After a few seconds uncertainty, he fumblingly undid his jeans and then let them slip slowly to the ground, where they gathered awkwardly round his ankles.

"Lie on your face." The words emerged indistinctly, because Frank was trying to speak through his teeth without moving his lips.

Simon stood there uncomprehending, handcuffed by the trousers around his ankles. "Frank," he said quietly, remonstratingly. "Let's go to bed."

In the background now, Piaf's voice stepped slowly down wide steps into a moonlit garden. "Quand il me prend dans ses bras, je sens mon coeur qui bat, je vois la vie en rose."

Frank nodded slowly and solemnly, staring fixedly at Simon. "Lie on your face, you little poof," he said spittingly. And punched Simon in the eye.

Simon lost his balance and fell over. His heart was pounding; he felt jarred throughout his whole body. The punch itself was not painful – in fact, even as it happened he had thought, that's funny, I expected it to hurt more – but the shock was like a pain: a pain composed of incredulity, of fear, of self-pity, of helpless outrage. He lay where he had fallen, unable to move for what felt like an age, transfixed by these emotions, staring at Frank.

Piaf's voice basked by a fire, eyes melting and grateful. "Je n'oublierai jamais," she sang, "la belle histoire d'amour."

"You liked that. Didn't you? Didn't you?"said Frank, his speech uttered like blows. "All these months you've let me drag you around by the hair! Yes, you like it. Don't you? You like it."

"I've tried to give you what you want," said Simon pathetically, groping for understanding as he might grope for glasses that had been knocked off in an attack.

Frank dropped swiftly to his knees and leant over him, bringing his face so near that his spittle sprayed into Simon's eyes as he spoke. "Turn over," he said, grabbing Simon's shoulder tightly. "I'm going to fuck you. Just once. Just so you know what it feels like."

Piaf's voice was sinking away in triumphant joy: "Et il m'emportera! Et il m'emportera!"

Simon rolled over and lay unprotesting but tense, smelling the dust of the carpet in his nostrils, hearing Frank struggling awkwardly with his zip. And then Frank dropped on him, he was heavy, he crushed him so that he could scarcely breathe. He jabbed clumsily with his penis, pushing Simon awkwardly apart. It hurt, and Simon felt as if he was stifling beneath Frank's lumbering weight.

Frank suddenly seemed to have become only an inanimate force, pressing him down.

He tried to cry out in panic, but as if in a nightmare he had no breath to speak.

"See how you let me do it to you," Frank said into his ear, so close he felt the heat of his breath against the lobe. "You're something that's easy to possess."

And then Frank pulled himself violently out, stood up, and began to do up his trousers. "And discard," he added.

Breath flooded back over Simon in warm waves of relief. He lay still, his eyes closed, watching a strange calm make its way towards him. Slowly he recognised it. It was the calm of decision.

"And now I'm going," he heard Frank say. "You got what you wanted, but you're not what I want. I've got things to do in the world. You can stay here in your chamber and pine. I'm going. Goodbye."

Simon did not look round, he did not even open his eyes. The door closed. Certainty put its arms around him and gently lifted him. He sat up, resolved, staring at the empty carpet stretching away towards the wall.

After its arduous journey through the length of the record, Piaf's voice had attained a sane firmness. "J'ai payé," she sang confidently, "balayé, oublié, je me fous du passé!"

As his body settled down, he felt a sense of his own adequacy that he had never known. As if shaken into place by the violence of a few moments ago, he felt the isolated blurred insights of the last two months joining together into a clear understanding. Compared to Frank, he was stable, he was positive about himself, he was forward-looking. He had never realised these things before. As he pulled up his jeans, a little smile tugged insistently at his lips.

Sitting still on the dampish grass, basking in the kind spring sun-shine, gazing endlessly at the loch, only a flash of bright water from here with the hills behind leaning over it like concerned figures, Simon found himself amazed at his own calm these days. It was only just now that he had told Philip and Annie of Frank's latest stormy departure – how many final departures did that make? – a scene which had kept him up the previous night, and made him, after all, so pleasantly drowsy today. It had not been the first thing that he had wanted to tell them when he woke, as once it would have been. Instead he had set off with them on the planned trip to the country without a murmur, and let more than half the day go by before he thought to mention it. And it could not disturb the comfortable quiet that had now descended on the three of them, as they wandered in their own thoughts and dreams. The silence about them began to come into focus, comprised of bird-song, rustling leaves and distant voices.

The sun was hazing over a little now and a breeze from the loch brought a hint of chill. Philip sat up. "I think we've had the best of the day, loves," he said. "Shall we go to the station? If we go now, we'll have time to make tea and have a wee pint or two."

They set off down the grassy hill, fragrant in the late afternoon, and soon were among the woods by the loch's side. Tree-roots criss-crossed the earthen arm of the path like its veins. Rhododendrons flaunted themselves, frail white to shameless crimson among the shadows. All three of them felt yet another quickening of gratitude for the reasserted generosity of nature.

Philip seemed to glance about and sniff the air like a dog on a walk. "Those clothes suit you, Simon," he said, with a playful warmth.

Rather daringly, he thought to himself, Simon had ventured a red chiffon scarf with his new short-cut corduroy jerkin. He smiled his appreciation at Philip.

"A dashing figure like you, I think it's time you started picking people up for yourself, instead of waiting to be picked up by the likes of Frank," said Philip, with an earnestness that hid itself cautiously behind an assured joking manner.

Simon did not know what to say, but he found the image attractive, or rather supportive. He could almost feel himself walking a little taller.

The trees batted their leaves in a final burst of sunshine, sending down a shimmer of tiny lights and murmurs like a soothing shower.

Frank had returned of his own accord only a few days after his second departure. There he was at the door, late one night, leaning drunkenly against the jamb, with the look of a little boy expecting to be forgiven. Half in weariness, half in amused astonishment, Simon let him in.

"You see, Simon," he had said later, with a certain unconcealed brashness, "I need you. I've come to depend on you. I'm lonely."

But when he stormed off yet again, rather unconvincingly this time, a week or so later, Simon was less sure than he had ever been that he needed Frank.

And in the course of Frank's regular but unpredictable returns that followed over the next month, he had found himself, if anything, becoming mildly annoyed at his reappearance. It was not so much that his patience had been tried too far, but a glimmering realisation that he had no reason to expect that it should be tried so much in the first place. There was more to be demanded of a relationship than suffering it in the faith that it would suddenly and mysteriously conform to the ideal at last. Quite clearly, this relationship was not going to do that.

Philip made a luxurious and inventive salad for tea, an inspired response to the blessing of the weather; and by the time they arrived at the pub, there was still a glimmer of light in the western sky, sealing the sense of oncoming summer. They sat drinking slowly in the glow of relaxation, Simon thought, that follows however minimal a contact with life beyond the city's wintry grave.

"How did Frank get on with his wee jaunt to London the other week?" said Annie, rolling herself a cigarette. "Did he tell you anything?"

"Oh, he seems to have enjoyed himself," said Simon, smiling as he remembered the pompous absurdity of Frank's account, so obviously full of wilful misinterpretations of events. "He said he went to some gay clubs down there. It sounds very different from Glasgow. Hard to believe, in fact. He took great pains to tell me in lurid detail how he ended up spending the night with a Japanese male model."

The picture seemed to amuse them all.

"Yes," said Philip, lighting his pipe, slipping his words out between leisurely puffs, "I believe there's quite a lot happening in London. You know Alan, who's in our Labour Party branch?"

"The little bearded man who wears a suit and is always laughing nervously," said Simon, with a slightly uneasy memory.

"I was talking to him at Thursday's meeting. He's just come back from London, and he mentioned that there's quite a thriving homosexual liberation movement, with a programme of meetings and demonstrations. Had you heard, Simon?"

"Demonstrations?" said Simon quietly, incredulous, even confused. "No, no, I hadn't heard that." He took a sip of his beer for its reassuring familiarity. "It certainly didn't make the front pages, did it?"

"Wasn't wee Alan saying something about an organisation in Edinburgh?" said Annie, a little anxiously, as if feeling obliged and yet timorous. "Perhaps Simon could get in contact with them."

"The Scottish Minorities Group," Philip said. There was a hint of restrained unease in his voice, as if forced to utter a word in bad taste.

"I've never heard of them," said Simon, his hand fondling his glass like a baby sucking its thumb. "Do they include homosexuals?"

Philip said sombrely, "Apparently they are a homosexual group."

"Oh." Simon pondered. "It's not a very upfront name, is it?"

"I gather they spend most of their time burrowing underground," said Philip gently, inviting Simon to join a somewhat wistful smile.

Vanessa came home with them after the pub. They were all feeling rather high. The night was mild, and a large moon hung yellow in the sky above the rustling trees. Longing secretly flooded Simon: dreams of freedom and companionship.

"Wee Simon, let's dance," said Annie, pulling him to his feet. His movements were restless, intense.

And then Philip said, "Let's change the music. Try this." The open window let in the scents of the spring night. He put on *Carmina Burana*.

The blatant naive passions of the music suddenly seemed to Simon transformed to subtle explicitness in his drunken response. His body was galvanised into action by the hammering chords and the disturbing transitoriness of the moment. His arms and torso, reaching out, became yearning made concrete, his perilous emotional balance became the tightrope walking and the leaping of his feet, the striding of his thighs his defiance. He was lifted and cast down, swayed and twisted by a clamouring surge of incomplete, unexpressed emotions suddenly struggling to be recognised. Again and again, his hands found rest for a passing second in touching his body with a tenderness, mysterious and unknown, that was confirmed only by the immediately reasserted ache of its absence.

When the music finally set him free and he subsided, panting and sweating, he realised that for a long time he must have been dancing alone. He laughed in embarrassment.

"That was wonderful," said Vanessa, in a hectoring, matter-of-fact tone, refusing to allow him to dismiss himself.

And it was true, he realised, reaching for some beer as his diaphragm still heaved: he felt more real, more himself than he could ever remember.

He went out to have a pee. As he was coming back, there was a knock on the door. He opened it, and there was Frank.

"Hallo, Simon," he said, as if it were a well-worn joke.

"Oh," said Simon coldly, his mind racing. "Hallo. What do you want?"

Frank was visibly taken aback. His eyes opened wide with surprise, and he put out a drunken hand to the door to support himself. Then he smiled, as if in recognition of a secret game. "I was passing, so I thought I'd just drop in," he said, assuming a raffish twinkle.

Simon held the door half-shut. "Well, we were just going to bed, actually," he said fumblingly, with a lot less purposefulness than he intended.

Frank began to look niggled. "Well, well, that's alright," he said sharply, "I'll just go to bed with you."

"Actually," Simon said, his heart thumping, scarcely believing the sound of his own voice, the feel of his own hand on the door, "actually, I'd rather you didn't." He felt the blood draining from his face.

"Simon," Frank hissed, irritation turning to a louring anger in his eyes, "you're being very difficult."

"Yes, I know."

Frank waited, staring at him. "Look," he said sharply, and paused, at last adding desperately, "I'm sorry."

Simon heard his own voice full of bleakness. "I know I'm being difficult. But I'd rather you went away. Goodnight." His hands trembling, he began to close the door.

"I'll put my foot in it," Frank said petulantly.

"No. Don't. Please go away." An unexpected intensity leapt into Simon's voice. His hold tightened on the door.

And Frank said nothing, looking pathetic and surprised, suddenly surrounded by a great loneliness, as if he had just been marooned.

Looking down, half in shame, Simon closed the door, and waited painfully until he heard the heavy steps going slowly and solemnly down the stairs of the close. Then he went alone to his room, wondering.

CHAPTER SEVEN

It was not enough to wait patiently for changes to happen. He must do something himself. But what?

A week or so later Simon bumped into Pansy and Dave. They told him they were driving through to Edinburgh for the day at the weekend, and would take Simon and Philip and Annie too, if they liked.

"Mind you dress up to impress all those artistic queers that live in Edinburgh," said Pansy, with a smile half of encouragement, half of satisfaction at her own worldlywiseness.

The day of the trip was one of windswept dramatic clouds and sudden momentary shafts of sun, all at once silhouetting the outlines of magnificent Edinburgh buildings against a roll of white satiny light tumbling from some dark baroque cumulus. In a holiday trance, the five of them wandered into cobwebby second-hand bookshops in the Old Town and cosy pubs full of old eccentrics; piled their plates with exotic salads and feasted their eyes with interesting faces at Hendersons'; and promenaded up and down Prince's Street all afternoon, admired and admiring. Ah yes, Edinburgh was a real city, they told one another wistfully. For Simon in his restlessness the people passing seemed suddenly illuminated by radiant spears of possibility as certainly as the shiny black roofs of the castle by the darting sun.

But as the shadows began to grow, Dave and Pansy announced that they would have to drive back, they had promised that night to go and see a friend of theirs in some amateur production in, of all places, Dumbarton. But perhaps, since the day had been so good, the other three would like to stay and go back on the train? Simon was already planning the evening's socialising: they would tour the pubs of Rose Street, and the Kenilworth would be crowded with Edinburgh's elegant cosmopolitan gay population – something would turn up.

"Annie and I will drive back with you," he heard Philip say. "We can't afford the train."

Simon felt his eyes cloud over with shocked hopelessness. He seemed to fall to the bottom of some dark well.

Philip's eyes were averted, but Annie looked down from an unreachable remoteness, clinging to Philip's arm, bristling with righteous defensiveness. "You could always stay on your own, Simon," she said.

In the desperation and resentment of dependence Simon wanted to hammer at all four of them, as though it were they who were the walls of his dungeon. But he knew they would not open and set him free; they were built of their own stones, unrelated to and unreached by his solitarily real pain, and yet at the same time defining the limits of his living space.

"You should do more things on your own," muttered Annie as they walked towards the car, looking down at her feet like a school-mistress awkward in her anger. "It really would be good for you." Standing arm in arm with Philip by the car door, she heaved the sigh that closes a hopeless case.

They were doing their best, he thought, to create a role that was capable of independence, and yet the very fact it was they who were creating it made independence impossible.

Annie sat beside him in the car. "Look love, Philip and I really can't afford the train. It would be nice, but –" she said, reduced at last, despite her determination, to pleading. Philip was silent, his brows drawn down in a problem-solving knot, trying purposely to shade from view altogether the useless guilt and fear that bobbed beneath the surface of his eyes.

Simon sat stiff and motionless, unspeaking, his face like a mask, trying to reproach them by looking as much like a murdered corpse as possible. They drove westward in silence, into the dying sun and the twilight, on and on across the dreary lowlands, their featurelessness relieved only by sinisterly dark slag-heaps, grotesque little mountains of waste. After a while Annie pointedly started up a conversation with Dave about his teaching, which Simon could not join in anyway.

Glasgow was forming itself around them, grey and repetitive, over and over again. The journey was finished and they shuffled tiredly along from one red light to the next.

"What are you going to do tonight, Simon?" said Annie tenderly, trying to break the mood.

"I don't know," said Simon curtly. Salt in my wounds, he thought, seeking to fuel his intransigence.

Annie was silent. She nestled up against Philip. "I'm tired, lamb," she said, softly and privately. "Shall we have a little snooze when we get back?" Philip painfully closed his eyes and murmured acquiescence.

"You could come with us to Dumbarton, if you like, Simon," said Pansy, making a bright nervous effort to relieve the tension.

He said, "Thanks. Maybe."

He went with them. He knew it would be horrible, but he wanted to steep himself in hopelessness and to scorn Philip and Annie. And Dumbarton suited him perfectly. After all, it was like the Platonic form of Glasgow: a city that had suffered a stroke, that lingered on in some paralysed vegetable existence, but whose blank soot-blackened tenement face betrayed not even the memory of humane life, let alone the hope of it; a city that was there only to be by-passed on the way to somewhere else. They left the car conspicuously in an empty desert of carless poverty, and Simon dawdled after Dave and Pansy along the cold grey ghost streets, between row upon row of identical fronts with windows like the pupil-less eyes of the blind, regiments of tenements like lines of gassed Great War soldiers in a faded photograph.

In the dark draughty expanses of the hall where the performance was to take place, the odd spectator or two lay distortedly on the uncomfortable seats like bodies left scattered over a deserted battlefield. Dave and Pansy and Simon sat down near the front, where their friend might see them for reassurance, and at last after a long and pointless wait for the audience to grow, the dusty curtain jerked spasmodically open, and Simon found himself sitting numbly through a seemingly interminable sequence of three acts by a local boy made slightly good. It chewed over such predictable issues as the general impossibility of love, and the emotional tug-of-war experienced by the figure of sensibility between the opportunity that was London and the nostalgia that was Scotland – with all the the torment and subtle nuance, Simon thought disgruntledly, of a Highland cow chewing the cud.

His mind slipped away and lost itself in fantasies of another London, fantasies that had become increasingly frequent ever since that conversation with Philip, even more since he had written off to the Gay Liberation Front. But the numbing of his toes brought him back to the chill draughty hall.

Indirectly the evening had a positive result on Simon, in that he returned home with his arrogance considerably boosted. He had stopped off at Dave and Pansy's for a drink, and in the process of sampling their latest home-made wine, the high spot of the evening for all three of them, he had got so drunk that when he leant over to pick up his glass, he fell off the chair. To his surprise he found this very funny.

Now he stood in the bathroom, swaying slightly, and stared at himself in the mirror assessingly. A realisation crept over him, for a second tugging the corners of his mouth into a flickering diffident grin. "You know, you really are quite good-looking," he said to himself in quiet surprise.

He turned away, losing his balance as he did so and bumping off the wall, and undid his trousers to pee. His head slumped forward and he could see his reflection in the water of the bowl, but it was hazy, indistinct now, and in a moment it was broken up by his piss. Yes, what good does that do me here? he thought. I might as well be in solitary confinement.

He went into his room. There lying on the bed were the two copies of *Come Together* that had arrived only the other day, but had already been read from cover to cover. He had found out the London address of the Gay Liberation Front through Philip and Annie's Labour Party friend, and, hand shaking, had written at once in a burst of crusading enthusiasm, asking to join.

A letter came back quickly, saying there was no membership – and there were no contacts in Scotland. The tone of the letter made Glasgow seem like the end of the earth.

But folded inside the letter had been the newspapers – incredible, and profoundly disturbing.

He flung himself half-clothed on the bed, and leafed quickly through them once again, still trying to convince himself of their reality. Here was an inconceivable world where not only did men visibly have real sexual relationships with one another, but they even discussed it; where not only did people claim the right to be gay, they even demonstrated publicly for it.

His eye caught an article that earlier had made him think of Frank. "Hiding and role-playing," he read again, " acting and pretending; leading the double life and denying his homosexuality. He buries what he knows to be the real him – lonely and afraid. Lonely because he's afraid of love and friendship."

And so somewhere there were indeed others who had seen and understood as he had. He was not alone in his strugglings. The paper spoke to him in a voice at once intimate and reassuring, and yet strange in its very existence. "For men like these," he read, "men like us, liberation is around the corner. GLF will destroy this obscene oppression. Be free. Be yourself. Come out and live!" The paper trembling once again in his hands, he stared at a photograph on the opposite page. There, unbelievable and yet real, in a public park in broad daylight some men were kissing mouth to mouth, while all around others – women, men, old, young – lounged arm in arm, their heads high, smiling, laughing. "Meet our brothers and sisters," he read. "They are homosexual and they are beautiful! And they are angry; because they are proud and love one another."

He sat there, choking back the lump in his throat. Tears seemed so inappropriate. The chance no longer to be alone; no longer to hide, no longer to belittle oneself – it existed. It actually existed. After all this time.

It was calm in the house. Outside the leaves of a tree were sighing in the wind.

A fearful and yet stirring purpose had already been forming at the back of his mind. On Monday he was going to see about finishing the writing of his thesis in London.

But he knew no one there. No one. It was so far. This was so desperate. His body tossed from side to side as if it were being pulled.

But he would not be alone. Holding the papers to him like a doll, he lay back on the bed and closed his eyes. He was afraid; but he must go.

There came the soft patter of spring rain against the window.

He took off his clothes, switched off the light, and climbed into his bed, pulling the covers about his ears. Its familiarity was at once comforting and inadequate.

Part Two: COMING TO GRIPS

CHAPTER EIGHT

The train south from Glasgow is like an emigrant ship to America. In the mid-morning Central Station, always pale grey because of the light that filters through the grimed frosted-glass vault above, is like an empty tarmac steppe, across whose vast wastes drift muddied pages of last week's *Scottish Express*. Travelling across it in tight knots, isolated by the great spaces of the tarmac, are the London emigrants and those who are seeing them off. At the platform gate they join in a jostling river and mill round, like ants pouring from a broken nest, and the police who have been circling aimlessly round the station are suddenly hovering ominously here, waiting to pounce on the reckless excitement born of the desperation of leaving. A voice snarls, "Haw hey, jimmy, who d'you thunk you're shovin', eh? Jist watch yersel, ok?" Beyond the gate, hanging from the window of the carriage nearest the bar, three chancers from Castlemilk, their faces pale and sick from lack of sunlight and food, chant together rhythmically to quell their nervousness, "We-arra-peepel! We-arra-peepel!" Further along a beaten-down young wife, with two uncontrollable small children already climbing over the seats, clutching the rim of the window as if it were the edge of a cliff she was slipping from, gabbling to her mother on the platform for the umpteenth time the same complaints and excuses with the desperation of a dying confession. "A hate ut down there, so a do. Bit Hector cannae get wurk here, he likes ut, he wants tae stay oan. A cannae staun ut, a'm tellin' yi, un the hoose a' day, naethun' bit the television, an' ut's a' Pakis where we luv. Isabel, get oaf o' there, or a'll kull yi." The mother, her latest beehive protectively covered with a yellow chiffon scarf, stands with her handkerchief to her face, dabbing at the tears. Here and there returning businessmen, in raincoats despite the summer to show their disgust for the northern climate, give the natives a wide berth, like aristocrats trying to avoid the peasants on a tour of their estates. And now a rickety dwarf of a guard, his face puckered with years of bad temper, pushes along the length of the train, spitting out warnings, flinging the doors to with a slam, and the whistle goes. A great mocking raucous cheer goes up from the chancers, breaking up into the only cry of exultation they know, "Cel-tic! Cel-tic!" The mother cries out like a wounded thing, "Ina, Ina, take care o' yersel, hen!" The young wife herself is now suddenly sobbing, "Oh mam! Oh mam!", again a small barefoot child deserted in a Drumchapel garden. And at once her own little daughter pouts, feeling suddenly trapped in the train as if in a cupboard, and breaks into loud crying, so that her mother grabs her by the shoulder like a doll, choking, "Uzza-bell! Stoap that greetin', or a'll punch yer heed un, a'm tellin' yi!" The brother with stoical male disinterest sits absorbed in a comic.

Slowly the long train pulls out over the Clyde, a wide slime-brown sluggish creature here, shaded almost into deadness by the sooty buildings overgrowing its banks, and then gradually begins to gather speed through the endless grimy red-sandstone tenements and shopping centres.

Simon found himself sitting opposite a meticulously tidy nervous granny, from Clarkston it might be, arranging and rearranging her hands in her lap. He stuck his face to the window at an uncomfortably exaggerated angle, hoping against hope she would not take advantage of the politeness he knew no way not to offer, deprive him of the teeming dreams of the traveller south.

"Are you a student, son?"

"Yes, sort of." He tried to sound at least distant and boring.

"My grandson Michael, he's a student. The other one's still at school. I'm just going down to stay with my daughter the now. I've never been to London before. It's a funny place, isn't it, you know, you see on the television all they flower people and the demonstrators, and a lot of blacks, they say . . ."

At Kilmarnock a timid neatly dressed young woman sat down beside Simon, and he knew he was rescued. Within a quarter of an hour the two women were already swopping sandwiches, nervously bolstering themselves up for their respective great expeditions by a dogged repetition of the minutiae of the normality they were leaving behind.

Simon turned and watched the heaving dark ridges and pale empty moorlands of the Southern Uplands go past, and then the foaming rushing rivers, scrambling here and there through rocky gorges, and above them, the Scots pines in embattled isolation, their foliage like torn rags frozen in the moment of being taken by the wind, on long muscular branches wrenched into protective gestures against the bitter sky. But once past Carlisle, the country becomes milder, the vegetation relaxes, and one knows one is already in another country. Here the trees do not cower, uncertain of their survival, but stand upright, their limbs fearlessly opened out, gathering together in groups. Slowly the train drags itself up Shap Fell, peak succeeds peak, the last gesture of the high country, reaching out after the traveller like an outstretched arm to bar his way, only to be pushed aside. For suddenly the hills fall quickly and quietly away, leaving go their hold, and the valley opens out into the plains, that roll here, on and on, studded with woodlands, till they lie flat and exhausted over all the south-east. And soon there come the cities of the midlands, black and squat, huddled together, crouching close to the ground, making the tall tenements of Glasgow seem defiant by comparison. Then the train breaks away, like a horse making for the winning-post, hurtling along unstopping, and the passengers stop the conversations they have been finding it harder and harder to squeeze out over the last couple of hours, and go silent with anticipation. Long before one has expected it, there come already hastily snatched away glimpses of the lazy aimlessly rambling rivers, the uncaring somnolent dark green trees of the south. Then at what point the liberal punctuation of brightly painted pubs with gardens and prim small factories and dowdy bungalows merges into London, it is uncertain, only suddenly the realisation that the country is left already far behind.

The three chancers, having spent most of the journey sliding this way and that across the swaying walls of the bar, were now finding their way noisily and unsteadily back to their seats, accosting the sour-faced businessman wincing past them in the narrow passageway with an aggressively cheery "How y'daein', pal, awright?", standing aside ostentatiously to make way for the shy young woman taking her last chance for the toilet, sweeping back their McEwan's cans in a wide gesture of mock gallantry. They fell over one another in a drunken pile on their seats, starting up odd fragments of Glaswegian songs, swopping obscenities. "A've goat the buggest wullie o' the loat o' yiz. You should see't!" "Aw, gie's a break." "Naw, gie's a luik." "*Get* yer hauns oaf, ya poof!" The ticket-collector passed through the carriage, calling loudly and imperiously in a London accent, and curtly ordered them, like little children, to take their feet off the seats. "Yes, sair!" one replied, complying promptly and theatrically, and falling at once into that wordless imitation of the swallowed sound of the upper-class southern accent that must be universal to every subject race of the English.

And now the train was passing through an endless narrow channel of high brick walls, just above which, by craning one's neck, could be seen the tops of Victorian terraces and tiny patches of the blue southern sky. The Clarkston granny composed herself in her seat, smoothing out any possible creases, and looked through her glasses with nervous disapproval at walls which, if nothing else, were quite obviously of an alien building material. Simon sat smiling, catching the summer heat on his face, pleased with this first blessing on his daring. They passed a sign saying EUSTON in bold letters above an arrow, charged by its situation with purposefulness, and within seconds they were drawing up alongside the shadowy platform, bustling with West Indian porters.

As the passengers poured and scattered from the carriages, one could tell the Londoners by their look of bored familiarity, the certainty of their sense of direction. As for the immigrants, even the chancers were awed into momentary silence, setting foot on London soil for the first time as if it were the moon. Simon struggled with his suitcase, step by step up the long platform, and passed through the crowd of expectant peering faces at the gate, and into the suddenly sunlit covered court-yard, looking more like an airport terminal than a railway station. He found a phone-box and nervously phoned the student accommodation service. An harassed woman's voice with a foreign accent asked him how long he was staying, and when he said he didn't know, she gave him the address of a cheap student hotel in South Kensington, and told him to come into the office the next morning to fix up something more permanent. He furtively consulted his underground plan in a dark corner, anxious not to be despised as an ignorant provincial visitor, despite his suitcase, and then with the number of stations and the line-change memorised, he hauled himself across the courtyard, the suitcase already becoming heavy, and merged into the never ceasing blank-faced flow of people descending the escalator into the hidden arteries of the tube, trying to look as if he had done it many times before.

A fluorescent world beneath the ground, flitted quickly through by figures drained of colour and any expression beyond confusion or impatience, the ticket-machines inappropriately lit like the fairground, the mechanical gates routinely barring your way with the inhuman metal stump of an arm like something from a cheap science-fiction film, the creaking swaying escalators spilling you only at long last into – will it be a labyrinth of white tiled cloisters, deafening with the ring of echoing footsteps, muffling the busker's frantic guitar and tuneless wail, or a dim catacomb of narrow brick tunnels, where borne on the sooty smell of the trains there drifts a disembodied flute playing Bach?

Slowly, in awe, he picked his way through South Kensington, a maze of silent streets brooded over by dignified trees, between high Victorian brick facades, the warm red of the brick a more dominant colour than the sky. Down the steps of the hotel babbled two sunburnt women in tee-shirts, arm in arm, talking in Californian accents with the habitual American tone of outrage at the primitiveness of all other parts of the world. Round the corner and up the steps lolled two tall Australians, aggressively absurd in shorts, displaying thighs as thick as Simon's waist, who flung clumsy looks of appraisal at the women and contempt at Simon, pale and sweating with the load of his suitcase. Inside the dingy hall a truculently efficient Malaysian woman behind the desk took Simon's name, pushed a key at him, and recited a list of house-rules like a tired teacher. His confidence already battered, Simon passed quickly, sheepishly, through the musty lounge, where two or three bodies lay in varying states of exhaustion with unseeing eyes aimed vaguely at the television, and up the dusty uncarpeted stairs. In the dormitory bedroom, close with stale tobacco smoke, a figure already asleep rolled over and growled at the disturbance of his entry.

He pushed his suitcase under an apparently untaken bed, trying to pretend that he did not care what happened to it, and left hurriedly, already longing for the comparative anonymity of the open streets. In the hallway a forlorn-looking man was speaking anxiously into the phone in Finnish.

Outside, the yellow light and long shadows of a summer evening, the singing of blackbirds. He began to walk street after street, insatiable, gazing into the proliferation of shop-windows, marvelling at the variety of restaurants. He felt now almost humbled by the place, and finally, venturing meekly into a trattoria, so insignificant it seemed a favour that the waitress noticed him at all. He ate his lavish pizza slowly and painstakingly, as if under scrutiny, while the light left the sky, but when he stepped outside again, the darkness was soft and warm, the final seal of strangeness. He passed several bright noisy pubs, too strange to go into, but finally seeing one that was quiet and empty, he slipped in and sat on a barstool as inconspicuously as possible. "Yes, guvner, what's yours?" "Pint of bitter, please." The alien name had its own thrill, even before the sweet yeasty taste of the warm southern beer. And soon the lethargy of the train journey, the foreign warmth of the evening, and the fear and anticipation that now hung in every shadow and rustled in the lazy leaves of the trees, all merged and swam in a sweetly lonely daze. From the pub's television wafted fragments of the British occupation in Northern Ireland, which seemed as far from here as it was possible to imagine.

He left the pub and walked back to the hotel, and slept the sleep of an excited child.

He woke early to the sound of too many people trying to use inadequate bathroom facilities. Dressing quickly, and with a school-boyish modesty because of the other people still in bed, he found his way to the crowded basement breakfast-room by following the over-whelming smell of hot fat. There was a spare place at a table where two young Germans were trying, energetically but with insufficient English, to explain to the worried elderly waitress that they wanted their bacon uncooked. "Raw!" she cried out in horror for them, the penny finally dropping, and then grasping out at a welcome native face in Simon, "Well, they say it takes all sorts, but raw bacon – I ask you!" Simon smiled several times, at the appalled waitress in soothing deprecation, at the Germans in concilatory apology, and at himself for this worldliness. He decided, as if to bless the opening of this day with extraordinariness, to eat the whole meticulously English breakfast that was being served, something he did not remember last doing, which he would normally have regarded in others with bemused incredulity. He chewed his way through it, watching the motes dancing and congregat-ing in the thin early morning sunshine that slanted through the high windows, like the crowds gathering on the morning of some momentous occasion.

At the student accommodation centre a mothering woman fixed him up with a room to himself in a postgraduate hostel in Camden Town. It was expensive, but it would do for a few days until, he told himself, he found his feet here. He made his way there without noticing much beyond the exhaustion caused in him by the unfamiliar heat of the bright summer sun. The room was sparse, though pleasant and sunny, but once he had moved himself in and unpacked a few things, he found himself at a loss as to what to do next. He lay on the bed and read a little, or sat at the desk and fiddled with his thesis, but again and again his mind kept turning to what had really drawn him here, and he would take out the well-thumbed copies of *Come Together* and pore over them, or study his A-to-Z for the exact location of the local Gay Liberation meeting-place, where, a fortunate omen he thought, there was to be a meeting that night. Once or twice he wandered out through the almost deserted corridors, drifted across occasionally by timid and studious-looking African and Asian students, and down the nearest sunlit shopping streets, where he stared in fascination at the profusion of soft fruits and summer vegetables in the greengrocers', returning this time with a bag of peaches, that time with a few salad vegetables and some cheese, which he ate with his bare hands.

The sunny daylight hours passed slowly, and yet in his memory they were nothing, and now he stood diffidently examining his appearance before the mirror, as the shadows of the lush green trees outside lengthened in the early evening light. He chose a favourite tee-shirt with the motif of a shiny apple being eaten by a worm, and slipped almost stealthily from his room, feeling unexpectedly exposed, as if he expected every passing stranger to know full well just where *he* was going.

The meeting-place, a hall with connections unidentifiable from its name and a dingy unnoticeable exterior, turned out to be not very far away at all, and he heard a clock already striking the meeting time as he drew within sight of it. In the very moment of telling himself that he was not going to, he had already walked past it and on up the street, beyond his knowledge of the street-plan, his heart pounding self-embarrassingly and his cheeks hot. With some difficulty, he turned off and found a circular route that would bring him back to it again, but again he walked past. There had been no sign of anyone going in; but he could not work out whether he would prefer to slip in amongst a crowd, or whether he would rather avoid being seen in such a group by anybody passing by, who would inevitably *know,* of course. By now his perplexity was giving him an actual headache.

Finally, at the third attempt, his tongue wet with fright, he made it through the street door. The predictability of the initial surroundings jarred with the unpredictability of what he was about to enter into. The dark scratched wood and concrete floor of the anteroom reminded him of the cloakrooms in a school. Even this far, there reached up his throat a pang of fear, as if from childhood, and he wanted to hesitate, were it not that someone might very well come in behind him. He walked into the main hall.

It was almost empty. There were only two other figures, almost lost in the shadowy spaces. One was a sickly-looking man in his late thirties, dressed dowdily in outdated American-looking clothes, who was pacing up and down impatiently, his rhythmical footsteps on the wooden boards echoing through the hall. His hair was lank and indeterminate-coloured, and his pasty face wore a resentfully adopted inconspicuousness. His eyes went straight to Simon, shiftily, but at once he turned away, with a look of angry disappointment, changing to universal contempt, which was meant to indicate to himself and anyone else simply "Not my type". The other person, sitting upright at the end of one of the rows of uncomfortable wooden seats, was of immediately indeterminable sex. She or he was dressed in a full white shirt and loose white jeans and red sandals, their hair was frizzed out, their eyes were gaudily made up, there was a very light growth of unshaven hairs on one small area of their chin. Without moving from their seat in the middle of the hall, the person said, in a voice that could have been a light man's voice or a deep woman's, "Hallo, come in."

Wanting reassurance, Simon said nervously, "Is this where the Gay Liberation meeting is?"

"Yes, that's right. Come in and sit down."

"I thought the meeting started at seven-thirty."

"Oh, but nobody comes till after eight. Sit down and relax." The voice spoke with a kind of remote disinterest, even when offering invitations, which made Simon relievedly certain that the person was not here to welcome him out of the sense of duty or any official capacity, which she-he confirmed by saying, still in a flat inscrutable tone, "I got here so early tonight by accident, you know."

Simon sat down awkwardly. The other man went on pacing up and down, frowning at the floor.

"Do you come from round here?"

"No. Glasgow."

"Oh. Oh." For the first time the voice was coloured by emotion, at first surprise, and then understanding sympathy. "Well, you're not alone now."

Simon wished he found this last remark more true. Silence. Only the sound of impatient pacing.

Then the person beside him resumed, once again in the mechanical emotionless voice: "I'll give you my address. I work in a hospital, and live in nurses' quarters. Here's the address. I'll write it down. You go to the Archway tube. Don't be shy."

Puzzled, Simon took the address out of unthinking politeness, but could think of nothing whatsoever to say. Suddenly the other man sat down beside them, dropping his head into his hands as if exhausted, and then in a quiet weary voice took up some conversation with the nurse that had obviously been going on before Simon arrived. Simon felt relieved, and sat still on the edge of his seat, looking round the dull familiar fittings of the hall anxiously, doubtfully.

People were streaming in all at once. They came in knots of three or four, laughing, talking together, loudly greeting others. Of every age and race and style, their variety seemed quite simply endless. No sooner had one group of relatively similar people passed in, than another, sometimes quite diametrically opposed, succeeded it. And with only one or two exceptions, in contrast to what Simon would have thought the more typical self-abasing air of the man who had been pacing, they all looked so brimmingly confident. Some of them veritably shone.

Only the older men, some even white-haired, were clouded with a self-protective distrust, a smothered resentment even, at this youth that was enjoying so openly a sense of freedom and solidarity they had never known, and which even now by sheer weight of numbers they would be intimidated from ever enjoying. Here and there they glared out from the rest, like cripple children among a troop of healthy ones, painfully asserting a right to be there, which their faces showed they knew they could not maintain.

Simon watched the unceasing parade go by and slowly fill the hall, in utter dumbfoundment. He felt as uncomprehending and as unconnected as a visitor from another century, let alone another place. But the sight he found as much as anything hard to believe was that there were even people there whom he might expect to meet in the circles he moved in, who might even be friends of his.

Slowly, as his sheer obsessive amazement wore off, Simon began to feel awkwardly isolated and at a loss what to do next. The hall was crowded now from wall to wall, but nothing seemed to be happening. He noticed several people glancing at him, curiously or interestedly, he was not sure. He was too overawed to even think of any action he could initiate himself, or what, in any case, it should be. He waited.

At what seemed like long last, a voice could be heard vaguely above the whirr of chatter, trying to draw people's attention from the other end of the hall, and a long-haired figure in a green satin shirt and dark red velvet jeans climbed on to the stage and looked impatiently helpless, followed by a plainly dressed middle-aged man with a bald head and heavy glasses, who quite unexpectedly gave an incredibly loud bellow of "Shut up, for God's sake!", the effect of which, through shock, was almost immediate, leaving the hall suddenly silent except for a few nervous giggles. The person in the satin shirt then proceeded, in a quiet gentle voice, with a tone of suggestion rather than direction, accompanying his words with deprecating downward glances and long fingers waved in elegant gestures of vagueness: "Well, brothers, we were sort of thinking that, now most people are here, I suppose, perhaps, that – well, we could sort of split up into sort of small groups, and do sort of consciousness-raising things. So if you could, you know, form little circle things of about eight people, I suppose we could – well, that's all really." He smiled widely with glazed beneficence.

It crossed Simon's mind that a much greater sense of purpose and cohesion had seemed to characterise gay liberation when he looked at it from Glasgow.

But at once a quite jarring sense of businesslike purpose and communality seemed to descend on everyone in the hall, and everywhere chairs were being eagerly pushed and dragged, scraping and squealing, into circles, into one of which, forming around him while he sat feeling embarrassedly ineffectual, Simon found himself being solicitously invited.

As the emotional dust of the invitation subsided, he dared to look with short, interrupted, childishly curious glances at the people he was among. There was one person to whom everyone was looking anxiously to start the discussion: he was very relaxed, so much so that he made the rigid wooden seat he sat on seem like a comfortable armchair, and his features were sharply focused by earnestness, rising definitely out of a strangely dusky complexion, while he wore with a paradoxical unselfconsciousness a tight-fitting flame-orange see-through shirt. Among the others in the group was a man of sixty or more, very obviously diffident, very obviously working-class and beaten down, but with hair, which still retained its colour, of a quite romantic Liszt-like longness, a wistful expression positively chiselled on to his face, and wide soulful eyes which occasionally rose from the floor in surreptitious, almost stolen glances at the younger members, including Simon. There was a tall elastic young guy, apparently called Dorian, with dyed blond hair and a sequinned tee-shirt, whose face seemed perpetually smiling, or rather leering, because the eyes above the grin twinkled incessantly in every direction with a studied salaciousness. Beside him was someone of whom Simon formed little impression, other than that his clothes were distinguished from most people's by their restraint, their almost ostentatious lack of flair, and that, while the plain regular features of his face seemed to be trying to show a serious-minded self-control, this was continually challenged by a haunting remoteness that seemed to surge into his eyes whenever he let his guard down. This person turned out to be called Richard. Of the others beyond him Simon took little visual note, partly because they were sitting in positions he would have had to turn specially to see.

"Well," said the dark man in the flame-orange shirt, who was called (for Simon not surprisingly) Angelo, speaking in a controlled but warm and flexible tone, "it's hard to think of something new to talk about. We seem to go over the same things every time. I – I was quite interested by that recent article in *Come Together* on ageism."

"I don't think we've talked enough about coming out," said someone barely audibly. He was a guy in his late teens, bristling with timidity, who now looked shocked that he had spoken at all, and his eyes went wide with alarm and shifted dreadingly from side to side, as if he expected a reprimanding slap to descend on him from somewhere at any moment.

"Yes, I don't think time's ever wasted talking about coming out," said Angelo soothingly, encouragingly. "Well, does anyone want to talk about coming out then?"

There was a long silence. At last, with a dramatic sigh, Dorian said, swinging one leg over the other and resting a long forefinger on one knee: "Well, some of us just seem to get dragged out, no pun intended, whether we're consenting or not. Sometimes I think I can't walk down the street without someone's asking me where I keep my magic wand, or something a little less subtle, my dear. I'm sure I can't think why. It's not as if I flaunt myself." He batted his eyelids.

"You people just go too bloody fast." It was a conservatively dressed man in his late thirties, with a besieged look. "Some of us find it a lot harder than others. We've got to do things gradually. Some of you just seem to want to rock the boat a bit too much."

Dorian stared pointedly at his painted toe-nails.

"I do think it's important we think positively about coming out, though no one's going to say it's not hard," said Angelo firmly. "We must always remember there are two sides to it. It's not just a matter of advantage for ourselves, it's a political act as well. But in any case, I don't think the purely personal advantages are to be undervalued. In my experience it does everything for one's self-respect, which we all need, and in fact that is only aided if it requires a bit of courage on our part to be honest.

"Politically, it's a question of whether you think we do better to confront or to run away and hide. And none of us have the right to knock the blatant gays, the upfront gays, who are in that confrontation every minute of their lives, just because we've found it necessary so far to allow ourselves the option of hiding behind a privileged mask of presumed heterosexuality."

The older man at first turned his eyes slowly away and looked uncaringly into the distance like a scolded dog, then with a sigh folded himself away, as it were, shaking his head as if to say, "They don't understand and they have no patience."

Simon found himself in his still slightly dazed state regarding the fluent and confident Angelo with something little short of childish hero-worship.

After the awkward pause that followed his speech, Angelo started up again brightly, "It would be interesting to hear from a newcomer to the group what they think about coming out, perhaps even someone from out of town." His eyes roved expectantly over the circle of faces. I must say something, I mustn't let him down, or myself, thought Simon, but he sat awkwardly shifting position on his chair, struck dumb with an immediate weighed-up certainty of his own ineffectuality, and a mere nightmare terror from somewhere long ago. "Perhaps you'd like to say something," Angelo said to Simon, half with a tone of polite invitation, half like a dentist setting his patient at ease.

"Well," said Simon, feeling himself at once sinking into incoherence, "yes, I think coming out is important. I – I've come out to all my friends. I suppose I can't really be friends with someone I haven't come out to, it feels – dishonest, like they would know only part of me, but . . ." His train of thought was suddenly sucked right under, and he blushed for his own discomfiture.

"Yes, honesty is important, isn't it? Especially since it's something we've been bullied out of," said Angelo, as if accepting and even valuing a point well taken, but now he too was momentarily embarrassed as he caught Simon's grateful and admiring look, embarrassed as much as anything because he obviously enjoyed it.

Someone else started speaking, and the discussion teetered on; but Simon was only half-attending now, shocked and sorrowing at what he supposed his mental and emotional handlessness in this company, waiting for another less demanding phase of the evening to turn up.

Which came. As the hands of the clock on the wall inched towards ten, there came a squeaking of chairs all about them, the sound of conversation came now not in a general murmur but in loud bursts spreading out from peals of laughter, and the groups were breaking up. All discussion died away under the barrage of noise, and the members of the circle were no longer looking at one another but staring over their shoulders.

"Well, time to go to the pub," announced Angelo, with the flat tone of one who is stating the obvious only because someone else is waiting for them to, and at once, like a class dismissed, pushing back its chairs and picking up its bags, the circle rose and formed little knots that moved in fits and starts towards the door.

Someone whom he had not noticed said to Simon, "Are you coming to the pub?"

"Yes. Where is it?"

"Just next door."

He mingled with the general exodus, trying unsuccessfully to feel calm about this new development. What, after all, would the pub be like?

But whatever he could have expected, this was not it. It was not a gay pub, at least not on any other night of the week, that was obvious. In one corner there was a billiard-table, hovered over by a pall of smoke, across which two pensioners with burnt-down cigarettes perched on their lips were leaning awkwardly, wheezing with the exertion. They were surrounded by a group of eagle-eyed old men, all with cigarettes and pints, scarcely visible for the smoke. Elsewhere, one in a dark corner near the bar, and one on a barstool propped against it, sat two old women, also smoking, watching over every coming and going with looks of calculating knowingness, occasionally exchanging short clipped comments with one another, deliberately indecipherable to the uninitiated. Bent over a couple of the tables were two adolescent couples with earnest eyes, struggling to become intimate through the barriers of nervous politeness and sexual trepidation. And into this sleepiest and most ordinary of London pub scenes flooded the Gay Liberation meeting, swamping half the whole area with its laughs and shrieks, kissing and cuddling and flaunting itself uncompromisingly as the alcohol began to flow, finding in the very power to shock and not to have to fear the consequences a strength that was only the more heady for having been denied so long.

"Can I get you a drink?" It was the person who had invited him to the pub, a rather gangly individual in dark clothes, with big glasses and a prominent nose that gave his face a prying look.

"Yes, thanks," said Simon gratefully, but in some wonderment at this generosity. "I'll have a pint of bitter."

He stood, feeling exposed as an incompetent alien by his solitariness in this laughing crowd, while the person went to the bar. He became aware he was hesitantly looking for Angelo, hoping indeed Angelo might come and talk to him (though he could not think why he should), in that firm and encouraging way of his. He caught sight of him at last in animated conversation with a distant group of people who looked similarly relaxed and earnest.

The person came back from the bar and handed Simon his drink. Simon expected him to start some sort of conversation, but instead he just stood staring at Simon, fingering his glass, and at last he said only, "Mmm, yes, well," in a curious tone, nervous and yet theatrical, which Simon could at first make nothing of until, with a shock, he registered that it was meant to be an ostentatious performance of sexual nervousness in the face of Simon's imputed charms. He looked down in embarrassed bewilderment, and busied himself with sipping his beer.

Suddenly Dorian had sidled up to him, and at the same time he noticed the silent drink-buyer go tense with a lour of impatience. Surely it could not be from jealousy, he thought.

"I haven't seen *you* here before," drawled Dorian, his eyes roaming up and down Simon like hands.

"No. I've only just arrived from Glasgow."

"Glasgow! Oh, my dear, you poor thing!" cried Dorian as if he were crooning to a baby; but then suddenly taking a half-step back and raising an elegant hand in a gesture of horror, he said, "But I hope you didn't choose to live there. I mean, what awful taste!"

"Well –" began Simon, preparing to launch himself into a balanced account of his home-city.

"Oh no, heavens, don't tell us about the nasty place," Dorian gasped, with eyes shut against the possibility, and then advancing and patting Simon's arm maternally, "No, I'm sure you don't live there on purpose. I mean, you don't look the sort that tears up railway-carriages. Never mind. London's the only place to live. I'm sure you'll *enjoy* it here!" He had the power of investing the most innocent of words with innuendo. "Well, I must go and get myself another gin. Life wouldn't be worth living without gin, would it? Oh, I see you're drinking *beer!*" And with eyebrows lifted high above a look of pity at Simon's lack of style, he swept off towards the bar, twittering a last minute acid greeting at the by then unsuspicious drink-buyer.

"Er, Dorian's alright really," he said hesitantly, quite uncertain of how to read Simon's reaction to Dorian, and whatever it had been, trying deliberately to find an ambiguity that would enlist Simon to his side.

Sifting through his own reaction, just as uncertainly, Simon said, "He's very – confident."

And at that moment, surprisingly, Angelo had joined them. He smiled at Simon, looked momentarily and uncharacteristically off-balance, and then, as if clutching out to steady himself, spoke blandly to the drink-buyer. "Hallo, Alan. It was quite a good discussion again tonight, I thought. We seem to be keeping up the numbers too."

"Er, yes," replied Alan abstractedly, "yes, I wonder how long we can, er, keep it up."

And then Angelo spoke to Simon, but looking down, and with a polite coyness, which was perhaps the last thing Simon had expected, and which made him not only bewildered, but almost disappointed. "Have I just been blind," said Angelo, with at least a sure practised music in his voice, "or have you not been at meetings before?"

"No, I've only just arrived from Glasgow." Once made, the bald statement of fact seemed to Simon to dangle uselessly there in the air, asking for nothing of the much that he thought he wanted to ask for, let alone offering anything.

"Glasgow. Really?" said Angelo, with a tone not at all of shock but of clear interest, and even somewhere behind it respectfulness, which was not just welcome to Simon but much more what he expected.

Lifting his glass to find inspiration in the beer, he found that it was already empty.

"Can I get you another drink?" came a new voice. He turned to look. It was the person called Richard, whom he did not recognise at once, who now looked as if he had been standing waiting on the sidelines for just this opportunity.

"Yes," said Simon, a reflex response only, very quietly.

"The same again?"

He nodded. Suddenly he could not speak. The final awareness that he was being treated as a centre of attraction fell on him where he stood, trying to keep his balance among the others, like an avalanche sweeping him away out of reach. There was nothing to hold on to, the situation was so very strange, so totally unfamiliar to him; it was as if he were blind and had been left suddenly in some place quite unknown to him to find his way. And when he did emerge from the daze, when slowly the sound of voices about him began to break up again into words, he wanted to weep: he wanted to stand there and weep for the person he had been, the person who was so sexually isolated he could not even recognise an advance when it was made, the person who had never known a world where sexual opportunities existed, who had lived year after year in the continually reaffirmed belief that for him there were none. He could not speak, and there was a lump in his throat, so that when Richard put the drink in his hand, he turned and cracked out the broken word "Thanks" as though it were in response to a rescue from a life-sentence, and the all at once distant-eyed Richard recoiled in timid surprise and humility before the nakedness of his pain.

"So you come from Glasgow?" he said softly, struggling to reimpose a bland normality on himself.

"Yes, that's right."

"I don't come from London myself. I was born here, but I grew up in Toronto." The words were delivered with a deliberate flat offhanded-ness, and yet somehow through them there sounded the mournful note of someone who would always be a stranger in a distant land. "When did you come to London?"

"Yesterday. On the train."

"You didn't waste any time finding Gay Lib." This time the surface was of a casual conversational joke, but now there came from behind it a chord blended from pleading anxiety and almost disappointed distrust.

Dorian had joined the group again. Simon had been aware without listening of his loud rising inflection of outrage and self-mockery and his scattered laughter, but now he suddenly heard, "*You*, what's your name?" flung violently against him as if he had been totally unreasonable in withholding it.

"Simon."

"Oh. A bit undistinctive, but alright as names go, I suppose. Anyway, I bet you've done it."

"Done what?"

Dorian sighed dramatically, and spoke as if humouring a stupid child. "Well! Made love on a beach."

"No."

Angelo said, "It sounds very romantic of you, Dorian."

"Romantic!" he shrieked. "My dear, the sand gets *everywhere*!" And he gave Simon a look that was so salacious he winced away from it as if he had suddenly been shown a particularly shocking photograph.

"Er, what do you do?" said Alan dully, making it very plain that he was trying his luck again. Unfortunately for him Simon, still in some shock at the tone of Dorian's conversation, thought in panic the question must be about these unknown mysteries of sexual activity, and looked momentarily horrified and bewildered, so that Alan added awkwardly, "As a job, I mean."

And so a long dull conversation started up. Dorian left, then Angelo. And it came almost as a relief to Simon when the closing-bell went, and it was time to leave the pub.

Simon was struck by the slow relaxedness with which the London pub closed. Unlike Glasgow there was no raucous barman bullying you to finish your drink and get out, trying to make you feel guilty for having been there drinking their alcohol in the first place. Instead people simply drifted at their own unhurried pace to the door, while the bar staff leisurely cleaned glasses and chatted still to the remaining regulars.

Angelo went by silently, but gave Simon a quick glance, almost diffidently, smiling gently only at the very moment of averting his eyes, with what seemed to Simon a wistful finality. Dorian, appearing yet again as if from nowhere, grinned at him from under langorous half-shut eyes and said suggestively, "Well, I expect I'll see more of you some time," and to Simon's dumbfoundment, he ran a hand up his thigh, and at once was gone. Even the old man with the Liszt hairstyle, who had been a member of the circle in the meeting, but who had not exchanged so much as a word with Simon, nodded to him shyly as he left.

"Can I give you a lift?" Again the voice of Richard coming from somewhere unexpectedly close to him.

"Oh yes, thanks," he said, in unaffected gratitude for an unlooked-for favour.

"Oh," said Alan coldly, and it was only his note of jealousy that jolted Simon into thinking for a moment that the offer might imply more than he took from it. But surely not, he thought, though all at once uncertainly.

They were in the actual doorway now, under the lighted sign that shone out into the street. "Well, in that case," said Alan, "I'll say goodbye here." And before Simon had time to realise what was happening, let alone think about it, he had kissed him on the mouth, standing there on the street, thrusting a big unfeeling tongue into Simon with a quick predatory lapping motion, like a chameleon lapping up a fly, and then withdrawing it with a grunt of approval, as though over the taste of a special chocolate he had bullied to be given but would not bother to try and taste again.

"The car's just here," said Richard, the plain words of information carrying incongruously a clear edge of rather outraged disapproval.

Simon followed him introvertedly, not wondering at why he had allowed himself to be kissed so peremptorily: had he had time to think he would have allowed it anyway, because he was in fact marvelling that he was so suddenly in a situation where he could be kissed at all so easily.

He got into the car. Richard sat stiffly, awkwardly, with his hands on the wheel. "I'm sorry, I don't know where you're staying," he said.

"Oh, just down in Camden Town."

He sat still. Simon waited for him to make a move to start the car. But then he said, "Well, I'll say goodbye now." And then he too was kissing Simon, dropping his hands from the wheel and leaning over a little clumsily. It was a gentle, but a searching, almost pleading kiss, which he seemed to leave reluctantly.

He said, "Would you like to come to my place?" Nervously but struggling for a rigid control of the nervousness, trying to hide it behind what began to seem an habitual blank casualness.

Simon said, "Yes." But it was as though he were listening to another person speaking, as though all this were happening to another person who was used to such things, who knew what he ought to do in such situations. Whereas Simon, in private, was drifting in bewilderment, just following someone else's sense of the situation, with which he himself felt no actual connection. As soon as the car ride began, he rapidly found himself simply staring out of the window, in renewed fascination at the city scene still alive at this time of night, only half-aware of the tension of Richard's driving, the overeagerness to start before a traffic-light actually turned green, the speeding-up to jump one turning red. When he heard Richard say, with a still nervous humility, "I didn't think for a moment you were going to come with me," he could think of nothing to respond with but a smile, and a smile that was nothing but part of the spontaneously invented performance as a willing knowing pick-up.

They passed through King's Cross, an intersection Simon flattered himself on recognising because of its unforgettable lunatic complexity, and then a little beyond that stopped at a square two-storey house in a small square full of solemn rustling trees. "Well, this is it," said Richard.

Simon followed him into the house. The ground-floor was in darkness and silence and smelt shut up. "The landlady lives down here," said Richard. "She'll be asleep." They went up a narrow creaking flight of stairs, patchily lit by street-light falling through a coloured-glass window. Richard opened a door at the top of the stairs and turned on a light. "This is my room," he announced tonelessly. Simon entered almost warily and looked about it as he might at the setting for some predictable incident in an indifferent film. Above the unmade single bed was a large drawing of a white-bearded Arab in a burnous staring broodingly into remoteness; on the mantelpiece were a handful of books – a Spartacus gay guide, an atlas of London, a single worn copy of the poems of Walt Whitman. There was an old-fashioned television in the corner, several expensive candles jammed into beer-bottles on top of a chest-of-drawers, from which the odd ends of shirts and jeans stuck out from where they had been untidily crammed. Simon looked to Richard to see if any comment on the room was expected of him, but Richard was standing there as if he were unaware of being in any particular room at all, even in any room at all. He looked no more at home in it than a wild stray dog might have done, or for that matter, a desert Arab.

Making an unconvincing gesture at a joke he said, "Well, I'll say goodbye again," but it turned out sounding more like a dismayed cry for help, as he awkwardly put his arms round Simon and kissed him for a long time. The only thing that Simon felt in this kiss was its pleading-ness, but he did not know what this stranger of a few hours was pleading for, what he could answer to him: and so he did nothing but act out the perfect kiss, letting his tongue slip and wander softly over and around the other's. Which to his surprise seemed to be an answer after all, because he felt Richard relax; and when they drew apart, he said, "Where did you learn to kiss like that?", the stereotypical bland-ness of the remark lying strangely on the deep genuine gratitude that sounded beneath it. Then he said confidently, "Shall we get into bed?"

"If you like," said Simon, only a little taken aback, submitting himself to the sudden course of events as to the first kiss.

At once Richard began to tear off his clothes, unselfconsciously, while Simon nervously detached first shoes and socks, then jerkin and shirt, and at last, hesitantly, jeans. But now Richard looked quite transformed, another person, at home in his nakedness in a way that explained the ill-ease he felt in the clothes whose drabness had first struck Simon. His face wore a new sense of certainty.

He flung back the untidy bedclothes and waited for Simon to join him. Then without speaking he lay down; and Simon followed his example, like a game of follow-the-leader.

At once Richard swamped him with caresses. Isn't this what I wanted? thought Simon. But beneath the caresses he felt no more engaged than a patient being examined on a table. He closed his eyes, and let his own hands search, running up and down the line of the back that wreathed around him, over and over, like a mouse endlessly running up and down the length of a new cage. He kept thinking, How should I make my hands behave? What should I try and make them show they are feeling?

When he opened his eyes, it was as though he found himself the accidental witness of a transfiguration. The very features of Richard's face were changed, the flesh of his shoulders glowed, he seemed to have entered a different realm of being, a realm where words were intruders, where there came only sighs with the ease of the sun moving out from clouds and suddenly illuminating something that before was indiscernible. And Simon lay and watched this thing happening above him, pinned there on the creased dirty sheets, feeling sweaty from the heat of contact.

"Now," said Richard, the monosyllable itself almost a sigh. Now what? thought Simon. He felt Richard push his legs apart, and then plug himself in like an electrical device, the slithery absurd connection paradoxically clinching Simon's sense of emotional separation. He lay there on the alien bed and looked at the great dark arch of the shoulders hanging over him, at the seemingly mechanical pile-driving motion of the pelvis, feeling at first bored, then uncomfortable, the discomfort stirring chilling memories of Frank's rape, until he squirmed away from it, reaching up his hands to push Richard's shoulders away. Which Richard must have taken for the writhing and clutching of desire, for he lifted his face, with his eyes shut, shut tight, further into the distance; and his mouth curled like a pout and all at once he was giving a cry as though of pain, as though he had fallen suddenly into his own hollow world of pain where no one could come near.

Simon felt him go limp, and was relieved that it was over.

Richard opened his eyes. He said, in unintentional confirmation of Simon's sense of being used and isolated: "I lost you there for a moment."

They lay beside one another, each gasping for air, unspeaking.

"That was beautiful," said Richard. "Did you enjoy it?"

But I should have, thought Simon. Why didn't I? "It's just a bit strange," he said.

"Have you had it off with lots of people in Glasgow?"

"No. Only – two." He did not see he'd had anything meaningful to himself with either of those two, but something in Richard's manner made him feel ashamed even to admit to that small number, let alone admit to less.

Richard had raised himself on one elbow now and was looking at him. He spoke at first with the hesitant feeling-the-way of someone who has not received the expected answer. "Well – well, I expect you – well, you could treble that number here over the summer, at least." The remark was delivered as an urbane compliment, but now again Richard's eyes, looking away, swam with an unsure pleading, like a starving child who had just finished an unexpected meal in the house of a stranger benefactor, so that Simon suddenly warmed with sympathy towards him, reaching out with a smile and stroking his arm, a stroke that was affectionate, but perhaps as physical contact inept, and seemed to go unregistered by Richard.

Who said only, "I'm hungry. Shall we have something to eat?"

"Ok."

Richard got up and pulled on his jeans. Once Simon left the bed, it seemed to him like the scene of an accident to which he did not wish to return. But likewise putting on only his jeans, he followed Richard into the kitchen.

"Do you like Philadelphia Cream Cheese?"

"Oh . . . yes."

He watched Richard take from the fridge (the strange keeping place betraying his Canadian origins) a packaged sliced loaf, but unexpectedly brown at least, and peel open a screwed-up package of cream cheese, and spread meagre sandwiches rather clumsily, almost helplessly.

There was a noise of someone coming in the front door and mounting the stairs. Simon had forgotten to think whether Richard had a flatmate. A voice called and suddenly in the door there appeared a young poetic-looking Anglo–Indian with long heavy dark gold hair and flamboyant clothes. "Oh, I'm sorry," he said in a worldlywise tone, "I thought you were alone. It doesn't matter." And he glided away.

"That's Roger," said Richard, as if enough were said.

Apparently forgetting his recent experience, Simon suddenly felt a rush of self-flattering excitement. Fancy being found in such a situation on only my second night here, he thought.

"Let's take the sandwiches into the bedroom," said Richard.

And Simon followed and climbed unthinkingly onto the sweaty ruffled bed beside Richard, and ate his way through the bland sandwich in a self-congratulatory reverie, seeing himself as he thought he had been seen, a casual sexual success instead of the mocked-at wrong-headed pathetic failure who was always alone; all memory of the unpleasant private reality of the experience just passed wiped out by the sense of having gained social standing, as easily as the crumpled sheets could have been smoothed out to present an unsuspicious appearance to a visitor.

"Did you just come to London for a good time?" asked Richard, who was sitting a little apart.

"Well, I wanted to see what was happening. But in Glasgow I was very . . . nothing happens in Glasgow," said Simon, purposefully repudiating his former self. He went on and gave a depreciatory summary of his post-graduate work. "What do you do?" he asked Richard.

"Oh, I'm not much of a brain-box. At the moment I'm a bus-driver."

At once another little thrill of self-congratulation ran through Simon. And I got a working-class lover, he thought, there's communication for you. And he almost smirked as he thought of the now still half-clothed half-wild Richard leaning against the bonnet of a bus perhaps and chatting to his work-mates in a sweat-soaked uniform at the end of a hot day.

"I used to be in the army," said Richard colourlessly.

"Oh really? The army," said Simon, suddenly deflated and embarrassed. Romantic visions could only embrace so much.

"Yes, I just sort of drifted into it. I didn't really think about what I was doing. We were sent to the Rhine, NATO troops. Then I got caught having it off with the troop-sergeant on the back of a tank. He got court-martialled because I was only a private. And I bought myself out and came to London."

The story with its little echoes of martyrdom played back into the hands of Simon's fantasising.

"I don't really know what I *want* to do," Richard said looking down, troubled. But then, turning with the most banal of smiles, which Simon now saw as one among ten thousand coming from above a uniform in a foreign town, he said, "But I know I want to do this, though."

And he grabbed hold of Simon again, taking a kiss from him now as the starving child might have stolen food from the benefactor, not because he was hungry, but because he thought he should take it while it was there since he might never see it again, perhaps even because he wanted the benefactor to feel shamed by the sight of his desperation. But Simon lay jammed against the wall and just let it be taken from him, because he could see no special value in what was being taken. Even his hands hung limp, not trying to perform, until Richard seized one and forced it against his genitals, as though they were the hands of a doll of his he could make do what he wanted.

"I'm sorry," he said, suddenly leaving go and sinking back, "we can't do it again really, because I have to get up early in the morning for my shift."

Simon's body hung where it had been left, but his eyes went soft and sorry for this human being whose wishes (alien as they were) could be destroyed by a work-routine. And he felt as if his body were no longer his own, while his thoughts and feelings had been detached from it, had been crammed into a drawer in the corner which had been pushed shut. And when Richard lost confidence, or actually turned away, as momentarily he did now, it was as if he ran to that drawer, and took out his thoughts and feelings and fantasies and tried them on secretively in front of a mirror, admiring himself in guises *he* wanted to be seen in by others; but which Richard did not seem to see him in.

"What are you doing tomorrow then?" said Richard quietly, hopelessness, even resentment somewhere beneath his words.

"Nothing that I know of," he answered, at once pitying and open. "I'd like to see some of the gay places in London, but I don't really know where they are, or – or how to go on my own."

"Well – well, I could take you to a few tomorrow night, if you like." And even now the quite childlike surge of utter buoyancy was held down, had to be guessed at, rather than could be seen.

"That would be nice."

"Well, I could pick you up about half-six. Could you – could you give me a ring a bit before then, just to confirm it's still ok?"

"Alright."

"I'll put off the light now, because I have to get some sleep. You don't have to get up when I get up. You can sleep in and let yourself out later. You can find your way to King's Cross tube, can you?"

"Oh yes," said Simon, suddenly reminded absorbedly, as if it were all at once the licence for anything he might do, that, yes, here he was in London, that distant city to which all spiritual wealth drains, and where one must go to recover a little to take back. "Yes, I can find my way to the tube."

Richard put out the light, and coming back to the bed, rather to Simon's surprise dropped at once into a wrapped-in sleeping position, his back to Simon, breathing heavily. Simon tried unsuccessfully to make himself comfortable on his narrow fringe of the bed, but when he closed his eyes there came readily, not sleep, but a semi-conscious jumble of dream-like images, through which he floated, a blasé worldly triumph, disturbed only once by a strange smell in the bed about him, which stirring uneasily, he recognised as the smell of love-making, but at once lost in his torpid dreaming.

CHAPTER NINE

At half past six the next evening Simon was sitting in the pale evening sunshine, waiting for Richard on the wall outside the hostel. He had done little all day but posture to himself in his imagination, even starting a letter to Annie that recorded what little had happened to him in London so far in a tone of revelation and unmitigated self-congratulation. It totally ignored the threatening presence of submissive timidity and sheer incomprehension. Even now, sitting here feeling the breeze lapping his newly-washed hair, he was pushing to the back of his mind the awareness that he was about to offer himself up as a plastic dummy, to Richard's dreams on the one hand and his own on the other, mutually incompatible as he already suspected these were.

Richard's car drew up punctually alongside the kerb. Simon stepped into it as if this were a moment in a film, celebrating the lover's car that would sweep the beloved off to excitement and happiness like a knight's white charger. He turned to Richard and was almost surprised to find how ordinary he looked, realising at the same time that he had carried no memory of his physical appearance with him through the day. Richard leant across and kissed him, and Simon took the kiss distractedly, as if this were an action of the scenario he recognised as necessary, but which belonged to Richard's part, not his.

"All day I've been thinking about how beautiful last night was," said Richard sincerely.

An uneasy memory of discomfort and emotional isolation rattled its chains in the dark locked room of Simon's mind where it had been shut from view.

"Where are we going?" he said quickly, diverting himself with the childlike anticipation of foreign entertainments.

"Well, we needn't go anywhere, we could just go home," said Richard hesitantly, a boyish hope flickering for a moment in his voice. But then, as Simon felt himself beginning to look worried, he said in an unexpected blasé tone, "No, come on, we'll hit the town, I'll show you the sights."

And so began the first of many similar nights.

In silence they drove right across London, through the brightly lit West End busy with entertainment traffic, to Earl's Court. It was a long drive, and as he began to tire of watching the crowded pavements and the endless parade of pubs and restaurants Simon began to wish that Richard would talk to him. But about what he could not say, and he searched in vain himself for a promising topic of conversation.

At last they parked the car, and got out and began to walk, still without speaking, under trees stirring drowsily in the mild night. Simon could hear the pub even before he reached it. A solid mass of milling people, shoulder to shoulder, completely filled the huge downstairs bar, almost spilling out onto the pavement. It made a Glasgow pub on a Friday night seem quite uncrowded by comparison. Simon was taken quite aback. All these people are gay, he thought, all of them.

He followed Richard and jostled through the crowd and up the stairs. The barnlike upstairs bar was only a little less crowded. He stood and waited selfconsciously among the chattering laughing hordes while Richard pushed his way to the bar for drinks, feeling as much at a loss as a traveller in a foreign-speaking railway station, and almost frightenedly aware of assessing glances falling on him from every direction. But he himself did not think to look around any more than if he had been a child left by its mother in a crowd in a certain spot. Only when Richard at last struggled back, after what seemed ages, did he dare to glimpse furtively about him, and marvel wide-eyed at the nonchalance of this great variety of people, all sprawled about as if the prospect of their leisure seemed not merely secure but endless.

Richard, scanning the scene with an apparently knowing quickness, steered him to a table in the corner where there was room for two people to squeeze in.

"I bet there are no pubs like this in Glasgow," said Richard with an uninterested certainty.

"No. This is so big."

"Yes, I guess this is one of the biggest. I come here quite a lot."

"Are there lots of others then?"

"Oh, about five or six. And lots of smaller ones scattered around."

Simon sipped his beer nervously, and peered round sheepishly over his glass. The people at the next table all seemed to have their eyes turned outwards, he noticed, as if each of them separately was looking out for somebody, and only spoke to one another out of the corners of their mouths. A few moments passed. Simon hunted about for something to say to Richard.

"Do you know people here?" he said, raising his voice to be heard above the whirr of chatter.

With a slightly surprised hint of a smile, Richard's eyes went quickly round the room. "I think there's someone over there I slept with once a while back," he said flatly. "We didn't really hit it off. I think it's him, anyway. I can't quite see."

"Do your friends come here?" said Simon, feeling somehow he had been misunderstood.

Richard fingered his glass, glancing away and then down, his brows furrowing strangely, like a small child who feels deliberately puzzled. He said thoughtfully, "Well, I guess I don't really have any friends. Not to speak of." He paused, and then added firmly, "I've always been a loner." It was one of those public announcements of a decision about oneself that is to be taken as unarguable. He gave a little shrug. "After all, most gay people are, aren't they, growing up among straights? Do you have any gay friends in Glasgow."

"Well – not gay friends, no."

Something seemed to have been touched in Richard. Staring into his drink with a helpless look, he spoke with an uncharacteristic earnestness. "Yeah, I used to feel lonely when I was in my teens, and all everybody else talked about was how big so-and-so's tits were, and whether she was really an easy lay – you know. Then I discovered cruising in the local park. At first it was just a kind of extension of being lonely, I suppose. I went there to walk on my own in the evenings because it was all I had to do. I was never sure what would happen. But once I knew I could get guys to suck me off, then it didn't seem to matter so much any more that I didn't have anyone to talk to. So long as you've got sex you're alright, aren't you?" Glancing up at Simon, he slipped his hand along below the table and tickled Simon's crotch.

Simon smiled back tentatively, flooded with pity for this bewildered lonely figure, and at the same time terrified of the responsibility that it seemed he had as Richard's lover. He felt sure he could not measure up to it. Especially when it seemed so hard to get near Richard. "Is that why you go along to Gay Liberation, because you're lonely?" he said.

"Lonely? Oh, no. I don't know. I suppose – well, I used nearly always to come here to cruise. But yes, I go to Gay Lib most of the time now. Because – well, they're a nice lot on the whole, especially the young ones. These days that's where all the best-lookers turn up." He winked at Simon.

"You know, I'm older than I look, actually," said Simon defensively, a little clumsily. And yet at that moment he felt inexperienced and naive.

Richard was taking a drink from his beer and did not seem to hear. "It is more friendly though, Gay Lib," he said thoughtfully, putting his glass down. "I suppose that's what's different about it really. All that stuff about not hiding what we are any more, it's important. I think that's why I went in the first place. It makes you sort of feel a bit more close somehow."

"I was very excited when I first read *Come Together* in Glasgow."

"Oh yes, the newspaper, I've read one of those. Some of those things, though, that they talk about, like sex-roles – they're always on about sex-roles – sometimes it's a bit beyond me. Or maybe I'm just not really interested."

124

There were two middle-aged Americans in loud suits sitting next to them. With unaffected American ease one of them suddenly intruded on their conversation. "Say, do you guys know of any other bars round here like this? We kinda like the atmosphere here. We're new in town."

"The Coleherne's just around the corner," said Richard.

"Oh, *the* Coleherne? Is that so?"

Suddenly Simon thought he recognised something in their tone, Richard's as much as the Americans': there was something in its relish of the football-fan or of the executive who, finding themselves in a foreign city, are interested only in seeing the fleshpots. I suppose this must be very liberating for me, he thought.

"Allow me to introduce myself," said the American. "I'm Howard, and this here's Earle."

"Hi there," said Earle, beaming.

"Richard. And this is Simon."

"Well, it's great to meet you, Richard and Simon. And are you Londoners? Do you come here a lot?"

"Well, I live in London," said Richard flatly, "but I was brought up in Toronto."

"A fine city, a fine city. And where are you from, Simon?"

"Glasgow," said Simon, a little shyly. "In Scotland."

"Scot-land? Well, it's great to meet a Scotlander. And tell me, are they all as pretty in Glasgow?"

Simon blushed and smiled, and was coyly silent, as he thought he should be.

Richard said uneasily, "Do you want to finish this drink, and we'll go somewhere else?"

"Oh, if you like," said Simon, taken by surprise, swallowing the remains of his beer quickly.

"Well, it's been really great to talk to you, Richard and Simon," gushed Howard, proffering a large pink hand. "So long now."

Earle too wished them goodbye effusively, as if they had been the high-point of his evening, and Simon left them feeling almost touched at their childlike American forthrightness. How easy it is to be sexually approached here, he thought, almost exultantly. He gazed curiously about him as he left, looking at first with fascination and then a little bit of longing at a young West Indian who was leaning against the head of the stairs. But the black looked back at him with a condescending smile merging into haughty disinterest for this boyish-looking white so obviously unaware of the situation he was in. Simon was suddenly and painfully reminded of his underlying bewilderment. He kept close to Richard as they made their way down the stairs, nervously holding onto the back of his shirt with two fingers.

And now they went to the Catacombs. Dark, hot, noisy, smoke-filled vaults, their shadowy corners full of scarcely discernible inter-locked couples, the patchily lit spaces between pillars crossed by wildly dancing scantily-clad bodies. A lithe figure in a skin-tight bright red cat-suit, with sunken cheeks and glazed eyes and untidy long-black curls, ran past them up the stairs, squealing with laughter, and goosed Simon along the inside of the thigh as he passed. Simon had never before seen so much overt sexuality as he saw here, not even among straights. Couples with naked torsos danced close, as if glued together by their sweat, whose pungent smell hit the nostrils at every turn. Giggling young men in provocatively tight jeans and shirts open almost to the waist writhed sinuously in dance, the hand of one of them clutching the crotch of the other.

"Do you want to dance?" asked Richard, in a routine sort of way.

Timidly, Simon said yes, overwhelmed merely by the opportunity of dancing with another man in a situation that would involve no tension. But the very strangeness produced its own tension, and he danced stiffly, unimaginatively, as much as anything because there was so little room to move in. Other bodies kept jostling him feeling him up. Richard was gazing abstractedly over Simon's shoulder, and when Simon suggested they sit down, he came to a stop as though a siren had sounded and he was leaving a routine job he did mindlessly every day.

They sat in a corner somewhere and drank lemonade. Again Simon found himself waiting for Richard to talk to him, but he was silent and apparently quite comfortably so.

"Do you like dancing?" said Simon tentatively.

Richard shrugged. "I've never really thought. I feel a bit awkward," he said slowly. "It's just a sort of substitute really, isn't it?" He grinned at Simon knowingly.

Tensely Simon swirled the ice-cubes in his lemonade. "I think I like dancing," he said rather timorously, feeling his words were melting on contact, "because it's a way of letting your body express something you feel. Things which one doesn't say outright because – because it would be too disruptive, perhaps."

Richard looked blank, and Simon felt embarrassed. "You look nice when you're dancing, though," Richard said, in an attempted tone of kindly reassurance. He finished his lemonade. "Shall we go? I have to get up early again tomorrow."

They climbed the steep stairs, and emerged into the soft fresh air of the street. "How long have you been driving buses?" Simon asked.

"A couple of years. I'll be stopping soon, because – oh, I'll tell you later."

"Do you like it?"

"Good money. A job doesn't mean much to me really. I do a bit of this, a bit of that. When you're driving, you get a good view of all the men walking along the street. But it's just work. Everyone sells them-selves, don't they?" He opened the car-door. "Shall I show you the rent-boys on the way back?" he said, leaning on the top of the door.

"The what?"

"I thought that one would get you. Come on, we'll stop at Piccadilly Circus. It's on the way."

As Simon settled into his seat, Richard leant across and gave him a quick surreptitious peck of a kiss. "We won't be lonely tonight, will we?" he said. And then they were driving, unspeaking – as usual it began to seem – on into the neon showground of the West End. They parked in a small street off Leicester Square, and Simon followed Richard docilely along the still amazingly busy pavements to Piccadilly Circus.

"Just stand here for a minute and watch," said Richard, stopping and leaning on a parapet where they could look across at the arches of Barclay's Bank. "There's one."

Simon gradually singled out from the coming and going a pallid young man with permed hair, tight-fitting clothes, high boots, and a leather shoulder-bag, who was strutting up and down rather impatiently in front of the bank, drawing on a cigarette with flamboyant gestures.

"Just keep looking around," said Richard, "and you'll see some more. Try not to let them know you're looking."

And sure enough, Simon was soon able to pick out from the passers-by several similarly costumed figures, moving here and there with a purposeful aimlessness, or simply leaning against walls like wares outside a shop on display. Some of them made their way to the mouths of the tube-station and disappeared down the stairs with a look on their faces of entering territory they controlled.

"Well, there we are, shall we go?" said Richard, in the manner of an uncle leading his charge away from the Changing of the Guard.

Simon rambled along beside him towards the car, gazing now at the flashing neon walls all around them, with the same tourist's fascination with which he had watched the prostitutes.

All this licence, he thought, all this licence.

"Shall we go back to my place now?" Richard said, a warmth hovering there somewhere.

"Oh yes," said Simon dreamily. "I'm quite tired."

"Oh. Are you?"

It was only the slight edginess of that reply that made Simon realise the abstractedness of his remark. In fact, he himself would have liked nothing so much now as to go home and sleep, and the reminder that he was playing the unaccustomed role of lover made him suddenly feel diffident and resourceless. "Oh, no, not really tired," he said, feeling clumsy, waiting for the certainty of the car's direction to relieve him of the responsibility of covering-up.

It was hard, if not impossible, for him to reconcile the sense of miraculous opportunity, that seemed to be opened up so certainly by all he had seen tonight, with the strange and inadequate reality of the experience with Richard the night before. Suddenly he felt a longing for the advice, the wisdom and encouragement of Philip and Annie.

Richard turned and gave him a smile at once generous and saucy. He pulled the starter. But the car did not start. He waited and tried again. He tried several times. It did not start.

"The battery must be flat," he said, as if it were a comment on something that might be happening to somebody else.

Feeling trapped, Simon looked helplessly away out of the window. He saw two policemen emerge from a dark alley and come towards the car. He felt a great relief. Help had arrived opportunely, he would not need to expose his uselessness. He smiled.

A policeman's gloved hand grasped the door firmly, flung it open, reached in and grabbed Simon by the muscles of his upper arm, squeezing them till they hurt as he jerked him off the seat.

"Ok, come on you two, get out!"

Simon found himself standing up in the middle of the road with his arm gripped tight by the black figure towering above him.

"We're having trouble with the car," he said weakly, still for the moment unable to adjust his sense of the situation. "The battery must be flat."

"The battery must be flat!" said the policeman, mimicking him, and shaking him a little.

Simon looked in uncomprehending dismay for Richard. He was standing on the other side of the car, held by the other policeman. He seemed to be patiently answering questions with a look on his face of mildly vexed endurance. The policeman was holding a small stainless steel butter-knife under his nose. "And who does this knife belong to then?" Simon heard the policeman say. "Jo Lyons it says on it. How come it's in your car?"

"A friend gave it to me to use for a screwdriver," said Richard blandly.

"Oh yes. Friend of Mr Lyons, is he, your friend?"

Simon felt the fingers about his arm begin to tighten, and go on tightening as if they wanted to squeeze the very bone. He winced and turned to look at the policeman in sudden fear, realising his incredible powerlessness.

"And just what do you think you're doing then?" said the policeman with a sneer.

"We were going home," said Simon under his breath.

"What's that? Speak up, can't you?"

"We were going home."

"Oh, going home were you now? And how old would you be?"

"Twenty-two."

"Twenty-*two*! Well, fancy that! What's your name?"

"Simon." He gave only his christian name unthinkingly, as if he were a child answering an adult.

"And what's *his* name?" The policeman gestured with a thumb towards Richard.

In momentary panic Simon hesitated.

"Don't even know his name, do you? Well Simon, and do you happen to have anything to prove you're twenty-two?"

"I've got an international student card." He fumbled for it awkwardly in his breast-pocket with his one free hand, and gave it to the policeman, who snatched it from him with a sidelong resentful look, stared at it for some time as though it were difficult to read, and then thrust it back at Simon like some object of disgust. Almost at once he released his hold on Simon's arm, and pushed him slightly towards the car. The other policeman noticed the gesture and looked across questioningly.

"This one's a big boy now," said Simon's policeman in a voice of playground mockery. "Now you're twenty-one, Simon, we can't stop you, can we? You can go home with him, if you want to, can't you? You can do anything you like. You can do all sorts of things together tonight, you and him, can't you? Now you're a big boy." The bullying thrusts of derision droned on and on, and he began to accompany them with little thrusts of the hand, pushing Simon into the car, till Simon sat down quickly and pulled the door shut, quaking and sweating, feeling sick for lack of self-respect, wanting to shrivel up in a corner and weep. Richard got in beside him, and slammed the door in a rush, and tried the starter with gritted teeth. The engine wheezed uncertainly into life.

Simon involuntarily gasped with relief, but turned to look out of the window with a sudden shock of nightmare pursuit. The two policemen were standing side by side in the middle of the road. One of them lifted his hand and flapped his wrist in a gesture of goodbye. The car began to move.

"Pigs," said Richard, but in a tone of explanation, not anger.

Simon was aware of his hand trembling convulsively, like something no longer under his control. "I thought they were coming to help us with the car," he said, as though he were describing how an accident had happened to him.

"They thought you were under twenty-one," Richard said off-handedly, and then was silent.

Only as Simon tried to distract himself with looking out of the window did he realise how shattered he felt. He had never before had to fear the police. Always in Glasgow when, as so often, they drew up in a car beside him as he was walking home alone at night, their opening aggressiveness would disappear at once as soon as they heard his educated accent and his address, and they would drive off in search of a more suitable victim. They had always been a threat to somebody else. Now, he felt already, he would never be able to so much as see a London policeman without a qualm of fear – and of hatred. He had felt their power, their unjustified, resistless and terrifying power; he had been made to learn what they were there to do; and he was ashamed that he'd had to have his nose rubbed in it before he properly understood.

He was still shaking when they reached Richard's place. He wanted to be comforted, and waited for Richard to do something. But Richard opened the front door in silence, and went on up the dark stairs. He followed slowly, fantasising that his lover was holding him close as he trembled, and muttering soothing words over him from some fond superior strength.

"Shall we go straight to bed?" said Richard, going into his room.

And there was nothing. No comfort, no fondness, no reassurance of talk. He did not want to go to bed. There seemed to be nothing there. It did not even fill any image of himself. That was not how the episode should grow to an end; it was something imposed.

"Yes, if you like," he said quietly after a moment, suddenly thinking, Well after all, two nights in a row is quite an achievement.

He took off his clothes, arranged them in a pile, and laid himself down tamely, waiting for it to be over. Richard's hands began to move all over him.

And since he could find consolation in nothing else, he began to seek it in at least the power to act well the part required.

But rapidly it began to feel like consolation in the power to deceive. He seemed to be lying there gazing up at a happiness which he was supplying, but from which he was shut out. He felt like a machine for the production of satisfaction, but a machine haunted by dreams.

Yet Richard seemed so much himself. His bland features softened and reshaped themselves; the movements of his body were now all purpose, now all pleasure, the flesh becoming as vibrant as marble in changing sunlight, and his voice dropping the chains of words, and dripping effortlessly in a soft wordless crooning sigh.

Until Simon noticed that his arm had gone to sleep, and asked to move it.

"Don't you enjoy it? You don't come," Richard said in puzzlement. "Don't you like being fucked?" He looked concerned, fearful even.

Simon found himself disarmed. "It's just – it's something I never thought about before." No, it's not that I dislike the idea of being fucked at all, he thought, but the actuality of feeling treated as an inanimate thing, with my consent sought only in retrospect.

"But you look – you look as if you wanted to be fucked."

Simon was appalledly silent, not understanding. How can one look like that? he thought. It seemed like the straights in Glasgow saying, "But he looks so feminine."

He was proud of what he looked like, it was part of his honesty, part of his daring. And besides, because of that, what could he now do? Even if, say, he tried to grow a beard, which he quite simply doubted he could do convincingly, he would wear it as though it were in play, or worse, a shameful attempt at evasion.

Richard began to wank him, with almost a little desperation. So that a voice in Simon said, He's doing it out of guilt. But just as Richard began to get excited, he suddenly found himself coming even before he himself had expected it. And it was all over as if it had never been. Richard looked surprised and then let down.

He sat up, a certain dismay seeming to settle on his face, and swung his legs off the edge of the bed, turning his back on Simon. "Do you want some coffee?" he said over his shoulder.

"Yes please," said Simon flatly, grateful at least for the diversion. Left alone, he felt a sense of disappointment emerging like a skeleton from a cupboard, which he rushed to hold shut.

He rolled over and lay facing the wall, drawing his knees up towards his chin. His eyes fell shut and unconsciousness began to beckon enticingly. But hearing Richard coming back, he quickly opened his eyes and pulled himself up on one elbow, blinking drowsily for a moment.

Richard handed him his mug, and lay beside him on the bed in silence, sipping the coffee slowly, looking grave and diffident. "There's something I haven't told you," he said after a while, an embarrassed bleakness in his voice. "I'm going to Amsterdam in three weeks' time, for a few months. It was all arranged a while ago. I'm going to stay with an old flatmate. The fare's paid for and everything. I should have told you."

A gust of wind suddenly rattled the window-pane, and after a few seconds, rain began tapping against it as if it wanted to get in.

For a moment Simon had felt relief. But now he found himself shaking. And yet he was not sure whether he was anxious about losing Richard so much as about losing what Richard represented.

Silence began to roar between them. "Amsterdam?" said Simon at last, genuinely curious.

"People are very free there. There's lots of places to meet, lots of sex," said Richard, an uncharacteristic gleam of enthusiasm flickering behind his eyes. He sounded like a would-be Russian defector talking about the West. "I sort of feel I've been hanging around in London long enough. Oh, I've had some good times, and slept with some good-looking people. But things don't seem to be going anywhere any more. I go along to Gay Lib meetings, I pick people up, and I keep hoping I'll find the ideal sexual partner. But I guess I'm never satisfied. So I just thought, it was time to try somewhere different." For a moment he looked lost.

"Well – we've got three weeks anyway," said Simon softly. With a stirring of real fondness, he stretched out and ran his hand down Richard's back. And then, with a sudden calculation that surprised him, he slipped his hand round and brushed it along Richard's thigh.

Richard looked relieved and grateful; as if an alienatingly mystifying conversation had suddenly switched to a topic he could join in on. He knelt astride Simon's thighs, looking down. "I like being with you," he said.

Simon turned his head, and looked at the drips of rain streaming down the uncurtained window. He thought, I cannot relate to people in Glasgow because I am so sexually deprived and isolated. And yet now I cannot relate to someone here because I do not understand the world they live in, because I have never known it. Perhaps anyone I relate to here could only turn out a victim, a victim of my unwilling naivety and my unwilling desperation, and their willing self-delusion and trustingness.

"I do, I really like being with you," said Richard again quietly.

But you don't know me, thought Simon. But perhaps no one has ever known me, because I am only ever half there, or less, much less.

And then all at once Richard had inserted himself. Like putting a coin in a pinball-machine. Simon shut his eyes, running away into himself. But the moment of irritation faded quickly away. Instead, he felt his hands ranging over the territory of the back above him in a new way, as though they were confirming possession. They even changed shape a little, sending pressure down to the tips and the nails, almost clutching.

The rain could be heard falling heavily now. It was quite cold for summer.

CHAPTER TEN

The three weeks passed slowly.

Simon spent almost every evening with Richard. Left to his own devices, Richard was quite happy just to watch television. But sometimes they would go to a new pub or club. Wherever they went Simon began to find he could always expect there to be someone who would have his eye on him. As the strangeness passed away, he began to feel more and more confidently flirtatious. And yet a farewell look of reproach, for instance, could make him lose his footing at once, and send him stumbling into guilt and shame and perplexity.

Once home after an outing, Richard would hurry to make love to Simon with the enthusiasm of reconfirmed possession. And Simon accepted tranquilly. Because he was beginning to realise that any exploitation was mutual, that he was using Richard as a protection, both a screen and a buffer, for his own ineptitude in a social situation he was only just beginning to grasp. The screen shut him off, and also stopped him seeing out.

But perhaps even more, he needed Richard in order to keep up his image, to himself and others, of having succeeded in doing what he set out to; instead of, as he knew in private reality, having only discovered a new level of helplessness in himself. Even in letters to Philip and Annie, he found himself posturing, deceiving, making the claim that he was enjoying sex.

And time jogged by. Sometimes at Simon's urging they went to one of the smaller Gay Liberation groups in other parts of town, each of which seemed to have its own character.

Notting Hill became a favourite of Simon's. Perhaps he would not have worn a bright yellow jumper with a purple crimplene frock like that man in the green plastic sunglasses, but he could not help looking enviously at the coffee-coloured lace evening-dress with a white cloth rose at the neck on the man beside. Despite a new embroidered Indian blouse, standing beside Richard in his plain cotton shirt and brown cords, he felt glaringly odd. He envied the drag-queens their courage, but at the same time felt helplessly remote from it.

To his left was a tall striking person, with sculptured face, thick tight-curled hennaed hair and turquoise eye shadow, a white daisy behind his ear, brocade trousers, and a general limber Angelo-like relaxation, coiling and uncoiling himself all over the table he sat on. He kept catching Simon's eye with a look of secret understanding.

Simon was trying to follow the discussion, but he found it hard.

Fragments of distant ideas seemed to fly back and forth between them, never settling, only glimpsed.

"Because I wear a dress and make-up," the one in lace was saying, waving agitated varnished fingers, "it doesn't mean I want to get put down like a woman. And it doesn't mean I'm itching to get laid."

"Yeah, right! Tip her over and fill her up, that's what they always think," said the one in sunglasses in an aggressive strident voice. "You don't know, you just don't know how sick I am of men pinching my bum. It may be beautiful, but it's not common property. It's part of *me*!"

The other one preened his cloth rose solicitously. "I'm into drag because I think men should *stop* acting like men, not because I want to encourage them!"

"You've got to remember some people grew up thinking sex is for proving you're desirable, not for showing you're fond," said the man on the table in a gentle voice. "Some people get off on having their bums pinched, or whatever. They never get over the stage of thinking it's flattering."

"Yeah, right! Ticking it off! All men are interested in is marking up notches on their pricks!" The man with the sunglasses dipped in his handbag and took out some crochet in tinselled wool, which he began to work on with angry jabbing movements. Some previously silent onlookers began to remonstrate.

His attention wavering, Simon glanced aside at Richard. He was standing with his eyes fixed blankly on the floor. "A bit hard to follow sometimes, isn't it?" Simon whispered to him, smiling nervously.

"Oh, they're quite a load of politicos here," said Richard looking up, tapping his foot in a bored way. "I wouldn't usually come, but I thought you wanted to, Simon."

"Oh, I did. But we can go soon, if you like," said Simon, feeling a reluctant obligation.

As he left hand in hand with Richard, the man on the table suddenly threw him a look of questioning impatience, almost, Simon thought, as though he were actually saying, What do you think you're doing, who do you think you're kidding? For a moment Simon felt afraid and bewildered, as much as anything because he realised that in this world of social relationships that he still found largely incomprehensible, where the only resource he could find was bluff, there were some who comprehended quite confidently, and only too accurately.

The week before Richard left for Amsterdam was Gay Pride week. It was to culminate in a march to Hyde Park. But Richard would not be on it. He was sailing that morning.

"There's a Gay Lib dance in Fulham Town Hall the night before I leave,"he said to Simon, rather distantly. "Do you want to go?"

"Oh yes! A gay dance? I can't imagine it!"

It was a rather muggy night, full of electricity. The air seemed to brush against one. They parked the car a little way away, and walked to the hall through warm dark streets, perfumed excitingly with the cooking smells of exotic restaurants. Before them the hall reared up in the form of a vast columned portico, from which there streamed bright lights and wild music, passed through by hurrying figures in gaudy clothes dwarfed by the height of the ceilings. Simon wandered down the wide corridor like a child approaching a Christmas party, rapt, almost oblivious of Richard leading the way. And so into an immense cavernous hall, dimly lit, packed with bodies, laughing, dancing, cuddling, stretching on and on indistinctly to a distant spotlit stage, where a rock group, writhing sexually over their instruments and flashing with sweat, were pulsing out glaring imitation Ziggy Stardust. He stood still in awe, and drank in the smell of sweat and spilt beer, as though it were the mists of hashish wafting the Hashashin into a delusion of the paradise that awaited their selling themselves to the cause.

The touch of Richard's hand on his arm, pulling him into the dance, jarred him with its physical reality. He hesitated to step into this unreal vision. As he did so, he felt the distant rays of the spotlights fall on his body, blurring it into just one of the magical tantalising hints of figures that filled the space from far wall to far wall; and he began to move, both sensing and watching the oblique light cut his movements up, till he realised he had become no more than flashes of graceful hand or thrusting hip or tossing hair. And he danced on and on, wilder and wilder, until at last physical exhaustion, and the perspiration making his clothes stick clammily to him, or tripping in a cold trickle down his ribs, brought him down at last to a sense of tangible existence. He stopped suddenly, looking about him quite differently. He saw Richard before him, paused questioningly, his hair plastered to his forehead with sweat; and beyond and around him real people, real expectations, and perhaps even real opportunities.

And now Richard looked at him searchingly, and came forward and said almost humbly, "Shall we split up and wander around for a bit on our own?"

And Simon found his fear forgotten. "Yes," he said definitely, almost enthusiastically.

"I'll meet you back in here later," said Richard, turning even as he said it, and merging into the anonymity of the crowd immediately and completely.

Simon stood for a minute, enjoying a sense of freedom, and yet uncertain what to do with it. He took a few steps forward, feeling emotionally as clumsy as an astronaut taking their first steps on the moon. He was almost surprised to find that he could do it, and he stopped and looked about him. Yes, he thought, now I too am a part of this. And he began to wander in the direction of a busy doorway, at once with a facade of self-concerned purposefulness lying, like sunglasses worn as discardible disguise, over a surveying aimlessness, as if he too had been doing this for years. He found his way down some steps into a large room with tables and chairs where people were sitting drinking, and beyond that into a similar room where the bar was. Finding this a dead end, he turned with a pretence of looking for someone in particular and not finding them, which felt almost practised, and sauntered back to the dance-hall, where he moved from one vantage-point to another, looking about him.

Standing alone, he saw one of the people, looking gentle but imaginative, whom he found sympathetic.

Suddenly Richard was at his side. "Why don't you ask him to dance?" he said, and walked on by before Simon had a chance to reply.

This was at the one time the challenge and the reassurance Simon needed. He walked across the hall, and said to the long-haired young man in a purple tee-shirt, "Would you like to dance?"

"What?" said the man, screwing up his face to try and hear above the band.

"Would – would you like to dance?" said Simon, if anything more quietly.

"What?" said the man again; then suddenly realising, "Oh, no thanks. I'm feeling tired."

Simon turned and walked the distance back across the hall, feeling both relief and contentment. He realised that he had achieved all he wanted to achieve. He had taken a first lesson in a new kind of confidence and like all first lessons it had to be simple and limited. The merely being able to acknowledge sexual possibilities all around was what he had wanted to confront. The merely having the courage to initiate some communication, however crudely, was all he had wanted to learn in asking someone to dance. And he was relieved that nothing came of it; for more and more he was beginning to sense that he was vulnerable to the power of others, in a way he could not pinpoint.

He wandered back to the bar at the back of the hall, and sat down on one of the bench-seats, wondering. Within a moment the feeling of contentment had been tinged with unease. Out of the corner of his eye he noticed a friend, or rather ex-lover of Richard's, whom he had met once or twice, coming across the room towards him with an anxious-looking stranger. He felt disinterested, turned in on himself.

"Hallo," said Richard's friend coolly. "I'm sorry, I've forgotton your name."

"Simon."

"Oh yes, of course, that's right. Simon, this is Vernon."

"Hallo," said Simon, smiling mechanically. The stranger looked very nervous and very flushed. He sank down unsteadily on to the seat beside Simon. "Hallo," he said, panting as if he were just about to run through a long urgent message.

"Well, excuse me for a minute," said Richard's relaxed friend, drawling a little. "I'm going to get a drink."

Simon looked marginally surprised at the briefness of his visit, but then turned to stare self-absorbedly at the table again. He virtually forgot the bristling Vernon at once, and got quite a jolt when he heard him saying stumblingly, "Where – where are you from?"

He turned round to answer reluctantly. "Glasgow."

"Oh," Vernon said. He stared wide-eyed at Simon. A hiccup shook him and he looked bewildered, as if uncertain what had happened. "Do – do you want another drink?"

"Well, no, not really," said Simon, and looked away again, drawn by his preoccupations.

A pause. Vernon said brightly, "I'm from St. Alban's. If you know where that is."

Simon turned back. "Well, I know it's built round Roman ruins. Somewhere just north, isn't it?"

"I've got a car. It's a short drive." He looked expectant and then lost. "Um – what's the gay life like in Glasgow?"

"Small. Rather secretive. Rather frightened." He added with a distant politeness, "What's it like in St. Alban's?"

"Oh, it's non-existent really. But I've got a good job. And a place of my own."

"Well, that's important."

"Yeah, it's a nice pad. You'd like it. I say, listen," – Vernon broke into a sudden gabble – "Would you like to come back with me tonight?"

Simon got a bit of a shock. Then almost at once he felt quite pleased. He paused, and said, "I don't think so." He did not want to say No bluntly, too aware of enjoying himself being admired; but like a piece of fine china in a museum case, that the viewer looks at, likes, but knows will never be for their use.

"Oh," said Vernon, obviously not expecting for a moment to have been turned down and caught with no plans. For a minute his pondering eyes rolled around in his head like bagatelle-balls teetering around a no-score hole. "We could visit the ruins," he suggested uncertainly.

"I have to see a friend off somewhere tomorrow morning," said Simon, and smiled condescendingly, almost aristocratically.

"We can get up early. I'll drive you back in time. I don't mind, really I don't."

Simon became a little incredulous. But what's all this for? he thought. Just one night of sex? Why is he so desperate?

At that moment Richard appeared at the table. Simon went to move along the bench-seat to make way for him, and beamed at him wordlessly, as if to demonstrate that someone who was allowed to use this fine porcelain had now arrived.

"Come and dance," said Richard, taking his arm and pulling him to his feet like a dummy.

As they left, Simon flung a sideways glance at Vernon. And saw him biting his lip to keep back the childlike tears at having been mocked and frustrated. A panicky flash of guilt burned up from the pit of Simon's stomach. He turned away and stared emptily ahead.

Back on the dance-floor, he moved his arms and feet around distractedly. The whole experience seemed now to be staring at him in a new light. He thought, Has feeling myself used like an object only resulted in my learning to make myself appear like one? Has it resulted in my learning to look other people up and down only as connoisseurs of such an object?

But that's got nothing to do with what I want, he thought. It can't be true. And he pushed the realisations away to the back of his mind, intending them to lie there for a long time.

Richard said, "I'm tired, I'm going to sit down. Dance with someone else if you like."

Yes, I could, I could, thought Simon, and it seemed that yet again he saw a pinpoint of light in the darkness. But no, I'm afraid. Will they know how to use me? If I'm an object, how will an object be able to tell them?

While the two of them stood uncertainly in the midst of the dance-floor, a man in a long maroon velvet evening-dress climbed onto the stage, and began to speak into the microphone in an inappropriately soft and gentle voice. "Listen everybody, we've been told there are some heavies hanging about outside hassling people. Someone's already been hurt. The police have been called, but we don't know if they'll come, and if you're leaving now, you'd better not go on your own. And be careful. We want to see you all in one piece on the march tomorrow."

The hostility of the outside world seemed to descend like an accident. Simon felt disabled. It was no longer possible to think about the intricacies of his position.

He and Richard went and sat down by one another in silence. Supported by two others, a young man was helped in, crying, his white cheesecloth shirt spattered with blood. The band put down their instruments.

But after waiting a bit, they had managed to get home without event.

The night was clammy. At any moment there would be a storm. As they lay in bed, even Richard did not seem to want to make love. But they both knew they ought to. Their sweating bodies kept sticking together and pulling apart with a noise like a raspberry.

When their duty to the occasion was done, they lay by one another both like taut strings. Simon sensed even Richard's disappointment, that in making love there had been neither comfort nor consolation. A flash of lightning spotlit their two faces staring stonily at the ceiling.

"We should shut the window or rain will get in," whispered Richard, with the obvious relief of finding something to say that had nothing to do with either whatever he was or should be feeling.

"I'll do it," said Simon, eagerly leaping out of bed, glad to be rid of the tense physical contact.

Thunder grumbled in the distance. He stood for a moment half-turned towards the window, letting the sudden wind blow raindrops in on his face.

"Well, I hope you don't have a stormy crossing," he said over his shoulder.

"I'll be alright. It'll be fine again by the morning," came Richard's voice behind. "And what are you going to do? Are you going to go back to Glasgow? Or stay in London? For more adventures."

No, he could not go back now, thought Simon, not while he felt still in the midst of something unexplained. "I'll stay," he said, courage struggling with trepidation.

He shut the window, and the pane creaked with a sudden gust. He turned and made his way to the bed in the half-darkness, inching forward fearfully. Experience seemed to be scattered before him like drawing-pins over a carpet trodden in bare feet and darkness. He wanted to lie down, but when he got into bed, it seemed as if it could no more support his resting weight than a swamp, he felt himself so heavy with future fears and threatening self-reproaches.

"Will you go on the march tomorrow?" whispered Richard.

"I'm not sure."

"You should. Show you're proud to be gay." The sound of Richard's breathing came and went more and more slowly. After a while he said, "Well, we've had a good time."

Have I? thought Simon. Instead of learning to cope with recognising myself as a sexual non-entity, I've learnt to cope with recognising myself as a sexual object. But I don't see what either has to do with being a human being. "Oh yes," he said at last, "I've enjoyed myself. It's certainly been a change." It sounded like the bleak self-consolation at the end of a wet break by the seaside.

Silence came. Only the sighing of wind and rain. They lay without touching.

CHAPTER ELEVEN

Richard had slipped away so quietly in the early morning, scarcely waking Simon, a murmured goodbye, a little brush of the lips. Simon had dozed again almost at once, and now, drifting into wakefulness, he could scarcely remember Richard's leaving at all. His dreams seemed more vivid.

He got up and wandered into the empty kitchen. He drew the curtains, and an expectant sunshine came dancing in. Fearful and yet exhilarated, he felt the decision rise slowly in him to join the Gay Pride March. Hastily he made coffee, and gobbled down a scanty bowl of cereal. He felt rather odd, sitting at the table alone, wondering if he would be likely ever to see Richard again, or what it would mean if he did. Tidying the vacated bedroom behind him, he stole down the stairs, as if anxious not to be seen or heard, and slipped out, shutting the door gently behind him.

The march was gathering at Cleopatra's Needle. Timid and uncertain of the way, Simon arrived quite late. As he came within sight of the waiting figures strung along the walls of the Embankment, tension came towards him in ripples, but it was hard to tell where excitement stopped and fear began. "Welcome, brother," said an apparent sentry in gaudy drag, touching him lightly on the shoulder, planting a quick kiss on his cheek – surely leaving a lipstick mark – and ushering him towards the crowd. "Join the others under this monument to an ancient queen." Simon found himself at once engulfed in a general nervous pulsation, hands fiddling, pacing up and down. Quickly it seemed it was the momentum of this alone that grouped them into a body of clusters and straggling lines, which stood for a few moments like a car revving its engine.

And then they were marching. A slow uneven motion surged back and forth around Simon, throwing out one group of people to the front of him, drawing another back, and so on, again and again. He looked about, a little overawed, for faces that he knew, but though he could see many that he recognised, there was no one that he knew to speak to. So he drifted along among the strangers, keeping his eye for reassurance on a bearded man pushing a child in a pushchair who, though he had never seen him before, struck him with a feeling of dependability.

After only a short time a sense of routine, even of aimlessness began to threaten. For a start the march seemed to be taking place virtually unwatched in this part of town on a Saturday morning. But as they turned towards the West End on their way to Speakers' Corner, excitement and purpose seemed to come back in a wave, sweeping the length of the march, so that one turned to see just how long it was. Near Simon a man with long hair and a flowing scarf cupped his hands to his mouth and began to bellow in a ringing voice that echoed from the tall buildings shutting out the sun now on either side. "Two, four, six, eight, Gay is just as good as straight." From somewhere behind came another voice, being joined raggedly by others, the volume seeping up. "Give me a G, give me an A, give me a Y," and so on. Simon saw that the man with the beard had lifted the child onto his shoulders, and was chanting exultantly. Even Simon himself tentatively joined his voice with the others, swallowing half the chant and weakly dribbling out the rest, but feeling within him a rising thrill of power through shared pain, a strange feeling he had never known before.

But then something happened at the front. Alarm spread backwards first; there was a flurry of questions, followed by a slowly moving wake of information. "It's the pigs! They're diverting us, making us go through empty streets. We've got to get back onto the route we planned." Everyone was looking about them, as if waiting for someone else to make the suggestions, but they still kept marching forward. Suddenly Simon could see that the pavement was studded with immobile policemen, standing like objects, bollards in the way of an escaping car, only their hands twitching behind their backs, their faces masked in impassivity, the pupils moving in their eyes behind their distant look as though from behind the arrow-slits of a medieval castle. All at once the long-haired man with the megaphone began to wave his hands and shout, "Go back, go back. We've got to get onto the main streets!" From the distance came the sound of a rhythmical chorus and hand-clapping. "Out of the closets, into the streets!" The policemen's hands moved and tightened round the end of their batons, their eyes narrowed slightly. The march seemed suddenly to lose all cohesion, as if it were being shaken loose. Great gaps appeared in it, and everyone looked anxiously all around, as if they were no longer walking in a body, but alone. And yet it kept inexorably moving forward.

Then all at once they were turning into Oxford Street. Crowds lined the footpath, jostling, staring, pointing. The march came together again, ranks formed around one; Simon found himself rubbing shoulders with two total strangers, flinging them sideways smiles, as they all chanted together. Righteous anger flowered among them like a joy. A man in radical drag – stocky and ginger-haired, dressed in a torn fur coat despite the weather, one eye painted with green, the other with purple, pink powder on his cheeks, and a huge ox-bow mouth in lipstick the colour of congealed blood – was striding along thrusting leaflets into the hands of the goggling crowd. An old man rode along the march on a bicycle with a placard attached saying "Woe to the sons of Sodom!'', loudly fulminating with religious abuse that was totally drowned by the chanting, which throbbed through the street like a great heartbeat.

Simon held his head high. He felt as he had never felt before that he would inherit the earth, that all their guilt, their fear, their loneliness would have an end, forever; it must.

And when they reached Hyde Park, there was nothing to do. Simon wandered around aimlessly for a while, as everyone else seemed to be doing, looking at least for someone he might know. The crowd spread out but did not disperse, as if reluctant to admit to impasse. A bearded man in a white cotton summer frock and big straw hat with roses on it came towards Simon, and they seemed to recognise one another, from some meeting or other. Simon smiled tentatively.

"Bit of a let-down really, wasn't it?" said the bearded man.

"I suppose so," said Simon hesitantly, looking forlornly around, sorry to find his own mood reflected. "Just now I felt as if everything was only just starting."

"You're new to all this, aren't you?" said the man, taking a pipe out of his handbag and filling it. "I know. It changes our lives at first – gay pride, gay solidarity. Me, this is my first time in drag, and that's the most worthwhile thing I've got out of today, the courage to do it. Knowing I'd have support. I suppose in a few weeks you'll see me walking down Oxford Street in fishnet stockings and a tutu as if I've done it all my life. But once we've won our gay space, what are we going to do in it – together?" He drew on his pipe, and clouds of smoke slunk up over the brim of his hat. "Where the movement goes from here, how it organises itself, I don't know."

A wraithlike man in a cardigan advanced timidly towards them, clutching some leaflets. He flung a quick sideways glance at the bearded man, like a hand whisking at a wasp, then pushed a leaflet into Simon's grasp, and hurriedly dissolved into the other stragglers drifting past. It was an announcement for gay coffee afternoons in a church hall. "Oh well," said the man in drag, "some people seem to know where the movement should go. Enjoy the sunshine anyway. I'll see you around." And he wandered off across the park swinging his handbag in a circle.

Simon sat down on the grass, picked a daisy, and twirled it frustratedly between his fingers. If the movement wasn't going to carry him anywhere, at least something might happen to him, he thought.

A small disgruntled knot of people ambled by in silence, with placards reading "Gay is proud" and "Gay is angry" slung across their hunched shoulders like some pantomine Dick Whittington's bundle on a stick. Simon sat and watched them vanish into the distance.

And nothing happened. Drawing circles with his finger in the grass, he thought, Perhaps after all, like Richard, I'm just a vacancy waiting to be filled by sex. He flung aside the now mutilated daisy.

It was a while before he realised how much at a loss he felt without Richard. The first full day alone he stayed at home in the dingy room in an Islington boarding-house he had moved to a week before, reading and studying desultorily, going down to watch television in the evening. But the next day found him more and more panic-stricken. A letter arrived from Philip and Annie, and he read it through intensely four or five times. Again and again the thought crossed his mind of giving up on everything and rushing back to Glasgow. Familiarity alone beckoned as a source of content. But then again it would seem impossible to integrate his experience here with his life in Glasgow, impossible to make anything of it.

Despite its early promise, it was turning out a cool wet summer. That evening as the dank twilight began slowly to gather, he felt at once unbearably lonely, and yet terrified of venturing out on his own. At last, he ran down to the off-licence and bought himself enough beer to get drunk alone in his room.

He lay on the rickety single bed, surrounded by the smell of damp dust, dreaming to himself of the places he could be. At last he had to go and pee. He staggered to his feet and lunged into the gloomy bathroom next door. There his face floated in the small square of flecked yellow mirror above the sink, detached from him, like a head on a plate. He stooped and gazed into it, as if it did not belong to him, judging the pallor of the skin, checking out the cheekbone shadows, scrutinising the haze of blond hair. There it is, he thought, that at least is mine. I have discovered my physical appearance, and from it I can create communication.

He propped himself against the wall and peed carelessly, showering drops over the edge of the bowl. No, he said bitterly to his vague outline in the bubbling water of the bowl, all I can create is a ware, of a kind which no one will actually keep, because there is no obvious use for it. I am deluding myself too with my own fancy wrappings.

He felt his head itching, in one place at first, then all over. He scratched it impatiently, savagely. A thin shower of dandruff floated down and settled over his clothes, like a light autumn snowfall, followed by a few hairs, like shed branches. As he lurched through the door and reeled off towards bed, he decided he would have to do something about his dandruff. He could not afford to lose his precious hair.

He treated it anxiously the next day with some foul-smelling commercial preparation, and the following morning it looked considerably the worse for this attention, and his hair was a knotted fright.

It struck him that his own body was trying to destroy the very physical appearance in which he himself was reluctant to place his trust.

But just because he distrusted it, he told himself, that did not mean he wanted to give it up. He needed it. He was too diffident to make an initial impression any other way. He needed to be able to put on his beauty to cover his fear and incomprehension, just as his clothes covered his cringing unexercised body.

However, the next day there seemed little wrong with his scalp after all. Very probably no one else would notice anything. He decided to take his courage in both hands and go to the meeting of South London Gay Liberation. He had made it to a meeting on his own when he first arrived, he could do it again.

He arrived there late, perhaps because he had waited for it to stop raining, perhaps because it was a long tube journey, perhaps because he knew from a meeting he had been to with Richard that it would be boring anyway. But then it suited him, after all, in the role of fey beautiful stranger. If he walked in late, it drew everyone's attention to his first appearance, and still gave them all time to look at him before the meeting broke up.

The meeting itself was dripping slowly like a tap after the flow has been turned off. A figure looking gaunt and church-ridden was speaking, with the tone of someone going over something for the umpteenth time.

"We've got to do more for the ordinary gay," he was saying. "Most people don't want to get involved in long heavy political discussions. Let alone terrify everyone by putting on dresses and war-paint. They just want somewhere to have a good time quietly with their lovers, or other gay men."

Hardly listening, Simon became fascinated by watching the rain still forming a spreading pool at the tip of someone's umbrella resting against the chair beside him.

After what seemed an age, people pulled back their chairs and started to move off to the pub. He stood up, gazing about like an owl in the daylight for a moment, and sidled over and attached himself to someone he vaguely recognised, with no more ingratiation than a half-smile. The person donned at once an uneasy look, much as he might have done if he had suddenly noticed that he had a flea.

Simon said nothing as they walked; but he did not want to say anything. What was there to say? The wind struck cool and damp and strong.

The almost empty pub was very poorly lit. The dinginess frightened Simon, it was like something reaching out of his schooldays to reclaim him. "Here's a pint for you," he heard a voice saying from a distance, and turning, found surprisingly near him the person he had come with, holding out a pint towards him with a puzzled look. "Oh thanks," he said, clipped and flat. He stood so that he was half-turned towards the group talking beside him, and half-turned outwards to survey the rest. He did not want to say anything. Silence, after all, is necessary for a beautiful stranger, he thought.

A neat little man whom Simon had met before was leaning against the bar. A dentist or something, Simon remembered; or was it a doctor? He came over when he saw Simon had seen him. His shoes were highly polished and squeaked a little.

"Hallo," he said. "You know, I find you very perplexing."

Simon smiled. Enigmatically.

Getting no further reply, the dentist went on, "You come along to these things, and the disco the other day, and you seem to spend all your time giving searching looks, and yet you avoid any possibility of getting off with anybody."

"Yes," agreed Simon.

"I mean, surely you can't expect to find a lasting deep spiritual relationship in the space of a summer's visit?"

"No," said Simon, with a secret uncertainty. He wants to have a short shallow unspiritual relationship with me, he thought. Indifferently he stored the knowlege, and obligingly looked away so that the dentist's eyes could roam over him.

A mountain of middle-aged flesh with tinted glasses, oiled hair, and a rum and coke lurched up to the little dentist. "Hallo, Jim," it said, with a kind of brash unctuousness. "Are you still off to Australia?"

"Australia?" said Simon turning, genuinely surprised. There seemed in the striped-shirted, almost dapper dentist little of the desperation that might conceivably drive one to Australia.

"Australian dentistry has a good reputation. I know of a vacancy coming up in a practice in Sydney," Jim said to Simon defensively, looking as if he wished the topic had not been raised.

"Oho, I envy you," said the fat loud middle-aged man effusively, in a grating voice, swaying slowly and spilling rum from his glass as he gestured vaguely with it, "the sun and all those surfers. Besides, get out if you can, I say. Britain's had it."

"I would have thought it would be a terrifying place to live if you were gay," said Simon.

"I would have said the same of Glasgow," said the dentist, standing on his dignity to try and hide his unsureness.

"You're not going back to Glasgow, are you, Simon? You're not leaving us?" said the middle-aged man, cajoling with all the subtlety of the luridly perfumed brilliantine that slicked his hair.

"Well, I suppose I'll have to eventually," said Simon.

145

"Have you thought of staying in London?" His tone suggested that it would be unreasonable to say no. He was shuffling closer to Simon, the wall of his body shutting off everything from view.

"Yes, I have." For he was sure that soon London would reassert its promise of escape.

"Well listen, Simon," said the middle-aged man, leaning unsteadily towards him, dropping his voice conspiratorially. "I might be able to help you out, if you do. A nice-looking boy like you could earn perhaps fifty, a hundred pounds a night. I've got friends in the club business, you see. You wouldn't need to do anything you need be ashamed of. Just dance, take your clothes off, a quick flash, the lights go out and you're off. You don't have to talk to the customers, or anything like that, unless you want to. Are you interested?"

"Well – I'm not sure." He stored it in his memory. The man started giving him his phone-number, but he did not really listen.

Drifting off into a daydream, he was struck by how worried his hands looked as they clutched his glass, clinging insecurely to its slidy surfaces. Unexpectedly he saw them belonging to the grotesque figure of a petulant frightened old man surrounded by chests and cabinets crammed with bric-a-brac, none of which was ever used: this was how he was storing instances of sexual flattery, proudly, undiscerningly, without any idea of using it. A senseless kind of pride, he realised in bewilderment, that vanished the moment one recognised it. For a moment he panicked. How was this awareness of his sexual attractiveness ever going to help him to get to know people?

"Last orders, please." He heard the barman calling from a great distance, and looked up, slowly focusing his eyes.

Ahead of him was the dark intense man with a mournful moustache. He looked rather awkward, with heavy untamed limbs forced into clothes that could not contain them, let alone grace them, and his expression, for all its brooding intensity, was strangely ingenuous. His moustache was wet and drooping at the corners with beer. After lumbering up unsteadily to Simon and looking at him for a while, he said in a positively lugubrious tone, "You're tearing me apart, you know."

Simon smiled. And automatically filed the remark away. "Not really," he said, looking down.

"Yes you are," the man continued, gruffly mournful, still fixing Simon with a look of sombre childlike pleading. "What's your name?" The words were grotesquely solemn and clumsy like his movements.

"Simon." He could not help feeling pleased with his own quietness and gracefulness as he displayed himself before the man.

"Mine's Kev. What do you do?"

"I'm still a student."

"Oh." Spoken disappointedly. "Well, I'm a sign-writer. Where do you come from?" Every word seemed to receive its own ponderous emphasis. Simon felt the magnetic desperation tugging at his detachment.

"Glasgow." He was aware of struggling to assert his distance.

Yet still the man pressed on, with childlike insistence. "Where are you staying in London?"

"I'm stuck in a really awful boarding-house. But it's cheap," said Simon. Gradually he was feeling penetrated by an unexpected unintended pity.

"Ah. Well, why don't you come and stay with me?" Kev said, with a note, to Simon's surprise, of humble generosity. "If you like. Give me your address and we can be in touch."

Simon laughed nervously. He wanted to fend off Kev's assumption of a special claim in something so obviously widely in demand. And yet he could not help as it were remembering that he would feel respect for this rather absurd courage, were he not a beautiful stranger. Confused, he began to give his address. He could always treat it simply as another incident of sexual approval to be ticked off.

But afterwards he deliberately moved away, feeling forced into action to assert his inert disinterestedness, bringing himself to hover on the edge of another group of talkers, aware of Kev's sad eyes following him. He was relieved when he heard the barman calling time.

He gulped down the remnants of his beer, and without saying a word to anyone, slipped quickly out of the door and began to walk towards the tube-station with an anxiously frantic step, as though he were being followed.

But no, slowing his pace, he realised he was quite alone.

147

CHAPTER TWELVE

"Clomping Kev," Simon dubbed him puckishly in his thoughts, the moment he opened the door to him. They had exchanged letters since they last saw one another. Even now, as he followed the lumbering taciturn figure down a flight of steps towards a basement, Simon remembered unashamedly how he had grinned over the single rather crumpled typed page, full of uncorrected typing mistakes, that had unexpectedly turned up in the mail a day or so after the meeting. A repeated invitation to stay, written with a strange blend of rough-and-ready homely concern and rather querulous inelegant pleading, its final effect rather like an intended light gateau that through the maker's inexpertise had turned out a steamed pudding.

They came down into a spacious basement flat, looking out onto a small grassed-in yard, the main room shabbily furnished, dusty, cluttered with dropped tools, half-sawn planks of wood, sheets of hardboard and so on, its corners displaying a range of bookshelves and a fair-sized record collection. There was a closed door in a far wall towards which Kev moved, stepping over the clutter on the floor with a kind of ostentatious longsufferingness but without comment.

"The bedroom's in here," he mumbled over his shoulder.

Even at the very moment of his following Kev into the bedroom, Simon was unaware of what sleeping arrangements Kev had in mind. In reply to Kev's letter he had tried to suggest his own preference for privacy, but only obliquely, anxious not to lose this opportunity whatever Kev's intentions. If Kev's superficial appraisal of me, Simon had thought, was enough to make him seek this relationship, he can rest assured that from me he will receive a superficial response. I will present a politely friendly appearance – and I'll even sleep with him if there's no way out – but he can't expect loyalty, he can't expect concern. So he thought.

What Simon wanted above all was a sense of shelter. A little harbour amidst the chaos to return to, to venture out from. And the moment any shelter seemed offered, he had snatched it up.

In the room there were two single beds.

"This will be your bed," said Kev, pointing to the rather untidily made-up divan nearest the door, "and you can hang up your things in this part of the wardrobe, if you want. It's not the most comfortable of beds, but you should be alright."

"Thanks," said Simon, a little surprised, and perkily tossed his case onto the bed, and went back into the other room, strolling around it with an appraising air.

Kev stood for a moment in the bedroom doorway, one arm leaning against the jamb, exposing a particularly large patch of sweat under the armpit of his shirt, his greasy slightly curly black hair dangling down with a seemingly cultivated untidiness over his dark eyes, which bored into Simon already with an obviously premeditated look of knowing patience. "What do you think?" he said brusquely.

"Nice place," said Simon, looking out of the window, his back to Kev. "But rather untidy."

"I don't have time to tidy," said Kev shortly, rather in the manner of some laconic peasant receiving nobility in a nineteenth century novel. "You do what you like. I'll go and make us something to eat. From tomorrow, we'll share cooking." He stomped arrogantly into the adjoining kitchen.

Simon dropped himself like a feather onto the settee, whose groaning broken springs engulfed him awkwardly so that his bottom slung below the level of his knees. He drummed his fingers on the arm and smiled around him smugly. "Can I put a record on?" he called out after a while.

"Why don't you?" said Kev gruffly from the kitchen, and at once began to clatter the crockery.

There was a very eclectic selection of music – heavy rock, Dylan, popular classics, Cajun music. After browsing a little, Simon put on the Concerto for Orchestra. Its camels-across-the desert opening theme mingled headily with his expectation and the late afternoon sunshine. So now from this base he could resume his adventuring. He settled back into the settee as best he could and waited for his meal. From the kitchen he heard the sound of breaking glass, and a muttered curse.

After a tea of corned beef salad, eaten largely in silence, Kev dragged out some strangely sawn pieces of wood and sheets of cardboard, of an obscure relationship to one another, and began to work with them, on his knees in the middle of the carpet, speechlessly absorbed. Simon tried to make himself comfortable with a book. He would have liked to have gone out, somewhere, anywhere, but he did not want to be impolite to his host on his first night. He twisted his legs this way and that in an effort to provide himself with at least a semblance of ease.

"You do fidget," came Kev's voice, but when Simon looked up, he was already once again impassively bent over his work, a nail between his teeth.

Simon turned back a little disappointedly to his book. A reluctant solitariness seemed to hang in the room like smoke. In the silence he could hear the tick of the alarm-clock in the bedroom.

Suddenly Kev rose up and began to move towards the settee, but as Simon lifted his eyes questioningly, he had passed it and gone to a cabinet against the wall behind. Simon aimed his eyes at the printed page, but did not read. He heard a chink of glass, and then Kev thumped back to the middle of the floor and flopped down with a bottle of black rum, a bottle of coke, and one large glass.

He said, not looking at Simon, unscrewing the bottles, "You'll have to get used to me. I drink about half a bottle of rum every night."

Strangely Simon felt relieved. He lowered his book, stretched out his legs, and tried to think of something to say.

"Always rum?" he asked.

"Yes, like pirates. Do you drink?" said Kev sharply, glancing up suspiciously from under his black eyebrows, indeed almost already bristling with accusation and indignation.

"I drink beer," said Simon, feeling himself suddenly and pointlessly on the defensive.

"Ah." Kev sunk back with a stiff little smile that was gone almost the moment it appeared, the first smile of his that Simon had seen. At once his look reverted to an intense stare, as if he were waiting to spring. "Do you like Guinness?"

"Sometimes." Simon kept his own eyes uneasily averted.

"So you should. Put some weight on you. You look like a bloody advertisement for Oxfam. Well, there's a couple of bottles of Guinness in the kitchen. Why don't you go and get them?" He turned back to the business of fixing his own drink, total indifference to Simon apparently dropping on him as at the flick of a switch.

Simon went to the kitchen and fetched the beer. When he came back, Kev had his back to him, crouched over whatever it was he was making. Rather reluctantly Simon sat himself back down and began to drink in silence, the book in his hands but nothing more, lifting his eyes regularly to look at Kev in puzzlement. As the soft dark beer began to touch him, he wanted to reach out to Kev, to learn more of him, of what lay behind his abruptness. But how could he do that, and not seem to offer more than he was willing to?

He watched Kev shuffle a little way awkwardly on his knees, like some elephant-seal on land, to pick up a hammer. With one hand he held a nail to join the corner of a frame, while, screwing up his face in agonised concentration, with the other he raised the hammer aggressively and brought it down with what looked like a ridiculously heavy whack. The nail bent, and there was the sound of cracking wood. "Oh bollocks," he said loudly, miserably, and flung the hammer from him. It glanced his glass, taking a chip from it and knocking it over, pouring the black rum and sticky coke into the carpet.

He said, "And don't you laugh!" looking up at Simon fiercely.

"I didn't," protested Simon quickly, as if raising a hand to ward off a blow. "What are you making anyway?"

"Well you might at least offer to clean it up," Kev almost shouted, rising as slowly and precariously to his feet as if his body were a human pyramid. "You bloody students, you're all the same. Not even a word of sympathy!" He strode into the kitchen, muttering over his shoulder, and returned with a wet cloth and shovel, louring as he dropped to his knees with a reverberating thud and fussily, awkwardly, cleared up the mess. Simon observed a diplomatic silence. Kev cast him a side-glance as he returned to the kitchen, where he deposited the broken glass noisily in a bucket, then came back with a new glass, knelt, and unsteadily poured himself another drink. Simon was pretending to read again.

"If you must know," Kev said suddenly, taking Simon quite unawares, "it's a light-show for the Gay Liberation disco on Saturdays, over the pub down the road. If you stop pestering me, I'll show you how it's meant to work." His voice was making the effort to sound gentle, but it was rather like someone trying to play delicately on a tuba.

Simon felt a touch of pity. In fact, as he lowered his book he actually smiled over Kev, whom he found looking at him now, as the rum rose behind his eyes, with something dog-like in his gaze. He dropped nimbly from the couch and knelt quietly beside him. "I'd have had it finished ages ago," Kev said in a tone of pathetic resignation, "if inanimate objects didn't keep ganging up and playing tricks on me." Resuming work, he proceeded to explain his rather Heath-Robinson contraption with an enthusiastic meticulousness. On and on he went, gradually getting slower and more tongue-tied, until the rum suddenly seemed to overcome his coherence.

Stopping all but in mid-sentence, he stood up, kicking his tools to one side, uttered a laconic goodnight, and lurched into the bedroom, where he dropped heavily onto audibly protesting bedsprings.

Simon stayed on with the pretence of his book, wondering about Kev, calculating how to stay safely detached, dreaming about possibilities – the Saturday disco perhaps. Unable to read a word. He waited until he felt sure Kev must be asleep, then he tiptoed into the bedroom and slipped quietly between the sheets.

The next morning he went up to University College on the tube and spent the day in the library. He came back early and had tea going before Kev came home from work. When Kev came in, he raised an eyebrow at the sight of Simon in the kitchen, and uttered an expression of incredulity. He turned his back and started to go out of the kitchen, but as he did so he tossed a small paper bag towards Simon. "I brought you a cake," he said over his shoulder, as if it had been an ordeal for which he expected no thanks.

Simon tentatively stared inside the bag at the sticky garish Florentine biscuit lying in wait on the greaseproof paper; he did not like sweet cakes, and for the moment he left it sitting there, wondering what to do with it. But almost at once Kev came back, dragging a huge bag of washing, and his eyes went at once to the cake bag. "Well, aren't you going to eat it, seeing as I bought it for you?" he said, in a tone of mournful outrage.

"Yes," said Simon, stirring unconvincingly at a pot, "I was just – busy." He put down the spoon, took out the cake, and took a large bite of it. Crumbs showered down him to the floor, like a little rock-slide.

"Trust you to make a mess with it," muttered Kev, barging past him with the plastic sack of sheets and shirts, to get to the bathroom beyond the kitchen. Halfway there the sack split and the dirty washing flowed onto the floor.

That night they went to the pub on the corner. Simon was glad to get out, and yet he still felt a bit of a captive, even if an acquiescing one, allowed out only as though on a leash. The pub was almost empty and rather dreary. "Do your friends come here?" said Simon, who would have welcomed company.

"I usually drink on my own," Kev said, studying his glass, drumming quietly on the table with his fingers.

For much of the evening they sat over their drinks in an awkward silence, Simon resentfully dreaming, feeling Kev's eyes fixed piercingly on him, waiting for something from him with a melancholy impatience. But what? A response? A proof of failure?

Once or twice, turning to his drink, Simon caught sight momentarily of a ghost of desire haunting Kev's heavy gaze, his mind's eye tentatively peeping beneath Simon's clothes perhaps. Turning aside again, Simon would feel his body suddenly glowing with smug elegance. He would lift his glass, or cock his head, or even suppress the smile of satisfaction that rose to his lips with such poise; such a delicate lightness, that made Kev seem by comparison an unshaped model of heavy clay stuck to its chair. But in a moment the smugness would pass, and he would feel resentful of Kev's unvoiced fantasies, his unsanctioned intrusion. And when Kev spoke to him, he thought he sensed now in the tone Kev's resentment at the fact of his own desire.

The next night was the night of the Gay Liberation disco. All day Simon was like a dog straining on its lead, knowing in a moment he is going to be set free in the country. Immediately after tea he had dressed before the mirror in a black embroidered Indian shirt with floppy sleeves, and he paced the sitting-room unspeaking and impatient, as Kev fumbled over his machine and staggered with it unhelped up the stairs to his van.

They had arrived early, and Simon was already drunk before the upstairs room had even filled. It was a warm evening, and he sat for a while watching the fading light from the bay-window, which was opened to let in the summer breeze, desultorily chatting with a rather well-groomed group who gathered to enjoy the cool. Kev was busy with his light-machine, which did not seem to be working too smoothly. As it grew dark outside, Simon's eyes turned restlessly inwards to the disco and began to prowl around the walls, watching the dancers; sometimes with envy at their agility, sometimes with contempt at their sluggishness, searching recklessly for someone to pay attention to.

Meanwhile, a greying man with a fixed smile and tired screened-off eyes, dressed in a neat white polo-neck, had joined the group at the window. "Hallo, you're Simon that's staying with Kevin, aren't you?" he said softly, holding out a hand, smiling at Simon like a doctor at a new patient. "I'm Bernard. I think I may have seen you at one of our meetings."

Feeling inwardly a little irritated at the man's polished beneficence, Simon shook hands politely, his eyes turned away to survey the room.

And there he was. A slender little figure, dressed in lush corduroy, with diffidently male-modelish good looks and wide almost doll-like eyes, following Simon with baleful longing.

"Are you a friend of Kevin's?" came Bernard's bedside voice, setting the patient at ease.

"Well, not really. I only met him about a week ago at one of the meetings," said Simon, feeling uneasy at his own words. "And – he asked me to stay."

"Kevin always strikes me under that clumsy exterior as a rather lonely soul," said Bernard, with a kind of spiritual confidentiality, like a vicar discussing a problem child with a parent. "It was generous of him to put you up. I hope you're looking after him well."

Simon was trying to keep his eyes on the man across the room, flooding them with a look of bashful pleading. His view was constantly interrupted by the luridly lit gesticulations of two drag-queens, who were filling their corner of the dance-floor with lithe and inventive movement. Long legs in emerald and scarlet stockings frantically flailed the air, floppy-sleeved arms fell and wavered through it like streamers. For all that it kept getting in his way, Simon was enjoying their expressive exuberance.

"It's a pity these people in frocks always try and take the place over," said Bernard beside him, a sour edginess in his voice.

"Oh, they're dancing awfully well," said Simon abstractedly, turning politely back to Bernard.

Bernard was still smiling impassively, but within the murky shade of his tense brows his eyes were letting a tangled distrust and irritation slip through. "But they do frighten people off," he said, in a measured tone of reasonableness, as impenetrable as a patient school-teacher. "They always come along whenever you've got somewhere new started, and they do make it so difficult for the rest of us. Don't they? Have you been along to our coffee afternoons?"

"Well, not yet," said Simon distantly, hardly listening. His eyes kept straying over to the watching face across the room, which flashed now green, now rosy in the stuttering gleams of Kev's light-show. At last in a pause between records he saw with some relief that his admirer was coming towards him, approaching out of the lost souls hovering over the dance-floor waiting for the music to breathe life into them again.

"Oh hallo, Michael," said Bernard to the little man as he joined them. "Nice to see you here."

Simon's eyes rose hopefully to greet their soul's knower. Somehow his face looked rather bland close to. But perhaps it was the light.

"Can I get you a drink?" said the little man, almost unctuously.

When he came back from the bar, the disc-jockey was already playing the slow smoochy music that announced the end and the purpose of the evening. "I don't suppose you'd like to dance?" said the little man.

He dropped into Simon's diffident embrace like a dummy made of soft rubber, his arms dangling limply over Simon's shoulders, his head flopping slowly from side to side. Simon tried to rest his cheek on the soft corduroy shoulder before him and gazed out with a look of unease through a vapour of sumptuous aftershave.

What was it he wanted? The prestige of a glamorous conquest? To know himself a beautiful jewel on the neck of a beautiful possessor?

The track finished and they had not said a word. They stood waiting for the next track to begin. Already despite himself Simon was beginning to feel absurdly as though he were dragging round an awkward and useless bundle; he had been given it as a present, but there was no one to tell him what it was for.

As the music resumed, the little man's eyes half-closed langorously while he shuffled on the spot. "What's your name?" he murmured with portentous earnestness.

"Simon."

"Oh, what a lovely name. I'm just Mike."

"Oh. That's – nice." Melting Mike, he found himself naming him in his imagination. He sought for something more to say, feeling as though he were in a dream, trying to reach somewhere important down a dead end, where he stood frantically running against the final wall. For the moment he let the music again take care of them, suggest to them what they should be feeling. It stopped and started again. "What do you do?" he ventured at last.

"I'm training to be a social worker." Mike's words oozed easily from him along sighs carefully modulated like teases. "What do you do, apart from look so tempting?"

"I'm still a student, a postgraduate student."

"Oh, how clever. Don't tell me. Music?"

"No, English, actually."

They stood swaying from one side to the other, wrapped around one another like two trailing creepers tangled together. To Simon it seemed their conversation moved on like a clockwork toy which he had wound up and then abandoned to run on meaninglessly in an empty room.

Now in the silence that had already returned between records a voice announced that the disco was about to close. Lou Reed's voice slid over the few couples that remained on the floor, like razor-blades in syrup: "Oh, such a perfect day . . ."

"How do you manage to make your hair look so lovely?" said Mike, stroking his own sleek well-cut hair. "Mine's such a mess. I expect you agree?"

"Oh no, it's not," said Simon politely, giving it a dutifully appraising look, and forced in the process to look Mike for a moment in the eye. All at once Mike's gaze locked pleadingly onto his and flooded with a look of dramatic imminence. Wondering in alarm what it was he was going to ask or reveal, Simon found himself engulfed unawares by an eager acrobatic kiss. His surprised tongue responded hesitantly, like his toes dipping into bathwater already feared as too hot.

Mike let go with a loud sigh of relief and a smile of contented accomplishment. "Do you come to this disco often?" he said with a new casualness, his head subsiding onto Simon's shoulder.

"No, I've only been once before. A little while ago. Do you?"

"It's my first time."

"Have you enjoyed it?"

Mike murmured into his ear, "It's been a surprise. You beautiful thing, you. I wasn't expecting to fall in love."

Love: the word struck Simon strangely, like an unaccustomed word reminding one of a childhood spent in a different region. Something irretrievably lost. On Mike's lips it sounded out-of-place, even somehow violated.

"Are you going anywhere afterwards?" Mike breathed, with an intonation of coquettish innuendo.

The moving lights suddenly juddered to a standstill, and in the pink glow that lay across the ceiling appeared a crack of white with ragged brown edges, that spread rapidly like a blood-stain. A smell of burnt plastic drifted across the room. Simon heard Kev's childlike muttered curse, and the clatter as he kicked the light-machine over, plunging the room in darkness, as though he were knocking down his coloured bricks because one would not balance in the right place.

Simon felt the strange unexpected unwanted voice of pity calling to him remonstratingly, from afar. In the darkness Mike put his slobbering lips over Simon's ear, and bit it. Simon started.

"Actually, I think I really should go back to the friend's place I'm staying at," he said clumsily, stumbling over shallow breaths. "I've only been there a few days, and I – I don't want to appear ungrateful for his hospitality."

"Oh, are you sure?" crooned Mike, managing to make his disappointment, if it was real, sound only like an iced topping. "Oh, go on," he wheedled, sticking his wet tongue into Simon's ear, which Simon hated. "I think you're just teasing." It sounded as if his peevishness came mainly from a feeling that Simon had proved a better teaser.

"No, really," said Simon anxiously, going tense, standing still. "Why not another night?"

Lights came on suddenly. In their sickly uncompromising glare Mike stood wide-eyed and blinking, his flesh pale and lifeless, hanging sloppily from the bones of his face like a coat slipped on in a hurry. Slowly he put on an expression, as tailored and showy as the soft corduroy jacket that lapped him from the shoulders down. "Oh well, tomorrow then," he sighed cajolingly.

I've got to go through with this, whatever it is, thought Simon, and what's more, I chose to. "Yes alright, tomorrow," he said, with a stiff twitch of a smile. At once Mike began to tell him where he lived, with a voice like treacle being trickled slowly from a spoon over an unyielding pudding.

When Simon went to look for Kev, he found he had gone. He had to walk back and ring the door-bell, as he had no key with him. After a while Kev could be heard stamping up the hall. He swung the door open and stood there in a dressing-gown, leaning on the door for a moment, staring at Simon with a look of smouldering scorn. "Oh, you're back are you?" he said, turning his back at once, and walking on ahead down the stairs as if disinterested. Simon followed timidly at a little distance, trying to make no sound.

"Had a nice time with your little friend?" snarled Kev over his shoulder. "You stink of aftershave you know!" He walked straight on through the sitting-room into the bedroom and shut the door behind him.

Simon was left standing in the middle of the sitting-room as if he had been dropped there. On the floor in front of him lay the remains of the light-machine and an empty bottle of rum on its side. He tried to quash his fear and guilt with the assertion to himself that at any rate he was not going to be owned. And for a while he just stood there, listening to the silence of the night, waiting until he felt sure that Kev must be asleep, as it already began to seem he had done many times.

When he woke next morning he saw Kev packing a bag in a corner of the bedroom. Kev turned to look at him as he sat up in bed, but looked away again at once with a scarcely hidden snort. "I'm going out for the day," he announced, flatly, and yet aggressively, lamming a pair of swimming-trunks into the bag as if he was swatting it. He drew the zipper shut quickly and strode towards the bedroom door.

As he was about to pass through it, Simon said, with an unconvincing attempt at cheeriness, "Where are you going?"

Kev turned slowly with a withering scowl, as if his patience had received a final blow. Then he simply went on his way, calling back only when he was out of sight, "I'm going to spend the day with some friends on the Thames." In the kitchen Simon heard him making tea, presumably for a thermos.

He sat wondering for a moment whether to let him leave before he got up. Then he thought that the least he might do would be to say goodbye. So he swung his legs out and dressed quickly, and crept shamefacedly into the kitchen as if he was going to face an angry teacher.

Kev was sitting at the table. He looked as if he had been waiting for Simon. He pushed a cup across towards him. "I made you a cup of tea," he said quietly.

"Oh," said Simon, taken aback, "thanks." He sat down and sipped the tea. It was lukewarm.

Kev stood up, towering above Simon, who glanced up at him sheepishly, his lips poised open above the edge of the cup. But he only thumped across to the sink, looking straight ahead, washed his cup and put it to drain. Then he walked out.

"Goodbye," he said from the hall.

"Have a nice time," called Simon, clutching his cup anxiously.

"I'll see you when I get home," came Kev's voice moving towards the stairs.

"I'll be out tonight," cried Simon timidly, in alarm, cringing as if he expected a blow to descend out of the empty air. "I'm going – to visit someone."

He heard Kev's heavy footfalls halt for a moment; there was a barely audible grunt, then they lunged on, falling slowly and regularly on the stairs like tired hammer-blows, fainter and fainter, and then out of hearing.

He reached Mike's place in the early evening. Its prissy garden frontage, evidently kept up by someone, was dissolved in a soft half-light as he wandered hesitantly up to the brick-arched door. He pressed the bottom bell and chimes sounded distantly inside. He stood waiting, wriggling anxiously within his own clothes, as though he were wearing something that did not fit him.

Later they had lingered over a pretentious but unsatisfying meal, which must have cost Mike a great deal. Smiling proudly, he proffered his insubstantial delicacies like a children's game: "There's some pâté de foie gras, but don't take too much. There's some olives, but I'm going to take them away after you've had two." They sat over coffee chatting in slow drips about music. So far the whole evening had the feel of a conversation in a waiting-room where the realisation dawns that the train is so late it is perhaps not coming at all.

"Well, it really is uncomfortable sitting round the table like this; let's go through to the bed-sitting-room," said Mike with the air of a rehearsed speech, perhaps deliberately unsuppressed, standing up and grinning nervously.

Simon went through and sat stiffly on one of the chintz-covered chairs, feeling exposed by the expanse of carpet around him, wondering what to talk about next, staring about forlornly for inspiration. Mike was flitting here and there, getting him a drink, turning down the lights, picking out a record. He's setting the scene, thought Simon suddenly, with a chill of disgust, feeling himself turning into a mere prop, used by Mike in a one-person show.

Mike rose up gracelessly from the record-player, and wafted towards the chair beside Simon, drink wobbling in hand like a tightrope-walker's umbrella. He had put on *Don Giovanni*. He passed the other chair and after hovering for a moment, he alighted on the arm of Simon's chair. Like a vulture watching a dying animal, thought Simon, feeling the soft chair about him like a trap. Mike's thin voice drifted down to him in a conversation about Mozart, to which he replied with a kind of terrified enthusiasm, as though he were engaging delaying conversation with someone holding him at gunpoint.

But they did not have much to say about Mozart. In fact, they did not seem to have much to say to one another about anything. "You said you were training to be a social worker, didn't you?" said Simon with a brittle last-ditch cheeriness.

"Oh yes, that's right," said Mike, as if reminded of something distant and irrelevant. He paused, swilling his drink in his glass, looking vacant. Simon tried to fix him with a gaze of interested anticipation.

"Well, I feel so sorry for people!" said Mike at last, his voice gesturing with an unctuous sincerity. "I mean, don't you? Oh well, of course you do. You're a really kind person, I'm sure of it."

Simon wished he felt so sure himself

"Actually," Mike went on in musically solicitous tones, "I'm finding the course a little bit hard, to tell you the truth. You know, I see some people and all I can think is, what you really need is some one to tuck you up in bed and feed you cups of warm cocoa." His eyes glazed over rather wistfully. "I sometimes think that's the best I can aspire to be. A sort of living cup of cocoa." There was another silence, and then Mike yawned loudly, unconvincingly, raising a delicate hand halfway to his gaping mouth. His hands with their clipped nails looked as if they were washed twenty times a day. "Well, I'd like an early night," he said, with ostentatious insincerity. "Have you finished your drink? You know, you hair looks awfully beautiful against the light like that."

Simon gulped down his gin like Dutch courage.

"I'd run out of gin, and I'd told myself I wasn't going to buy another bottle. But I thought – well, for a special occasion." He had lifted off and fluttered over to the bed. "I hope you don't want a goodnight cup of cocoa, because actually I haven't got any. Rather non-U really, isn't it?" He flung the covers back, exposing a huge triangle of candy-striped sheet. "Well, there we are. All ready for you." Simon thought, Soft lights and sweet music, and now he wants to pose me on the couch like a painting. I wonder if he'll set my arms in position for me to look inviting. But Mike was leaving, murmuring something with that tone of practised dishonesty about cleaning his teeth; leaving, so that he could return for a discovery scene.

Simon went over to the bed, undressed quickly, and jumped into it like a cold swimming-pool, at once pulling the covers up to his chin and clutching them there, lying with his knees curled up, staring out along the gentle rise of the pillow.

"Oh, you're in bed already, are you?" said Mike rather disappointedly, appearing in the doorway. He was combed and washed, his shirt unbuttoned. He wore his good looks as he always did: like someone who wears an ostentatiously expensive suede jacket whatever the weather, whatever the occasion, and even though nothing seems chosen to go with it.

He moved to a position where the light might fall on his good side as he undressed. Simon looked doggedly away. How did the search for closeness come to end up like this? And at what point did it become so impossible to say no? He was still staring broodingly across at the blank cream space of the wall opposite, feeling mocked by this cheap romantic melodrama, mocked by his own futility, when Mike sunk into bed behind him, stretching out creeper-like hands around him, saying as one might to a child one is teasing, "Now I've got you." Simon half-turned, sadly wondering, but then he rolled back and lay inert, scarcely present.

And yet it was not as if Mike seemed to notice anything lacking. His rubbery hands manipulated Simon's lank body half-heartedly, in the merest tokens of foreplay, and then he was rolling Simon onto his stomach, throwing a leg over him – like a dog about to mark a post, thought Simon.

"No," said Simon, suddenly rushing back into the present, wriggling beneath the weight above him; "no, I don't want to."

"Oh go on, why not?" wheedled Mike's voice above him, unbelieving, wheedling, enjoying the game. "I think you're teasing me. "Anyway, everyone says I'm very gentle."

Pinned down on his stomach, Simon could no more easily actively rebel than actively respond. He gave up. A Mozart love-duet was drifting across, full of all Mozart's slick serenity. He felt like a painting of a nude torn from an art-book being masturbated over by a sickly adolescent.

And it was all finished remarkably quickly. A sudden snore made Simon realise that Mike had already fallen asleep. The record was spinning round finished on the turntable, making a rhythmic monotonous click.

In the morning Mike had to leave early to go to his training course. Simon lay in bed for a while, but he could not sleep.

He got up and with little appetite made himself some breakfast. The flat was dark, although summer sunlight could be seen slipping under the doors and curtains. Simon purposely left them closed, afraid at the thought of light rushing in. Mike had invited him to a concert that night, and as he hesitated in his reply, still half-asleep, he had read in Mike's waiting eyes the evidence of his power. Half flattered, half frightened, he had agreed to Mike's face to go. But already he had decided to stand him up. Well, what a pity I had to pick him, he thought; there must have been lots of more attractive people at the disco. He went to the record-player and put on the banquet scene, where the Stone Guest carries Don Giovanni off to hell.

After he had finished breakfast, he set off for Kev's place, without washing the dishes behind him.

He was in the middle of cooking tea when Kev came home that night. He heard Kev talking to himself as he tramped slowly down the stairs; obviously he supposed he was alone. Simon listened to him enter the sitting-room and drop heavily into a chair with a deep groan, which he repeated a few times. Simon felt embarrassed. He clattered with a saucepan.

Kev appeared in the kitchen doorway, ogre-like. "Had a nice time?" he snarled leaning against the doorpost.

"It was ok," said Simon sheepishly, looking down at his cooking.

Kev just stood there, breathing loudly and as if with difficulty, his contemptuous gaze falling on Simon's face like a physical sensation. Then he turned and silently went back to the sitting-room.

Just after they had finished tea, the telephone rang. Simon knew who it was, but made no move to answer it. He sat watching Kev get up laboriously and lumber through to the other room, then reappear in the doorway and sit himself back down and lift his tea-cup to his mouth without looking at him, before he said quietly, "It's your little friend for you."

Simon lifted the receiver awkwardly to his ear, as if it were a machine whose workings he did not understand. He said with a cultivated breathlessness, "Oh hallo, I hoped you'd ring."

"But what happened? Why aren't you here?" came Mike's frantic and yet suspicious whine.

"I'm not feeling well," Simon stumbled, shutting his eyes in the face of the enormity of his own lie. "It must be something I ate. There's something – well, not right with my stomach." He had never heard a more unconvincing lie.

"Oh, you poor thing," crooned Mike, with an unexpected sincerity. "Oh dear, I hope it wasn't all that rich food last night, was it? Oh well, do look after yourself. Are you in bed? You should be tucked up in bed."

Simon had been totally unprepared for his belief. He did not know how to react.

"Oh no, I'll be alright. It's nothing much. Listen, I would have let you know, but I didn't have any daytime phone number for you."

"Oh that's alright. The important thing is that you get better." Mike sounded almost clucky.

"Yes. Well – I'll phone you later in the week. I don't really feel like talking just now."

"Of course not. You just look after yourself, you poor thing. I think you should go straight to beddy-byes."

Later that night, as he sat reading with his dutiful Guinness, it was as though he could feel Kev's rum-soaked smouldering gaze filling the room. He heard it crying out darkly in the plaintive writhing fiddles and whoops of the Cajun music that Kev was listening to, crouched over on the floor near Simon's feet. Simon stared hard at the pages of his book, trying to forget that Kev was there, the disco sign that he had been painting cast aside, his rum bottle half-empty, but it was as if Kev's eyes bored through the pages of his book like lasers. He was saying to himself, I'm not going to be owned or used, I can do what I like.

"Are you just going to sit there reading every bloody night you're here?" Simon did not look up. The voice sounded hollow, bitter in defeat. He looked up. Kev was staring into the carpet, his shoulders hunched, his eyes misty, his hair lolling lifelessly over his forehead. He had a paint stain on his cheek.

"I'm sorry, I wasn't trying to annoy you," murmured Simon help-lessly, caught in an ambush of guilt and pity.

Kev said almost apologetically, "No, of course you weren't." He gulped like someone with a lump in their throat. Then his big clumsy hand felt behind him for the bottle, groping uselessly like the newly blind. At last he flung himself round, like a sack of potatoes sinking on to its side, and snatched at the bottle angrily. "Why don't you have some rum tonight?" he snapped, squinting up at Simon. "I suppose you wouldn't. Because I'm offering it."

Simon was silent, rigid, waiting in fear to see where his guilt and pity would lead him.

And then Kev began to stand up. Simon watched him rise slowly, as if each action took not seconds but hours, the knee bending, the big hand pressing against the floor, the leg drifting upright; and then he was there, towering over Simon, but still, quiet, with a look of sorrow in his eyes. Simon's muscles tensed, he braced himself to dodge. But Kev just stood there, his long clumsy arms hanging down as if they had been disconnected, his broad shoulders lifting and falling with his sighs, and on his face a look as of contemplating something broken beyond repair.

He said with a gracelessly mournful voice, like a trombone trying to sound plaintive, "Why don't you give me a cuddle? Just once, just tonight."

Simon said nothing. He gave himself up to his pity, but even as he allowed himself to be carried away, another voice within him was saying, as though with clenched teeth, But I won't be used, just because I'm good-looking.

Kev dropped down on the settee beside him, the springs groaning beneath his weight, the cushion beneath Simon shuddering as with a wake. He dropped like a precariously balanced child's tower of bricks toppling at last. For a while they sat beside one another, immobile, each staring ahead, as if in shock at what had already happened. Tentatively Simon turned his head, and saw Kev's bloodshot eyes drifting away on a dark tide of introspection, his awkward bundle of a body settling already again into hopelessness. He reached out, and embraced Kev with a clumsy incompetence, as one might lift an awkward weight. He held the cumbrous sweaty body in his arms like someone else's shopping he was holding as a favour.

Kev began to speak, his low lugubrious voice muffled to Simon by the position of his head, reverberating indistinctly in his chest like a voice calling from a great distance in a cave. "I suppose you think I'm repulsive. That great lump. I know I'm no bloody Mister Universe, but just now and again you might show something for me. Christ, I've put you up, haven't I?" He stopped, and heaved a deep breath, his expanding shoulders forcing apart Simon's awkward grasp, so that he started, as if the shopping were spilling to the ground, and clutched the cumbersome shoulders back to him. "No, no," Kev went on, murmuring dolefully over Simon's shoulder, "you're not interested in being kind. You're just interested in being admired. They're all like you. I might as well go back to the cottages. I know your type. But why? I don't understand. You're a nice person. At heart. I can see that. Why don't you act like one?"

Simon said fearfully, "I'm sorry. But I don't want to be owned by you. I want to experiment, go my own way. Anyway, you made the offer for me to stay here, I didn't ask you." He was not sure whether Kev could hear him, whose warm body went on breathing agitatedly in his arms, while he stared coldly out over the heaving shoulders as at a crossroads of obligations, all of which he wanted to avoid – obligation to pity, obligation to host, obligation to his own cultivated attractiveness.

"You didn't have to accept," said Kev suddenly after a while, so that Simon for a moment could not remember what he was replying to.

"What?"

"You didn't have to accept my offer to stay, did you? But you did. And I was pleased, then, when you did." He began to shift, and slowly, lumberingly, like some stranded whale, he pulled back from the embrace and sat, grotesquely huge before Simon's cringing confusion, the dark drunken eyes gazing into Simon balefully. "Why don't you come to bed with me, just once, just tonight?" he said sadly. "Just lie there with me. I won't do anything. Look at me. I'm too drunk to be able to do anything anyway. Don't you understand? I'm lonely." Simon watched an absurdly little tear well up in one of the unfocusing eyes and trickle circuitously down the big cheek, petering out even before it reached the drooping moustache. "Drink's the only companion I can rely on." Suddenly he was shouting, flinging his head with its sweat-tousled hair against the back of the settee, staring up at the ceiling. "I have to fucking drink because I can't cope. I can't cope with being alone. And I can't cope with all that bloody affected gay scene shit. Slam the closet door behind you, they say. But they've made no place for me. No place for anything clumsy. No place for anyone who actually admits to being confused, helpless. You seemed so lost. I thought you'd understand."

He sat rigid, his limbs tensed as though holding off a great weight, fallen now all at once deep into silence. Simon reached out an uncertain hand and quickly brushed his hair, no sooner there than gone, like a small child approaching and quickly patting a dog. Kev rolled his head over on his broad shoulders, glimpsing him reproachfully as he passed, before looking down, crushed, sliding into torpor.

"I get so angry at everything. You've been very patient," he said, barely audibly. "I'm going to bed now. I don't suppose you'll come with me, will you?"

Simon nodded, although he knew Kev could not see him, and sat on, silent, watching Kev rise wearily to his feet, watching him sway a little as if his own height struck him as precarious, watching him make painstakingly for the bedroom in a series of staggering lunges, without looking back. Then slowly Simon got up and followed him. I couldn't refuse now and I wouldn't want to, he thought, and yet what right had he established to expect it of me before?

Kev was curled up in bed in a great untidy heap, his eyes open but staring blankly into the pillow. Simon put out the light, felt his way across to Kev's bed, and took off his clothes carefully, folding them for the morning. Drawing back a corner of the sheet, he slipped neatly onto the tiny edge of single bed that Kev did not occupy, without saying a word.

"You shouldn't have bothered," said Kev into the pillow. He tossed over, his weight flinging the bed about, and laid a big padded arm around Simon, who lay taut and uncertain. But almost at once Kev was snoring, leaning against Simon like a fallen wall, filling the dark air with the smell of sweat and rum.

The night was close. A car whined along a distant main road, going purposefully somewhere. Simon lay perched on the edge of the bed, confused and restless.

CHAPTER THIRTEEN

How much I want there to be a time when I want to say yes; but if I mean no, I ought just to say no, Simon thought. It seems one of the hardest things to learn.

Now he had saddled himself with going to a party with Mike, which he did not really want to do. He had put on new jeans with wide embroidered flares, of which he was rather proud, but Mike seemed to have misgivings about their appropriateness. "Are you sure those aren't women's jeans?" he had said when they met.

It had been a cool rainy day and to Simon the party itself seemed full of the same sodden greyness. People hung limply about the room, small-talk dripping slowly from them like raindrops. Simon lounged against a wall, anxiously gulping at a rough Spanish red from a paper cup already soggy at the bottom, trusting at least to drunkenness, staring blankly over Mike's shoulder at the dingy wallpaper, unaware of what was being talked at him.

"I said I got the tickets for the Berlioz at the Proms."

"What?"

"*La Damnation de Faust* I'm taking you to. I got rather expensive seats. Only the best for you."

"Oh yes, yes, good. When is it?"

"Oh, I forget exactly. Early August some time. A few weeks off."

A few weeks, thought Simon, looking down into the sticky purple lacework of wine clinging to the crumbling walls of his cup. He heard Mike saying, "And I thought perhaps at August Bank Holiday we could go and visit my parents." What does he think is happening? Simon thought. His nervously drumming thumb went through the bottom of his cup.

"Oh dear, is your cup broken?" cried Mike solicitously. "Here, let me get you another one. I say, you drank that rather quickly, didn't you? Be careful of your tummy."

Simon held out the crumpled cup to Mike with a weak smile. Two people whom he had talked to at the disco came up to them.

"Hallo, Simon. Hallo, Mike."

"Oh hallo," said Mike, giving a charming and prolonged smile, then ducking past them, wafting them with French aftershave. "Excuse me a minute, I'm just going to get Simon another drink."

Simon relaxed a little when he had gone. He liked the two people who had arrived, both schoolteachers, and respected their earnestness and sensitivity.

"How are you finding the party?" said one of them, with a cynical look that showed what answer he expected.

"Well, yes, it doesn't seem to have quite got off the ground yet," said Simon, pleased their opinions converged.

"That's one way of putting it," said the other with a smile. "A rather lifeless crowd. Mike's a really nice person though, isn't he? We're both so glad he's got himself a good boyfriend. He's such a sweet kind generous person, and I know he's been feeling a bit insecure and lonely since he came to London."

At that point Mike returned, his owl-like eyes preoccupied with not spilling the overfilled cups.

"There you are," he said, with a note of fussy achievement. "Don't drink it all at once."

Simon took it in silence and swilled it down nervously. All at once he felt extremely uncomfortable, and kept trying to avoid the eyes of the two teachers.

When he had finished the wine, he used it as an excuse to wander off alone. The party hung from the corners and was festooned over the armchairs like cobwebs. Even the record-player seemed to be playing as if its motor were running down.

"Hallo, do you remember me?" Hearing the smarmy drawl beside him, Simon felt as if he had stepped in something slippery. He turned sharply and saw, posed against a mantelpiece, a slim mischievous figure in a black scoop-neck blouse with inlaid mirrors and tight fitting gold lamé trousers. "I remember you," the figure said knowingly, with a preposterous leer in the eyes.

A nostalgic recollection stirred in Simon of his first Gay Liberation meeting, which already seemed long ago. It was as much as anything a sudden gush of nostalgia that made him stop and say to the man with a smile, "Yes, I do remember you. We met at a North London meeting. But I don't remember your name." Already the warm self-pitying nostalgia was a flood, sweeping him away helpless towards dangerous rocks and rapids.

"I don't remember your name, but I certainly couldn't forget your face," said the man, trickling his words slowly, looking across at Simon as though posing for a centrefold. "My name's Dorian."

"I'm Simon." He had caught hold of an idea, and was already trying to stretch himself out on it, precarious as it was, the nostalgia slowly running off him.

"Of course. How silly of me to forget! What do you think of my trousers?" Dorian ran his hands sinuously down his thighs, and pulled a grimace of simulated ecstasy.

"They're very nice," said Simon openly, but momentarily embarrassed by Dorian's shamelessness. He faltered. "I was on my way to get a drink, actually."

"What are you drinking? I've got my own private store of gin and tonic stashed away in this corner." Dorian gestured lethargically with his elegant long fingers. "Why don't you join me?" His words oozed with innuendo, as he sank balletically to his knees to reach the gin.

With a smile at himself, Simon conceded eagerly, sitting down to play in the innuendo like a child with a sticky cake. The conversation slid along the thin ice of clothes and drinks and parts of London, but with Dorian as it were effortlessly performing pirouettes and dashing leaps, continually tossing come-ons to the teetering Simon as he did so. "It's so dreary south of the river! You wonder if they ever really drained the swamps. You should have stayed in North London, with me."

"Oh there you are!" Mike's voice floated down from above with a kind of motherly outraged relief. "I wondered where on earth you'd got to. I've been looking all over for you." He seemed to hesitate for a moment as to whether or not to sit down, but then remained standing, with a wide-eyed puzzled expression, like a baby that has just been played a trick on by an elder child.

The sound of Mike's voice, seeming to coo like some pigeon, sent an icy shudder of irritation through Simon's body. He stared into the carpet, biting his lip. Then he leaned gracefully back on one arm and looked up at Mike, his eyes cold and aggressive, saying softly, "I'm quite alright. I'm just talking to Dorian. He's a friend of mine from North London." He felt himself bristling with a violent wish not to be intruded upon, he could feel it coming out of him like an electric glow.

"Oh – oh alright," said Mike, sounding like a string snapping on a violin. He stroked his paper cup nervously. "Oh well, I'll come back in a minute then," he said falteringly, and wandered off with a hesitant weak smile directed pointedly at Simon alone, leaving a faint scent of aftershave fading behind him.

"Who's that?" said Dorian theatrically, in a tone that invited Simon to be complicit with him. And, in fact, the slighting description of Mike that Simon found himself all too readily giving seemed indeed to seal something between himself and Dorian. Perhaps it was the gin, but he even thought he found in himself an increasing volubility from that point on. They lounged debauchedly on the carpet opposite one another, pretending to weave a tie between them with their exchanged flippancies, Simon momentarily believing it; while now and again Dorian leant across and knowingly patted Simon's knee or his hand, and light reflected from the little mirrors in Dorian's shirt would play over Simon like spotlights.

After a while Mike came back. Simon saw him edging towards them with a look of martyred reproach. He said coldly, "I'm going home now, Simon," and waited. Simon looked down, his fingers gesturing nervously as if to brush the reproach away like a fly. "You can share a taxi with me, if you like," Mike resumed, switching his tone now to one of "But-I-forgive-you-anyway". Simon thought, I suppose he thinks I'm just teasing. He looked up at Mike slowly, and saw him smiling ingenuously, as if the game were now over.

Gradually under Simon's silent gaze the smile cracked a little at the edges, the glazed eyes began to almost smoulder, he was becoming impatient to claim his own. He spoke, almost whining, "Are you coming?"

"I think I'll stay here for a bit," said Simon at last, blandly, smiling apologetically as though at the rejection of a chocolate or a cup of tea, so that there might be nothing for Mike to seize hold of. "Thanks for the offer of a taxi, but I'm quite enjoying myself. I'll phone you." He had not the slightest intention of doing so.

"Oh. Well, goodbye, then." Mike's nose puckered as though at a bad smell, his wide eyes actually narrowed with disdain. He sniffed, flinging a quick look of contempt at Dorian. And then all at once, as if he had been hit by a sudden pain, his face seemed to collapse into a waste of self-pitying panic loneliness. To Simon for a moment it was as if a toupee had fallen from someone he had never known was completely bald. Mike turned on his heel and tried to stride out, his little body seeming pathetically shrunk within its lush corduroy suit.

"I don't think he was very pleased," drawled Dorian, his eyes under their eye-shadow gazing into the space that Mike had just vacated with a look of mock puzzlement, a deliberately naughty smile spreading across his elfish face. He brushed Simon's thigh with a nail-varnished finger and added, "Well, I wonder why. Don't worry. He'll get over it."

Suddenly Simon was totally unashamed. Serve little Melting Mike right, he thought, for thinking he could keep me like some plaster statuette to paw over.

"You're not going home to that awful person you said you were staying with tonight, are you?" said Dorian ingenuously, peeking over his glass of gin. "Why don't you come back to my bed-sit in Chalk Farm?"

By the time he got out of the taxi in Chalk Farm, Simon realised that he was very drunk. He stood on the pavement, thinking earnestly about his balance, while Dorian handed over the fare with much effusiveness to the acidly laconic driver. On the stairs each step seemed to veer towards his foot before he expected it, his legs moved themselves lethargically, and Dorian's protesting prattle about the driver's comment on his eye-shadow slid past his ears like a breeze.

He found himself sitting swaying on the edge of Dorian's bed, his head dangling loosely as though he were top-heavy, staring into a mud-coloured mug of coffee, with a vague uninterested awareness that Dorian was still there, apparently expanding on the virtues of his bed-sit into the empty air. I must get some sleep, thought Simon, that's what I need.

Dimly he felt Dorian approach, something was said about bed, and he looked up with a weak sheepish smile, feeling a sudden twinge of nausea. Dorian laid him out on the bed, pulling off his clothes as one might undress a doll, and he closed his eyes. He felt the bed heave like a ship beneath him. Dorian seemed to be clamouring about at the end of it, and then he began to suck Simon off noisily. At first, as he tried to put together what was happening, Simon felt little more than a pleasant tickling sensation and a distant puzzlement, then suddenly and quickly with some alarm he realised he was about to come.

"Stop!" he cried sharply, slightly slurred.

Dorian's face bobbed up absurdly between his legs. "What on earth's the matter?" he said.

"I'm going to come," said Simon, in the panic-stricken tone of a child about to wet their pants.

"My dear, that's the whole idea," sighed Dorian, and burrowed back down, making dramatic noises of relish. Though Simon's dimly felt orgasm had all the abandon of a cold water tap being turned on to wet a rag.

He fell asleep straight afterwards, without even shifting his position.

When he woke, Dorian was still asleep beside him, sprawled across the bed like a heroine's corpse in an opera. Simon sat up uncertainly, guilt and fear rushing in on him as he put his hands to his jarred head. He got up carefully and put on a kettle, trying not to wake Dorian, whose actual woken presence would seem like a sudden rush of evidence against him. Painstakingly he began to prise open the lids of the ornamental jars ranged beside the gas-stove, trying to make no sound, in the search for coffee which he found in the very last jar. He dropped the teaspoon.

"What are you doing?" From behind him the slow outraged drawl rose to a shrieked crescendo and subsided, like a slow-motion film of a drop of liquid breaking a surface.

Simon turned like a guilty child. In the sunlight creeping under the curtain Dorian was still stretched full-length with one arm flung out and his eyes shut. "I'm making coffee," said Simon, as if it were the confession of a misdemeanour. "Do you want some?"

"Oh not now, for heaven's sake! It's far too early," said the sleeping figure without opening its eyes, only twisting the head a little restlessly.

Later, when Dorian did get up, slipping into wakefulness with enviable efficiency and poise, he proceeded to make them kippers for breakfast. It was meant as a gesture of style, but kippers turned out to be the last thing that Simon's system wanted. A stale fishy smell seemed at once to permeate his consciousness like a fog, and an acidic discord in his stomach began to echo his mental unease.

"Oh well, I'm going shopping now," said Dorian, turning his back and rising gracefully from the breakfast table, giving his hair a little pat as he swept past the mirror. "I'll walk you to the tube station. It's not far." He put on a pair of sunglasses and took a few balletic steps back from the mirror to examine the effect. "Are you ready? Some of the shops will be closing soon, you know."

Silently Simon gathered himself together and followed Dorian down the stairs, as if he were being led to the dentist's chair. He dreaded what he now had to face.

But as he stood at the tube-station after a silent walk, fumbling over what suggestions he could make about their meeting again, he realised, at first with amazement, then with relief, that Dorian was calmly saying goodbye. There he stood by the ticket-machine in his dark glasses and striped tee-shirt, a bag hanging over his shoulder and a hand on one hip, rippling his long fingers in a child's gesture of goodbye, the words sliding syrupily from him. "Well, I suppose I might see you around some time. It was nice. Look after yourself. Don't do anything I wouldn't do." He leant across and stroked Simon's thigh in the middle of the tube-station, then turned with a histrionic sweep and slunk felinely out into the street.

Simon stood for a moment in puzzlement. He had never expected so calm an attitude to sexual flippancy from anyone, so far was it from himself. He did not know what to make of it. Had he allowed Dorian to use him for a cheap thrill? But he could not make resentment rise, because it occurred to him he himself had been making use of Dorian. They had joined briefly in a state of mutual exploitation, asserting to one another the use-value of their bodies, and then they had swept on, like shoppers carried along in a crowded market. At least there seemed a kind of honesty here, which Mike, even if he had been well-meaning, lacked in the romantic idolisation with which he mystified his treatment of Simon.

And what of Kev? He pressed his coin into the machine and took his ticket. Usually he let the escalator carry him down, but today he decided to walk.

He had forgotten his key. He rung the bell and waited, hoping that Kev was at home, feeling momentary anger at a sense of Kev as his turnkey. Kev opened the door, and stood holding it, looking Simon up and down. "Where the bloody hell have you been?" he shouted, going red in the face, suddenly struggling for breath to say more.

"I was at a party," Simon began quietly, his eyes on the ground, his voice swallowed up with fear and embarrassment.

"Just come down and look at this," stormed Kev, striding on ahead down the stairs, panting and clenching and unclenching his fists. Simon followed meekly like a cowed schoolboy to a punishment.

Kev went straight through the living-room and through the kitchen, Simon still trailing unquestioningly after, and into the bathroom. Kev stood there silent, his shoulders heaving with quick breaths, his brows in a black V-shape, towering over the bath: it was full of dirty sheets, which Kev had put in it to soak a week ago, which were now stagnant, smelling like a ditch.

"The water's a bit stale," said Simon tentatively, registering the smell, but for the moment uncertain of the point Kev wanted to make.

"Of course it's bloody stale! They've been in it for a week!" shouted Kev, his voice momentarily cracking as though he was about to cry instead of rage.

"They should have been washed and hung out," said Simon helplessly offering advice.

"Of course they should have bloody well been washed! But who's here all the fucking day, sitting around reading books and playing records while I'm working?" He took a step towards Simon, a stiff mechanical step, as if he had become the automaton of his own anger, then stopped. Simon became suddenly terrified, but then at once resentful of his terror. Kev was lifting his hand, but he turned it back to furiously scratch his own head. "What do you think you are? Did you think you could just go on staying here without rent and without – without even doing one bloody thing about the house? Bloody students! Isn't my life enough of a mess? Well, I think it's about time you looked for somewhere else to live." He pushed past Simon, who leapt out of the way like a startled cat, and went into the living-room.

Simon stood there hesitating. Then he went shamefacedly to the bath and pulled out the plug. He went through to the kitchen and got soap-powder and rubber gloves, and went back and began to wash the sheets. Swilling the unmanageable tangled mass ineffectually from side to side, he thought, What did you ask me to stay here for? What did you want of me? You just wanted me to feel sorry for you. But how can I relate to you: when all you can do is feel sorry for yourself?

He bent over the bath, his back aching, and hauled the heavy trickling sheets into a plastic bucket. Poor bloody me, he thought. The sheets still smelt slightly stagnant. Panting and waddling, he carried them through the living-room to the backyard. As he passed, Kev was sitting on the edge of the settee with a glass of rum, hunched over a magazine, brows furrowed. He did not look up.

Simon lifted the cumbersome mass of dripping material onto the line, and started to aim pegs at its dangling amorphousness. And now what am I going to do? he thought.

At the disco that night he arranged to move into a spare room in the house of Bernard, whom he had spoken to the night he met Mike. Bernard was sure Simon would be comfortable. There was a garden, and a piano – did Simon play? Bernard himself taught voice and singing at a small theatre school nearby.

And what part am I acting? thought Simon later. I thought I had a ready-made role: but in fact what I have still to do is work out what the play is about.

CHAPTER FOURTEEN

For a moment warm sun streamed deceptively across the back lawn, through the geraniums and into the small sun-lounge. Here Bernard was sitting at the breakfast table opposite the house-guest Neville, a suave middle-aged man from South Africa, whose annual summer trip to London would be over in a few days. Bernard's eyes shot up nervously from the crust of toast he was playing with as Simon came in through the glass door from the sitting-room, tousled and clumsy as usual in the morning.

"It's your new lodger," said Neville, leaning back and riding on his chair, picking at his big grinning teeth with a nicotine-stained finger. "Hallo, Simon. Sit down." He waved a hand used to imperious gestures, as if the house were his own.

The sun retreated back behind the scudding clouds.

"Good morning, Simon. Did you sleep alright?" said Bernard with a strained fussy politeness. He was like an aging hamster, bundled whatever the weather into a tight but cuddly jumper, timorous, his chubby face with its Mickey Rooney-like boyish looks continually twitching, as if chewing a secret hoard of anxieties. Simon felt a little uneasy with his insistent veneer of cheery goodwill. "Good morning," he said, sitting down at the place set for him, fingering the cutlery indecisively. "I slept well, thanks. An indecisive sort of day."

"Oh, it might brighten up," said Bernard, with the mock enthusiasm of a scout-master in a rained-out camp, pushing away his plate as if it were a bad habit.

Neville reached across a vast healthy hand and picked up an apricot from a bowl in the centre of the table, and thrust it into his mouth whole. "Hev an eppricot, Bernard," he said with his mouth full, lifting one and holding it out. Bernard took it and nervously bit into it, picking out the stone and laying it neatly at the side of his plate. He reached out and took another, after toying with it for a moment. Simon tremulously poured himself a cup of tea, feeling conspicuous, and dozily contemplated what he might eat. Bernard took a third apricot.

"Three already," said Neville, dropping four lumps of sugar into his tea with self-conscious aplomb. "I thought you said you deedn't believe een lexatives?"

"That's why I'm having them," said Bernard, in a quietly burdened tone, glancing into the distance out of the window.

Simon had noticed the bristling ranks of constipation remedies in the bathroom. He took a piece of toast, and found himself trying to crunch it quietly in the sudden silence.

"Yes, eet's a dreary dye," said Neville, with the air of one who cannot easily be long without the sound of their own voice.

"Are you going to the all-London meeting tonight, Simon?" asked Bernard, unsuccessfully obscuring a little edginess.

Simon was caught with his mouth full. He swallowed awkwardly and said, "Yes, that's right."

"Meetings!' said Neville, lighting a king-size cigarette and flamboyantly breathing the initial thick smoke down his nostrils. "Everyone makes such a fuss in London. People in South Effrica are so much more relaxed about the whole thing."

Simon said nothing, politely. He finished his tea and toast and got up to go. Bernard jumped up as if at a signal, and started hastily clearing up, as if he had been impatiently waiting for Simon to finish, while Neville sat on, still riding on his chair, smoking and grinning a little provocatively.

Simon went to his room and lay down. The bed was soft and plush, and yet somehow, no matter what position he lay in, he seemed to find himself feeling continually uncomfortable.

I must become more careful about letting myself get involved with people, I must become more responsible, he thought.

He picked up one of the old *Come Togethers* he had brought with him, and which he had recently been re-reading, trying to sort out what had become of his high hopes. "Hiding and role-playing; acting and pretending . . ." The words caught his eye. This was an article he had once read with Frank in mind, but now quite different phrases seemed to stand out, quite a different meaning seemed to emerge. "Engaging in the 'hunt'. Playing 'games' with each other. Games of destruction . . ." He read on looking anxiously for explanation and encouragement.

"Playing roles in a society which demands gender definitions, sexual role-playing, masculine versus feminine," he read, "what can we do? As time passes, tenderness, sensitivity are frozen out . . ."

He stared disappointedly at the paper. "The meat market smells!" it ended. "Have a revolution in your life!"

That was just what he wanted to do. But how to achieve it, after all? He put the paper aside, and lay back, eyes closed, his mind pacing restlessly.

Much to its surprise the little city pub was crowded that night. People were drinking with a kind of enthusiastic cameraderie, combating the atmosphere of fragmentation and directionlessness that had hovered about the meeting, second attempt as it was to gather from the assembled dreams and memories of a few activists, already feeling themselves aging, a centrally reunified single-purposed Gay Liberation

Movement.

Simon was sitting at a table with the dentist who was going to Australia. He looked both relaxed (he had even ventured into a pink short-sleeved shirt) and abstracted. "I'm afraid I felt as if I was already observing the meeting from a great distance," he was saying with a leisured self-awareness.

"Are you looking forward to going?" said Simon, sipping his drink slowly, his eyes wandering around the room.

"Well, I'm apprehensive in some ways, of course. But it's the kind of challenge I must get something out of. Don't you think? Life won't be the same again."

The scruffy young man called Julius whom Simon had met at the same meeting a fortnight ago was sailing towards them through the jostling crowd. "Can I sit here?" he said, even as he did so majestically. Simon acknowledged him with a little bemusement. He was an extraordinary-looking person; with his long sallow face and deep-set glazed brown eyes framed by sleek long black hair, he looked for all the world like a drunken Greek icon.

"I'm drunk already, Simon," he said, showing a craggy range of rotting teeth as he smiled cavernously, his big eyes lolling in their deep sockets as if in comfortable armchairs. "I had a whole bottle of red wine before the meeting started, I couldn't help myself. I love red wine, don't you? I have this passionate thing going with it. I'd drink it all the time, if it were humanly possible, all the time. It's so dark and Mediterranean, you know, a sort of liquid blood-consciousness, but laced with sparkles of sunshine lying there in waiting, don't you think? And now, I've got to drink humble old beer – because I've got no money, not till my next dole cheque. In fact, I haven't even got enough money to get home, if I had a home. I'm absolutely stony. But no matter. I'm drunk and happy. Well, Jim, and how are you? Not gone yet?" He turned suddenly to the dentist and hung there leering at him.

Jim had looked a little nonplussed by Julius's presence at first. He said quietly, "Not yet. The week after next."

"That's wonderful," said Julius enthusiastically. "Well, Simon, aren't you going to say something?"

Simon felt rather dazed. "Well, I can't think of anything, no," he said, defending himself with a little laugh. He found Julius fascinating. He was ready to sit and absorb, and yet he found his talk bewilderingly alien.

"No, well, you're not exactly an unstoppable artesian well of speech at the best of times, are you?" Julius responded, with hammed earnestness, looking fixedly at Simon. "You're rather the mysterious silent type, whom everyone thinks is so sceptically intelligent, and that you must know so much more than you say: even if in fact very often you don't. But what does that matter when you do it so well. Because you do, you know. Yes, well, you *do* know. And after all, I don't mind. It makes you a good listener, and me, nothing reassures me like being listened to. After all, I can hardly keep my tongue still long enough to get drunk. I even talk in my sleep. Geoff says so – he's my ex-lover, my ex-grand-amour!"

Jim interrupted briefly, with a puzzled look, "I thought you were back together again."

"Oh, it's on again and off again – the drama, the passion!" cried Julius, gesticulating like a tormented prima donna, his eyes rolling towards the ceiling under their fringed heavy lids. "The doors slamming at midnight, tumbled onto the streets naked and unprotected as a peeled potato. The frantic telephone calls, hearts pounding, weeping on one another's shoulders! I don't suppose you go in for much of that, Simon?"

Simon found himself put on the spot by an unexpected silence. "No," he said quickly, looking away like a dog that knows it is being talked about, "but then I haven't really had the motivation recently." He could not reconcile Julius's fluent self-mocking theatricality with the fact that everything he said about himself was obviously perfectly true.

"Well there you are, look at that," said Julius, lighting a cigarette, changing the subject as if he had not been listening even to himself. "My beer's gone, run out, such as it was, pathetic watery pretence against the rigours of sobriety. Oh well, how fleeting are life's little joys. And they are, they are. Except for the easily deluded. Simon, you've nearly finished your pint, won't you give a thirsty beggar eighteen pence? Or whatever monstrous price they charge here, for the benefit of all those prints of race-horses on the wall, I suppose, all those steaming flanks." His eyes roaming aimlessly round the decor swooped down in a sudden glissando to Simon, where they hung like lanterns bobbing above the black deeps of his smile below, where there lounged the untidy guard of shabby brown teeth.

"Oh yes, alright," said Simon, downing his pint and preparing to go to the bar.

"No, let me get a round. I can probably better afford to," said Jim, gathering up the glasses and rising, seeming glad to find something to do.

"He's quite soft somewhere underneath, isn't he?" said Julius, watching him go. "Australia should be good for him, put him in touch with his vulnerability. And, ah, the sun-drenched coral reefs, the wide empty spaces waiting for you to cross them! A gay liberation movement still in its infancy, still filled with all those heady dreams and hopes! Don't you wish you were going too? Actually, I'm glad he's left us alone for a minute."

Julius planted his elbows on the table and leant towards Simon, who looked down guardedly. But Julius's intense face resting on his hands was like a full moon at twilight framed in a window, mesmerically drawing one to look at it. "I like you, you know, even if you haven't got two words to put together. But I know you all the same – intuitively, inspirationally! And you, at least, find me fascinating. Which is something. It's one of those momentary attractions of opposites, doomed to failure – thank goodness – or we might have lived to see ourselves end up like Geoff and me, almost marriage. What a fate! Like prison. Shuts you off from the outside world. And once you do get out, you go off and make the same mistake, and you're back in again. Though I don't suppose you think that! By the way, where do you live?"

Simon felt a little ashamed of answering, and fingered his glass nervously. "I've got a room in this man's detached house in Balham. He's a voice trainer, or something. He's a bit neurotic. The place is full of constipation remedies. It's all a bit suburban, very middle-class – but it's alright really."

"It sounds dreadful," Julius cut in, pulling a face, staring at his grubby fingernails for a moment as if he were going to do something about them, but then setting them aside. "I haven't got anywhere to live at the moment, nowhere. Not since I broke up with Geoff. I'm just drifting, drifting, crashing at people's places, then wandering off into the beckoning light of dawn. There's always a bed in the commune if I want it, but most of the time, I don't. Drifting like a stick down a dark river, touching friends for a moment, and then gone, on, on into the fluidity of history. I like it, it suits me, don't you think? Anyway, why I was telling you all that is because I was going to ask if I could stay with you tonight."

"Well – I'm not sure," said Simon puzzledly, quite uncertain of what he would be letting himself in for, and yet curious to find out.

"I don't mean we have to sleep together," Julius said with a little sigh, as if he were explaining something to someone he had not thought to be so naive. "Though, of course, I don't mean we won't sleep together either."

"I don't know what Bernard would think." This was true.

"Oh, him! That! What does that matter? A shock might do him good, loosen up his sluggish system. Poor old soul! So that's settled then. And here come our drinks."

Jim loomed up beside them, and lowered the three glasses held confidently together to the table.

Julius raised his glass to him, smiling monotonously and almost audibly. "Jim, you're kind, you really are, isn't he?" he said, glancing at Simon quickly. "A great soft heart pounds beneath that neat exterior. Here, have a cigarette." He lifted his crumpled packet and opened it, but it was empty. "Oh well, never mind. You can give me a cigarette instead. It's the sense of sharing that counts."

In Jim's face a moment of struggling outrage was at once subdued by a willingness to be charmed. "I've only got a few left actually," he muttered under his breath. "Cheaper cigarettes is one thing I'm looking forward to. They're so expensive here."

"Oh yes, yes, aren't they? It's really nice of you to give me one," said Julius, nodding, taking a cigarette from the packet and sliding it back almost into Jim's lap with an elegant flick of the wrist. "You'll have one with me. Of course." While Jim put a cigarette to his mouth as if following a command, Julius struck a match with a flamboyant gesture and moved it across as portentously as if he were about to light the Olympic flame.

His eyes hovered like hawks for a moment on Simon's fingers drumming on the table in a rhythmical pattern. "Simon, do you play the piano or something? I expect you would with your background! And what would you play? Well, it wouldn't be Chopin much, or all that rich creamy romantic stuff. Ouch!" He dropped the still flaming match from his hand, which he left poised for a moment in mid-air, open in horror.

"I hate being burnt. Don't you? I'm sure it's a sort of tribal memory. You know how in the Middle Ages they used to roast us over slow fires, and then they used to use us just to get the fires going to put the witches on – that's why the Americans call us faggots. Ah yes, there's a lot for us never to forgive, you know. Anger burns in me, an inexhaustible bitter anger against that straight straight world all around us, anger that won't be quenched until the world's changed and we're avenged. And we will change it, you know. Oh yes, eventually. But it's a slow hard struggle." While he spoke his paradoxical eyes bobbed about light-heartedly over the fury of his words, like brightly coloured beach-balls bobbing on a storm far out to sea. He saw his cigarette still waiting between long fingers and lit it. "Now, what were we talking about?" He beamed expectantly.

Jim said, "Do you play the piano, Simon?"

Simon felt embarrassed, after Julius's offhand comment about his background. "Oh yes, a bit, when I visit my parents' place. And there's a piano where I am now, actually," he said, brushing the words from him as if they were a stain on his clothes. "I don't play very well. Bach, Beethoven, mostly." He sipped at his beer self-reassuringly, casting a diffident questioning glance at Julius, waiting to see what he would say.

"Ah yes, Bach, Beethoven. Of course," he said, breathing smoke leisuredly down his nose. "They're remarkable really, aren't they? I have to admit it. It's as if they stand at one remove, watching themselves. So intensely – cerebral. That's a good word, beautiful but coldly insidious, those syllables wrapped around one another like the calculating coils of a beautifully patterned snake. Ah, poetry!" His eyes leapt self-mockingly towards the ceiling and down again, and he gestured with the hand that held the blue-smoking cigarette, turning up the palm to reveal, after all, its emptiness. "Geoff likes all that kind of thing, you know. He sits up deep into the night, tangled in fugues and brooding over morbid trios, lost to the world but finding himself. Pity the record-player was so awful, it used to sound as if the needle was being drawn round by an asthmatic mule. Oh, you've got to admire them, Bach and Beethoven and all that, I mean, haven't you? But me, I prefer something more self-indulgent. Tchaikovsky, Richard Strauss. Which I suppose you hate. I like Tchaikovsky, I do, it's like chocolate, unmitigatedly bad for you, but quite delectable.

"But you know, the kind of music I like best is Near Eastern music, and Egyptian music, especially Egyptian music. Oh it's in my blood, that Mediterranean thing, it must be. Have you ever seen an Egyptian concert? There's this sumptuously curtained stage, and the orchestra wailing there below, and slowly out into the hovering spotlight comes this enormously fat figure, brown eyes already wet with tears of maudlin torment, earnest sweat and cheap perfume flowing down their faces like the promised milk and honey. Even from their photographs you can almost smell the sickly sweet smell, it's true. All their singers are fat, the men and the women, tremendous wobbling mountains of sensual flesh, the men rippling all over with mindless possessive Islamic lust. Oh incredible! He stands there, looking limpid, and at last he starts to sing, not sing like we mean it, it's so much more blatant, a sort of endlessly unravelling groan, being squeezed out of him like toothpaste from a tube, in loops and coils, from the bass depths of his manly strength up to the frantic falsetto heights of the piteous injustice of it all, so wronged, so grieved that he cannot get and use who he wants. Oh, his soft uncaring heart is broken! And the audience sway, back and forth, with the wailing music, all together, the odd tear trickling from them too, and they say 'Ugh-ff, ugh-ff,' – it means 'Too much, too much,' – thousands of voices gulping 'Ugh-ff, ugh-ff,' like waves breaking on the shingle. I don't suppose you'd enjoy it at all, Simon." He took a last passionate drag on his cigarette, then stubbed it out resignedly.

Simon felt at a loss as to what to say. He looked across tentatively to Jim, but he was looking expectantly to Julius. And Julius dangled there before them in silence, smiling irrepressibly, content within himself. Simon felt that he and Jim had become like fish drawn towards a spotlight. The barman called last orders.

"Come on, let's go," said Julius, suddenly cascading with animation, swallowing the remains of his beer in one bravura swig, tossing the empty cigarette packet into the ashtray, and sitting at the edge of his chair as if ready to spring from it into a race, his eyes all the time running round the room like dogs about to be let into the open.

"Well, in case I don't see you again, have a nice time in Australia," said Simon nervously to Jim.

"Oh. Thanks," said Jim absently, watching in bemusement as Simon got up to go with Julius.

"He'll have a wonderful time, won't you?" said Julius over his shoulder, already floating towards the door.

It was a soft warm evening outside. Before they got to the tube station, Julius stopped, and taking his arm pulled Simon aside, looking at him darkly. He seemed about to make some dramatic, even tragic pronouncement, and Simon suffered a growing qualm of apprehension, pinned against an office-block wall under the dingy street-light. "Simon," said Julius hollowly, "I haven't got any cigarettes. I must smoke. Or I'll have to kill myself. Will you buy me some? That's wonderfully generous of you."

"Oh," said Simon, going warm with relief, smiling eagerly, "yes, of course. We'll find a machine."

"I know where there's one," Julius called over his shoulder, already a few steps ahead.

A train was just about to close its doors as they arrived on the platform, but Julius made them run for it. He did an Errol Flynn leap through the closing doors and pulled Simon awkwardly after him as they began to slide open again. Two elderly people clutching theatre programmes stared at them with a routine disapproval of their recklessness. Simon felt embarrassed, but Julius strolled to a pair of empty seats and sprawled with his feet up. "Sit down," he said generously, as Simon appeared beside him, gesturing with his hand, making Simon feel momentarily that the two of them were the only ones who had any right to be on the train at all.

"Ah, nicotine! Lulling cloud of insouciance!" Julius leant back and his voice floated up and down, almost as though he were singing to himself, his hands peeling the paper from the packet and pulling it open as though they were undressing for a longed-for bath. He stroked out a cigarette and lit it lovingly, breaking into a coloratura sigh as he played the smoke from him like a famous fountain, his head lolling on his shoulders and his moony eyes gazing with a fixed amusement at Simon, who was sitting studying the pattern of dried mud on the floor, brooding on what was going to happen when they reached home, feeling like a naughty child waiting to be found out, though not knowing why what it had done was wrong. "You never smoke, do you! I can see," Julius launched off, turning to stare at the carriage ceiling as if into the heavens of inspiration. "I have to, because it dulls my sensations. If I don't smoke I just can't cope with the barrage of sounds and colours and tastes that cry out to me on every side. I've got to keep them screened off. When I stop smoking, the blue of the sky drowns me. I turn a corner and I'm flung on my back and beaten by the red of a pillar-box. I weep when I so much as hear a guitar string plucked, the intensity of the vibration is so great I dread it will change my heart-beat. And so I smoke, and I love it, I do, veiling me away from the world. Of course, it ruins my health, I can't run a step, I cough my lungs out from November to March, my heart's probably affected. But everything has a reverse side, every hill's beside a valley, I wouldn't want it any other way. Ah, proverbial wisdom! So dialectical, so true! Me, I wouldn't even enjoy the daylight if I didn't know it was going to get dark. Let my relationship with Geoff break down, let gay liberation disintegrate! It's only part of an ongoing process."

He stopped speaking abruptly, and smoked, while the train swung them from side to side, hustling through the blackness with a sense of direction that, Simon realised, looking about him, no one thought to doubt.

Julius lurched a bit as they made their way through the silent night streets of Balham, suddenly bouncing off trim privet hedges and rough-cast walls and juddering out in front of Simon. "Ha, drunkenness always takes a long time to catch up with me, I always outrun it," he cried with a laugh to no one in particular, as though this were a moment of private triumph.

Simon said nothing. He opened the door to Bernard's place as though he were robbing it, and crept stealthily after Julius, who had already sauntered down the hall, looking critically about him, like a rich client in the foyer of an hotel. "I think Bernard will be in bed," whispered Simon, easing the door painstakingly into place behind him and delicately slipping across the chain.

"No he's not, he's here," said Julius loudly, in exactly the tone of someone complaining about a fly in their food. Simon looked round in alarm, and saw Julius standing there, grotesquely half-lit in the lurid light seeping from the sitting-room, swaying as though he were suspended from the ceiling by a string, his mouth fixed tautly in an ingratiating grin as though he had been surprised by an unwelcome photographer, his eyes glimmering with distaste. A faint shadow drifted across him from the doorway, and Bernard appeared dimly, ruffled and defensive, like an unexpectedly woken hamster venturing from its straw, looking expectantly to Simon while he fidgeted with his hands.

"I – I've brought someone home," said Simon fumblingly, throwing the ball back into Bernard's court awkwardly, as though he did not know how to play.

"So I see," said Bernard quietly, with a great politeness that had long ago ceased to be a routine and become a burden. "Well, aren't you going to introduce me?" He looked across almost sadly at Julius, as he might at the turds of a visitor's dog on the carpet.

Julius remained there before him, large and steaming gloriously. While Simon was still trying to swallow his confusion, he said, "Hallo, I'm Julius," pulling an unwashed hand out of his scruffy jacket pocket, and breathing alcohol over Bernard as he leaned precariously towards him.

"Pleased to meet you," Bernard murmured, taking Julius's hand by the fingertips, like a friend's baby's wet nappy, his face like a schoolboy pretending not to be hurt by a cane. "Well Simon, I'll leave you two, if you'll excuse me. I was just about to turn in. Please check that all the lights are switched off, won't you? Goodnight." He was edging back even as he spoke, and now he turned suddenly and walked away towards his room, very quickly, as though only his dignity restrained him from actually running.

Julius looked at Simon and laughed. "Wasn't he absolutely charming? Though I don't think I managed to charm him. Not that I really wanted to. What are you looking so aghast for? Where's the kitchen? I've hardly eaten a thing all day, I can't afford food as well as wine, and one has to have one's priorities right." He walked into the sitting-room, casting a disdainful inspecting gaze over it.

"I don't think he was very pleased," whispered Simon, following solemnly, moving his feet as though walking barefoot on stones. "Careful!"

Julius put down a fragile-looking ashtray with a sigh. "He'll probably ask you to leave. And a good thing too. What would you want to live here for?" He strolled around the room, patting the baby grand patronisingly, turning his nose up at the fan-shaped light-fittings sunk into the wall. "I suppose I should have taken my shoes off so as not to defile the carpet . . . Though it already has one of the most tasteless patterns I've seen. Ah, is this the kitchen through here? What's he got? Any Bath Olivers? Camembert? The pick of Fortnum and Mason's? Just what I feel like. Have you ever eaten pheasant? Delicious!"

He already had the fridge open as Simon came in, standing back admiring it like a burglar before a cracked safe.

"Aren't you going to make us a cup of tea?" he said over his shoulder, predatorily unwrapping a small packet. "Pâté! And pumpernickel! Divine! Does he have any Earl Grey?"

"No," said Simon, washing out the teapot, half-oppressed with guilt, half-tremulous with a sense of adventuring into confidence in a way he felt he had longed for without knowing it, "only Typhoo."

Julius laughed enthusiastically. He was eating olives with one hand and heaping pâté onto pumpernickel with the other. "Are you a marxist, Simon?" he said, apparently out of the blue, fastidiously arranging the pâté beneath the knife like an artist working on a canvas. "No, I don't suppose you are. Geoff's a marxist. He reads books about it endlessly. He could probably tell you the history of every Trotskyist sect in Britain, or the argument of chapter three of the second volume of *Capital*. Such dedication! I'm a sort of intuitional marxist, I know virtually nothing about it, but I know intuitively that it's right. I suppose you're a liberal. Never mind. It's probably just a phase. You'll grow out of it."

Simon's grip tightened on the teapot, but he said nothing. It was not indignation he experienced, but an irritation at his own incomprehension. He felt not so much perceived as foreshadowed, and the effect was to make him realise his intense ignorance of himself and his situation. His hands became strangely clumsy, down there at the end of his arms, trickling the tea precariously into the floral china cups and splashing the saucers. "Tea's ready," he said subduedly.

"Ah, wonderful!" said Julius. "Here's two pieces for you. Let's take it all through into your room. I've had enough of this place. I don't want to see it again till we're looting it after the revolution."

"You've used all the pâté."

"He can buy some more. I'll leave him a note wrapped in the empty paper. It will say, 'What, no Bresse Bleu?' Now, where's your room?" He poised the pumpernickel expertly on top of his teacup, and mooned questioningly at Simon.

Simon led the way silently. "Watch the steps," he said, opening the door.

"Do we have to descend into your room like the nether regions? My God! I know you're a neat little package, Simon, only a skeleton covered in skin, but even so, it's not very big, is it? Not exactly the Albert Hall." In fact, Julius's expansiveness itself seemed to make the dingy little room, tucked away to the side of the house, even smaller. It could have been a cupboard, thought Simon, and he suddenly detested it himself.

"We'll have to sit on the bed. There's nowhere else."

"I can see that." Julius lunged onto the bed and spread himself out, flinging his head back and pouring the pumpernickel into his mouth like a scene from a Roman orgy. He caught Simon out of the corner of his eye and patted the tiny corner of bed that he was not occupying. "Aren't you going to join me?"

Simon stood teetering for a moment, and then perched himself on the edge of the mattress, propping his back against the wall. He began to eat warily.

Julius pushed the last of the pumpernickel into his mouth in a great wedge that would hardly fit, and began to speak with his mouth full, showering Simon with a fine spray of sodden pâté. "I'm not going to sleep on the floor, you know. We'll have to sleep together after all." He swallowed his tea in a few noisy gulps. "I can see that you don't exactly relish the idea, but I must say I'm quite looking forward to it. I think you're nice. And you don't have to say anything. But do hurry up and finish eating, I'm getting tired." He yawned grotesquely, peering out reprimandingly at Simon from above the monstrous cavern that had swallowed his face, and began to tear off his clothes as though stifling, hurling them from him higgledy-piggledy onto the floor.

Simon demurely finished eating and drinking, refusing to move. He felt no reluctance about the situation, no sense that he was being exploited, or even significantly prevailed upon; only a great bafflement, not just at Julius now, but that he too could somehow become involved with the issue so lightly. He turned quietly to observe Julius, who was now already naked, sitting with his arms folded, staring at Simon impatiently, heaving his shoulders with a bored sigh. He reached for a cigarette.

"I'll turn the light off," said Simon, rising gracefully and going stealthily to the door.

"Oh, we have to have the dark already, do we?" sighed Julius, caught in the flare of his match as the blackness fell. "Yes, I suppose we would have to. Where are you?"

Simon undressed slowly, folding his clothes and laying them on the chair. Then he advanced with a pretended casualness as far as the bed, where he stood trying to make the pretence convincing to himself.

"We only need to lie and cuddle, you know," said Julius, just visible beyond the glowing tip of his cigarette, lying on his back with his arms behind his head. "It's just nice sometimes not to spend the night alone, to slide into the isolated prison of unconsciousness knowing there was someone there beside you as you went."

Simon climbed gingerly into the bed. The thought had never occurred to him. He lay there, consumed only with curiosity. Nothing happened, and a kind of smug calm descended on him. Everything will be alright, he thought, everything, and his eyes fell gently closed.

Suddenly a pair of arms were thrust about him as in a scuffle, a hot sweaty body crashed against his, and a warm wet mouth was dabbing his face all over with kisses like sparring blows to a punchbag.

"Hey, you're very violent," he said in surprise.

"That's not violence, that's passion," said Julius, stopping at once, and sitting upright as if his mood could be changed at the flick of a switch. "I like you! Why shouldn't I give you a squeeze and a few kisses? Aren't you going to cuddle me?" He dropped back over Simon's face and resumed energetically as if he been only pausing to mop his brow. His arms surrounded Simon and hugged him tightly.

"Your breath smells of garlic," said Simon.

Julius went instantly limp again, as if the air had rushed out of a balloon. He rolled over to the other side of the bed. "You're very talkative, all of a sudden," he said, with a little self-caricaturing sigh. "It's hopeless, isn't it? You haven't a clue about sex, have you? It's a closed book. You see, your trouble is that up there with all those intense friends in Scotland you told me about last time, you get lots of love, but no sex. While I get lots of sex but no love. Not that I'm sure I can find a use for love when I have it! Just like you with sex, it would seem. But what does it matter? We'll just fall asleep together, in the warmth of each other's bodies, and the smell – oh, I forgot, you don't like the smell. You're still hoping it's going to be like it is in the movies." Julius shuffled about making himself comfortable, and laid an arm gently over Simon's shoulders.

Simon's eyes were open. He was staring into the emptiness, the emptiness of the past and the future, as if for a moment, just a moment, plucked aside from the insistence of time, looking at it from a far vantage. "You're right," he said quietly. "I don't understand sex, and yet I'm obsessed with it. I want to experience it."

"Oh, you sound so glum," said Julius, his voice muffled by the pillow, "so dismal. Poor Simon! There, there. Of course, you're obsessed by it. How could you not be? It's part of the great romantic myth that pervades our culture. Sex is supposed to make you real in a way you aren't otherwise. There you are, it's the same with me and love. I don't understand it. I don't enjoy it when I get it, and yet I'm obsessed by it. You see, perhaps you've got something I haven't."

"But I can't integrate my sexual longings and my experience of love – I mean, love with my friends," Simon said, gazing into his own vision of himself in the ephemeral calm.

"You're in a transitional phase," Julius went on, his voice becoming lost in sleepiness. "Maybe you'll always be. Maybe you'll never reconcile theory with practice. You ought to see yourself in a wider context. And learn to live with fate's essential half-heartedness. But never give up your dreams, your goals. Liberation. Perfection. Not for a moment, not for a moment. Life – life's easy when you acknowledge that it's hard. Ah, my horrible literary glibness! Turn over and put an arm around me. Really, you've got to go some way towards other people when you can, you know."

Simon turned, and moving his hand across the distance between them – tiny in actuality, but a far, venturesome journey – he held Julius's shoulder. It was solid, strong, like a buttress.

"That garlic pâté will make me fart all night. You won't forgive me that, I suppose. Tomorrow I'll leave early so you can tidy up your life again behind me." Julius murmured on and on. "Or perhaps we'll go for a walk together on Clapham Common. We'll see, we'll see what happens. Advance with poise along the precariousness of life, delighting in your balance. Become a piece of life's rich" – he yawned – "dialectical pattern."

The sound of their mingled breathing came like the sea, advancing, retreating. Sleep came and went from Simon; he was intensely there, and then at once fading away. "You know," he said painstakingly, in a surge of clarity that even at the moment of its articulation was already sliding away, losing itself in a vague, even sentimental haziness, "you – you make – make me hope."

CHAPTER FIFTEEN

Bernard had come to ask him to leave the very next day after Julius's visit. He must have been waiting up for Simon to come in, sitting tensely in his chintz-covered chair, listening for the turn of the key in the lock, because he had shot into Simon's room even before Simon had had time to slip his bag from his shoulder. Confronted, taken by surprise, Simon had fumbled to maintain a wounded dignity; the ease of which before the fearful and incompetent Bernard had almost made him feel guilty. But seizing the advantage, he even managed to imply a certain smallness of mind on Bernard's part. Rather mawkishly, he held up his own attempted social mobility as an achievement which, it seemed, Bernard could not share. "Besides," he added humbly, lowering his gaze, "Julius had nowhere to sleep and no money.

"He had enough money to get drunk," said Bernard defensively, pulling at his jumper, his eyes looking everywhere but at Simon, his feet wriggling rhythmically.

In many ways Simon was relieved to go. He was uneasy with Bernard's reticence and attempted complacence. There seemed to Simon so much rather to be angry about, so much to question.

And he was beginning to realise that he must choose friends and lovers from motives of solidarity. Not because it was convenient for him, nor because it flattered him – or them.

He would have liked to tell Julius that one of his predictions, at least, had come true. Several times he phoned a number that Julius, when pressed, had left as a possible contact: but there was never any reply. He shrugged – as he supposed Julius would have wanted him to; but decided to keep trying, now and again. Anyway, he was bound to bump into him again, sooner or later.

Not without some difficulty he found himself a place of his own through *Time Out*. It was a room in a weathered terrace-house in the no-man's-land of Mornington Crescent, near the tube station that the trains all seem to bypass, in a street so small it was not even named on the map. If he walked to the end of the street, his way was stopped by a high brick wall, beneath which lay the lines that run into Euston, carrying the Glasgow trains back and forth, time after time, day after day.

The house was one of those London houses where no one does much more than exchange politenesses when they happen to meet in the kitchen or on the stairs. But the solitariness, the quietness, even the rather cell-like bareness of his room seemed strangely to appeal to him for the moment. He wanted time to be alone, to think.

It was the end of August when he moved, and September came in quiet and misty. Simon woke on his first morning to find the tiny patch of lawn outside his window scattered with dew and golden leaves. Already autumn had been walking in the garden at sunrise, leaving behind a lingering aura of sorrow and serenity. For a moment he saw his whole summer as an endless – and friendless – succession of brief encounters. If as such it did not seem to differ greatly, so far as he could tell, from the lives of those he had met, that afforded neither reassurance nor explanation. It had been a loose string of episodes that seemed unrelated and yet somehow unified.

Waiting for him downstairs was a letter from Annie. Eagerly he opened it and read it, standing there half-dressed in the shadowy hall. There was an uneasiness about its tone, and it raised twice the earnest wish that he was being careful not to hurt people unnecessarily while in London. Nodding, he pushed it back in its envelope and put it into his pocket, ready to re-read, but not now.

After breakfast, he sat gazing at the slowly lifting mist, and contemplated the fact that his grant was finished. He had no money and no job. Already once or twice he had leafed through the barman's jobs in the evening papers. But really he did not feel up to working. He needed as much time as possible to sort things out. So for the time being he decided to beg a little life from social security, a whole approach to life he knew so well at second hand from years in a mortifying Glasgow, shut off from the wealth that flowed so easily still in London.

That afternoon he took the place left for him among the others on the hard benches of the social security office, surrounded by coughs and snuffles and cold draughts. And in fact, he found it gave him a momentary sense of communality, a strange dignity. It seemed to him for a moment he could at last share in the emotions and self-respect of a group with common economic interests.

And so, when it was discovered that the old man with a torn coat had been sitting silently waiting for six hours, unable to hear his name called because he was too deaf, he shared in the outrage that flared hot and loud in one corner, and glowed on warmly even as far as him. He shared in the admiration, raucous in some, timid in others like himself, for a young Irish woman with a child, her breath steaming in the cold air as she spoke, saying quite blankly that if she wasn't paid something on the spot, she'd leave the baby right there on the counter and they could look after it. Beyond the counter, fenced off by bars like a big cat maddened by a cage too small for it, was a madwoman, spitting and rearing, intransigent, unable to feel anything any more for her fellow human beings beyond annoyance. The Irish woman dumped the strangely silent baby and turned to walk out, but they called her back in a childlike panic, and sent her through to the other room.

Simon discovered that in the other room there were little screened-off boxes – as if encouraging one to confess to the sin of poverty. The weary clerk that dealt with Simon's case filled in his form wrongly for him, so that a day or so later, when he was down to his last few pence, a letter came saying he was not entitled to anything. Where the system could not protect itself by cheating, he thought, it had inefficiency to fall back on.

Though exhausted by the long walk and the long queue, it came strangely to Simon on his return that, in fact, behind the clerk's performance of faceless indifference lurked the memory of someone essentially well-meaning, perhaps even idealistic, who had simply been eroded into a state of embattled confusion.

After that the cheque came: telling him what he was worth. Not much. Fourteen pounds fifty: six pounds fifty for rent, just over a pound a day for food, transport, heating, beer to help him dream, and that was about it. But just now it would do.

Once or twice a week, scuffing the growing drifts of fallen leaves before him as he went, he would walk through the increasingly chilly evenings to the odd gay movement alternative venue he could afford to attend. Out of a kind of habit he still found his eyes straying, found himself thinking of getting picked up. But it had become no more than a half-hearted mechanical gesture, with no momentum and no real expectations. He always came home alone.

He was concerned now only with retreat, a monk-like retreat, in order to reflect, to try and make sense of what he was doing. Indeed he had descended willingly into his impoverishment with a sense of its appropriacy.

For a while a few hopefuls would still come over and speak to him, still phone him, make invitations, with one clear end in view. He listened to their phone-calls, and their conversations when they met, more carefully than previously. But it often felt to him as if they were speaking to a different person. And he would find, after all, a certain relief in ending up sleeping on his own, wrapped in his own caring embrace.

If sexually he was indeed a blank screen, he wanted now only to wait until he had an image of his own choice and making to project there.

Soon the phone-calls and invitations tailed off.

But he no longer had any need for lovers as decorative but useless possessions. The realisation made him feel for a moment the kind of transient freedom that he supposed someone would feel who gave up everything to become a tramp.

The open road stretched dauntingly ahead. It was up to him to choose the route. Once, that is, he felt sure he could read the map.

He did bump into Julius again. At long last.

He had been feeling cold waiting for the tube. But now he could hear the distant sighing in the tunnel that heralded the arrival of the train, and his eyes were turned to the gaping black mouth from which it would finally rush, bright and noisy and present. A hand tapped him lightly on the shoulder, and as he turned, he saw that it was gloved and ringed, and belonged to a figure in a shabby fur coat with frizzed hair and lurid eye make-up, obscuring rather than highlighting the langorous icon eyes that at first he did not recognise.

"Hallo," said Julius, his untidy beam hovering expectantly like a hand waiting to be shaken, "it's me."

"Yes," said Simon, trying to smile back more certainly, "so it is. I haven't seen you for a long time."

The train roared in, drowning Julius's reply. The doors hissed open in front of their faces, demanding entry. Passengers came and went on either side of them.

"Where are you going?" shouted Simon, drifting forward.

"Same place as you are," said Julius brightly, taking his arm, shepherding him to a seat. "To the dance. That is where you're going, isn't it? I thought so."

"Yes, it is." Simon sat where he was put, not resentfully, watching the other passengers staring at them, while Julius smiled back regally from above his mangy fur.

"Another old dance!" he said blankly. "Not so long ago they were a shining symbol of progress. Now they're just another stall in the meat market. One bumps into one's friends and remembers happier times. You struggle for a corner big enough to dance in, and never get off with the one you really had your eye on. But who'd miss them? Hope springs eternal! Pity I didn't know you were coming, I got this wonderful shot-silk dress the other day. Much too small for me, but it would look good on you."

The train jolted, glided past the emptied platform, then swept into blackness.

"Where have you been?" asked Simon. "I haven't seen you."

"I went to Yugoslavia." Julius gestured expansively. "On the dole. I had to hitch and beg and starve. I had a wonderful time. Ah, the Mediterranean sun, it makes me grow, it makes me blossom. I sometimes think I'm always dormant in England, an undernourished exotic, barely kept alive by the graces of a few wishful and inspired sympathetic spirits, for whom I keep at least in leaf. What do you think?"

"You seem to blossom here. I don't know how you managed to go abroad with no money."

"I had to live off sunshine and red wine and love."

"Did you sell yourself?" said Simon, curiously, trying to sound blasé, but the words came out too eagerly.

"Oh, that wasn't what I meant. Of course, yes, I did that now and again, how else do you think I made money at all? No, I meant love, the real thing, or rather, the unreal thing. It's so convenient for that kind of holiday, isn't it? A free anaesthetising drug, emotional coca-leaves, that makes you forget you're hungry, unbathed, and at a loose end."

"I thought," said Simon, "that you didn't know what to do with love."

Julius lolled back, his eyes sparkling. "Well, there you are, I found a use for it. Besides, it's easier when you're on holiday, momentarily detached from your real world. Isn't it? And then, he was Yugoslavian after all, and hardly spoke a word of English, and I certainly didn't speak much Serbo-Croat – what a name for a language, it sounds like an insult – so, well, that saved us from a lot of problems. And after all, we've got to indulge love now and again, even if we don't enjoy it, it's the same as needing to have sex. Even if we don't enjoy it. Are you getting any these days?"

A middle-aged woman across the carriage was listening intently to their conversation, eyes wide with shocked fascination. Simon felt awkward. "No," he said quietly, "I've given up trying really. It was the wrong approach. That's not what I want." He was pleased at his own certainty.

"Well, at least you sound pretty decided," Julius sighed languidly, batting his painted eyelids and lighting up a cigarette. "I'm sure that's a forward step." He patted Simon's arm with affectionate mock patronisation. "What are you going to the dance for then?"

Simon shrugged and looked away uneasily. "It's somewhere to go."

"Lonely, are you? Ah, aren't we all? Have you got a job?"

"No, I'm on social security."

"No money and no sex – you should be hanging around Piccadilly Circus. You can make five pounds a time, maybe more."

Julius stirred up a tiny glow of bitterness in Simon. Since he had got no emotional reward from selling his sexual attractiveness, the prospect of actually selling it for a cash reward filled him for a moment with a kind of vengeful satisfaction. Why not? "Oh, I don't think so," he said hesitantly. "Anyway, I don't know how you set about it."

Julius looked reproachfully at Simon and spoke with a voice of painstaking explanation. "Well, you just stand in a suitable place, looking expectant, and wait for someone to come and ask you the time or something, and then you go off for a cup of coffee or a drink –"

"But how does money come into it?"

"You talk about it – before you do anything. It's nothing to be ashamed of. Economics is bigger than you, you've got to defend yourself as best you can." Julius sighed, and folded his hands over one another conclusively.

The train rocked them gently, brushing them against one another. Simon knew he had already rejected the idea. How much he wanted to believe there could be something affectionately agreed, something equable; though just now this was only an act of faith in a haunted darkness of uncertainty.

"Poor Simon, you must be leading a wretched life." Julius drew on his cigarette relaxedly, speaking through a haze of smoke. "Never mind, I'm sure it will do you good in the long run. A little insecurity, a little deprivation is necessary now and then, it makes us discover what we really need. Though in your case, yes, well, it's not exactly a little deprivation. Willingly or unwillingly, you're a proper ascetic, aren't you? Simon Stylites! But I'm not too worried about you, you'll be glad to hear. These emotional and economic sanctions exercised against you by our cruel historical conjuncture will only pave the way for self-determination in the end."

Simon looked at his own swaying outline reflected vaguely in the glass. "I wish I had your faith," he said.

"You do have," said Julius, unruffled, exhaling smoke. "When you're ready to use it."

The end of the tunnel slid past the window, and the train carrying them glided slowly through the half-light of a station, peered at by confidently expectant faces, into a momentary motionlessness that only asserted the purposefulness of its onward movement.

As winter set in, his breath would steam in the morning in the unheated room when he lifted his head above the bedclothes. He would lie there in the warm for a while, listening to the police cars and ambulances in the distance rushing along the Euston Road to another IRA bomb scare.

Sometimes it seemed to him that the availability of mere sex, offered so liberally on every side in London, had been only a numbing drug, anaesthetising him from the complex reality of his situation. Tucked up beneath the covers, he knew that he wanted to be able to confront and make use of that complexity: but it was like his learning to swim – he had wanted to be able to swim, but he had sat out half his lessons shivering on the edge of the pool, reluctant actually to enter the chilly water.

These days London was gloomy, flickering with premonitions of unrest and change. The miners were striking and the government had cut off the electricity. It was nearly Christmas, but the shop-windows were unlit and the street-lights glimmered at half-power. In the darkness familiar streets had become as if unknown.

Simon went as often as he could to visit some gay squatters who lived nearby. They were friends of Julius, who had introduced him to them at the dance. Sometimes Julius spent the night there, and when Simon inquired after him, he would often find that someone remembered finding Julius napping in their bed a day or so before, but no, he had not said when he would be back. The squatters were supporting the miners by burning all their heaters on full and leaving on all their lights, because they were not going to pay the bill in any case. Simon would curl up in the luxuriant heat, and listen to their frenetic debates about this strike in particular and politics in general. He himself was unforthcoming, and yet placidly accepted. Sometimes his reaction was watched and sought for, often he was left benignly to his own silence. There were two or three among them who dressed always in rather lurid drag, and no debate would get far before one of them would start proclaiming raucously that everything came down to the power of men. If anyone interrupted, they were shouted down for acting like a man.

"Listen, sweetheart, if we all gave up our male competitiveness, there wouldn't have to be employment struggles, because no one would ever want to be boss. Think of it."

"Yeah, it's male to be job-defined. All of us should be on social security as a matter of principle."

"Then we lose contact. We should be out showing our involvement with the miners' struggle. And the Irish struggle. Instead of just stewing here at home, literally. We used to go on workers' demos once upon a time."

They were always talking about the good old days, though sometimes Simon would discover these particular good old days were as recent as a few months ago.

"That was when we thought we were among the oppressed. Before everyone decided that all that mattered was having somewhere to dance and screwing around."

"Don't you mean, having gay tupperware parties in St John's Wood and asking your local MP to open a gay flower arrangement for charity!"

And so on, here, there, and everywhere. Simon often found the wild tangle of their half-glimpsed ideas quite impenetrable, but always wonderful to observe.

More and more, he was becoming sure of where his feelings lay, but he lacked the clarity to open his mouth and put them into words.

Indeed, confusion and inaction were becoming addictive.

It occurred to him that he was frittering most of his time away now. Hours were consumed in the mere calculation of the day's meagre expenses. In the mornings, when he did not have to sign on, he would do a bit of shopping, or creep off rather secretively to earn a few pounds on the side by cleaning wealthy homes in Hampstead and Finchley and so on for an agency. It was dull discontinuous unrewarding work, of course, affording nothing more than a glimpse on the one hand of the nervous indolence of the well-off, and of the mindless arduousness of most people's work on the other.

In the afternoons he would go to the library and fidget half-heartedly with the tail-end of his thesis. Not so long ago, he thought often enough, such a thing would have assured him of an academic career. But now there were precious few jobs on offer. Education was being cut back as cavalierly as the power supply. He was not even shortlisted for those one or two posts he did apply for. Though he still went on applying, dreaming of doing something helpful and rewarding.

Sometimes there came strange moments when insights suddenly seemed to stick together. Once, it was very cold, he was sitting bundled up on the tube when a young European couple, Italian perhaps, got on and sat opposite. They were both dressed in white furs; the thick high collar set off the man's trimmed black beard. The woman's little hands holding her camera lightly to her were gloved. The skin of their faces had the creamy luminescence of pearls, except where high on the cheeks a mingled rose and tan dappled through; like sun through water while their eyes were like jet beads, impassive, unmoving. It seemed that light radiated from them. They were beautiful.

And suddenly Simon hated them. He hated their beauty born of wealth, their warm furs, their skin nourished by good food, their trips to exciting places. He hated their beauty born of heterosexuality, the reassurance of one another, the world's admiration of a lovely couple. He thought that always in the past the sight of any human beauty had filled him with a kind of naive joy. But now that he saw, as if for the first time, what was necessary to create it, to feed it, he felt not contempt, not horror, but a hatred so intense he wished it might make them drop dead before him.

But such emotional intensity was becoming all too rare.

With little to occupy him – staring day after day into the indigence of his present, the open-endedness of his future, haunted by fleeting visions of the comfort and optimism of his long-ago – in a moment of perception he saw himself: a disinherited bourgeois, shut out forever from the life of connubial bliss and good things promised him by the book-lined liberal humanism of his family background, where the academic bank-manager's son had lain down to sleep with the un-learned bricklayer's daughter.

But if he had not inherited a space to live in, he was still unsure of what space to seek for himself.

The end of the year was rapidly approaching. His mother had asked him home for Christmas. And Annie had written saying surely he would be coming back for Hogmanay; there would always be a place for him with them.

The contours of his hopes, his expectations, his reassurances – the landmarks of his way – seemed to him now flickering behind swirling mists. To find out where he was he must again make a move somewhere. And where else to go? He did not see himself with the confidence or clarity to take off for the beckoning horizons of Amsterdam or Australia, for instance. No, the open road before him did not lead that far, not at the moment. At least he could be assured of a community of friends in Glasgow. And that was important. There was no point any longer in pretending that he had not become very lonely in London.

Besides, in deciding to return now, he revived the distantly remembered image of Glasgow, hard but loved city, as a place of important beginnings.

Julius was the one person he would have liked to see before he left. He asked at the squat, but no one, it seemed, had seen Julius for weeks. When last heard of, he had been talking, they said, about finding some way to get to New York.

Never mind. Something at least of Julius would stay with him in his memory anyway.

And then, a day or so before he was due to leave, he saw him in a gold lamé turban and red pendant earrings going past on a down escalator as he himself stood on an up one. Simon waved frantically, and even moved as if to walk back down the ascending steps, causing a momentary angry jostle all around him. But Julius simply glided by, smiling serenely at Simon from above what was now revealed as an ankle-length Afghan coat, whose newness and lushness could surely only mean it had been shoplifted.

"I'm going to Glasgow," Simon shouted, trying to mouth the words exaggeratedly, so at least they could be lip-read.

"What?" Julius called back, already slipping away out of earshot, and added in a clearly audible bellow, which caused the passengers on either side of him to stare in cold amazement, "You're going somewhere? We're all going somewhere. I hope you get there soon!"

And waving a visibly dirty hand regally from out of his wide shaggy cuff, his face fixed in a clownlike beneficence, he vanished out of sight.

There was a rail strike, and he had to take the earliest train in order to be assured of getting right through to Glasgow. It was still freezing; the pavement glistened in the lamplight, as he shut the front door quietly behind him and picked his way with his suitcase tentatively through the unaccustomed early morning, through a darkness not like the night: a cold darkness, full of dim bustle, expectations and beginnings, that seemed alien and unfamiliar.

Simon remembered Julius's voice, that night at the end of the summer. Every hill's beside a valley, disintegration is only part of an ongoing process. And he thought: The darkness before dawn.

Part Three: GOING BACK

CHAPTER SIXTEEN

And there he was that evening, standing with Philip and Annie at the bar of the Kist o'Whistles, happily sipping his pint of heavy, babbling endlessly about London, his experiences slipping out one after another. Over the bar the landlady smiled at him from behind her horn-rimmed glasses, an uncharacteristic gesture of her dour face; and the eyes of the regulars, even the ones who did not particularly know him, went to him in recognition.

Vanessa bustled in, darkly glowing, and brushed him softly with her lips on the cheek. "You're looking a little older, a little wiser, you know," she said, surveying him with her knowing look, and adding in a low chuckle, "and all the better for that! Don't you think?" Shouting imperiously, she arrested a man who was passing, whom neither of them knew except by sight. "Don't you think he's looking well?"

Simon recognised him now. He was one of those who used to gaze soulfully at him from across the bar in a furtive drunken silence; but if it ever looked as if they were about to be drawn into one another's company, would vanish suddenly into thin air. Now, caught by Vanessa, he blushed to the roots of his hair. "Oh yes," he mumbled, since her gaze refused to allow him to ignore her, and passed quickly on, visibly trembling. Once Simon would have felt hurt, threatened by lonely despair. But now he found himself laughing along with Vanessa, at the assertion of his own difference.

"I'll get you another drink," she said. "A pint of heavy? Wee Heavy, that's what I'm going to call you now!"

For the moment he basked in the affection of his friends, soaking it up, while he watched the deep warm red of the tee-shirt he had chosen seem to spread out over them like the radiance of a fire.

Familiarity proved a great source of content. But as much as anything, the return to old surroundings brought clearly home to him just how much he himself had changed. He no longer thought he was the only gay in a world where possibilities were closed off by heterosexuality like a high wall.

Now and again he took himself to the gay pubs he knew of in the city, something he could not have braved before. The knowledge of his possible attractiveness still hung on him rather awkwardly from London, still not quite assimilated into the rest of his manner. People would mill near him like coy schoolgirls, casting shy sideways glances, giggling, muttering to one another in camp accents that dropped from them the moment they stepped outside. It might be that with the ostentatious recklessness of a child answering a dare a perfumed man with immaculately groomed hair would begin a conversation with Simon. But when the topic of gay liberation came up, his eyes would go fixed, uneasily, warily, like those of a pet that suspects for a moment it may be about to be betrayed by someone it knows. "Do you not think they go a wee bit too far?" he would say stiffly. "I mean, do you not think we should keep ourselves to ourselves?" From a bar-stool on the edge of their conversation a man (drawing attention away from his frightened wrinkled eyes by the daring brightness of his shirt and his overbearingly lively chatter) would interrupt, "Och, liberation! Here! My goodness, even if they changed the law, what difference would it make to us? Nestling behind the storm-doors of our flats in Hyndland. With our cats and our classical records and the memory of our maiden aunts. Deep down in our wee red sandstone hearts, we're all douce, aren't we?" Beside Simon a good-looking man dressed with subdued trendiness in a corduroy suit would murmur softly, "You don't change things overnight, do you?" And so on.

But the fact Simon found nothing in common made him now feel above all impatient with their dead-end view of themselves. A view which he no longer shared, he realised. Although he decided to go on paying the odd visit – to avoid contact would have seemed now a kind of betrayal – nevertheless, he had little expectation that it would be from here any new companionship would emerge.

The old sense of hopeless isolation, the sense of living in a vacuum might have gone completely, yet the problem of how to establish a gay relationship with another man remained. In London he had expected the problem to disappear: but instead he had found himself simply looking at it from another angle.

He resolved to go on thinking a bit more before he decided to act again.

But he could not suppress for long a certain restlessness, the resurgence of longings still unsatisfied. Time passed slowly. It seemed as if the spring, apparently so near, in reality would never come. Days lengthened only the more to affirm the absence of the sun, still lost behind endless clouds.

"What are you going to do?" said Philip, in his edged voice of practical challenge, as he leant against their favourite corner of the bar.

"I don't know yet," said Simon thoughtfully. "I know a lot more things now I didn't know before. I feel more determined to achieve what I want. And yet more puzzled about how to. And even uncertain of just what it is I'm looking for."

"Well, remember," said Philip gently, "you stay strong only by continually reminding yourself that you're strong."

"That's one thing I'm certainly going to go on doing."

"We hope you'll stay on with us now, m'dear," said Annie, venturing an arm a little awkwardly round his shoulders. "We missed you while you were away, you know."

He smiled. He too had missed the closeness the three of them shared. And yet already he was beginning to sense that now his heart was no longer wholly in Glasgow, any more than his heart had ever been wholly in London. Even if the reasons in each case were different.

Annie drew breath and paused, her face troubled by a characteristic look of diffident contemplation. "You know, I've been thinking, m'dear," she said, laying her words out tentatively, "from what you say about what happened in London, you could learn a bit from thinking more about what women have to put up with from men."

Philip looked impatient and defensive, his mouth twitching as if chewing over what he was about to say.

Once Simon too would have wanted to say that he knew all that, that it wasn't the point. He would have said that surely what gay people had to put up with was different. No one, after all, had ever said that women either didn't or shouldn't exist. Had they? But for some time now so many remembered fragments, mostly from drag-queens, about the possessiveness, the overbearingness, the unawareness of men had been sticking to remembered moments of his sexual experiences in London like pairing cells, building up a pattern. And yet – as if to prove the point about the tenacity of male privilege – he found himself unexpectedly uneasy about admitting as much to Annie. "Well yes," he said at last, his voice seeming to take upon itself an unexpectedly masculine tone, "I do think our problems have certain points in common." Feeling his way carefully, he drew breath to say more.

"I may not be gay and I may not be a woman," Philip said measuredly, "but I can't just deny myself any right to try and have an effect on the world." Simon felt a twinge of guilt; he owed so much to the model of Philip's strength and purposefulness. "Anyway, who's for another drink?" It was as if Philip took the conversation by the hand and dragged it away.

Annie's face clamped shut in a brooding silence. Simon wished he could feel more detached than he did.

The persistence of winter brought an intensified recklessness; which proved to have its own uses. The three of them, Simon and Philip and Annie, had been invited to a comparative stranger's fancy-dress party: and Simon decided to go in drag.

It was an act of self-assertion, and above all of defiance. If there was one thing he had got clear in London, it was that outrage and confrontation were amongst one's best weapons if one was ever to broach the walls of convention.

Putting together his costume carefully, he could not suppress the hope that he might for a moment deceive men who did not know him. That seemed a terrible risk; but perhaps one of his few real chances of an interesting sexual encounter.

And yet, as it was, what he really gained from the experiment was something quite different.

Philip was dressed as Pan, naked except for leggings made from an old jumble-sale fur coat, with his hair teased into horns, and daffodils behind his ears. His costume brought out in his characteristic gestures a certain magnificent vitality.

Simon was shivering as he changed before the fire, but more from nervous excitement than cold.

"We'll all be keeping a watch to make sure you don't get into any trouble, m'dear." said Annie, glimpsing him in the mirror, as she adjusted her bow-tie Simon was surprised at how much, as it seemed to him, she had hidden herself. She was dressed as a vampire, her long athletic body in an austere evening-suit, a full black cape falling from her shoulders, her hair drawn back from her high forehead, the firm bones of her face accentuated by white powder: the very image of some ruthless vigour, stretching down centuries beyond the grave.

"Whee, I feel wonderful!" said Philip suddenly, leaping into the air, and as he did so, catching his foot in the flex of the table-lamp and jerking the plug out, so that the room was plunged into the flicker of firelight.

He swayed and capered before Annie, butting his head like a young bull, his weaving hands casting fantastic shadows, the orange light glinting from his torso. Annie flung open her arms and lifted the full spread of the black cape, swirling and flapping it about her, her head tossed back, lifting and lowering the length of her legs slowly in great steps. They dived and pranced around and over one another in the glimmer of the flames, touching, kissing, seeming to Simon as he watched to become powerful alien creatures, filled with an easy energy and self-possession which he had had to struggle so hard to come within sight of.

They had stopped while he was still dreaming.

"Come on, loves, it's time we were going," said Philip, striding across and plugging the lamp in again.

In the sudden rush of light Simon surveyed himself. Annie's long black velvet dress hung from his shoulders to the floor; his hands clasped the ends of his grandmother's stole; Vanessa's beads swayed about his neck; his hair was bound up in his own red chiffon scarf, knotted at the side with an ostrich plume, twenties-style. The unaccustomed sensuosity of it all was like a euphoric drug. Without prompting his body settled itself into position, shoulders yielding backwards, head langorously to one side, eyes peeping out from under hovering lids.

"You look magnificent, Simon," said Philip, standing back approving.

The eyes bobbed across in Philip's direction, looked up shyly, then down, then up again invitingly, and then drifted off and dangled in a lonely vacancy, waiting to be rescued. The mask seemed to come naturally, it already had complete possession of Simon's body. But he began to watch the mask itself, with as much fascination as he watched its effect.

"A perfect image of conventional femininity," said Annie solemnly. "Now, let's see what happens."

They went to Maryhill Road to get a taxi. A cold steady rain was falling.

"Simon, m'dear, it's up to you." Annie pushed him forward to the kerb, and retreated with Philip to the shadows. "A taxi's not going to stop for us dressed like this."

"They never stop for me," said Simon forlornly. "I don't know how to make them stop. I don't have the air of authority."

A taxi was racing purposefully past, raising a ridge of rain-water shining in the orange lamp-light. Simon leant out tentatively and waved a helpless gloved hand. The taxi swerved to a halt, splashing Simon's stockings, and flung back its door. "Come on in, hen. You'll catch your death."

But entering the party was hardly a joke. Never had he known such fear, he thought. It was as if he were at war, at any moment he expected violence to strike him down. Male hands holding glasses or cigarettes seemed to him only waiting to become fists. The blood pounded in his ears above the frivolous music. This was the fear he lived with among straights transformed from an ever-present slight ache to an exposed nerve. It screamed within him, as he picked out the eyes of those men who visibly hoarded vengeance for any who dared to suggest that their virility and its privilege were arbitrary. And they were there, of course, framed by token disguises as sheikhs and tsars and cowboys, while the crowd milled around them, acceptingly.

But they did not notice him. Amazingly, it seemed they were fooled. He watched his own mask as meticulously as a spy, correcting immediately a gesture that threatened to become masculine, a stance that betrayed the centre of balance. Beneath the dark eye-shadow he kept his eyes timorous, self-aware, seeking approval.

And he found that he was also a spy on – men. An unexpected spy on the reality of their policy; like the employee of a firm rumoured to be corrupt, who accidentally chances on proof that it is indeed yet more corrupt than he dreamed.

Going to look for more wine, he found Annie in the kitchen. A drunken bearded block of a man in pirate costume, swaying precariously on the edge of the kitchen table, was trying to chat her up. His weight was falling this way and that like potatoes in a sack, thin streams of beer and saliva trickled from the untidy fronds of his moustache. Annie stood still and straight beside him, her sense of self seemed stretched tight like a wire; she was completely detached, mockery showed through the curtain of impassiveness before her eyes. Simon drew near to the table, open, curious.

The man's big hand came round his waist and pulled him in like a fish. The grip tightened as on a package that had just been claimed in a shop. "Hallo, darling. So you've come to keep me company," said the man sloppily, his glazed eyes sliding about as if they were loose in his head, not managing to focus on Simon, but holding him firmly against him.

Simon smiled slightly and said nothing, because he was terrified of the consequences of breaking his cover, while a fascinated utter horror grew all over him that one human being dare claim possession of another so mindlessly.

The man's free hand fumbled clumsily for his glass, aimed it uncertainly at his mouth and drank noisily. His eyes roamed up and down appraisingly, not like a prospective buyer, but as if assessing a casual purchase. "Oh yes, you've got a very pretty neck," he said, low and slurred. But it was as if Simon was not meant to hear; it was not a compliment to Simon, it was a satisfied statement to himself of his assets. His big mouth began to chew loosely at Simon's neck, sweeping it with the soggy brush of his moustache.

"Of course," said Annie coldly, "you realise that's a man."

The hold loosened on Simon's waist, the wet moustache drew back, a shocked effort at concentration struggled in the lolling eyes, staring at Simon, almost giving way for a moment to incredulity. The big hands moved from Simon's waist to the table. The man said, "Fucking Jesus, you're not."

"Yes," said Simon carefully, calculating the situation second by second, "I am." He was not sure what was going to happen. He was still reeling with horror at the sudden clarity of the situation, at how he had been consumed like food, how he had been treated as an appurtenance.

The man looked away, avoiding Annie as much as Simon, and shook his heavy head, making laughing noises, as if submitting to having been well fooled. Then he spat several times on the floor, cleaning his mouth out. "Well, darling, you've got a very pretty neck," he said. But now the words, the very same words, were not appraisal, but contempt.

Simon wanted to leave while he was safe. Moving across to Annie's side, he said to the man, "Thank you," and poured himself some more wine. Some other people came into the kitchen and greeted Annie. Simon slipped away quickly as they moved up to the table, feeling the man's eyes burning into his back with fury at his challenge as he passed through the door.

And the other room seemed to him now full with another kind of men, men who thought he *was* a woman; who looked at him casually as part of a birthright, which they might take up, use, or discard at will, which had no other purpose; who were alert and ready to use violence to maintain that right, to assert that purpose. A new world he had never properly appreciated. It was a strange new relief to find amid this the face of a gentle man, who seemed to have tentatively set his power aside and come out to mingle with the people. There was one there at least, dressed as Nureyev in a white blouse and tights, and Simon warmed towards him with a certain tenderness and respect.

"How's it going?" said Philip, coming up beside him.

Simon found it hard to say. "It's terrifying," he said, fingering his beads. "But that man over there's nice." The man dressed as Nureyev was dancing with a tall woman dressed as a gipsy.

"Why don't you ask him to dance?" said Philip, almost boyishly eager to create some progressive confrontation. The music was coming to a stop, another track was about to start. "I'll help. Come on."

"I haven't got the courage."

"Yes you have." It seemed that Philip had already crossed the room and asked the gipsy to dance, and without his fully realising that he had done it, Simon had followed and stood opposite the ballet-dancer, trying to think of what in the world he should say, a much greater problem than how he should look. The ballet-dancer, smiling simply and sweetly, said with a gesture of polite invitation, "Are you dancing?", and by that time they already were, propped by the music in their mutual diffidence. The question to which he could not immediately see the answer was whether the ballet-dancer knew.

He surely didn't, because he suddenly looked at Simon with such idealisation as surely no man ever awarded another, so that Simon felt himself secure in the man's imagination, as the man showed no interest in his reality. The man spoke to him as if he were not human, his words were made to touch Simon like fingers touching a fragile precious object from some distant time or culture; they attributed to him an otherness and an unimaginable frailty, which had nothing to do with the casual friendliness and charm of their sense. The man said, "Am I saving you or are you saving me?"

The mask replied, with eyes moving in humble flattered gratitude, in response to the tone and not the words. And it said, "I don't know."

A bearded man in uniform came out of a corner, and catching Simon with a slow dark look of malicious outrage, whispered something in the ballet-dancer's ear. The ballet-dancer faltered in his dancing, for a moment he looked clumsy and at a loss, he half-turned away to talk to the man in uniform. By then Simon had already stopped dancing and was looking about the room for a friend to talk to. He found he felt hurt, disappointed. But the ballet-dancer turned back and said in a soft generously polite voice, "Thanks for the dance." For a moment Simon's mask dropped, he looked back in sad surprise. The ballet-dancer blushed, and drew his hand mawkishly across his face in a self-mocking gesture of shame as the music stopped. He gazed round forlornly for an escape route, and at that moment Vanessa, who was dressed quite breathtakingly as Cleopatra, came up and began to talk to him.

Simon walked to the wall and slouched against it, no longer taking care to look like a woman. Seeing Annie coming towards him, he turned away in shame. His ostrich-plume slipped and dangled askant. Clasping the glass to him, he downed his wine doggedly, and the party began to fade beyond a sealed-off drunkenness.

All next day he seemed to tremble with shock, as if he had been the witness of some near fatal accident. The knowledge of institutionalised violence he had received felt like a secret which he dared not admit even to himself.

Later, when he was more able to reflect, the intensity of this experience seemed to confirm the glimpsed explanation for the situation in which he had found himself in London. If heterosexuality had once bounded the possibilities of his world in Glasgow, it was as much as anything its reflection which had bounded his possibilities in London. It was indeed time for him to look at the relationships between women and men more closely, in order to understand the relationships amongst men.

He began to read some of the books on feminism whose titles he had heard bandied about in London, venturing, at first tentatively, to discuss them with Annie. Soon there were times when they talked about them late into the evening. The clarity of what he read was at once a consolation and a challenge.

CHAPTER SEVENTEEN

The weather, at least, had not changed at at all. There had been a glorious spring: but it rained all summer.

Already August. Soon it would be autumn. First one drip of the afternoon's rain, then another fell against the window and dragged its slow tear-stain the length of the pane. Simon rose from the floor, where he had been crouching over a book, and went to stand looking out. Once again successive barrages of dark cloud seemed to be driving in over the city like the surf of an incoming tide. The rain, falling steadily against the glass, began to merge its aimlessly wandering solitary streams, turning the view to a patchy blur.

The spring seemed to have shown a treacherous kindness. Day after day, Simon had lain in the sun by the Kelvin, listening to the wind moving gently among the willows, drinking in the heady smell of warm grass.

Image succeeded image of himself in his mind, turned over, discarded. It was like the far-flung search for some spiritual Rumpelstiltskin.

And yet time after time, in spite of his determination, he ended up slipping away into a vision of himself as cursed and feckless. Why? Simply because he had not managed to become part of a couple. He knew that was why well enough; and questioning the value of couplehood however seriously seemed unable to change what he actually felt.

The brief sunny spell passed. And the everlasting Glasgow clouds returned like a challenge.

Now he stood with the summer drawing to a close, alone in the house, watching the rain fall over the endless rows of black tenements. Philip and Annie, Vanessa and a boyfriend of the moment – it was one of those recurrent periods when she was effortlessly juggling several at once, and clutching on to none – they were all in the country on their bicycles, defying the showers. Cycling had become something of a fad among them. But so far Simon had found himself unable to master the bicycle. He could not find his balance; the best he could manage was a swerving aimless course that came to an abrupt end with his falling to the ground. Meanwhile the others sailed by him, venturing further and further, ascending the mountainous distance, their wheels like the newly-allocated wings of young angels, he thought morosely, leading them skyward while he lay earthbound.

But if indeed Philip and Annie, for example, were the saved, the blessed, one thing they had seemed singularly unable to do was to intercede on his behalf. Simon had abandoned faith in them: blind faith, which seemed to him now to have been unthinking of himself, and unfair on them.

Because although it might be true that their entering the state of couplehood had once wrought in them some irrevocable transformation, there was nothing final about that transformation. Like everybody else – himself for example, or Vanessa – they still had to progress; adjust to changing circumstances, live through lean times, find reasons to go on.

And yet . . . And yet, belonging as they did to the privileged class of couples, they had such resources of emotional wealth to help them cope. Sometimes Simon felt himself an emotional beggar, begging scraps from their tables, cradling a bare flicker of existence, drowsily dreaming now and again of utopia.

Life seemed to be confronting him continually in the form of contradictions. He longed to escape its complexity: and yet, of course, most often what presented itself to him as the escape into simplicity was the entry into the complexity of couplehood.

The rain was easing off. From behind the ragged blanket of black cloud tumbling overhead, a sepia sunlight filtered through an oncoming veil of light haze; far off on the horizon, another wall of darkness was already advancing. But it would be fine for a spell.

He looked over at the book open on the floor. He was immersing himself in history now, suddenly struggling, as if time were running out, to understand the endless interweaving of power-relationships, that included the power-relationships of men and women. Possession and violence in its defence surrounded him, it seemed, in layers, which fitted together somehow into a system it was vital to understand if one was ever to escape from it.

But for the moment he was too restless to go on reading. He caught up a jacket, and ran out to take a walk.

The air was mild and damp. Once outside he remembered there were holes in his shoes, because he could not afford to buy new ones. His socks quickly became wet from the steaming pavement. But soon he would have some money. He was getting a job in a few weeks, in a part of the university library. He was glad to be getting a job. That seemed, at least, to offer an appearance of playing a useful part in the community. But he was a little resentful about this particular job. His father had persuaded him into it, even almost arranged it for him. And Simon could not help thinking that he was depositing him there, among the silent dusty shelves, in accord with some image he had of Simon as a destined timorous old maid.

He passed two small girls sitting on the steps of a close, deep in conversation. One had muddy bare feet, from the other's nose hung a stalactite of green snot. They giggled as he went past, talking secretively to one another. "Hey, she fancies you," one of them called after him in a shrill mocking voice, adding in a burst of scornful laughter, "even more than Donny Osmond." Yes, with a face like mine, thought Simon rather wistfully, perhaps the only people that can be relied on to fancy me are the fans of teenage pop idols. Sometimes these days I feel my physical appearance like a prison, in which I did not ask to be isolated.

The other day, on one of his occasional visits to the nearest gay pub, he had not found himself without what could best be called admirers. And for a moment, longing bathing all details in a golden haze, it had been tempting to seize the opportunity. But as he got a little drunk, the memory of the emptiness of his relationships in London had returned like a frost. Instead, he finished the evening in stark practical discussion with a visitor from Edinburgh, who told him about the hesitant efforts under way to get a gay liberation group going there. Why didn't Simon try to do that in Glasgow? he had asked. Simon hedged, loth to admit what he feared was most to the point; that he still allowed a sense of his singleness to persuade him that he was ineffectual.

The man from Edinburgh left Simon with a recent copy of *Come Together*, in which he pointed out an article headed "The Myth of Sexual Attraction". Some of its words still stuck in Simon's mind even now as he walked. "Few people seem to realise that sexual attraction is a hallucination," he had read, "a type of hero/heroine worship that doesn't see people as real people, but projects an ideal image onto them." He could not help wondering to what extent in the past it was just this hallucination which had led him like a will-o'-the-wisp into a pathless tangle. But later in the article was the sentence: "Once this illusion of sexual attraction is nailed, people can stop saying that they 'fancy' X, and they can start summing people up rather in mental and emotional terms – X is interesting or intelligent or gentle or sympathetic or whatever." Fragments of the sentence bobbed to his lips as he turned it over in his mind, like a little song of encouragement sung quietly to himself as he wandered.

He reached the park gates and slowed his step. Late summer sprawled about the park. The foliage hung thick and sleepy. The smell of damp earth lingered in the heavy air. For a moment, the luxuriance of nature was like an affirmation of joy.

Couples strolled past him, whispering in one another's ears. The park seemed to be full only of couples. And all at once, as so often before, he felt ashamed to be found there, wandering in a solitude that he must wear like some medieval punishment mask, condemned for all to see as useless to anybody. He turned and walked up the hill, as if seeking the consolation of a vantage-point, a distant overall view. Pausing for breath halfway up, he caught a glimpse of a couple alone in the midst of the wide sweep of a grassy bank. Or rather, he did not see the couple as such; he saw a man's muscular back in a tight-fitting white shirt, the head bent forward, while a woman's hands clasped the shoulders, slipped and ran down the length of the back, going limp with the feel of it. And Simon was consumed by envy, an envy that was like a pain. He could almost smell the warm moisture of the man's sweat beneath the caressing hands. How long, how long it was since he had felt the warmth and firmness of another's flesh. Envy, envy of them, made him helpless, made him writhe within his clothes as though they were chains. His own flesh rubbing against the stuff of his shirt ached to be touched, to be acknowledged, to be proved real.

Dazed, he wandered on to the top of the hill. Everything was vanishing into the spreading grey stain of the oncoming storm cloud. A huge drop of rain hit him violently on the forehead like an unexpected blow. From every direction couples appeared running for shelter, holding onto one another, shrieking and laughing. The sky went suddenly dark as twilight.

He made his way slowly home through echoing empty streets, heavy rain running from his hair down over his face. It was one of those moments when he felt himself confronted by the glaring oddness of his solitariness, which, resist as he might, it was often hard not to see as irrelevancy. Even as worthlessness.

When he got home, the hall was crowded with bicycles. The air smelt of damp carpet where little pools of dripping rainwater had formed about their wheels. From the living-room came the noise of laughter, and a wavering moan of sound that only after a moment did he recognise as Vanessa's mock operatic contralto. In a rather convincing imitation of Wagner, he could hear her now turning the epic misfortunes of their journey into a spontaneous performance of self-mockery.

Embarrassed at himself, he slunk quietly into his room and shut the door. He took his jacket off and his sodden shoes, and stretched out on the bed, taking his book solicitously in his hands. But he could not concentrate.

The door opened and Vanessa came in, her cheeks still red from exertion. "My goodness, what are you going in here?" she said, standing at the door looking down on him. "Aren't you going to come and join us? We were just having a little opera, you know."

"Well," he said, looking sheepishly about him as if for something he had lost, "I thought nobody would want my miserable bachelor company."

"I certainly would!" said Vanessa, almost sharply. "We're your friends. Don't you think we need and value your company? All kinds of companionship are important, you know."

Vanessa could change a mood with the sudden certainty of music. He swung his legs slowly off the bed. "Alright, I'm coming," he said. "Who's there?"

"Just me and Annie and Philip. Archie's gone to see his other girlfriend."

"His other girlfriend?"

"Och yes, I packed him off there. I wanted to be with my friends."

As he came over and stood beside her, she took his arm gently. "Listen," she said earnestly, "you have things to tell us that no one else has, Simon. And we want to hear them. We need to hear them." She looked him purposefully in the eyes, and ushered him ahead of her into the living-room like a special guest.

Simon found his job in the library tedious. But at least, when there were no superiors around, he could take the opportunity to sit at his desk – and go on reading.

Winter approached, settled in, and ground on. Hogmanay began to draw near. The time of huddling together for strength and warmth, the celebration at once of solidarity and individuality, the great ritual purgation by alcohol and sleeplessness, in millions of lives, all across the sun-forsaken country. One could feel people gathering their pieces together, ready to stand in that dead place of the year, and know that they were going on living.

Philip and Annie left to spend Christmas with Philip's parents in England. They were going to return on the 30th in time to prepare their place for what had become an established party, on what was after all also their wedding anniversary.

Christmas Day arrived inevitably. Simon spent it as always with his family, and the usual bevy of brothers' girlfriends and questions from visiting relatives. This year one of his brothers had chosen Christmas Eve to announce his engagement. The artificiality of the Christmas spirit only made Simon feel all the more alienated. And resentful for having to hide it. At least there was the relief of a gathering at Vanessa's in the evening.

He tried to talk to his mother, but she was absorbed in frantic preparation of the Christmas dinner. He wondered at her dogged excitement. There she was bent red-faced over the stove, hauling out the naked baby-sized bird in its pan of spitting fat, watching three or four pots at the same time, while the family trooped in one after another to whine about just how much longer it was going to be. He felt with consternation as if he was seeing the situation in its reality for the first time.

"Can I do anything to help?" he asked, but the offer was so strange that his mother found it an embarrassment.

Just as the turkey was about to go on to the table, the phone rang. By some chance it was everyone else who had their hands full and his mother who was able to run out and answer it. She came back beaming with a kind of Christmas tearfulness and said to Simon, "There's Philip on the phone for you, love. That was nice of him to ring."

Simon went to the phone, feeling for a moment quite mindlessly touched himself.

"Hallo, Philip! Happy Christmas!" The banality slipped effortlessly from him.

"Happy Christmas, love!" And yet there was something immediately distant and preoccupied about Philip's voice. "How has your Christmas been?"

"Oh – not bad. How's yours?"

"Listen, Simon, we've run into a spot of bother down here. It's turned out that my sister and her husband aren't turning up until the 29th, and then both my parents have gone down with a heavy cold. So quite honestly, one thing and another has completely sabotaged the happy family reunion they were bent on. I know it's going to cause a bit of awkwardness, but we've decided we really ought to stay on down here a bit longer than we planned. Which means that we won't be able to have our party at Hogmanay. People will need to be told, and we thought Vanessa's little party tonight would be a good place. Are you still going?"

"Yes – yes, I'm going, yes – I'll tell people what's happened," said Simon, feeling a sudden unexpected wave of dismal loneliness sweeping him far away.

"Perhaps," said Philip's voice from the lifeless plastic, "you'll feel like holding the party yourself."

He was drifting back to dry land. "Yes, well, that might be the best thing. I'll certainly think about it."

"Well, I'd better ring off now. Your mother said you were just about to eat. Give my love to everyone."

"Yes of course. Give my love to Annie."

"I will. Goodbye, Simon."

"Goodbye Philip, and – thanks for ringing."

Philip hung up. Simon lowered the receiver carefully into place. A sense of responsibility gushed up in him in a warm surge, and he turned and walked back to the dinner, calm and upright, finding himself involuntarily smiling.

His youngest sister had made everyone put on paper hats out of crackers, and she ran to him and put a purple crown on his head. It was too big and slipped down almost over his eyes like a blindfold. At once he was swamped by the excited dinner-table discussion of his brother's forthcoming wedding.

Later, he went to the Kist o' Whistles, where people were meeting before going to Vanessa's. It was a mild moist night, without so much as the hint of a frost, even though it was very still. Almost, Simon thought, serene.

He pushed open the pub door with an unaccustomed purposefulness. Vanessa, ever quick to catch a mood, noticed him at once. There were only a few people drinking. The pub looked alienly empty, like a shopping street on a Sunday, pale in the dingy light whose inadequacy one never otherwise noticed, and with so much unoccupied space one could see how dirty the floor was. The predictable faces were there, though even they looked slightly out of place in the vacancy. There was only one face he did not recognise, some predictably ordinary-looking, eminently heterosexual man who was with Jean's husband Duncan the electrician. Jean taught at Vanessa's school and they seemed to be great friends, though Simon could only explain it as the attraction of opposites. Jean seemed at heart a happy wee housebody, with a look of contented humility and a manner of polite generosity,

It was into Duncan's smart red car that they all piled at closing-time. There was not room for all of them. Vanessa said, "Och, Simon's light enough. He can sit on someone's knee." Everyone else got in, and when Jean said chirpily from inside, "Right Simon, in you get," he found himself sitting on the lap of Duncan's friend.

"Simon, you haven't met Rob, have you?" said Duncan, with a kind of clumsy relish at the seeming incongruity of the situation. Duncan, after all, would scarcely have allowed Simon to sit on his lap.

Simon twisted awkwardly to look at Rob for the first time, having noticed nothing more as he sat down on him than a donkey-jacket. In the dim streetlight filtering through the car window he picked out a round unassuming face of about thirty, modestly shielded by rimless glasses, but with a frame of cheerfully exuberant red curls, leaping over one another like gambolling puppies. It said "Hallo," quietly, but like a phrase of distant music caught on a breeze, with an immediately distinctive and attractive Central Lowlands accent. The face seemed to be trying to retreat behind its hair, as if he wished in providing his lap to be an invisible host.

Simon felt rather embarrassed and apologetic. "Hallo," he said quickly, and looked nervously to the front.

"Are you all settled back there?" called Jean.

"They're fine," said Vanessa. The car started to move.

A voice behind Simon said, "Have you been to the fair in the Kelvin Hall this Christmas, Simon?" Gently, kindly. Almost compassionately.

"No," said Simon turning back, startled yet gently touched at the one time, and feeling that his reply was almost a shortcoming. It was for a moment as though a small child had run up to him in the street and taken his hand and looked up expectantly, and he had looked back bewildered.

"You should go," said Rob softly, invitingly, and Simon saw now in his face a great courageous perseverance; he was in some battle with his shyness and his sense of awkwardness in the situation to be not just humane, but something more, something more active. "There's a kind of magical absorption you can watch on people's faces there, as if it were real magic. A wonder–cure. For a moment a real escape. It's a very reassuring thing, you should go."

"Oh, Duncan, watch that car!" came Jean's shrill voice. "There'll be a lot of drunks on the road tonight."

Simon turned to look, and immediately forgot Duncan's friend. He edged forward and rested an arm against the car door, so that he was just perched on the man's knees, loading him with as little obtrusive weight as possible.

As soon as they got back to Vanessa's place, she took his arm gently, as though something special and delicate, and led him across to the lighted Christmas tree and crouched down with him beside the presents beneath it, so that they seemed sheltered and apart from the others for a moment.

"You're looking very much in control," she said exploratorily, half–compliment and half–question.

Simon found himself telling her the story he had brought with all the ready fluency of a prepared script. She listened attentively, looking away darkly but nodding now and again. When he had finished she said, "Och, you know, it won't be the same without their Hogmanay party." She turned to him quickly and gave him a sharp look, followed instantaneously by a barely perceptible nod. "You're going to hold it yourself," she said in a low voice.

"Yes, I thought that might be a good idea." He was anxious for her approval, and yet already excited in the half–belief he had it.

"Oh yes, yes, I think that would work," she murmured, as if it scarcely needed more than the acknowledgment of the obvious. He felt dismissed with her blessing.

Someone there must have had a fascination with old films because the television had been turned on in the middle of *The African Queen*. Hepburn and Bogart were just making it through the rapids to their mutual surprise.

"I love this film, don't you?" said Vanessa, curling up by Simon.

Some of the others were sitting apart, talking quietly and sporadically. Simon overhead Duncan's friend say, "Yes, I'm going through to Falkirk tomorrow."

Jean said, "Has your wife moved back there now?"

"You know, wee Simon, you shouldn't underestimate the impression you can make on people in your quiet little way," said Vanessa affectionately, filling his glass for him. "I expect you're really quite looking forward to Hogmanay in a way now."

On the small screen Hepburn and Bogart were firmly locked in an embrace of incredible exhilarating elation, while the all-seeing camera moved to a distance, and showed the steamer approaching the unexpected waterfall. Simon and Vanessa stopped talking and watched, waiting for the triumphant end.

During the week he discovered a remarkable new combination of clothes: a purple brightly embroidered Indian tee-shirt that had been Vanessa's Christmas present, with a black cord jerkin which Pansy had given him long ago because she no longer wore it, and some icy blue jeans he had bought in London. He paraded up and down in front of the mirror with a kind of revelatory joy he had forgotten, all those dark turbulent colours and misty colours, the cold shading into tentative warmth, and his hair above it contrasted into veritable spun gold, his eyes darting about underneath. It was a moment like one of those midwinter days that seem suddenly to hint at spring. Someone somewhere was having a party he had heard, to tide everyone over between Christmas and New Year; and when he walked into the pub and caught Vanessa's eye, he knew the clothes were a success.

The party was being held by a painter, a charming and effusive middle-aged habitué of the Kist o' Whistles, in a spacious mansion-flat lined with his soulful wispy drawings of women. When he got there, Simon found he did not know many people other than those he had come with. He hoisted himself onto a table in the crowded kitchen, where he had wandered in search of a corkscrew, and sat patiently waiting for the luminous flickering he felt steadfastly within him to draw some event towards him.

But nothing happened, of course. He just got drunker, and looked increasingly askance at the milling unreachable ebullience that seemed to surround him.

After a while a small dark figure came and sat gnome-like beside him. It greeted him tentatively by name. Turning, he saw it was that friend of Duncan's. He racked his memory for his name, and finally found it lying somewhere, though he did not use it.

"You don't mind me coming to talk to you?" Rob said, diffidently winning. "You look as if you were doggedly waiting for something to happen."

Simon smiled at the pleasant nearness of the observation. "But I've come to feel my place is just watching, really," he said, as a piece of complementary information.

Strangely Rob seemed to spin the thought out, sitting there looking down at his own little legs in heavy boots swinging over the edge of the table. "Watching a party can give one that flattering feeling of being purposefully uninvolved, can't it? Even of feeling that other people are the victims of their wants and fears in a way that for a moment you are not – perhaps. Do you sometimes find it that kind of relief?"

Simon as always was a bit taken aback at being asked about himself. "Well, yes, I suppose so," he hedged, but at once felt guilty for the reflex hedging, which seemed scarcely necessary. "Yes, perhaps it's like all these careful drawings of women around the walls, where you feel that in the act of observing, the painter has been able to set himself free from his relationship with the actual person." His fluency, banal though he at once thought it, surprised him by its sudden ease.

"What do you do, Simon?" asked Rob, with a note of such genuine concerned fascination that it readily transcended the question's ordinariness.

"I've often thought about good answers to that question," replied Simon willingly, smiling and taking a drink. "I've often thought I should say something like 'I get by'. The customary answer is that I'm working at the university library. Last year I was on the dole, and before that I was writing an English literature thesis. Or as one friend of mine, Philip, put it, 'I was selling my acquiescence to the Scottish Education Department.' What do you do?" He found that he looked forward to knowing.

"I'm a carpenter," said Rob smiling widely; an extraordinary smile, Simon noticed, because few faces would dare so confidently to look so absurd, cut in half by this cartoon-like semicircular crack. "But I don't think that says a lot about me either. I suppose I should find a thesis on literature overawing, but you hardly make it seem so." He glanced straight at Simon from under his clown's wig of red curls, at one and the same time like a brief handclasp of grateful respect and an exploratory click of a camera-shutter, quickly submerging his gaze again on his own feet dangling unsupported in mid-air.

"Tell me about your friends Philip and Annie. I've heard a lot of people talking about them." He sounded for a moment like a child asking for a story.

"Oh, well, Philip – I was going to say Philip's a teacher and Annie works for the Corporation, but that isn't a good start," said Simon, realising at once his inability to reply to the question, which posed too complex a problem. "I find it hard to talk about them, in a way, because they've had a great influence on me. You know, I have to admit that I've measured my own achievements against theirs. Especially the

216

achievement of their marriage."

"Do you think that was a bad thing?" The light breeze of his voice, soft and lilting, came again with a tone of sincere and even humble curiosity.

"Well no, in that I think it was a good yardstick," said Simon, finding himself gently stirred into spreading rings of thought, like a pool by a stick twirled contemplatively by one who sat looking for their reflection in the water. "But yes, in that it often makes me feel unrealised. And dependent."

"I know what you mean, but I don't think I could ever want not to feel dependent on other people – and vice versa." He looked up, haunted by uncertainty for just a moment, his face crossed by a spring shower of old age; then he turned and smiled, and everything fell into the simplicity of a child's painting, with bright orange hair and pink cheeks and a crescent beam painted in a determined line.

His words seemed, Simon thought, sensing the unusualness of this easy conversation, like some sort of replying phrase as in a musical dialogue. The soft singing voice might almost have been whispering in his ear. He said, "I've been struggling for ages to convince myself that I should be able to live a fulfilled life completely on my own. It seems a sort of ultimate dream of invulnerable strength. But I know that's not possible. There is no way I can separate myself as I see myself from how others see me. The two are locked in a continual state of interaction. And mutual modification. One could not exist without the other. Even in talking about 'seeing' myself, I suppose I'm admitting that I create my own sense of self by trying to look on, pass judgment on myself, give counsel to myself, like an outsider."

Rob gave a little murmurous shrug of a laugh, speaking with a kind of subdued exhilaration, like an unexpected harmony to Simon's theme. "Yes, our lives are such inextricably relative things, aren't they?"

"Oho, so you're out here where the drinks are, Rob!" Duncan, loud and fresh like a sharp sea wind, broke in upon them, out of nowhere it might have been, and flung a half-derogatory half-puzzled look at the pair of them perched side by side on the table. He called over his shoulder. "Which is your carry-out, Vanessa?" Vanessa followed him in, analysing the kitchen with one quick surveying glance.

"Simon, I must go to the toilet," said Rob rapidly, apologetically, slipping off the table and landing a little awkwardly on the ground, looking across at Simon almost sheepishly, the eyes behind the reflecting surface of the glasses shrinking away with what could even have been regret, struggling unsuccessfully to wave a parting smile.

But Simon nodded and smiled gratefully. It had been a strangely pleasant conversation, he thought, and now he might as well go home anyway. He emptied the last trickle of wine into his glass with a conclusive flourish.

Vanessa came up beside him and looked at him expectantly. "Well, any luck?" she said after a while.

It was several seconds before Simon had any idea what she meant.

"Oh," he said in breathless surprise, pausing, going on clumsily in his shock. "No, no, it's not that." He found the suggestion outrageous.

They ran through the rain, he and Vanessa and some friends of Vanessa's from school, to reach home in time for the first guests. After the pub they had stood talking in the doorway with the barmen, long beyond closing time, and ambled off at last in a jostle, arms linked here and there and endlessly exchanged, through a drizzle brushing and merging with their faces, until it began to rain in earnest. He ran beside Vanessa, ahead of the others, and her heels galloped against the black shining pavements like hooves, and she snorted and laughed, and cried out little encouragements, while he could almost feel the vibrating of her heavy body making the air ripple about her as with tropical heat. The tall staid terraces veered wildly up and down. The others could be heard just a little way behind.

"This is like a horse-chase at the end of a western," said Vanessa, the words jogged out in broken pieces like hiccups.

They reached the house and clattered up the stairs of the close, and Vanessa bent over panting and laughing while he fumbled for the key, and then they tumbled in. Noisily, all heavy steps on the concrete and excited snatches of conversation, the others streamed up behind them. Simon and Vanessa busied themselves setting out the food they had been preparing all afternoon. A few neighbours from elsewhere in the close were the first to wander in. Everyone carried a beaming face, like a placard proclaiming there are no strangers at Hogmanay.

It drew near to midnight, and someone switched off the record-player and switched on the radio, so that they could hear the chimes of Big Ben.

"Simon, open the window for the hooters," cried Jean, glowing above a glass of sherry.

As he jerked the stiff window up as far as it would go, the smell of cold and wet trees gusted into the room like music, and there came simultaneously the first tinny distortion of a chime from the radio, bursting like water flowing after a stoppage into the loud solemn deep climax of the university clock nearby, each note leaping monstrously and unexpectedly out of the night around them and disappearing back into it like a whale suddenly leaping out of the water before a small boat. The reflected light flashed from the liquor in their glasses as their arms reached out all round, chinking once, twice, six or seven times across the room. Belief and hope for some wholly transformed future slipped from them exultantly, as if they were black slaves at a gospel meeting, crying "Happy New Year!" again and again as if for the very first time, while out of the lurid orange glow of the night sky came the ships' sirens, like the wailing of the damned heard distantly by souls rising to the turrets of heaven.

It was all over, but it was all changed. There was Highland music coming from the radio, irrepressible, and Simon watched Jean standing with a half-eaten mince-pie in one hand, her head cocked as though listening for something tiny and far off, saying, "Isn't that an eightsome reel?"

"Come on, we'll make eight," whooped another of Vanessa's teacher friends drunkenly unafraid, pulling a scarcely protesting Jean into the middle of the carpet, and reaching out to grab others by whatever was handy as they tried to slip from her grasp like an armful of struggling cats. But at once and imperceptibly the clumsy dance gathered them into itself, into some timeless momentum of its own, entered into everyone's quickening pulses, faster and warmer, so that when they concertinaed into one another as they tried to count the steps, each seemed to feel nothing but the joy of physical contact. Simon found himself flung out first into the middle, alone, while the circle revolved around him, faster and faster, till it juddered to a stop and throbbed with hands clapping. He faced now Vanessa, now a total stranger, and leapt as if he might at last take off, flinging his hands above his head as if they were long bright banners unfurling in a high clear sky; into which he leant across and carried them up, whirling the weight of one after another easily by the arm, as they wove in the figure-of-eight, which he wanted to prolong exultantly.

People streamed in. The room became rapidly quite crowded.

The record-player was back in use. Drunk, Simon stood leaning against the mantelpiece, looking out over the flux of momentary groupings. It kept changing and regularly flinging out someone towards him, with whom he would talk for a while, with a strangely confident nearness that crept out of his drunkenness and took him by surprise, before he would urge them back into the general ebb and flow of fondnesses that filled the room. After a time he moved out into the middle of the crowd and sat on the floor, as though diving into it and lying at its bottom like a pebble over which it brushed gently and endlessly.

Sitting down there he saw, a little to his surprise, Rob drifting in through the frame of the door, with a few people he had never seen before. Rob was looking around gropingly, uncertainly, apparently for Simon, because when he saw him he came straight towards him. But he had to stop and wait awkwardly on the edge of Simon's territory, as it were, because a couple of Vanessa's friends moved in before him to say goodbye. The two women bent over and kissed him on the cheek and went out. Simon raised his eyes to Rob, in a questioning greeting, and yet thinking that really he was touched to see him.

Rob gestured with his stumpy hands and half-shrugged, as if to say, "I'm here but I don't know what to do about it." Then he let loose his smile, his vast absurd unarguable smile, upon himself and everything about him.

"Happy New Year, Simon!" he said, as if apologising for the words' inadequacy. "Can I – can I kiss you?"

Simon was astonished. Then he laughed.

"Yes," he said.

Rob bent over, looking about clumsily for somewhere to put his hands and not finding anywhere, and sort of nuzzled against Simon's cheek. Then he buckled onto his knees and laughed himself.

Simon wondered why they were laughing. Was it that they had found themselves caught out by some double meaning like the end of a joke? At any rate, it defused the potential tension for a moment, which now after all Simon could feel starting to shimmer from him like waves of mirage-making heat, despite his drunkenness.

"It looks like a good party," said Rob concernedly, out of the calm that lingered in him for a moment after the dying of the laughter.

"Oh I'm not sure, I hope so," said Simon, finding himself involuntarily shrinking, like a sea-anemone at the curious touch of a child looking among rock-pools. How on earth had they ever spoken to one another? The unease was irresistible, it was sawing its way relentlessly through the fences of his drunken self-confidence. "I'll be back in a minute," he said, and stood up, at once breathing deeply as if gasping for fresh air.

Someone came up to him and asked him if he would like to dance. He accepted, and found an immediate and unexpected relief in the simple directness of the language of bodily movement. He danced his tight-rope walker's dance now, his arms stretched tight to steady himself, and yet continually yearning to break into flight, while his feet balanced precariously on a thin line stretching on out of sight above a bottomless blackness. He glanced about the room, and it seemed that figures all about him were lost in dance. In a corner of the room he saw Rob now dancing with one of the women from the group he had come in with, staring apologetically at his gangling hands and earth-bound feet. He looked away again, into the emptiness beneath him, and the rhythm of the music flooded into him like morphia.

When he had to rest, Vanessa came over at once, as if she had been waiting for an opportunity, and dropped a string of encouraging words about him which, though above the noise of the music he could not even hear them clearly, felt like a wreath of flowers about his neck. A great intoxicated surge of joy in her shone from him and mingled momentarily with her responding gleam. Then she went away again, and he leant back against the wall alone.

And Rob was there again in front of him, his hands seeming to hang embarrassingly from him, groping the empty air as he spoke, like the hands of a baby reaching up out of an all-embracing nightdress. "Simon, can I dance with you?" His voice handled the preposterous risks it persisted in confronting with such a light delicacy, the words tiptoeing out of his mouth.

Simon heard himself saying, "Of course."

His thin arms hovered before Rob, like a butterfly hesitating to settle in the sunlight, his head ducking, his feet bobbing back and forth. Rob reared and swayed slowly, as though made himself to feel a mere larva, watching Simon's flickering hands.

"I'm fascinated by the way people look at you," he said earnestly, "as if they needed to keep check of something."

"I never knew that," said Simon, feeling he was offered not flattery but a revelation, to make use of as he wished.

"You dance with such an amazing combination of movements: you like it."

"Yes, that's true, I do. I find a rare certainty in it."

The music paused to draw breath between tracks, and they stood still opposite each other, like feathers held stationary for a moment in breathless air. One of the group that Rob had arrived with came up to him and silently offered him a joint, retreating at once as if he felt in alien territory. Rob took the joint distractedly and drew on it, pulling it slowly from his lips and staring at the smoke curling from the bulky paper tube.

"It's noisy in here," he said. "Isn't there somewhere we can go and talk?"

The smoke drifting between them could have been a thick fog, where only one step ahead could be seen, while all beyond that might have shown the aim of the journey was muffled from view. Simon took a tiny step forward in the small circle of clarity. "There's my room," he said.

As they walked towards the door, Rob looked around for someone to return the joint to, but could not see anyone. They took it with them.

They sat down at opposite ends of the bed, turned at once into stone by silence. For a moment, Rob covered his face with his hands. Then he surfaced, shrugging, trying to smile, and held out the joint to Simon. "Here," he said, "have some of this anyway."

Simon was gazing with a kind of helpless wonderment into his own perplexity. The world seemed suddenly quite without points of reference. He reached for the joint sheepishly, like a child taking a sweet from a relative they are unsure of.

"It's your vulnerability as much as anything that makes me feel close to you," Rob commented softly into himself, so that Simon felt as though he were an eavesdropper.

He put the unaccustomed joint against his lips and sucked on it clumsily. Everything slowed up around him, like an express train pulling into a station. He handed the joint back to Rob across a distance which seemed suddenly nearer, and yet which took ages for his hand to journey across.

Rob clasped the joint to his mouth, screwing up his face around it, and then subsided very slowly back against the wall. He said, "I feel a great closeness to you, but I don't know how properly to express it. You seem – elusive."

Mists encircled Simon, shrouding all before him in a menacing indefinability. Even his words loomed out of a frightening indistinctness, known only at the moment of their breaking the barrier of utterance. "I know, but at least usually there are some certainties – this will be a casual friend, this could be a good friend, this could be . . . We usually know which . . ."

The noise of the insistent dance music, the laughter of the Hogmanay party in the next room, hung in the background of his consciousness as if it were a thousand miles away, as if it were taking place among total strangers. He said, awkward, slurred, "The grass doesn't really help." He turned and peered at Rob, struggling to make him out.

Rob raised both hands, palm open, pasty clumsily pathetic creatures, and lowered them again, the fingers wilting in helplessness. Simon watched as his ever resilient mop of red curls flopped forward over his chest. Then with a sigh he rose smiling, like some ungainly sea-animal breaking the water near a boat in friendliness, and leant slowly over towards Simon, emerging out of the misty flux into emotional focus, even as the pink face coming closer turned into a shapeless blur. Between them both for a moment in their prenatal blindness there was only touch, the solid reliability of touch, encircled beyond by a great sheltering protectiveness, the arms that lay knotted before the walls of one another's backs.

Simon opened his eyes and felt alarmed. It was as though he had woken in some strange place, some far alien country, which he could not yet recognise. He was aware of himself smiling, as if it were some muscular action out of his control, and then he felt some part of his own body moving away from him, and realised that it was Rob drawing away his arms.

Rob looked helpless, clumsy, like a baby that has just somehow dropped an object from its pram. With a laugh that was like a sob, he said, "I don't even know how to make love to you."

Simon said, "I don't know how to be made love to." He sat still, alone, cold as a distant mountain, and the mist rolled down over him, making him feel mysterious, indiscernible. He wanted to emerge from it, but he was inanimate, merely waiting to be discovered once again. Rob was a stranded climber, looking down at his untidy clumps of fingers, knowing no handhold, no route.

Then Rob said, "Do you ever feel the joy with a man that you seem to feel among women?"

Simon felt seen, in sharp detail, watched. He was real. He said with a quickened self-knowledge, "Joy? No."

He looked at Rob, his eyes and hands reached out, yearning to confirm his actuality. Rob opened his arms and took him, inelegantly, as if his arms were too small for the embrace, as if he were a child left to mother a younger child. Together they overbalanced awkwardly onto the pillow.

And all at once Simon felt a great wave of tiredness come in and sweep him out towards unconsciousness, struggle against it as he might.

He roused and felt Rob's hands trickling through his hair. It was as though compassion ruffled him like a wind.

"You have hair like no hair," Rob said, softly and uniquely.

Simon ached suddenly with a sweet pity, for that vulnerable absurd face like a balloon on a string above him. He laid his hands on the urchin curls, but they would not let him in; no matter where he ran to, they would not yield.

He said, "You have hair like Harpo Marx."

Rob said, "Everyone says that."

And Simon was asleep. Out of nothingness he woke with a start, feeling that something was lost, forgotten, so that he wanted to leap up and search. But sleep lay on him like a great stone on his chest; all he could do was turn his head. It was there beside him, he could hear him breathing, the sound of life rising and falling, like expectation blending inevitably into resignation. Rob's eyes were closed and his face was turned into the shadows of the pillow, so that nothing could be made of it. He wanted to touch it, lightly and tenderly, but he was afraid; and sleep had hold of him firmly, like a father with a protesting child, and was dragging him masterfully away, just as Moses felt his eyes dimming as he sank down in sight of the promised land.

CHAPTER EIGHTEEN

He was blundering through sleep, staggering out now and again into a momentary clearing of consciousness, then swerving back into the tangled darkness, where fear and grief pounced out at him, caught at him even as he burst again into wakefulness. There was a tiny square of grey light a little way before him, which only after a while he realised was the curtained window, and beside him a warmth, and a smell of sour drink. He rolled over and saw Rob's eyes, naked and defenceless without their glasses, waiting for him under the shelter of red hair, guilty and uncertain.

"Hallo," Rob whispered almost inaudibly, as if he were reluctant to admit that he was there.

But he was. His actuality overwhelmed Simon, he dared not touch it, dared not confirm to himself what had happened. His tongue hung uselessly at the bottom of his mouth, dry and fishy.

"I'm hung-over," said Rob. "I think I'll lie here for a while." He turned over quickly, bringing his knees up, pulling the blanket over his ears, trying to disappear.

"I'll get up," said Simon, sitting up and pulling away, feeling suddenly convinced of the need to flee. "Shall I bring you some coffee?"

Rob's voice bobbed up, grateful. "Yes, yes, please."

Simon extricated himself carefully and with difficulty, making sure not to touch Rob, and stood up with relief. Both of them had fallen asleep with their clothes on. For the moment he could forget what they had actually done. After all, it was nothing. He walked to the door, breathing freely.

They were locked in. There was no door-handle. It had worked very loose recently, and must have fallen off on the other side when he threw it shut behind them the previous night. He pushed at it with a shrug, as one might wave to someone already out of sight. He stood still, cold in the unheated room, feeling gooseflesh rise up his legs.

He went back towards the bed fearfully, like a naughty child. He said, "We're locked in. The door-handle's fallen off."

There was a silence. There came a little murmur from under the covers. "What?"

"The door-handle, it's fallen off. It was loose."

"Oh."

He began to shiver. "I suppose we should find this funny."

Slowly the bundle under the blanket bunched itself up, then Rob's legs swung out, still in their jeans, and his tousled head reared up and rested for a moment on his hands, hidden from Simon, looking down at the floor. Then he fumbled for his glasses, put them on, and stood up.

Their eyes met, both stranded, both crying out. For a moment they stood, looking at one another, and acknowledged their relationship.

"Well," said Rob, shuffling over to the door. "Is there a knife or something like that lying around?"

Simon wondered if he would have thought of that for himself. He looked around the room. On the table was a small screwdriver he had borrowed from Vanessa. His clock had stopped a day or so before, and he had tried unsuccessfully to repair it.

"Will this screwdriver do?" he said doubtfully, holding it out.

"It should," said Rob. He took it from Simon and opened the door easily. Simon smiled, but Rob's face was blankly pensive. He went through the door ahead of Simon, not looking back. Simon crept after nervously.

The room next door was a scene of desolation. Little heaps of empty cans and bottles and crushed paper cups were strewn like rocks from one corner to the other. Cigarette ends with long tottering growths of ash were stacked along the mantelpiece, while others were trodden higgledy-piggledy into the carpet. A chair had been overturned and lay like the carcass of some drought-stricken animal in a desert. The air stank with the putrefaction of stale beer and smoke, some of which still hung motionlessly in the room like a poisonous exhalation. Picking his way across the floor to the kitchen as though across a battlefield, Simon found that someone had vomited some flecked orange substance into the sink.

Rob stood in the middle of the room, at a distance from Simon. "Let's go for a walk and get some air," he said, twisting his head restlessly within his collar, like the gesture of a caged animal too demoralised to pace.

"Alright," said Simon, gingerly running water into the kettle above the stinking sink. "That's a good idea." But what was more, he thought, it was just what he would have wanted to do had he been on his own.

He switched the kettle on and put coffee in the pot. He came back into the room and stood looking reluctantly at the scattered jigsaw of litter. He wanted to speak but did not know what he wanted to say.

"Parties do make a mess," observed Rob, but with a note of gentle rallying consolation quite dominating the flatness of the words, like a hand reached out in support.

"I'll clean it up later," said Simon, defensively despite himself, bending down and picking at a pile of rubbish, dropping a few cans into a convenient empty brown paper-bag.

"Leave it just now. Untidiness doesn't worry me," said Rob.

Simon shrugged and padded back into the kitchen, made coffee and brought it through. They drank it in silence, brooded over by the stench of the dead party.

"Shall we go for a walk now?" said Simon anxiously.

It was mild and sepia outside, and a fine drizzle still softly dabbed their faces, touching their cheeks quickly and lightly. The air smelt heavy with moisture, and the naked spindly branches of the trees glistened with a thin patina of dew, while above the grass there hung a soft haze. They walked slowly downhill towards the river and the park.

"I don't know what to make of last night," said Rob suddenly, his head buried in the collar of his donkey jacket.

Simon fumbled for words. He felt like some creature swept in on some great tide of emotion that had vanished overnight, now gasping for air among rock-pools fast drying out. "I don't know what I expect of it myself," he said.

"I felt close to you. I wanted to be close to you. That's all. But it seemed as if the only way you would allow anyone to get close to you was by making love to you." There was for a moment a note of resentment.

Simon thought, More and more I knew what I wanted of you, if not what now to expect: because you, in your form, are so unexpected. He said, "I don't want you to feel any obligation." The moment he said it, he realised it was a lie, and it sounded it: and yet it was something he would have liked to be true, the expression of an unreal ideal, addressed perhaps to an unreal ideal.

Rob stopped for a moment, and kicked impatiently at a half-empty beer-can left standing forlornly by the railings.

"Let's not pick at it," he said, looking down. "At any rate, I don't regret what happened." He raised his head. Simon waited tensely for him to smile. And he did at last, all over the place.

They sauntered on aimlessly for a while; it might have been spring instead of midwinter from their gait.

"Are you hung-over?" Rob asked simply, but as if he demanded a complex answer.

Again Simon felt a confident openness begin to rouse in him. "A little, I suppose. But it doesn't hurt. I think I enjoy the shocked reflectiveness almost as much as the abandoned honesty of the night before."

"Why do you like getting drunk?" And so it began again, the near probing, the stirring in the stranded little pool that awakened the secret little life there, bringing it scuttling out of the shadows. He felt Rob bent close over him, he felt Rob glimpsing his patchy reflection in him.

But why do I not reach out for him then? he thought.

They came to the bridge, and stood looking at the trees stretching their branches down towards the water in remote longing, hopelessly separated, while the river rushed by beneath, full and muddy, not even granting them a picture of their frozen tantalisation.

"Let's go and look at the weir," said Rob, so close beside him, so very close.

A bond is there, thought Simon; and yet sexual attraction has nothing to do with it, on either side. He is not gay; he looks, objectively, almost absurd. And yet for a moment it feels again and again as if everything is falling into place.

They walked together, talking as they went, the words flowing as if from a source of years. They stopped and leant against the railings, surrounded by bare weeping willows like fountains carved out of wood, gazing into the weir. Young and flashing, the water leapt tirelessly into the swirl beneath, and surged on trustingly towards the Clyde and out to sea.

Simon said, "I know that I want, but for all my searching, I don't know what I want."

"Is a sexual relationship very important to you?" Rob was fearless, watching the moving water.

"Yes, but I feel as if I haven't even glimpsed what a sexual relationship is. In spite of myself, I keep thinking it should appear ready-made, that that's the real kind. I suppose, even after everything I've been through, I'm still waiting for all my problems to be solved by walking off happily ever after into the sunset with someone."

"But it doesn't work out like that?" There was a trace of a bitter laugh in Rob's concerned softness.

"No. Every time I think I'm getting somewhere, I find it wasn't what I wanted after all."

"It's hard," said Rob, gentle to himself and Simon alike. "We're so misled and mystified. So many things they told us to expect that aren't realisable! So many pitfalls on the way they never warned us about! Sometimes I think in the end the only thing to do is accept that life is fickle and tantalising."

"Perhaps you're right," said Simon unconvinced, at once unable to believe that the fondness he felt could be either treacherous or unsatisfying. Besides, he realised, there was something in the words that struck like an assertion of chaos.

"Shall we go to the top of the hill, and see what we can see?" said Rob.

They crossed the avenue and left the river and began to climb. Towards the top the paths grew steep, and their panted breath steamed past them like a layer of cloud. At last they came out from the tangled trees onto a flat summit, where there stood a statue of a triumphant figure astride a horse.

227

The view stretched out before them in layers of daguerrotype browns, each more faded than the last. Beneath them, the park fell away to the khaki river, cobwebbed with dead woodlands, enclosed by the sooty Gothic melodrama of the University and the Art Gallery. Beyond that lay the docks, where the ugly metal trees of cranes stood poised in tiny silhouette against the pallid Clyde. Further out sprawled suburbs and housing schemes in a great circle, studded with high-rise flats that looked from this distance like small white tombstones, all fixed still in a relentless clarity. Beyond, Simon knew, seal-like hills slid into the widening firth and the open sea, while to the north great volcanic shoulders embraced the city, and far, far away, peeping above them, dreamed the snow-covered peak of Ben Lomond. But all that was invisible, lost in a dim colourless remoteness.

Rob came back to the flat to pick up his scarf. As they marched into the front-room, steeled for the smell and filth, they found it clean and tidy about them, with the strange peace of a reaped field about it, in the midst of which stood Vanessa, leaning on the vacuum-cleaner, eyes turned intently to greet them. She must have let herself in by the key under the mat.

"Were you out all this time?" she said with surprise and half-laughter.

"Yes," said Simon, not understanding, feeling ashamed. "We went out for a walk. But you shouldn't have cleared up."

"Oh well, it didn't take long," she said, giving her head a purposeful toss, "and besides, I did my bit to make the mess. But"– her tone changed to one of exaggerated reproach –"here's me tiptoeing round and sliding cans into bags ever so carefully because I thought you two were asleep, and I didn't want to wake you."

Simon felt awkward, even guilty. "No, we were out," he said flatly. "Thanks for doing it."

"Well, it wouldn't have been very welcoming for you both to get up to that. Was it?" she said at Rob, sweeping him into the wide embrace of her smile. She unplugged the vacuum-cleaner, and began to coil the flex with self-absorbed efficiency.

"You were certainly very quick, Vanessa," said Rob amicably, looking a little lost.

"Well, I'll leave you to do the mopping-up campaign," she said, bustling past them, eyes blessing them with a quiet glow. "It's time I had my breakfast. I'll see you later on," And she was out of the door.

"Yes, see you later on," Simon called after her, after a distracted moment. He looked around the tidy room rather helplessly, as if searching for something to do. He saw Rob's red scarf dangling very obviously over the window-sill. He said, "Well there's your scarf," and walked over, picked it up and handed it to Rob. Then he looked at the floor, into the carpet, till he noticed that the cigarette butts had gone. He said, "Well, shall I see you again?"

"Soon."

"Soon?"

He had transformed them both through some magic of his own to creatures of glass; the slightest rough touch would shatter both of them in fragments. And all at once the world outside, the very room around them, laid siege to them. It was hostile, desperate. This incredible shimmering fragility that they were could never survive it. The words came slowly, cautiously. "It seemed as if Vanessa had decided we had slept together."

"I'm sure she had." Rob's words broke like the gush of a sob, and he stifled them quickly. Behind his glasses his eyes drifted vulnerably on a flood of fear, as much Simon's fear as his own. "Listen, Simon," he went on hesitantly, "I shall be out of Glasgow for a few days. You know I've only just moved back up? I've been in London for three years. I went there to work after my marriage broke down. I'm going through tomorrow to see my son – it's his birthday, so soon after Christmas, poor wee boy – he'll be five – and I'm taking him on holiday to London for a few days. I don't see him much. My wife took him to live with her and her family after – after the break-up. I'm sorry, I suppose I should have told you things like this before."

"It doesn't matter," said Simon, looking down, only half listening.

"Anyway, I'll be back in a few days, and surely, yes, you must come and visit. I'll give you the address. Do you have some paper?" He raised an awkward hand and pulled his glasses from his nose, as if they were a great weight, and rubbed his brow like a tormented dog scratching against a wall.

Simon handed him a pen and a sheet of notepaper as if they were a present. Rob's big pink fingers scrambled down and clutched the pen, revealing naked little eyes half-shut in perplexity. He pushed his glasses back on purposefully, and wrote in big careful letters. Keeping his eyes on the paper, he handed it back to Simon, and slung the useless yards of his glowing red scarf determinedly over the shoulder of his jacket.

"You'll be off now?" said Simon softly, not moving, wondering whether they could touch one another now without breaking.

"Yes, I'll see you soon, Simon," said Rob, with a hoarse jauntiness. He suddenly looked up, pulled his hands from his pockets like tools, and grinning tentatively, he grabbed Simon like an awkward parcel and gave him a quick hug. Simon received it rather passively; he had not been expecting it: but then, a little to his surprise, he found himself stroking the warm donkey-jacketed back that lay against his shoulder almost consolingly.

They drew apart sharply, and both walked at once to the door without speaking. Simon swung the door open. "Goodbye, Rob," he whispered. Rob gestured with his eyes, hands in pockets. Simon shut the door quickly, and walked back to his room, yet he could hear the footsteps dying away down the stairs of the close.

He sat down, and gazed out of the window at the sky. After a moment he began to feel an unaccustomed surging calm within him. He seemed to be sailing the rain-clouds that were rolling past. Between them a guessed-at sun had begun to slip pale hints of brightness. Perhaps tomorrow it would be clear.

Time passed slowly. He decided to write Rob a note that would be waiting for him when he got back from London.

In the meantime, Philip and Annie returned. He wanted to discuss Rob with them, but they seemed preoccupied with secretive problems of their own, and in any case, it was hard to make clear Rob's significance. He went back to work, but his mind was not on what he was doing and he kept making silly mistakes. Day after day dragged by.

At last a letter came. But it was only the formal invitation to the wedding of his younger brother, the favoured family topic at Christmas, which he had all but forgotten about. He wished it were possible to avoid it. The uneasy alienation of a wedding was the last thing he wanted at the moment.

In spite of himself he felt his fears hovering over the few hours with Rob like vultures.

And then there came a postcard from Rob, brief and opaque, but suggesting a day they might meet. It was the day of his brother's wedding. The fact that it should interfere with his meeting Rob gave the occasion an added poignancy. It was an untimely reminder of the insistence of the straight world – the world from which Rob himself came. Simon wrote back suggesting another time.

And to his surprise and excitement, agreement came by return of post.

Now, as he reached the landing and rang Rob's bell, he noticed that his hand was shaking. In the silence and stillness that followed, he felt how cold his feet were.

With a quickening of the pulse, he saw Rob indistinctly through the red glass panels in the door; and then he was there, large in the doorway with the light behind him, so that his face could not be seen, only a rather shapeless grey pullover, and the blurred edge of his curls catching the light.

"Hallo, come in," he said, apparently warmly, with all his soothing lilt, standing aside and gesturing inwards with spraddled fingers, so that now a little weak electric light partially showed his smile. "It's good to see you."

"Thanks," said Simon, tongue-tied, realising only now that he was quite unprepared for anything. He stepped in gingerly. Rob shut the door behind him.

"Did you have any trouble getting here?" he said solicitously.

"No, no, I got a bus." There was a kind of temporising relief in such ordinary problems.

Rob brushed past, in the shadows like some faceless cuddly toy in his woolly jumper and curls, and pushed a door open. "Here we are," he said. Simon followed tentatively, and stopped just inside the doorway.

The room was bleak, four white walls in the featureless glare of a bare bulb, not quite bright enough for comfort. In one corner there was a table, from which the varnish was flaking, piled haphazardly with books, many with broken spines; and near it were two battered armchairs, and a very old single-bar electric heater, louring aggressively but ineffectively into the cold. There was an ungainly glass-fronted cabinet which seemed empty, but boxes and books and tools and even a guitar with broken strings lay scattered all over the floor. Rob was pushing some of them aside with his foot in order to clear a space round the two chairs.

"I'm afraid everything's still rather in a state of flux," he said. "Are you cold?"

"Yes, I am rather."

"Well, come and sit over the heater then. It doesn't penetrate very far. I'm sorry the chairs aren't very comfortable." He peered out pathetically from behind his glasses.

Simon picked his way through the bric-à-brac and perched on the chair nearest the heater. The bar gave out a dry irritating heat in a narrow ray, surrounded on either side by a quite unmitigated cold. He reached his hands towards it. The tips of his fingers were dead and yellow.

"You said you had to go to a wedding?" said Rob, sitting on the edge of the other chair, playing nervously with a tin whistle that was lying on the arm.

"That's right. One of my brothers."

"And how was that?"

"Not too good. I felt like an irritant substance in some communal cocoon. Rob, it's nice – it's nice to see you." He paused for a moment and bit his lip: his dead fingers were shooting with pain as the blood came back into them.

"Tell me about your brother." Rob settled back in his chair, like a child for a new story.

"He frightens me, as much as anything because I find him a sort of distorting mirror." He rubbed his still throbbing fingers. "He rushed to get married and set up his own safe cosy little monogamous world almost as soon as he left school. But it seems to me it's going to be so unsafe and so uncomfortable, not a world but a prison. And above all so inflexible: it makes me think of the fable of the oak and the reed. And yet I recognise only too well the fear and the longing that drove him to behave as he has; because I know it, in its own way, in myself. After all, who would choose to be a fragile reed exposed to the elements?"

Rob was gazing at him with a kind of awed fascination, as at logs being consumed in a fire.

"Yes, the marriage model is so attractive," he said, pulling a face, spitting out an unwelcome truism. "And yet recently I feel I've really found it fading in myself." There was a childish mixture of subdued exitement and shy humility in the way in which he spoke of himself. "I no longer feel, as I did once, that it's the only way to fulfil oneself."

Now that he had adjusted to the temperature Simon was beginning to feel cold again. He said, distractedly despite an effort at concentration, "I expect you're right. I keep trying to convince myself of the same thing. In the abstract."

"It seems to me important to have a network of relationships that balance out," said Rob, furrowing his brow, "one compensating what the other is lacking in, and so on. The answering of our wants and hopes turns out to be a very piecemeal thing."

A strange sense of unreality was threatening Simon, as though he were observing his own present as already finished history. He found himself gazing at the tin whistle, aware of the silence around them. He hunted about for something to say, a sign of animation. "Can you play the tin whistle?" he asked. "Oh, not very well," said Rob, a little embarrassed, but very earnest. "I love folk-songs. I can pick out a few tunes. There's nothing piecemeal about folk-songs, is there?" His face was cracked by a broad smile, while behind his glasses his eyes looked wistfully away. He lifted the tin whistle and toyed with it for a moment as if it was something incomprehensible, then he put it to his mouth and closed his eyes. A thin hollow aching sound drifted out like curls of smoke, so pathetic and yet resilient in its defiance of silence despite its lone tininess. The melody of *My Young Love Said To Me* formed itself like a hallucination. For a moment the room about Simon seemed filled with something he had forgotten.

The music stopped. Rob looked down with a kind of sweet troubledness, and recited quietly, like a distant mournful echo of the music:

> Last night she came to me, my dead love came in,
> And her feet they moved so softly that she made no din,
> She came up to my bed, and this she did say,
> 'It will not be long, love, till our wedding-day.'

He looked up questioningly.

"Yes, I know it, it's beautiful," Simon heard himself say. He felt as though some vast wave that had nearly drowned him had now flung him down on a strange shore, dazed and alone.

Rob's voice came near to him, friendly, resourceful. "Would you like a drink? There's a pub on the corner."

Simon smiled and stretched himself. "That's a good idea," he said, eagerly pitching himself up off the chair.

Rob put on his snug donkey-jacket and Simon followed him slowly down the stairs. The air outside smelt cold.

"A broken pattern improves an evening, do you think?" Rob said, their footsteps ringing off the empty frosted pavement.

"It makes it seem longer," replied Simon musingly, turning up his collar and burrowing his hands in pockets. "Actually, I'm always yearning for something continuous myself."

"I've come to feel reconciled to life as something discontinuous," said Rob calmly, soothingly, "and something constantly evolving. I thought to myself the other day that my attitude to life at the moment was a bit like the testing of the maiden in the ballad of Tam Lin. I hold on to it with a patient loving embrace even though it turns continually in my grasp into an adder or a bear or a red-hot ingot."

"And so," cut in Simon lightly, feeling a fascinated but wry smile on his lips, "at last should we expect it to turn into a handsome knight with gouden hair and twa grey een?"

"Ah, maybe that's the difference between ballads and real life," Rob answered softly, with a low acknowledging laugh, distant, like music overheard.

Inside the pub it was bright and warm, but too noisy. Customers were singing over a microphone to a piano, imitating sentimental singers of the fifties. The beer made Simon feel relaxed and mindlessly close to Rob: and yet it was impossible to carry on a conversation. Occasionally one would make the effort to shout something in the other's ear, but even so it was hard to hear above the crooning. Yet Simon was anxious to stay on, because he found that here he could feel assured that Rob was with him, without having to put it to the test in words. Besides, perhaps if he got drunk, it would bring some sort of dulling of the consciousness.

It brought nothing of the kind, of course; rather some sort of allergic sensitivity of the consciousness, such that the merest word from Rob rasped against Simon's thoughts and feelings, leaving a lingering in-flammation. Far from more confident, he felt more restlessly diffident. He hovered, standing with his coat on, inside the four blank walls of Rob's room to which they had returned, where now the light seemed to give out only some thick glowing vapour. He said, flexing his numb toes within his boots and stroking the back of the chair, not so much nervously as appropriatingly, "What time is it?"

Rob had sat down as soon as he got in, sprawling loosely and as relaxedly as possible on the awkward chair, following Simon with his half-timid, half-courageous eyes. He said hesitantly, "About half past ten, I think. But if you're worrying about buses, why don't you stay here?" His gaze had dropped to his feet, and his voice dwindled.

"Yes, I'll stay then," murmured Simon, but for a moment made no move to sit down, only clutched the chair-back like a guard-rail, feeling that he had got what he wanted, and at the same time knowing he had not. At last he let his hand fall free with a gesture to himself of resignation, took off his coat, and sat himself stiffly on the chair as though in a waiting-room.

"I was going to say," said Rob, drawing in breath for courage, "there's only one bed. But I can always sleep in here on the floor."

These last words flashed like a knife, drawn and waiting, in one of the lamplight pools of clarity that illuminated Simon's drunkenness. He glanced up, suspiciously, like an animal that has caught an ominous word in a conversation. "Oh, I don't mind where I sleep," he said irrelevantly, finding himself trying to sound polite even in this inappropriate situation.

But Rob was not so easily fooled. He too was sharpened by drunkenness, and seemed to have found in it a momentum of courage which he would not now let slip. His elbow was resting on the chair-arm and he was resting his head on his hand, furrowing his brow above his sheltering glasses. He said, "The one thing that I felt uneasy about at the New Year, and that I've worried about since I got your letter, was that it was obviously so important to you that our relationship be a sexual one. But I know that I can't really fulfil that aspect of it. No, it's not 'not really', it's not at all."

This is it, thought Simon: the knife struck him, as it did so becoming some massively strong lion out of a childhood nightmare, which pinned him helplessly to the ground with its red-hot claws. "Oh well, that's alright, it's not everything," he said, wondering which of them he was really telling lies for.

He saw Rob beam at him in gratitude, his curls like rays drawn round his shining face, but at once the beam faltered, dwindled, as he saw the deep panic behind Simon's fending words. He stumbled into speech, like one starting to run in alarm. "Simon, your gentleness, your thoughtfulness, your refusal to be pushy, they're important things to me, very important. They make me feel very fond. But sex – I just can't imagine it. I suppose sometimes it crosses one's mind, say, that it must be nice to suck a big juicy cock, but – it's an idea quite isolated from anything real. There are no – passions involved." His chin rested still on the cup of his hand, while his fingers were spread out before his face, their tips against his forehead, his eyes peeping through their fretwork like a colonial through a wattle fence that protects him from some dark hostile incomprehensible natives. "I don't know why. But it's just not something I crave or need. Just not something I shape my life around."

Simon wanted to throw the crushing weight of darkness off him. He struggled to get up, searching for a helping hand among Rob's muttered words. He said fumblingly, "I don't really know what I want in terms of sexual activity myself. What I feel, I suppose, is only a kind of abstract craving, that longs to become palpable – somehow."

"We all want to cuddle and be cuddled," said Rob gently, his chubby hand lowered and rubbing his chin beneath a tentatively resurgent hint of a smile in spite of still troubled eyes.

"Yes, I suppose so," Simon acknowledged. He shivered, feeling a draught.

"My own sexual relationships these days are very partial, very piecemeal," said Rob, the quiet confessional tone verging momentarily on the pedagogic, and then flowing with the ease of tears or blood. "There was this woman I knew in London, she taught philosophy at a polytech, I was doing some work on her house for her, and I found her very beautiful, and we were very close. But she wouldn't have a sexual relationship with me – or rather, that's not true at all, we had a sexual relationship, but it wasn't like they're meant to be. We were physically affectionate, and yet I suppose I wanted her at first to be physically passionate. But now I don't regret or resent anything. And I found that it answered more closely to many of my longings and expectations as it was."

"Yes," said Simon, politely demonstrating that he had been listening. And certainly he had heard Rob, but the words had vanished on contact, like snowflakes that are not settling.

Silence embraced them. Rob sat with his hands clasped between his knees, gazing into the floor. Simon was saying to himself, We can still be friends after all, that's what matters. And yet the fact was he felt alone, utterly alone; cut loose from his own lifeline and falling endlessly through his own inner space, the whole world slipping irreparably away into unimaginable distance.

Rob shifted uneasily on his chair, trying to draw attention, and yet frightened to intrude. "Actually," he said quietly, "I have to get up early and go to work tomorrow. I should really go to bed now." And yet he made no move, such stillness still hung over them.

For a moment Simon dreamily wondered whether, if he went to speak, any sound would emerge from the remote place he was in. He opened his mouth soundlessly for a while, and said at last, slowly, "That's alright. I'm quite tired."

Rob stood, unsteadily at first, and passed a hand across his forehead. He came and stood by Simon's chair, slung between his open feet like an unsure rope-bridge. "Come on," he said hoarsely, the voice tremulous with fragility. "You'll have to excuse the bedroom. It's even more untidy than here."

Simon closed his hands on the edge of the chair, pushed down, and found himself rising. Smiling, he said, "Even more untidy?"

Rob went ahead, across the hall where the floorboards creaked, and merged into the unlighted other room. As Simon followed him, a pale bulb came on, throwing a pool of half-light on the floor beneath, spreading a grey indistinctness all around. The room was filled with a raw cold. The floor was piled with clutter, including a dismantled bicycle. There was a double bed, with only one pillow.

"I feel very secure in this lack of apparent order," said Rob, looking momentarily like just another part of the clutter beside the bed. "I do actually know where everything is, or at least might be." He smiled helplessly, and bent over to try and unravel the tangle of sheets and blankets.

"I used to be very untidy when I was a child," said Simon, standing in a tiny space of cleared carpet in the middle of the room, waiting for directions on their sleeping arrangements. "I suppose I remember that untidiness with a kind of nostalgia. Now I like everything to seem tidy, even though there are always little forgotton untidy piles in corners or untidy cupboards out of sight." The cold made his jaw muscles tense, making his words flat and jerky.

"There," said Rob, panting, giving the top blanket a pointless brush of the hand, "that's as fit for sleeping in as it will ever be."

Simon nodded, rooted to the spot.

Rob said awkwardly, "Well, I have to pee. I'll – I'll leave you to it." And he slipped past Simon, looking away.

Simon went straight to the bed, and undressed in a rush, shivering violently. He jumped between the ice-cold sheets, which closed on him like metal, and pulled the blankets around his shoulders. Their hairy edges irritated his neck. The bed seemed vast about him; he was a tiny dot of anxiety curled up alone in its frozen midst.

Rob appeared, hovering in the doorway, looking embarrassed and clumsy. "I'll put out the light for you, shall I?" he said, after a moment.

Darkness fell on Simon, stranding him even further. There was silence. Then in his blindness he heard Rob padding lumpishly across to the bed, then pulling off his clothes quickly, gasping with the cold. In the yellowish glimmer from the window that he could now just make out, he saw his peelywally chest, with a light growth of red hairs, and one pudgy shoulder lurch towards him. The bed creaked and tilted beneath his weight, there was a smell of sweat, and then a cold smooth hand scrambled gracelessly round his back and came to rest leaning awkwardly over his shoulder. Simon turned, his forgotten body was already a stone betrayed to the wintry wastes of an empty bed.

"I'm sorry," whispered Rob, invisibly, letting his cold hand scrabble down Simon's upper arm and pulling the unmalleable body to him, bravely, compassionately. "It's the best I can offer."

"That's alright," Simon whispered back. Hesitantly he reached out his arm around Rob. A stiff puppet-like embrace; it seemed to bear no relation to his words or his thoughts. Yet slowly the warmth and the sweet smell of skin began to soothe him, like a drug closing off anxiety.

Silence, so profound he could hear the occasional drone of a car passing purposefully in the distance. They lay immobile. Simon's position was uncomfortable, and both arms began to hurt. Then he was in a half-sleep, his mind running frantically, like a stationary engine revving: not conscious, yet not dreaming; an incessant purring of disconnected unease that tightened and bounced him back like a rope the moment he seemed to be moving into actual unconsciousness. Though that came at last.

At least, briefly. His eyes came open and he saw a steely grey gleam over an indiscernible shape of blankets and pale flesh, with the feeling that he had only just fallen asleep. But at once consciousness seized hold of him, as if it had been waiting patiently for just this momentary slip to reassert its mastery. Simon tossed over onto his back, as if trying to wrench away, feeling a slight nausea at the pit of his stomach, noticing that his breath steamed outside of the bedclothes. He tried to imagine that being awake brought with it no consequences, no obligations.

Once they were up, it was hard to find anything to say to one another. Over a rushed cup of coffee Rob told Simon to drop over some time again, any time. And he told Rob to do the same. Like two acquaintances of long ago who meet by accident on the street and do not know how to finish their conversation.

Outside the morning was still frosty. Their brief goodbyes moved visibly from them as tiny clouds of frozen breath, which did not meet, and were dispersed almost at once. They turned and walked in opposite directions, only their feet ringing on the pavement in each other's ears.

He walked back through the Botanic Gardens. They were empty. Covered with a thick hoar-frost the lawns stretched about him, totally deserted, as if they were walled off. No figures moved among the trees, whose immobile silent existence possessed the place. It possessed the foreground on one side, dark, smelling insidiously of pines, the ground dead beneath an ash-shower of pine-needles. It possessed the horizon where, their tight-stretched limbs no longer discernible, there were the grey shapes of trees only in the haze, motionless, speechless, unhearing, sightless existences, like life after some unimaginable accident, centuries old.

Walking in under them, he came upon a bank where there was a miracle of snowdrops. At the top of the bank the ground was in the permanent night of pine-needles: but then there were snowdrops, tiny, fragile, but present, their heads hanging humbly, but their precarious stalks arched with arrogance. He sat down among them on the cold grass, and held the head of one, gently, carefully, in his hand, and stroked the stalk with his fingers. He looked up, up into the sky, misty and huge, looking for the white disc of the winter sun, which he knew must be there. But just now he could not find it.

CHAPTER NINETEEN

If only he could have the chance to start completely afresh, he thought, yet knowing all he knew now. Somehow, somewhere.

In the meantime he resumed reading frenetically, and no longer troubling to hide the fact at work: as if only in reading, in history and theory, could he keep in contact with what he had learnt and what he was persisting with. Because often, for a moment, he could not help feeling as if he had been led astray from the course of his life by a dream, which had masqueraded as a hope.

But it was hard to concentrate, even when he was alone at home or when there were no tedious enquiries at work to interrupt him. Again and again he found himself lost in a sentence that seemed long since to have become meaningless, and putting the book down, he would get up and gaze from the library windows into the sky, neglecting his desk. Or at home in the evenings, he would stare intently at a bowl of crocus-bulbs in his room, which had broken the surface but were still refusing to flower, as if he could find in the inevitable prospect of spring some replacement for the sense of progress he had sensed so certainly in the prospect of his relationship with Rob.

He was struggling to keep his grip on his sense of purpose, which seemed to be slipping from him.

He tried to fantasise about finally achieving a rewarding job as a teacher, about becoming someone his friends turned to for advice, about setting up gay liberation in Glasgow – but all fantasies seemed to be swallowed up into a great central absence almost as soon as they were formulated.

He was on his own again after all.

And the weather became as still as the grave. A great winding-sheet of freezing fog descended. The light and the heat were locked out. Outside it was impossible to feel more than frozen meat, animated by a pathetic wisp of discontent.

And overnight the snow came, out of a great stillness, falling slowly, persistently, meticulously, till it could be sure the city was completely smothered. When its job was done, the sun rose low in the sky, hazy and small, and mocked from a clear pale blue this earth where even the very air still froze at midday.

Simon too felt mocked. He had wanted to shoot up and grow in what was, after all, only a brief mild respite, like some rash daffodil. And now the snow had cut him down, destroyed all his life; the snow which he had known must return, which he should have been waiting for, merely tending a little growth ready to break the surface in its time.

He went to the pub with Philip and Annie. But there was no consolation there. And he could see that Philip and Annie were unhappy themselves. They stood before him in silence, like dark shells brooding on their own suddenly sensed hollowness.

"The cold gets inside your brain," said Philip distantly, like a comment on someone absent.

They drifted to someone's party at closing-time. But even there a pool of dinginess hung over the room, ghost-like figures hovered stiff and yellow-faced in the dimness of the bulbs burning low, because the power-supply was cut through over-demand. They squatted together in a corner, sheltering by their carry-out bag as by a fire. An icy draught still found them out. Philip's eyes bored sightlessly into the floor immediately before him, blankly incredulous, and yet still calculating. Annie fidgeted restlessly, like a feverish child.

Philip said, "Simon, I'm afraid we're both feeling rather under pressure." His words came like telegrammed reports of a disaster in a distant country.

Simon was fiddling nervously with the carry-out bag. At last he pulled it open and thrust two cans across, taking a third for himself. "I'm sorry," he said in pain, "I'm no help."

"Wee Simon, you can't help because at the moment you're part of the problem," said Annie softly, hanging her head.

"What do you mean?" He felt ashamed, and then perplexed.

"No, I mean your despair is part of the problem because it's part of a world we've encouraged to grow around us in our likeness," said Annie. She and Philip were sitting without touching.

As in the past, Simon could not decide whether without Philip and Annie and what they stood for he felt set free, or cast adrift. He swigged on his can. Into his mind there bobbed the words of confused outraged incredulity from one of Donne's sonnets addressed to God – the source itself, he thought, part of a literary world the three of them had once often discussed and sought themselves in. He said out loud, talking at the gaping mouth of his can, " 'Thou hast made me: and shall thy work decay? Repair me – now . . .' " The words vanished like bubbles.

But Philip closed his eyes and winced. He whispered, "Donne," as though it were the name of a pain. Nodding slowly, he went on quietly, " 'Despair behind and death before doth cast such terror . . .' Christ, is that what lies ahead for us?" His tongue was slipping a little, like shoes on the ice outside.

In the momentary silence that fell amongst them, Simon heard someone cry out denyingly, "It's snowing again." He looked lethargically across to the window, where two women were holding back the curtain in awe, and saw through a triangle of street-light the white flakes drifting down, infinitesimally slowly, like God shaking out his nervous dandruff.

Simon sighed. "The other day," he said, "I almost thought of writing off for this lecturing post I saw advertised in New Zealand. After all, there's no chance of getting one here. I need something to give me a new sense of purpose."

Philip said, in a deep voice, the nearest approximation to his tone of sternness that he seemed able to manage, "You're in a desperate situation, you could do worse than try a desperate solution." He paused, veiling his eyes.

Annie looked hurt. She hunched over, her pointed shoulders rode up and curved around her, like the wings of a vulture. "So you'll just walk out on us," she said slowly, the words slurred, a sudden violence of feeling snatching at Simon. "Simon, you think that the world consists just of couples and potential couples. That they've got something you haven't. And that somehow you've been mysteriously excluded from the possibility, which is rubbish."

Simon was taken by surprise, shocked and hurt. "No, it's true," he said, pain giving way rapidly to just indignation, "it's true."

Annie swayed, muttering like some incantating shaman. "You want to spend all your time grieving over it. You want us to feel you suffer in a way we don't. And what about us? You think everything's easy when you're part of a couple, that all problems are over. You don't realise what it's like, you don't understand what we feel. You don't even try to, so busy feeling sorry for yourself, as if you in all the world were singled out to be lonely. And now you'll just walk out on us. It's easy for you to take off, you're on your own, and the only thing you want to do with your life is look for a happily-ever-after relationship. But we have to work to keep one another, we have to decide what we're going to do with our lives, we can't drift."

She fell silent, and then looked up at Simon, softening her eyes, confusedly affectionate.

"Come on, let's go home and go to bed," Philip said wearily. "Unconsciousness is probably the best thing for all of us."

Over the next few days Simon struggled harder than ever to fit the jagged fragments of his life into a pattern that might hint at a way ahead. But instead reflection became more and more impossible. A sheer sense of loss became all-consuming. It was like a new universe, with its own laws.

He became ill. A skin complaint that had not troubled him seriously since he was a child reached up out of the distant past and took control of him as assertively as some instinctual longing. When he lay down to sleep, it was as if a core of despair writhed within, and burst out over him, casting red-hot boulders down the slopes of his arms and legs, leaving great craters as they bumped and tumbled down. A crust of lava, seething, transforming the known landscape as it went, oozed out from his scalp and down his neck and forehead.

Looking at his devastated surfaces, he saw an image of himself going blurred round the edges, fading out.

The doctor, a large and powerful man, made Simon as always feel helpless in his hands. Knowledge of his own ailments was withheld from him through mystery, drugs were kept at prescription's length. He was dismissed peremptorily with a battery of ointments and stern advice: and a supply of tranquillisers.

The tranquillisers crumbled in the mouth into a sweet powder. They spread first through the body like a kind of tangible mist rising from the centre of the sugary aftertaste deep in the back of his throat; then like hanging veils of heavy gossamer they trapped in their sticky threads his fears and memories, as they came flying like sparks down the vortex of coming sleep, entangling and anaesthetising them. On waking the next morning, his consciousness would lingeringly soak up their grey sweet vacuity like slow blotting-paper, as far as the sunset.

Philip and Annie brought him flowers and kindness to his room. As they spoke to him one cold long-shadowed afternoon, he had the impression that their conversation was like a letter with holes in it; their words kept disappearing into gaps of vaguely luminous stillness and silence. They had come, like a delegation to an exile, to persuade him to keep his self-respect: but for his part he received their daffodils and their speeches of encouragement as his confirmation as an invalid. They sat opposite him and watched their intentions crumble, their words faltering in the face of his misunderstanding passivity, while he lay far back in his chair, white from drugs, static, one hand laid on top of the other on his lap as if sheltering it.

When they had gone back to the kitchen, he sat for a long time looking at the opening daffodils in the vanishing winter sunshine. One peered out curiously from beneath a petal folded before it as if to shield itself; another had a single petal thrown back nonchalantly from an otherwise cautiously screwed-up bud; while the tallest leant back on its stalk and trumpeted into the air, a *daphodyl rampant*. He smiled at them dreamily, feeling fond but hopelessly remote, aware at the same time of a creeping comfort in his skin.

By night, he would often wander into the pub, like a revenant, steered there as much as anything by loneliness. He would stand, stiff and silent, impassive, his eyes empty pools from which the darting fishes of being were quite gone. As he got drunk, he would seek to seem a reproach to the world's indifference, while the world, seeing him lost within himself, assumed reproachfully that he was indifferent to it.

A stone world had overgrown him from the inside out: lifeless, silent, as unreachable and impassive as the moon. His skin, especially where the ointment had lain on it, glowed itself white and stony, while everything about him seemed to him to take place in a dim bluish luminescence.

It was only one night several days later that it really occurred to him to see what was happening. In fact, there had been nothing at all unusual in his catatonic silence of that night; but what was unusual was that he noticed it. He was saying goodnight to Philip, the first time he had opened his mouth all evening. And suddenly it was as if something in Philip's manner – patient, almost humouring as it was, the way one might speak to a friend who turns up drunk in the middle of the night after a long absence – something in it found its way to a tiny spot of awareness, an Achilles' heel unbathed with the general dreamy insensibility.

God, Simon thought as he turned and walked slowly into his room, these pills are like an elephant sitting on me. There was something in the humorous grotesqueness of the observation itself that harked back within him, even as he formulated it, to a forgotten consciousness.

He stopped taking the tranquillisers. And slowly, very slowly, they lifted off him.

There came a certain quickened clarity.

It was less cold now, but still grey and dank. On weekend afternoons he would wander aimlessly down to the park by the river.

And all the time his thoughts kept running like hands over the wall that marked the dead end of himself, seeking a way out.

Like most jobs, his job at the library had turned out at best boring, and frequently wearing to the point of despair. Like everyone, he had begun to long for a job where he could give of himself, little though there might be to give. He had applied regularly for the small trickle of lecturing posts for which he had been trained, but without success. After all, in these times there were so many people chasing so few jobs. As things were, the state had no use for him. It would let him beg through life. The promise of a privileged career that had been made him by his family and his education had proved false.

His situation with regard to a job was rather like his situation with regard to a relationship.

Finally, in some confusion and desperation, he had gone ahead and applied for a job in New Zealand. Perhaps there was more chance there. On the other side of the world. Wryly, he remembered his incomprehension of the little dentist in London who was emigrating to Australia.

He entered the park. All around him the leafless trees stood naked in the cold breeze, their limbs frozen into the embattled positions in which the wind had made them grow. He wandered among them, his eyes lifted to greet them.

There seemed nowhere to turn. To be gay in this city was to live in an ancient world of fear, guilt, and hypocrisy. And yet to be gay in London had been for him to live in an alienating world of objectification, exploitation, and hypocrisy – his own as much as other people's. He was not at home among straights, nor yet had he found a home among gays. What was to be expected of anywhere in the world?

Glasgow: London: Glasgow: and so on. For a moment he saw himself a rat in a maze; himself the conductor of the experiment – utterly uncertain of its objectives.

A couple ran past him, bumping into him without saying sorry. Hand in hand, they ran laughing up the steep slope ahead, their unbuttoned anoraks billowing around them, their hair lifting in the breeze. To Simon trudging slowly after, they appeared, despite himself, like angels ascending a baroque ceiling.

The wind had dropped. And as he reached the crest of the hill, incredibly the sun appeared for a moment through the clouds, poised just above the horizon: a dull red orb that one could look straight at, without light, without heat, and yet there. Somewhere, somewhere it must be warming the earth.

Coming slowly up the incline towards him was a solitary figure, seeming from a distance to be wandering aimlessly but as it drew closer, focused by an alert enjoyment, like a dog in the country. Only after a while did Simon recognise Vanessa. She came on towards him, her face lost against the light.

"I didn't recognise you, I didn't expect you," he said, a little embarrassed, as so often, to be found out in his solitariness. "Are you out walking on your own?"

"Oh yes, I enjoy walking on my own," Vanessa said quietly and measuredly, stopping beside him and turning to look at the sunset. "Especially now that spring's on its way."

"Spring?" said Simon, disconcerted. "I hadn't – I'd hardly noticed."

"There are buds already on some of the trees."

He followed her gaze to the bare trees, arching into the air all around and below them, and saw for the first time, in the glow of the sunset, the branches hung with little buds, glinting like raindrops. And on the ground, amid the small shadowy valleys of their roots, the spears of daffodil leaves beckoning on one another's assembled ranks. Even the lawns looked young and vigorous.

"Och yes, winter's over," said Vanessa, her face tinged rosy by the rays of the sun, her eyes turning to Simon, solemn and affectionate. "And it's time to let your winter end too, you know, Simon."

He felt stirred almost painfully to life. "Do you often walk alone?" he said distractedly, holding her words at bay for a moment.

"Why not? It's a little pleasure of its own."

The breeze gently ruffled Simon's hair, no longer seeming so cold. "I want my winter to end, as you put it," he said. "I want – happiness. I do try."

The light was fading, but for a moment all around the grass itself seemed to be glowing with a blue luminescence, suddenly filling the air with its fragrance. Somewhere nearby a blackbird began to sing at the setting sun, resourceful and trusting.

"The real joy of life is growth," said Vanessa softly, taking him gently by the arm. "There isn't a still point of rest and contentment. Whether you're on your own, or not, life is always growing. And it has its growing pains." Her voice came in soft little breaths. She paused, and suddenly with a gust of laughter she went on, "We're like trees. You're a little willow, and I'm – I don't know – a copper beech?"

"A laburnum?"

"Sometimes a laburnum. Like trees, with our flowering time and our time of dying back. Like trees, growing slowly. And hard to cut down."

"Let's walk together a bit," said Simon, pulling her arm towards him. They began to walk towards the river, facing the last pink smudges on the horizon, while behind them night was already spreading like a great ink blot. In another hemisphere, dawn must be breaking.

"I remember a friend of mine in London trying to point out to me that a sense of failure or disintegration was only part of a process. Like winter being followed by spring, night by day," said Simon.

"I think he was right," said Vanessa. "After all Simon, you've changed as much through your disappointments as your successes, you know. And you have changed. And you'll go on changing. One day, you won't recognise yourself."

"Do you think so?"

"Oh yes. You'll have lovers. You'll have gay friends. You'll have a job that's helpful. In another country, on the other side of the world. Full of sunshine."

"I might not get that job."

"Och yes, you will, you will." She squeezed his hand gently; and he squeezed hers back in gratitude. "And in the sunshine, little flower," she said in a low mutter of laughter, "you can open up."

He smiled. Twilight was all around them now, smelling of grass and river water. Half seen, the pennants of daffodil leaves seemed to be beckoning in the breeze. The paths stretched ahead on every hand, wide open and silent. "And yet, I wish I'd already found the relationship I'm looking for," he said.

"Simon, there's no perfect relationship, is there?" said Vanessa, as if reminding him of something he well knew. "But every relationship brings us just a little nearer what we're looking for. From every relationship we learn just a little more. Isn't that right?"

"Yes, it is," he said calmly.

"And it won't be the next relationship that will answer all your wants," Vanessa went on. "But it will answer some that haven't yet been answered. It will teach you some things you don't yet know."

They came to a halt on the bridge, peering into the dark whirling waters of the river, whose ripples caught the last faint glimmer of day. It surged beneath them, purposeful and tireless.

"And Simon, you don't *find* relationships," said Vanessa, slipping her arm about his shoulders now, and looking into his eyes in the dusk. "You know that. You've made that mistake. In London you thought sex was just something there to take, to consume." Simon nodded slowly. "But a relationship is something that you create. Something that you create."

"Yes," said Simon, "I'm beginning to understand that."

It was quite dark. But for a while they stood there together, unmoving, watched over by gently nodding branches, listening to the onward swirl of the water.

Part Four: GOING FORWARD

CHAPTER TWENTY

From where Simon lay, remembering and planning, he could see the city below, clambering resourcefully up from the sea over the tumbled hills: thousands of tiny frail white cabins clinging and balancing in the most precarious positions, transforming the landscape by their daring, changing an expanse of sea and mountains into a harbour laid out before him. A refuge where people arrived, rested, and exchanged; from where they set off for somewhere else: incessantly beneath one's gaze, as one found oneself at one vantage-point after another in the course of one's daily movements. Beyond the city, in one direction the purposeful cleft of a wide valley seemed to lead through gambolling rolls of land and out of sight, to a distant range of blue peaks lying along the horizon like some fantasy castle, whose turrets vanished in white streaks of cloud; while in the other the gates of the mountains opened, and from above planes rose and descended slowly through them, glints of silver in the distance. Below in the shadowed channel ragged reefs, like the teeth of snarling watchdogs, stood guard before a glimpse of the Pacific, opening out as far as the eye could see into a pale indeterminate freedom, pathless and endless.

His scarcely read book propped against the sprawling roots of a pohutukawa, whose crimson flowers were just now breaking bud, Simon lay half in and half out of the characteristically undecided sunshine. It was still warm but already the wind was beginning to mount again, the pages of the book kept flapping themselves over annoyingly, and flecks of white were once more visible on the previously unruffled turquoise surface of the harbour below. He settled himself more comfortably. Sometimes living in Wellington seemed like living in the sky: when one was not climbing arduously as if to meet the clouds, they themselves were slipping down the sides of hills, like groping clammy hands, to engulf one; or now, these summer days, rushing past about one's head like some majestic silent stampede, borne on the ever-present vigorous Cook Strait gales.

It would soon be time to go and meet Martin. As the time grew nearer, the thought had continually distracted him from his book. It was just as well that marking was over and the holidays had started in earnest a few days ago. He gave up his pretensions to serious reading and closed the book's cover, gazing into the expansive distance, the wind flicking his hair. This was one of the most important periods in his life.

The very first meeting with Martin had been strange, even mystifying. He had remembered the experience, rather than the person. It was a long time ago now, back at the end of the autumn. His friend Amanda, who had the office next to his, had asked if she could swop tutorials with him, for some reason he no longer exactly remembered, and he had been surprised and pleased by the confidence with which he already faced a group of strange faces. But afterwards, however successful the tutorial as such had been, what he remembered was an electricity of the atmosphere that had nothing to do with the discussion. It was as if there had been literally a loud gay vibration in his ear, filling him with a disembodied eroticism, which only after a while he realised was emanating from a quiet yet restless man, all but out of sight in a corner by the window. He was some part Maori, with a beard that was almost not there, and his eyes, when they occasionally ventured tentatively up into the late afternoon light falling obliquely through the glass, were like those of a stray dog. He was with a particularly self-confident ebullient young pakeha woman, dressed loudly and imaginatively; and when the tutorial had finished, Simon was able to identify them from the roll as a pair whose names he had heard frequently linked by Amanda as though they were a couple: Martin and Suzie.

The moment faded rapidly in his memory. And he was surprised to be reminded of it some weeks later when the same man stopped him on the windswept street, as he was walking head down unheedingly by, and shyly but graciously asked him how he was. He found himself replying unexpectedly clumsily, and as the wet gusty southerly made prolonged conversation difficult, they smiled, and Simon moved off in puzzlement. Over the next few months, as the great winter storms whirled over the city in regular succession, he bumped into him several times, looming suddenly towards him around the university; and each time Martin dropped a few brief but friendly passing words, in his quiet wandering voice, somewhat to Simon's bewilderment. Once Martin had even knocked lightly on the door of his office, and come softly in to ask some advice on an essay, because he was unable to find Amanda.

One cold late winter Saturday evening, as had become almost a habit, Simon was having a drink with Nick, who was busy persuading him to come along to a socialist fund-raising social. Already in his head he had agreed long ago to come, but for the time being he was preserving a diplomatic air of uncertainty. "Martin Walker will be there," said Nick suddenly, opening his eyes wide in deflatory self-mockery of the lip-smacking grin appearing beneath: as though offering a delicacy that was a mutually recognised extravagance.

Thrown as much as anything by this recurrent manner of Nick's, Simon looked back questioningly in silence.

"You know him, eh?" said Nick, already purposeful and businesslike once more. "He said he knew you, when I mentioned you a while ago."

"Yes, well, I know him by sight," Simon said cautiously.

"He's neat, eh!" said Nick emphatically, inviting Simon to join in one of those enigmatic broad smiles of his that somehow managed to combine sexual appraisal and genuine appreciation, an inscrutable contradictoriness that constituted much of Nick's fascination for Simon. "And a reassurance. He's so calmly self-accepting. One of those gays who are young enough to have benefited from our struggles in the gay liberation movement, who makes their importance real."

Simon nodded enthusiastically, saying nothing. And so Martin *was* gay: this casual and unexpected confirmation made him realise how much, through all his doubts and indifference, he had half-believed this; and how often, if not always, it turned out that one's intuitions as a gay person oneself were to be trusted after all.

And at the social, Martin and Suzie – who seemed to be there because she had been dared to attend dressed in skin-tight purple denim with stars on her face, rather than for her interest in politics – had invited Simon round for tea, with the air of doing something rather precocious; which quite surprised Simon, who accepted in humble gratitude. There had followed a series of increasingly frequent visits and outings, at first with Suzie always present, but later not always. Simon was struck now by the naive expectation of the normal that could have allowed Amanda ever to believe that these two were a couple. Suzie, who was a lot younger than she appeared, seemed to spend her days screwing a succession of handsome hunks with a confident and purposeful cynicism, and an extraordinary facility for holding them at a distance and yet dangling. The fact that she lived with a homosexual she seemed to regard as stylish evidence of her wordly-wiseness, like the presence of the two junkies whom Simon stumbled on to his alarm one day, shooting up in the front room. Which was not to say that she and Martin did not have a quite deep rapport, if in nothing else, in their approach to adult life as a rare adventure. Simon was delighted at, and grateful for their companionship, seeming as it did so revivifying in its casual spontaneity after the formality of average New Zealand social converse. He had been lonely here for so long; this seemed more than just another star in the darkness: perhaps it was the approach of dawn.

Yes, he thought, lying now watching the shadows lengthen, watching the changing kaleidoscope of light and shade over the now familiar landscape, picking out a wooded slope here, a particularly white house there – how much his life had changed since his arrival.

He could never forget the outward journey. The plane's inexorable onward movement through an endless night had seemed like time in stasis, making the present meaningless, while the past seemed intolerable and the future only uncertain. At long last, as the darkness changed to a drifting contourless expanse of colourless cloud, there appeared a broad crack of scarlet half-light, but for the moment it seemed to Simon impossible to tell whether the sun was rising or setting. Nevertheless, the body responded to the mere presence of light, like a plant. He must have crossed the equator then; the distorted hours of half-sleep were over, yet neither did he feel awoken.

And on dazed first sight, what had struck him most about Wellington, as he was whisked purposefully through it in a car by strangers with strange accents, was its air of impermanence, of transience: just so many wooden erections scattered over windswept hillsides, whose vegetation seemed to be in a process of continually reaching out to engulf them.

First contacts had left him feeling quite at sea. He had been invited hither and thither to dine formally with a succession of stolid married couples, who all dwelt in smart but characterless eyries, balanced on some hillside where their vast windows could command framed panoramas strangely half empty of houses. Despite their position as wealthy intellectuals, their proudly presented food seemed to have always a brashness, sometimes a veritable garishness, that Simon would once have associated more with the convenience recipes of a second-rate women's magazine. Their conversation lapsed so often and so fondly into jokes against New Zealand itself: like the one about the historian who specialised in the nineteenth century, and liked to visit New Zealand because there he felt he could actually live in it. Simon had never dreamt there could be a nationality so constantly apologetic about itself. This jumble of strangenesses left him so confused that it was months before he came to appreciate the sheer generosity these people had shown so persistently to one who must have seemed so odd and distant to them.

In any case, the gay community had been equally bewildering. To his surprise he had found one day a small local gay newspaper gathering dust in a radical bookshop, and had made contact with the tag-end of a wave of gay liberation that had already come and gone. Confronted by them with the city's busy gay pub – crowded with loud-mouthed Maori drag-queens, six feet and sixteen stone in make-up and evening-dress, and silent Japanese sailors eating dried squid instead of chips, the most boring of closet white clerks and the most beautiful of ambiguous Samoans, all side by side – he had been unable to do anything but watch in deep amazement, and utter remoteness.

He had felt alien and lonely here for so long. Even the very air felt strange. In the huge night sky above the shadows of the mountaintops even the stars were not in their right places. At first, amid the wild swirling weather of a rapidly advancing winter, it had been a constant effort to glean the tiniest fragments of companionship wherever he went: he felt as if he had to beg for them, and even then he was not given what he needed. But the very rareness of companionship made it so precious that he responded with warmth and gratitude and openness; and soon he realised that it had not been crumbs dropped from the table of the emotionally rich after all: but rather seedlings he himself had been nurturing which were beginning to flower and bear fruit all around him in return for his willingly bestowed care.

And finally, over the past few weeks, with the warm moist gales ushering in the early summer, the pohutukawas silvery with new growth, he had come to the slow amazed realisation that this growing closeness to Martin represented nothing less than the beginning of a whole new era. The categories of friend and lover were about to merge at last.

At first, there seemed to hover about Martin an atmosphere of tender yearning: as though he were a stranger from another world, a world infinitely strange but infinitely sweet, where he longed for you to be united with him, but knew no way alone to take you there. One watched him, as one could not help watching a wild animal caught sight of unexpectedly – graceful and proud, and yet timid, alert to an environment full of dangers. And his eyes followed you, changing with every mood that passed between you, like huge brown moons waxing and waning in a white sky.

But Simon felt now something quite other than just a dreamy fascination. Rather, he felt the tentative but increasingly certain recognition of kindred. To him this unexpected person in a small and remote country seemed to embody so much of the form of the gay experience as he had known it – this lost longing, this pride and this fear, this hope and this desperation. He had never felt before that he stood within reach of coming so close to another human being, nor another human being to him. It was as if they knew one another's inmost pains and dreams, and this had been the premise of their conversation, not something later suggested by it. Simon thought speech had never flowed from him from such deep wounds and sources.

He was only waiting for the moment when this intense communication must be made tangible, must be made real. He longed to urge the moment on, and the sexual failures and frustrations of his past felt like some encumbrance, almost like some limb swollen with elephantiasis that he must trail about with him, rendering him hopelessly shy and clumsy when this was least appropriate. But at heart he was certain that their bodies must inevitably enter into the communication, as it were, of their own accord. If it was not this occasion, well, it would be the next, or the next.

Never had a relationship seemed so right and so complete. And thus so simple.

He looked at his watch to see what the time was, and the sunlight that fell on his hand, as he moved his wrist out of the shade, was still comfortingly warm. Another five minutes and he would get up to go. He lay back, closing his eyes, drowsing, picking out the song of a grey warbler, embarked on again and again, setting out, hesitating, and then falling slowly away. Perhaps, he thought, it would be this time.

The ground on which he was lying lurched and juddered, as though the earth had suddenly stirred and rolled over, trying to shake him from its back as if he were an irritant substance. He opened his eyes and sat up, his heart beating involuntarily. Another earth-tremor.

He stood up, brushed himself down, picked up his book, and set off down the hillside towards the city. Once he started walking, he realised that the wind was already strong; he had to struggle to keep moving. Fingers of pale cloud were reaching up stealthily from the horizon to snatch at the low sun. Sometimes life in Wellington seemed so vulnerable. The very earth was continually shaking beneath one's feet. The wind was continually rising to halt one in one's tracks, to tug at roofs and trees, to send solid objects flying past or towards one through the air. Nothing was stable. Simon had come to love the feeling, to feel more at home in it than he had felt anywhere.

When he got to the cinema, Martin was not there; but then he had not really expected him to be. Martin was not known for his punctuality, and in any case, there was plenty of time before the film began. He studied the inscrutable stills suspiciously. They had both felt eager to see this Hollywood treatment of a story with a gay element, but Simon was filled already with apprehension.

Time passed slowly. He raised his eyes and surveyed the street. Dust drifted along the gutters in the wind. The centre of the city always looked at once ramshackle and prim. The shop-signs, squeezed higgledy-piggledy beneath the wooden awnings, were neat and proud, and yet somehow dowdy. A bus stopping too suddenly had lost its trolley, and the driver, shirtsleeves up, was round the back heaving it into place, while a jam built up patiently behind him. From the bus stop the scene was watched by a stocky tanned man in suit-jacket and shorts, with a look of satisfaction at the rough-and-ready handiness that kept this efficient little heart of his plucky country running. He turned and spoke to the stranger queueing beside him, a blankly smiling housewife in clothes that looked like they belonged in the fifties, her body held tight in a complacent reticence. Beside her there stood relaxedly a young woman with alert eyes in a bright headscarf and long patterned home-made wrap-around skirt, a bookshop purchase in her hand. Next to her was an impassive elderly Samoan, rigid in an old raincoat, with his long hair tied in a knot and a shark's tooth hanging from his ear. The whole scene was a typical rich jumble of elements.

At last, with only a few seconds to spare, Martin came loping round the corner, unbuttoning his bulky cycling gear as he walked, holding a glove in his mouth as he awkwardly swopped his crash-helmet to his other hand, so that he looked for a moment as if he were struggling with too many parcels. His eyes rose huge with unaffected apology above this commotion below; amidst which he still retained, apparently effortlessly, a certain childlike gracefulness.

"Here I am, my friend," he said softly. "Did you think I was never coming?"

Simon smiled tenderly, and yet almost afraid, in his own comparatively tidy clothes and fussy timekeeping, to claim his interest in this wild spontaneity. "Hallo," he said. "It's alright, nothing's started yet. And anyway, there's a short, and then an interval."

When they had got their tickets, Martin wanted to buy some "lollies". Simon watched bemused as he made his careful and by now familiar selection from the display of lurid perfumed sweets in the café next door, so serious and so enthusiastic. He began eating them before they reached the auditorium, and offered the bag routinely to Simon, who as usual hesitated, and then refused. Simon did not know what to do with something so transitory and sensuous, whose lasting nutritional value was quite uncertain.

Martin's childish excitement at the cinema made every visit promise to be a joy. There was something about the very way he settled himself into his seat that made Simon aware of the thrill of the giant moving pictures up there in the dark as if for the first time. A film became more than ever a moment apart.

Martin's physical proximity in the next seat seemed to Simon to make the stuffy air between them electric, and yet still he did not dare to actually bridge the gap. For a moment, amidst the smell of dust and old cloth, the intensity of this closeness alone seemed something he had never known before.

But when the film finished, even Martin's willingness for enjoyment turned out to have been unable to redeem it. The besieged gay bank-robbers had been portrayed as bizarre, even alien. When gay liberationists appeared to demonstrate outside the bank in their support, they were treated as a joke, and though Simon and Martin had turned to one another with a murmur of exhilaration and pride, all around them there had come dismissive laughter at something seen as merely outrageous. The world seemed indifferent, even hostile, as they filed from the cinema, jostled by young straight couples, shaggy men in torn and faded tee-shirts with big bare tattooed arms slung swampingly over the shoulders of sad-eyed women with heavy, timidly imitative make-up, the mockery still loud in their voices. Outside the wind swaggered noisily down the twilit street like a drunken mob.

"Let's get something to eat, eh," said Martin, as if humbly offering some meagre but real consolation. "I'm so hungry I feel cold."

They walked down the street and turned without discussion into the dark wooden doorway of the Casbah, one of Martin's habitual haunts in his wanderings by day and night, mainly because it had a juke-box. Martin slid along one of the plastic bench-seats and made straight for the selecting buttons. Music began to seep up, and sigh quietly but anxiously around. The Eagles: "All alone at the end of the evening, when the bright lights had faded to blue, I was dreaming . . ." Martin slipped out of his cycling jacket and settled back, eyes gazing into the future. A smell of fresh sweat and a newly laundered shirt drifted over Simon.

The waitress came up, smiling in recognition, and they ordered their usual – a cheese salad and coffee. To Simon it seemed she watched them questioningly, almost as if expecting an announcement. Simon began to dream.

The thin sigh of the juke-box came: "But the dreams I've had lately keep on turning out, and burning out, the same. So put me on a highway, and show me a sign . . ."

Martin drew a breath, like a sudden breeze rustling a forgotten paper beside one. "Simon," he said, and his voice seemed to alight gently and yet a little wearily on the name, seeming thus to define it as the welcome end of a long journey in thought. "Do you think you'll stay here now? Or will you move on? You've sort of got that air about you of always being just about to pass through."

"I don't know," said Simon; thinking, I'd stay if you asked me, yet I don't dare ask you. "I suppose, once one's travelled such an unimaginable distance, it seems it would be easier to do it again."

"Take it to the limit," sighed the record, "take it to the limit, one more time."

"I hope you stay, eh," said Martin softly, turning, bowing his eyes. "It's hard to think of you going."

The waitress reappeared and thrust their meals between them, with the kind of tiredness that made the food itself promise to be drab. Yet Martin began at once to eat with an enthusiasm that was indomitable, cutting a swathe through his plate as if he were mowing a field.

"I suppose I don't really know where I feel at home myself," he said wistfully, his mouth full. "I was brought up in Rotorua, eh? I lived for a while in Auckland, then I came here. I guess I'd like to go overseas one day." His eyes took wing, like two ravens, and drifted for a while on the sound of the wind caught between records.

"We're all rootless, really – gay people, I mean," said Simon, a locked-out sadness trying to get into his voice. "There's no home been given us in the culture and the history we grew up with, is there? And so we're lost everywhere; always looking for a past, even a present. Or giving up on that, and wandering after a future."

"Yes, yes," said Martin, the moment of acknowledged clarity seeming to make his eyes shrink into black pinpoints of focus. "That's true, eh? I'd like to feel that makes us freer to be who we want to be."

"I'd like to be able to feel that too," said Simon wistfully.

Martin chewed his last mouthful beneath contemplative eyes. "Nick, he's another wanderer," he said.

"He came to Wellington because the Party asked him to, didn't he?"

"Oh yeah. But he's always been a wanderer, you know. Did he ever tell you about the time he spent a year on his own on a bit of land in Coromandel?"

"No, no he didn't. He seems so strong," said Simon with affection.

"Yeah," said Martin, "and yet sometimes so sad."

They stayed for a while after they had finished eating, putting on records, talking. Martin's very features were eloquent. His face flickered with emotions like a river in a changing light; to listen to him talking was like watching the flotsam going by on the current. And to Simon it seemed that the river had come from a country that he knew.

Time seemed to have retreated.

But when they finally stepped outside into the rushing air, it returned. Simon felt uncertainty like alarm. He hunted about for the power to urge the moment, but for a while neither of them spoke. Then Martin cupped his hands and called against the wind, "Do you have to go back to your little basement now, or" – and his eyes, followed by his whole face, ducked down – " or would to like to come to my place for a while?"

"I'd love to come to your place," shouted Simon, trying to hold the reins of his voice, trying not to let it bolt beneath him.

They walked through emptied streets to the motorbike, saying nothing because of the wind. A gang of Australian spring tourists, hunched in parkas, wandered past shouting audibly about the dreadful climate and the lack of night-life.

All the way home the motorbike swayed beneath them, caught by gust after gust that slammed into them at every corner. Simon leant forward, eyes half shut, dazed by the closeness of Martin's body. They reached the bay and the city lay opposite them, strings of light laced hither and thither across the black shoulders of the mountains. The bay itself was a dark confusion of creaking masts, dimly visible here and there in small patches of lamplight.

They dismounted and struggled up the path and inside. The clump of sleek flax by the door had become a flicker of dark spears, flailing haphazardly at one another.

Martin went to make coffee, while Simon sat himself alone in the empty sitting-room, softly lit by an old-fashioned standard lamp. He could hear Suzie's voice in the distance upstairs, mingling with the voice of an unknown man. There came the first clatter of raindrops against the window, and he looked up from his feet to see the uncurtained glass already weeping with trickling streams, turning the outside world into a distant blur.

I must make us wait till we are sure we need our closeness, thought Simon. If you jump straight into bed, you force the relationship, it has no chance to grow. It will have no savour and no hope, it will die young.

Martin came in with the coffee in cracked and chipped mugs, and set it down on the floor, squatting beside it, gazing up at Simon. "It's funny, eh," he said affectionately, "sometimes when I come into a room where you are, Simon, it's almost as if you're not there at all. It's a moment before I notice you, eh? You used to be a bit like that in your office."

Your looking at me makes me feel more real than I have ever been, thought Simon. He slipped lightly off the chair and sat on the carpet opposite Martin. "I suppose," he said, "I feel somehow unconfirmed. As though my existence in society was still a bit like a rumour, rather than a fact. Rather like the existence of gay people as we first learn of it, only as a rumour."

"I think I know what you mean," said Martin, nodding slowly. "I guess I wouldn't say I feel so much unconfirmed, as incomplete."

"Yes," said Simon, "I think – I think we're both searching to be somehow fully realised,"

The house creaked in a strong gust, and the noise of rain grew more insistent.

Martin's hand lay only a few inches from Simon's, fingers loosely outstretched. Simon looked at it fondly, as though it were a helpless small animal. We are so close, he thought, and yet it must be both of us is afraid to touch. Afraid to break out of the comforting cocoon of fantasy into real life and its risks.

"You know, perhaps it's because other people have defined us so incompletely," Simon said. "I mean, have defined us only by our sexuality. That's why we come to feel ourselves it's only through sexual relationships we can be made real. And I suppose that feeling's only made the more pressing because our sexual relationships are so very beleaguered, so very isolated."

"Yes," murmured Martin, the merest wisp of sound, staring at the floor, "yes." His eyes rose, but moved beyond Simon, pacing sadly to and fro.

Beyond the window the weather had imposed its characteristic siege conditions.

Martin drew a breath. "You won't go home in this, Simon, eh?" he said quietly, looking down. "You might as well stay the night."

Softly, saying nothing they went upstairs, both treading almost like cats as if, thought Simon, they were fearful of admitting to their reality, so oddly must it sit on both of them. Martin had gone first, and for a moment he stood on the unlit landing, half lost in shadow, turned back towards Simon, looking concerned, even questioning.

"There's a spare mattress in Suzie's room," he said under his breath, swallowing the words, his eyes hither and thither, caught in a bar of dim light. "But this is my room here."

Simon came up beside him. But still he dared not touch. "Let's go into your room," he whispered.

Martin turned on the light. The room was small, sparsely furnished, haphazard rather than untidy. There was a scanty double mattress on the floor, the bedclothes thrown loosely over it. On the pale walls were one or two posters for concerts and political events, some postcards of New Zealand landscape, a small photograph of Martin with a pack on his back lying on the shingle by some mountain river on a cloudy day. Simon stood looking at it for a while, wondering what to say.

Behind his back Martin said, "You might as well sleep here, Simon, eh?" Simon turned, now feeling as if the sun had finally broken through. And found Martin not even looking at him, busy tidying the bed in an absorbed way, and then beginning silently to undress, his face blank. When he came to take off his jeans, Simon looked away, feeling suddenly as if it would be impolite to do otherwise. He felt confused, fumbling with his own clothes, removing them awkwardly as though he were a child unused to it. Although he could not see, he could hear that Martin had not got into bed. He must be standing there naked, and he wondered whether he should turn now.

"I'll put off the light," said Martin. He did so, and padded back across the thin carpet and got into bed. Simon pulled off his jeans in the darkness. And found nothing before him but normality. He turned back the sheet and climbed wearily but uninterestedly into the bed, as if it had been in a hotel.

And yet the warm sheets smelt of another body, for a moment they seemed as alien and beautiful as the bush, where one felt that if one were lost, one might almost forget it amid all that beauty. And as if it were inevitable, the smooth warmth of Martin's arms reached out and held him, the kind fingers touched his body knowingly, for they already knew it in expectation, thought Simon, they must. And his own arms had found Martin at last; they surrounded him, confirming his material presence, drawing them towards one another until Martin's light beard gently brushed Simon's cheek.

"It seems like the logical extension of knowing you," said Martin softly, and Simon could feel his words as puffs of breath against his face, as vibrations against his fingers.

"Yes," he said, "it is. Martin. Can I kiss you?"

"Yes, you can."

But when he leant over he found only Martin's lips puckered to peck at his and withdraw: like a child kissing an aunt. Again he was puzzled.

But then Martin began to talk. And he talked on and on, calling up memories, stories of childhood, of special places, visions, hopes, dreams.

Simon had become accustomed to the half-dark, and in a bar of lamplight that slipped between the flimsy curtains he could see Martin's eyes: they were like fires, where the possibilities seemed to flare and crumble. And Simon watched like a fascinated child, unafraid of being burnt.

The ebullience of Martin's speech caught him up like a wave; and he found himself joining in, laying his own life as bare as his body. Their longings and histories touched one another, intertwined with one another. But their bodies lay as innocent as those of the two small children they were half-remembering themselves to have been, and seemingly half-wanted still to be.

"If only we could reclaim the joy of our childhood friendships with the knowledge we have now," Simon said dreamily. "If only we could have known then we were gay, we might have made those friendships what they really were."

"I guess I'd like to be able to re-create those friendships just as they were in the present," came Martin's voice.

Outside the wind moaned and rustled in the leaves of the tree beyond the window; the house shuddered continually in its gusts. To Simon their quiet voices in the night seemed to wreathe round and respond to one another like some musical duet repeating themselves, over and over; until they were overtaken by tiredness.

He realised, starting from a silence, that they both must have fallen asleep.

He could just make out the sound of Martin's regular breathing, and their hands had dropped from one another's shoulders. The twilight in the room seemed changed, colder, harsher: perhaps the sun was rising. For a moment he felt wide awake, alert. He looked to his side, and saw that Martin had rolled over. The golden brown, gently curving expanse of his back lay stretched out before Simon like a beach on which he had been washed up: but Simon could not touch it, could not grasp it, the sand trickled through his fingers, his hands were empty. Drowsiness was coming over him again.

He rolled over himself, and drew his knees up towards his chin, cradling them. He felt like a starving child that had been taken off the street by a benefactor, and then offered only a cup of tea.

But it was real. He was lying there beside the first gay man with whom he wanted to lie. Lapped against by his warmth, by his smell. This was enormous, incredible, enough: the rest would come in time. It would all work out in the end. After all, they were such friends.

He was sleeping.

CHAPTER TWENTY-ONE

Already it was January.

Even for a Saturday night, the pub was uncomfortably full and hot and stuffy inside, though outside the wind was cool and lively.

Someone on their way to the toilet barged against Simon once again, spilling the beer from the glass he was just raising to his mouth. He put it back on the edge of the crowded table they had claimed for themselves, and shrugged. Nick smiled, and took a cigarette from the packet lying gaping beside his rum and coke, counting with a free finger the few that remained, and shaking his head solemnly. He lit up.

He was a few years older than Simon, son of a religious farming family, solid and bearded. For a while, before he came out – first as a gay, and then as a socialist – he had worked as a lonely teacher in the country, loving, creative, and respected. Now he was a park gardener; and, had he not been gay in a predominantly straight male party, he would already have been a party-hack. After so many years of living alone, he lived now with another gay party member, Peter, quite unlike himself – quiet and retiring, with a passion for keeping methodical files and for absorbing pulp television.

It was in this pub that Simon had got to know Nick. During the lonely months that followed his arrival he had come here rather furtively of a Saturday night, and hung about on the fringes. He has felt lost and yet fascinated by the alien scene, with its towering heavy-weight Maori drag-queens, its carefree Pacific Islanders, its Japanese sailors, rubbing shoulders with the most conventional and conservative of white gay men, whose clothes and camp style seemed to belong to a distant decade, yet who were equally rubbing shoulders with the city's handful of aggressive young activists. There was thus a strong sense of community here, in what was virtually the one gay pub in the area, which could never be reproduced in some larger more cosmopolitan city, gay mecca though it might be. Nick, an habitual visitor, remembering Simon from some seminar on gay liberation at the university in the very first weeks after his arrival, had spoken to him whenever he saw him here; and from mutually cautious fragments of conversation, to one another's surprise, had slowly grown a friendship in whose strength both could shelter.

Tonight, in the momentary lull in their conversation, Simon's eyes strayed tiredly over the dull familiar faces around the table. And then to Nick's face, which he caught in an unexpected moment of repose. Lines of weariness showed strangely around the eyes which were so often alight with a seemingly indefatigable animation.

But Simon's mind kept coming back again and again to the same place. "Martin's still not back from his jaunt round the East Cape, though he said he would be two days ago," he said wistfully.

Nick's hand patted Simon's shoulder in a gesture of exaggerated sympathy. "There, there, you'll survive," he said, in the tones of a mock doctor.

Simon smiled. What he sought in Nick was this quality of his to draw from him the strength he had. "Yes, well," he began wisely, "Martin's elusive at the best of times, and sometimes downright inaccessible. For every six times you phone, you'll find him in once."

"But it's that elusiveness that's such a part of his charm," said Nick with relish, taking a mouthful of rum.

This made Simon uneasy. "I don't know. Perhaps," he said, playing nervously with his glass. "No, I mean – I just miss him because we're such good friends."

"I don't believe *that*," said Nick in the voice of some towering guardian aunt, "for a moment! You're as well aware as anyone else" – and his manner changed momentarily to the moonstruck adolescent – "that he's simply divine. And he is, eh?" He stubbed out his cigarette, and spoke again plainly and seriously. "Anyway, it's necessary for a great romantic love that its object be inaccessible."

"But it's not romantic," said Simon emphatically. "That's just the point. We're not remote and pining for one another, we're very close."

Nick looked persistently incredulous. "Well, there's one cure for romantic longing," he said measuredly, as if pondering the problem in the light of personal experience, "and that's a good screw." He took a drink, peering challengingly over the rim of his glass. "Now look at him, for example! Gorgeous, eh?"

He gestured with his eyes towards a Pacific Islander at the next table. His black curly hair gambolled thick over his head, as if one could sink one's hand into it, and his alert eyes were at once fiercely proud and very gentle, even caressing, seeming to belong to some totally different concept of manhood, capable of combining seeming opposites of behaviour into a strange beautiful richer whole. How often on the street these men, fierce and yet gentle, self-possessed and yet yielding of themselves, showed up the mass of white men as drab, inflexible, slatternly of dress and manners, stiff in their emotions. With the island women, looking like strong, thoughtful, laughter-loving Gauguin portraits in flesh and blood, they had first awakened Simon to the magic and to the hidden restlessness that haunted this land.

Nick's voice came as if from inside his own head. "You always did have a fascination with islanders." This way that Nick had of suddenly inserting himself into Simon's thoughts seemed a repeated assertion of their closeness; and yet in many ways, as he was constantly aware, they were very different, almost diametrically so.

"A fascination, yes," he said, smiling almost coyly, "but that's all. I don't think I could ever be a friend to one. There's too much difference in culture. And in power."

Nick said archly, "I wasn't talking about being friends."

"When I thought of power, neither was I. One-night stands are so unsatisfying. All they've ever done is leave me more aware of the emptiness afterwards."

"But ah, the thrill of the pursuit before !" said Nick flamboyantly, breaking into a little low stutter of a laugh.

Simon frowned. "I'm not interested in being predatory. I want to be affectionate."

Nick stroked him gently on the arm. "Let's have another drink. The night is young. No, the pursuit is just a game. It doesn't mean anything sinister, eh? And anyway, its thrill is subverted by the boring reality of the capture."

Simon paused, their empty glasses in his hands. "Now *you* seem to be saying casual sex is unsatisfactory," he said.

"It's real," said Nick, smiling. "Reality is constantly unsatisfying, unlike fantasy. Fascination, pursuit – they're both made of fantasy. Of course, in reality, as it happens this time, neither of us would stand a chance of getting off with any islander, as you observed."

"But the thing is, with Martin," said Simon, his mind homing back to its central concern, "my closeness is reality."

"Or do you blend your fantasies with its actual reality?" As Simon looked sceptical, Nick flapped his hands in a shooing gesture, and turned away with histrionic pride. "Well, well, don't listen to your Auntie Nick, then! Anyway, where are these drinks? I'm going to have a pee, and I expect them to be here when I come back."

Simon pushed out into the swarm of people between the table and the bar. The wall opened just enough to let him through, and then closed indifferently behind him. On his return, he saw Nick emerging from the toilet door just as two enormous Maori drag-queens in tight and plunging red and turquoise silks were on their way in.

One of them eyed Nick flirtatiously with quick generous eyes. "Are you gay?" he said challengingly.

Nick looked embarrassedly flattered. "Oh yes," he said, screwing his face up in a suddenly confused mixture of blush, smile, and look of pride.

"Oh, what a pity!" the drag-queen said disappointedly.

The other drag-queen beamed at Nick. "Good on you, girl!" he said. They glided by magnificently.

Nick returned to the table, scratching his head. "Did you hear that?"

he said, his hands reaching for a cigarette. "The world is made of contradictions, eh?"

Simon nodded, uncertain from the glibness of Nick's tone whether he was expected to take the remark up. He said, non-committally and yet ponderously, "Well, yes, that's true."

"Which means," Nick said, breathing smoke down his nose, his eyes filling with a momentary calm, "reality is made up of contradictions. Including the reality of your relationship with Martin. It's only in fantasy that absolutes exist."

"Yes," Simon heard himself saying reluctantly, staring blankly ahead of him, "ok, I agree."

"To live in reality we have to accept its contradictions and work with them. Even though that means accepting reality will never be what we want." Nick was leaning back against the wall, talking half to himself. "While trust in absolutes brings – entails a withdrawal from society. Society which is made up of real contradictory human beings."

Simon half-smiled. "Like you," he said affectionately.

Nick gave a little camp shriek and descended on his rum. "I can't think why you say that!" he said, gesturing with his eyebrows, and crooking his little finger as he raised his glass.

"I meant, actually, in your sexual relationships as much as anything. You live with Peter in what, so far as I can see, is rather conventional domestic bliss. And you often say how good that relationship is for you. And yet, as soon as the pubs close, while Peter still sits at home watching television, you seem to spend most Saturday nights, at least, prowling after strangers through every public toilet in the city. And you're ready enough to tell me later how much you enjoy and need that."

"We all have a range of different needs, eh? One relationship can't fill all our needs."

"Oh, I know that – on an emotional level, at any rate. My relationship with you, Nick, is just as crucial as my relationship with Martin, but in radically different ways." Simon stroked the freckled back of Nick's hand gently, and Nick's tough fingers closed round his own in a brief earnest clasp. "But what I don't understand," Simon went on, withdrawing his hand and frowning into his beer, "is what you get from these fleeting mechanical sexual contacts with people you've never even set eyes on, usually, let alone spoken to. I don't understand what these can fulfil, when to me, and from your own words, you seem to have such a good friend in your lover.

"After all, sexuality is an aspect of communication, isn't it? I realised that most clearly when I realised that I had never before felt the sexual joy I feel with Martin, because I had never before been able to be sexually involved with someone to whom I was so close."

Nick interrupted in exaggerated expostulation. "And yet you haven't had sex! Or so you tell me. I don't understand that."

Neither did Simon. He felt dazed, lost for a moment, as if he had been struck in some particularly vulnerable place. "Well," he began, but his mind seemed to be panting, "our relationship does already have its sexual side."

"And on the same topic," said Nick, warming to his argument, rapping the table underliningly with the flat of his hand, "why don't you have sex with me, then?"

"Yes, well, I've often wondered about that, about why I don't even want to," said Simon quietly. "I suppose – I suppose it's because from my point of view, the intensity and the strength of our relationship is from a closeness in the way the mind *manipulates* the world: not the way the world *feels* to us.

"Well, I agree," said Nick, laughing softly out of the darkness of his beard to dispel the tension that lay in ambush. "And I'm flattered to have someone who loves me for my head. But not just my head, but my head seen in relation to the rest of my body, and other people's."

"But one of the things that puzzles me is that in your politics you have such respect for other people, you have such respect for their right to be able to realise the fullness of their possibilities – and yet these casual sexual contacts you take such relish in seem to me so reductive of other people. So genuinely objectifying. You're not interested in relating to them as a real – as a full and contradictory person. Only – well, if not just as a body (and I'm not sure about that), certainly only as an inflexible pawn in some game, some realised fantasy of your own."

"You can't enjoy playing with someone unless they want to play too," said Nick, after a pause, toying with the stem of his glass. "Anyway, I make no claim to being free of the contradiction of a baser nature. I wouldn't want to be."

"But it's not nature, it's conditioning. As men we're conditioned to be proud of being predatory and unthinkingly promiscuous."

"Yes, you're quite right. Of course. But conditioning doesn't go away overnight, any more than everyone forgets about wanting to make profits as soon as a revolution happens."

Simon was silent. He began to feel a little drunk, a little weary of having to think. His eyes wandered over to the islanders at the next table, their white teeth flashing in laughter. "Perhaps you've never been the object of someone's predatory fantasies," he said half-heartedly, not looking at Nick.

Nick patted his hair fussily. "Oh, how wounding! I'm sure there's life in the old thing yet," he said campily. "And perhaps it's time you actually indulged in some predatory sex, if it comes to that. Come on, this is all getting too much like hard work for a Saturday night. Besides, we were meant to be discussing how to get gay liberation on the move again. Without gay liberation we wouldn't have been able to have conversations like this. Finish that beer, and I'll get you another one before closing time. If we can't resolve our complexities, at least we can drown them. Until they bob up as good as new tomorrow."

Simon downed the last of his beer willingly, and handed the empty glass to Nick with a grateful smile. Nick put his arms around his shoulders and squeezed him gently, before sweeping off – an action which few could have achieved in the space – towards the crowded bar.

Summer was in flight now, rushing away on showery winds, every day seeming shorter than the last.

One brief sunny day, Simon had been trying to write an overdue letter to Philip and Annie, when Martin appeared at the door with a spare helmet and a look of anticipation. Simon was glad of the interruption. He had found himself putting down his pen again and again. In the months after his arrival, he had written frequently to Philip and Annie: their world still seemed criterial, and it was important to keep in touch with it. But recently, he had felt it becoming more and more distant, its concerns less and less directly relevant.

It was Martin's day off. He was working as a bus-driver now, perched behind the wheel with the enthusiasm of a child in a pedal-car: he had found the prospect of more university life too stifling. In his characteristically impromptu way, he had come to take Simon for a walk in the bush. Willingly, Simon had allowed himself to be whisked off.

It was warm, and unusually, almost eerily still. They found their way to a small dam in a steep, thickly wooded hollow, a place that seemed shut away. On the dam itself, some young Maoris were fishing for eels with sharpened sticks. Almost out of earshot, Simon and Martin lay stretched out on a flat rock at the point where the creek slowed as it formed its tiny lake behind the dam. To one side of them, the white waters scrambling along amidst the overhanging foliage showed the apparent timeless placidity of the lake for a momentary episode. Above them, only a small patch of cloudless sky was visible above the tops of the hills, caught in a stillness that equally could not last. All around and beyond, the bush lay in shade, undisturbed except for the steady hissing of cicadas; but on their rock the sun fell, cascaded onto the shimmering leaves of a flax bush just ahead, and out over the odd magical tree-fern and tawa tree rising raggedly out of the dark undergrowth that went plunging down the slope opposite.

Martin had closed his eyes, but Simon had kept his half-open, turned on his side so that he could ponder dreamily the peaceful golden landscape of Martin's face and body, naked except for his underpants, spread out beside him. Drowsily, he wanted to know their history, how they had come to be there, these generous sunny slopes, laid with such calm and abandon so near him, and yet still so far. Some mystery still seemed to lie beyond them.

Suddenly awake and restless, he sat up, clutching his knees. There was some distant jubilant shouting from the dam, and leaning forward he could just see one of the Maoris pulling an impaled eel from the water. It thrashed helplessly, and a stain of blood was just visible from where Simon was watching. He leant back, brushing dust from his jeans. As usual he had not taken his own clothes off, faltering at some hurdle of vulnerability.

A sense of great loneliness was beginning to fill him. The bush was so still, almost lifeless; indifferent. "Martin, are you awake?" he said anxiously. He did not dare to touch him.

Martin stirred, and his eyes opened a fraction. "Yes," he murmured, raising a hand to brush a fly from his cheek.

"We should watch the time," said Simon. "We don't want to be late for the gay liberation meeting tonight."

With a yawn Martin raised himself on his elbows, staring ahead at the dappled water, blinking. "No, that's important, eh?" he said quietly. "You think so, don't you, Simon? And Nick's certainly put a lot of work into it."

Yes, thought Simon, Nick is indefatigable. He may be taking care to play no significant personal role, but it's him who has provided the inspiration, the impetus for this revival. "It moves like the tide, the gay movement," he had said one night, as the two of them sat together on his verandah with a bottle of wine, watching the moon rise behind the jagged black line of the mountains on the other side of the harbour. "There we all are sitting alone in our little rock-pools, and a wave comes slowly in and gathers some of us up and goes back a little. Then another wave comes in and reaches people that hadn't been reached before and lifts them up with it, and goes back a little less. And on and on until the whole beach is covered."

"That's very poetic, Nick," Simon remembered saying fondly.

"Oh, scratch a political activist and you'll always find a poet underneath. I still keep a drawer full of my early work!"

"Yes, yes, we owe Nick a lot," said Simon, looking down; knowing that he could not let Nick and the others down by not going, yet secretly half resenting the fact that he and Martin had to rush off to a meeting, when they might perhaps have captured and kept with them this wild moment. "I don't think any of us would have had the confidence to put in the time and energy we have, if it hadn't been for Nick making solid suggestions and giving encouragement in the background."

Martin nodded slowly, yawning again. He stretched. "Are you surprised it's taken off like it has?" he said through his yawn.

"I suppose in a way it's always a surprise to find there are so many other gay people around – after all. At any time, in any place," Simon said, lying back on his side, supported by an elbow. "A very invigorating, stirring sort of surprise. And I suppose that in itself has got something to do with the number of people that do turn up."

"But it's happened here in the past and petered out, eh? Well, failed, really."

"Yes, I know. I came into contact with the tail-end when I first arrived."

A sense of cyclical failure seemed suddenly to cross Simon's mood like a dark cloud. He struggled with it. Memories swept in – the disintegration of gay liberation in London, the collapse of his own hopes there, and in Glasgow. "Well, in everything one has to have immediate goals, I suppose, as well as long-term ones." He scrabbled in his mind for an image of success that would dispel this sudden louring feeling of personal fecklessness. "Like our picketing of the Labour Party conference about law reform. But if you fail in those goals, I suppose it's not surprising if – if you temporarily lose heart."

Martin was nodding slowly, eyes still and deep with thought. "Anyway, like you said Simon, it's important to have a gathering-place. And a lot of people have obviously found one in gay liberation, when they hadn't found one elsewhere, eh?"

"Seems so. There's certainly quite a range of people we seem to have coaxed out of the woodwork."

"Yeah, yeah. Well, it's hard to find places to meet other gay people," said Martin softly, sadly, looking away across the lapping water. "I know you like the pub, Simon, but I don't really. So crowded and so noisy, and I don't like to get drunk, eh? I've always preferred the sauna."

From somewhere in the bush nearby there came the sudden shriek of a bird's alarm-call, one simple sound that had to cover a wealth of possible warnings. It was lost at once in the reasserted, seemingly peaceful monotone of the cicadas.

Simon's eyes bored into the grain of the rock beneath him, his body tense and motionless. He knew that Martin went to the sauna, Suzie had mentioned it casually over the phone one day when Simon had asked where Martin was, and later Nick had mentioned bumping into him there. And yet still its reality from Martin's lips came as a shock to Simon – though as yet he was quite unsure why. He dimly sensed, and at once feared, something that was about to bring unwanted light to the long slow dawn of their situation.

"I've never felt able to go there," he said quietly, uncertain from where to come at the subject.

"I find it relaxing, eh?" said Martin, turning to look at Simon. "It's a lazy atmosphere. And everybody's free of clothes, so you all somehow seem the same."

"I think that's one of the things I wouldn't like," said Simon, his mind working hard. "You wouldn't necessarily be able to tell whether the person beside you was an anarchist or an arch-reactionary, a bus-driver or – a policeman. I don't want to move on illusory equal terms with a policeman or a member of the National Party."

He paused, stroking at the face of the rock with his hand as if trying to physically mould his thoughts into precision. "The whole thing is an escape from reality, a fantasy. It's an attempt to make sexual fantasies real: by denying the reality that created the fantasies in the first place."

Without his intending them to, his eyes, moving busily, glanced Martin's naked body, at once strong and gentle, reconciling opposites; and another thought occured to him. "Besides, people don't *seem* the same when they've got no clothes on, not even then. A tall, heavily built, bearded man is not going to seem the same as pale thin hairless little me. Is he? A tacit assumption would be made about my position and my sexual wants – if anything, even more when I was naked than when I was clothed!"

There was a silence. A tui was singing almost inaudibly somewhere in the distance.

Looking timorously up at Martin's veiled face, Simon wondered if he had even been listening.

But his voice began in response, shy and yet persistent, confessional and yet assertive, the kind of voice that might be used to tell a possibly unsympathetic parent that one was gay, thought Simon. "I've never thought about any of those things, eh?" he said. "But I know I've met some good people there. And if I don't see them again, that only stops us getting so involved we start playing games. Yeah, some neat people, eh?" He hesitated, and his voice came almost imperceptibly. "One especially."

Like the sudden symptoms of an illness, Simon felt his heartbeat quicken, sweat appeared in little drops that he could see on his hand, and his throat tightened as though it were sore. The song of the tui came again, closer, clearer, a mournful contralto melody. "Oh yeah?" he said softly, trying confusedly to sound to Martin encouraging, and to himself indifferent.

"He's in Canada at the moment," said Martin wistfully. "Joe." His voice seemed to take the dull monosyllable in a shy gentle embrace. Simon's name had never sounded like that on his lips.

270

And so there's someone else, thought Simon, it's as simple as that.

Suddenly, with a deep crystalline burst of sound, the tui flew from the bush, big and glossy blue-black, and alighted on the flax just a few feet ahead of them, clinging precariously to a shaking brown flower-stem, its ruffed head twitching suspiciously from side to side. Surprised, stirred, Simon caught it in his view, he wanted to hold it there, but it flew off again immediately, a speck blurring into the dark bush on the other side of the water.

No, he sensed it was not as simple as that at all. Nothing is. Why had this Joe never been mentioned?

He felt cold, and his hands were shaking. Quickly, like a panic-stricken rat in a test maze, he experimented with how he might react. Yes, it should be with resignation, an acceptance of the hard facts. Free from resentment that for some reason they had been kept secret. What difference need it make anyway? Wasn't he trying to accept the complexity of life? He felt his lower jaw pushing out into a grimace of stoical resistance.

But he wanted to know more, and was afraid to at the same time. "Tell me about him." His voice sounded strange to his own ears, deep, toneless, as if it came from someone else.

"There's not much to tell, eh?" came Martin's voice beside him. "It was about a year ago, Simon. We were both on our way out of the sauna one night, neither of us having found anyone. And we saw one another. Funny, eh? Just in the doorway. Well, we only had that one night, because Joe was shooting through on his way to Canada. But it was enough, you know. He'll be back later this year, eh?"

Romance, thought Simon, it's romance. Our friendship, our closeness is being blocked from realising itself by some illusory faith in romance. I should have known. The whole sauna thing is founded on the myth of romance, the beautiful bronzed stranger who gazes into your eyes and whisks you off to perfect bliss.

Romance, he thought, gazing steadily out across the lake, his face passive and unmoving. Romance is an instrument which keeps us apart, by making us put our faith and hopes in the charm and beauty of a stranger, unknown and so treacherous, instead of consolidating the real bonds that might exist between those who are close to one another.

He had not spoken. The air was filled with the quiet lapping of water, the endless trilling of the cicadas. He said casually, "What's he doing in Canada?"

"Well, his father lives there now, eh?" said Martin, his voice handling even these circumstantial details tenderly. "But he was brought up in Christchurch. He's got a wife and kid down there. They're separated, but they still see a lot of one another. He's working selling

271

advertising space in Canada, and when he's made enough money, he's going to come back and buy up an old house in Wellington. Maybe – maybe I'll move in too, if it works out."

Simon felt stunned. Time seemed to be coming in waves, very fast, and then very slow. And yet he still sat there, his body unmoving and seemingly placid, even to himself. "What does he look like?" he said curiously.

"Well, he's blond," Martin began softly. I'm blond, I'm blond, thought Simon: it was like the unexpected glimpsing of a ship's light when one had given up, drifting lost in an open boat in the dark. He wanted to shout, before it moved away. "And tall," Martin went on, "bearded, quite stocky really."

The sun went behind a cloud, the first that Simon noticed passing. A light cool breeze shivered the leaves of the trees around them.

"Time must be getting on, eh?" said Martin, leaning over and reaching for his shirt. "It'll be a cool evening, I think. We ought to go home and pick up a pullover or something before we go to the meeting."

Simon latched at once wearily and eagerly onto the trivial details of everyday necessity. "We won't have time to go to your place and mine, I don't think," he said flatly, turning slowly, and venturing to look at Martin once again, half clothed now, with the kind of rapidly routine self-steeling with which one might venture to look a second time at an ugly injury.

Martin's eyes bobbed up from following the donning of his socks, and caught Simon by surprise in their playful tenderness. Simon struggled to harden his heart in resignation. "You can borrow one of my pullovers, eh?" said Martin. "Doesn't matter if it swamps you. It'll give you – what do you call it? – a waif look." He bent over the other sock. "No point in going to your place. After all, it'd be nice if you came back and stayed after the meeting," he said gently, "my friend."

My friend. In the midst of his rejection, Simon was pulled back by the very fact of their closeness. How could he break from a bond that was so mutual? Martin might as well have laid hands on him: he had to turn and look – fondly, warmly. "Yes, that would be nice," he said.

And at once the old hope stirred within him. It was like some insinuating Rasputin, reactionary and mystical; though it had been battered and drowned and taken surely for dead, now it rose and came at him again. "That would be nice," he repeated softly.

Martin stood up, his back to the light, almost a silhouette, framed by a rim of bright sunshine. "Ok, Simon, let's hit the road," he said. "Liberation awaits us." He smiled amid the shadows, and his great eyes glowed.

Simon clambered to his feet. Somewhere in the distance he heard a tui singing again, probably on the other side of the dam. They began the ascent of the hill, which had not seemed nearly so steep when they were coming down. While one paused for breath, the other would step ahead and turn back to give a helping hand.

CHAPTER TWENTY-TWO

Some months later, in the dead of winter, the news filtered through to the gay liberation group that the National Party was to hold its conference in Rotorua. The first reaction was a defeated sneer and a shaking of the head. How predictably defensive of them, to hide away in a small town in the midst of a term of government, safe from the demonstrations that everywhere must be straining at the leash to break free and snarl and bark around them while they cowered hopelessly at bay.

"You know what we should do," said Simon, disappointed and dreaming, "we should hire a bus and go and picket them just the same."

At the moment of his saying it, it seemed to him a forlorn fantasy; but so inflammable was the mood of the group now, such was the impetus already behind it, that others caught the idea like a spark.

Behind the scenes Nick did all the fanning he could, and by the next meeting it no longer seemed incredible or even reckless when Marje, the teacher of handicapped children who dressed like a bikie, rose grim-faced and asked confidently, "How many people would be prepared to go up to Rotorua for the weekend of the conference?" She herself and her lover raised their hand fiercely, and Simon and Martin lifted theirs with a sense of heroic optimism. Slowly, in the damp dimly-lit chill of the hall, hands, however hesitantly, began to flower here and there, and then at once came a shower of half-promises and ashamed excuses. The picket was on.

After a long discussion of what it should contain, Simon was delegated to go home and write a leaflet. It was a hard one to write, having somehow to strike a balance between the acceptable disguise of a reasonable tone and the outrage of which it was born, as well as the clean sweep to which it aspired. But by the next meeting, only a few days before the conference, there it was set out in fierce black print on wasp-yellow paper.

But Simon had made a mistake, carried away by his sense of initial success into carelessness.

At one point the leaflet cried, "The National Party is continually proclaiming its championship of the right not to join a union, of the rights of the unborn child, but what of the individual's right to practise their sexual preference as she or he chooses?" At once there came the voice of Nancy from Sydney with its characteristic Australian whining twang, like a circular saw cutting with unerring accuracy through Simon's almost conceited impetuosity.

"Just wait a minute," she said. "Aren't we laying ourselves open here to the possibility of someone saying, 'Look, even Gay Liberation believes in the rights of the unborn child'?"

"But – not if you look at the context," said Simon defensively, ashamed to admit he recognised his blunder.

A discussion sprang up, though it hardly seemed necessary, and eventually the wording was changed to, "The National Party is continually proclaiming its championship of the so-called 'right' not to join a union, the 'rights' of the unborn child, but what of the very real right of the individual to practise their sexual preference etc.", which Simon had to acknowledge (even if not vociferously) was an improvement. And so he had to take the whole thing shamefacedly back to the party headquarters that Nick had arranged for them to use, and not only reset it, but publicly confess to his clumsiness.

"Never mind," said Nick, patting him on the shoulder as he sat down wearily to confront the pasting up. "Come up to my place when you've finished and I'll have tea ready for you. We'll have pumpkin soup, and hot corned beef with roast kumaras and a salad with lots of garlic in the dressing, and guavas and ice-cream. And a spot of wine. Does that make it worthwhile, that as well as learning from your mistakes?"

In the event, there were eight picketers: Marje and her lover, Nancy and hers, Simon and Martin, his friend Rodney the dormitory-suburb hairdresser, and a painful spectre of a person called Bruce.

They gathered on the Friday evening in a rented van parked on the edge of the city centre. Late night shoppers kept passing indifferently in busy family groups. It was a cold clear night. Everyone was there except Martin and Rodney. Martin did not finish work until seven-thirty and they were waiting on him. Rodney was to be picked up near his work. People were already cold and knew they would be colder. People were already cramped and knew they would be more so.

In the back of the van with Simon sat Bruce. Simon found his presence hard to endure; the pain that bristled around him like a force-field was dazzling, Simon could not bear to look it in the face. There was always an air about him of being quite out of control: his clothes were always hopelessly scruffy and ill-matched; he was awkwardly overweight; his lank hair was unkempt and unwashed; his beard was uneven, he breathed noisily and desperately through his mouth as though choking; his bulging eyes writhed this way and that in terror and resentment like penned sheep in a slaughter-house. He lived in Wainuiomata, the tiny monotonous prim industrial suburban town, just too far from the city for easy access; and everything about him was shouting at you that he was trapped and slowly dying in an agony of deprivation and hopelessness from which he expected no escape, though what was worse was that he also knew it was not really his fault. The clumsy desperation of his gesture in coming on the picket, as he saw it, seemed reflected in how irremediably uncomfortable his bulky body looked in the confined space of the van. Someone who rarely spoke, but sat staring down at his nervously fumbling hands, only occasionally all at once catching fire from an overheard remark in someone else's conversation and gasping out something like, "That's just it, you can tell people and they don't believe you, they don't believe that you're gay." He undoubtedly already knew that when he returned from this desperate foray to the drab routine of Wainuiomata, his workmates would not so much laugh at how he spent his weekend, they would quite simply ignore it.

For Simon his presence on the journey was a reminder of a past not completely forgotten, and a *memento mori* to them all. We can't rely on the grace of God to save us from that, he thought. It's up to us ourselves to do something to prevent its ever happening to anyone ever again.

Martin was characteristically late. Conversation wilted, fingers began to drum. At last he appeared, a crammed duffle-bag slung jauntily over his shoulder, so overflowing with reasonable apologies that no one said anything. He glowed with obsessive excitement like a child being taken on an excursion.

"'Right," said Marje briskly, "we're off then."

As the van's engine jerked into life and it began to move, they all found themselves smilingly exchanging glances, as at the take-off of a plane to distant parts.

But as they made their halting way out of the city, every red traffic-light seemed to sabotage their excitement. One or another of them would try to strike up conversation, but all that came out were little nervous reassurances about the length of the journey, which everyone knew well enough. While Bruce sat incommunicative and occasionally sighing.

Until they picked up Rodney, where he sat waiting on his case by the end of the motorway. They were half an hour late. He burst into the back of the van, an explosion of lush Afghan coat and shrieks of aggrievance. "Where have you been? I was beginning to wonder if you'd meant *next* July! God, it's antarctic out there. I thought you'd just driven past me. I've been waiting so long I probably need another shave. I didn't dare nod off to sleep because there's no anti-freeze in my mascara." His dumpy body enveloped in his enormous coat, and his big expensive suitcase, seemed to fill every available space. Apologies were proffered. But Rodney's flow of speech stuck on grievance like a scratched record. Simon soon cringed into a corner and tried to show the unconcern of an inanimate object. The women began to talk among themselves. Only Martin appeared to be listening with a look of saint-like patience.

Irrepressible, Rodney fixed himself to Martin like a giant leech, sucking sympathy out of him with a stream of elaborate plaints as regular as the nattering thrusts of a drill, trying to prevent him from congealing with a digestive lubricant of diminutive "Marties".

Simon was disappointed. He had wanted to swop anticipation and self-wonderment with Martin, to build a fire of softness on the hard cold journey. He turned away and stared out of the window, into the vast black sky with its alien stars, Orion upside down and the Southern Cross, feeling alone in a strange land.

"Simon, stop sitting over there looking like Rodin's Thinker," said Martin, "and come and sit here by me." At once Simon felt ashamed of trying to act indifferent.

He got down and sat by Martin, and Martin snuggled up beside him, slipped out of one arm of his coat and put it round Simon's shoulders, so that the pair of them were wrapped together. Rodney turned away sulkily, hurt and silent with nothing to take hold of, and at once Simon felt guilty about having looked jealous.

Soothingly, Martin began to ask him about himself, to ask him, for instance, how he was enjoying the socialist youth group, whose meetings he had been attending more and more frequently, usually with Martin.

"Well," said Simon, "one thing at least it's done for sure is make me feel at home in history."

"What do you mean?"

"Well, I used to feel I'd simply been unlucky, that I was growing up in a hostile incomprehensible disintegrating world, which was not my fault – but which I had no control over. You know?"

"Yes, I know."

Simon did not feel ashamed of the naivety of his thoughts with Martin, as he would have with Nick. He felt gratefully free to say simply what things felt like to him. He said, "But now I feel I understand. What is going on around me is only the inevitable result of a process, I may live out my life without this misery ever changing for most people at all, except to get worse. But just as inevitably there will come a time when the disintegration is over, and something new and whole and sane and hopeful begins to grow. And what is most important, I realise that I can have some control over it, I can do something to change it. Maybe not much, but however little it is, if I do it with others it will be a contribution. I don't suppose I'll live – not in these times – to see any more than piecemeal changes. I don't suppose I'll live to see a world organised to fulfil human needs, anywhere. But at least I can have been working towards it, and know how it will be possible. I've got a place. I am no longer – no longer an aberrant loose part in a machine that grinds unsteadily on, totally uncaring of my existence." He stopped, thinking suddenly, If only I could attain the same overview of my personal relationships.

"I'm not sure I know what you're describing," said Martin carefully. "I think for me being in the socialist movement is more just a gut-feeling, eh? I can't bear to see people put down and hurt everywhere the way they are. I want to do something about it. But I can't really see things in that remote way, like you do. Perhaps that's why I feel uneasy in the group sometimes. Our ideas are so big and so good, but we don't seem to actually manage to do much, to change what people go through, eh?"

"Yes, I know, I feel that tension too. But good ideas do make things happen. That's how come we're going on this picket, eh? And it'll help things change. Slowly. But it will. We know that, because things have been changed for us in the past by people doing just this sort of thing."

"Yes, I guess you're right," said Martin quietly, his eyes luminous in the half-darkness, looking into the distance. "Let's try and get some sleep now, eh?"

He squeezed Simon gently, and Simon touched his hand – like a child's, so soft, so definite and determined in its affection, and yet still a little helpless, a little inept. Suddenly, catching sight again of the stars, Simon thought of Glasgow and of London – so far away in time as well as place, it seemed now. He lay there with Martin in an embrace, and the van carried them on into the icy inland night, up the endless double bends that inch their way round the waste edge of the huge indifferent volcanoes, up into the plateau, towards the confrontation.

They reached the motor-camp in Rotorua a few hours before dawn. At one point shortly before, it had been so cold that ice had formed on the inside of the windscreen. Now they each unfolded themselves from their crumpled positions and went into the hut to stretch out for at least a glimpse of sleep on a real bed.

The pale sunshine of a winter morning, the lush grass heavy with dew, the air thick with the smell of sulphur. From the window of the hut a thin ribbon of volcanic steam could be seen rising among the conifers beyond a small glinting lake. Dark hills gently undulated along the horizon.

It was already quite late. The women had been up for a while and were just coming back from the camp's mineral pool. Rodney was officiously and noisily preparing breakfast, while Bruce sat slouched over the table, staring broodingly into the knots of the wood. Simon went outside and sat on the step, gazing into the mysterious landscape. Martin slept on unruffled.

After breakfast Marje brought out the leaflets and the petition forms, and she and Nancy counted them and parcelled them out. Then everybody piled excitedly into the van, and they drove to the conference rooms, ready to catch the delegates and party members as they filed out for the lunch-time break.

They set up their two brave little banners in a mood of stoically ignored trepidation, watched curiously only by a small television team.

And then people began to emerge. It was only the first two or three who were taken unawares. Men in neat suits, they stepped out of the dark hall into the glare of the sunshine, dazzled, perhaps hardly noticing the banners let alone what they said; and suddenly found their way barred by a polite but unmoveable Marje, thrusting a leaflet into their mechanically responding hands and asking whether they would like to sign a petition for the repeal of laws against – homosexuality. They looked down dumbfounded at the petition form and then at the leaflet in their hands as though they had been defiled. But they being gentlemen, and Marje being, strangely they thought under the circumstances, a woman, they simply said very restrainedly, "No thank you"; and walked away quickly, joining each other at once to calm their nerves with some exchanged flippant comments, fingering the yellow leaflets awkwardly in their hands until they were out of sight and could crumple them into a rubbish-bin with a clear conscience. But the news spread back into the hall fast, and people came out forearmed. Visibly steeling himself, Bruce – who had put on a suit specially for the occasion, an ill-fitting one needless to say – stepped up to a small old lady in a pink two-piece and blue rinse, and said softly, almost stammering, "Madam, would you care to sign a petition for the repeal of anti-homosexual laws?" "No way!" she barked at him, eyes fixed ahead, flinging a vague irritated punch, and striding off, laughing to herself in derision. The MP who had failed to get an unsatisfactory bill through parliament the year before emerged sheepishly with his wife on his arm. Marje and Rodney both made a beeline towards him, but his wife steered him past, saying, "My husband went through a lot of trouble for you, you know. You've just got to be patient. This kind of thing does your cause a lot of harm. Why don't you pack up now and go away?" "Traitor!" Rodney called after him operatically. Meanwhile men could be seen hovering just inside the glass doors, trying to work out the line of least resistance along which they could make a dash for it.

Simon felt totally consumed by a precarious blend of fear and exhilaration; which struck him almost as a concentrated form of his last few months. He kept trying to watch Martin's gentle but unabashed approaches, but the crowd kept getting in the way. At one point he himself found a huge wall of a person advancing on him like a golem, who pushed the proffered leaflet aside contemptuously, and leaned over and said raucously, "No thank you, young fellow! I'm a decent ordinary New Zealander and a farmer, married with three kids, the backbone of this country, and as far as I'm concerned, you're unnatural and you should all be lined up and shot. Shot! And let me tell you, there's a lot of people who think like me!" Simon winced away, biting his lip, only to find himself by a bespectacled prim elderly woman who said earnestly, "Don't you think this has all gone too far – this Gay Lib thing? I mean, all this bra-burning!" Nonplussed, he found himself smiling politely and drew a hesitant breath to answer. But she just walked off shaking her head gravely.

It was only when they found themselves alone that Nancy drew attention to the fact that the television cameras had been filming them. They looked at one another flattered by a sense of achievement after all. One of the crew came across and asked them, with the manner of sharing a favourite running joke, whether they knew that the Prime Minister had called them "those pathetic creatures begging at the door".

Well, from outside it might have seemed a hopeless gesture, thought Simon, but there are hopeless gestures one can learn and gain strength from. He knew that well enough.

Now it was all over, they suddenly collapsed in laughing relief, swopping stories of their favourite rebuffs, turning ignorance and prejudice to a source of wondering amusement. Nancy and her lover squatted on the spot and counted the signatures. There were sixteen in all, more than they had expected.

Simon felt the confirmation of a growing sense of having done something he should have done. At home with his actions, as it were. It was a small achievement but a real one. He looked forward to telling Nick about it. Nick's response always seemed to add another dimension to things.

Marje said, "Well, I think we deserve a drink."

In the pub a wall of Maoris against the bar watched the eight of them smilingly. The high spirits they were sharing were infectious. Even Bruce was seen to show the ghost of a smile now and then. Martin, quietly glowing, stayed by Simon, murmuring to him an amused commentary on the apparently unconditional elation of the others. Now and again Rodney, who found it impossible to express his smug satisfaction without physically grabbing hold of someone else, would come up and paw at Martin, like an unsure child with a teddy-bear.

Martin whispered to Simon, "Now the picket's over, let's you and I go off and leave the others for a while. It's funny being back in my home town again, I never thought I'd come back to it for a gay picket, eh? We could go and visit my sister and brother-in-law, give them a surprise."

"What are they like?" asked Simon.

"Oh, just ordinary, just married," said Martin.

"Do they know you're gay?"

"Well, they know, but they've never acknowledged it."

"Right," came Marje's voice, loud and inviting. "So here we are in Rotorua with the rest of the day to ourselves. Who's for a drive to the Waimangu Gorge?"

Martin said, "Simon and I are going to go and visit my sister and brother-in-law."

Rodney's face fell. Simon felt an unexpected twinge of fellow-feeling for him, knowing well what he was going through.

Martin said, "Can you give us a lift back to the motor-camp so we can pick up our things?"

Simon was surprised. "Are we going to stay there?" he asked aside.

"They'll put us up, eh?"

"How will we get back to Wellington if they decide to take the van back tonight?"

"We could hitch. I've got enough money to fly. It's not expensive."

"Yes, I've enough to fly. Shall we do that then? It's a long way. And anyway, I like flying."

After they had picked up their things Marje dropped them on Fenton Street, and they waved goodbye with childlike ostentation until the van disappeared round the corner.

"Which way?" said Simon.

"Let's cut across the sulphur flats," said Martin.

"But it's dangerous, isn't it?"

"I used to do it when I was a kid. It's fun, eh?"

Simon smiled. It seemed a typical Martin gesture.

They made their way up to the gardens and turned into them. Beyond the gates they passed the trim artifical rock-formations, where trained volcanic steam curled elegantly in little wisps, surrounded by regularly planted trees. They followed the inexorable ponderous avenues, past the mock-Tudor mansion and on towards the lake where the smell of sulphur grew stronger.

And suddenly the gardens stopped. Where the path petered out there was a fenced-off wild geyser, an untamed vicious spitting thing that belched out tall clouds of steam through the half-dead trees around it with a smell like frying offal and a noise like a great hissing cat. But if they stood on this spot and turned their backs to the geyser, in the other direction they could see only neat avenues and flower beds and the little blue wreaths of trained steam round the rock-heaps by the gates.

"Come on," said Martin, "this way."

Simon followed him, into a totally alien landscape that might have belonged to another planet. The colours were so strong: the bright yellow of the sulphur, splashed here and there with the rich gingery brown of algae, striped and blotched with clear turquoise mineral water; and then the dazzling white of the steam, the heavy green of the distant conifers, rippling in the breeze along the horizon. They moved by strides and reckless leaps on tiptoe across the pools and rivulets of boiling water, coming to a stop sometimes on dead crusty yellow islands, while they searched for a way onward through the swirling steam. Martin would stand and laugh when it seemed they were stranded, while Simon grew afraid; and then suddenly with a childlike whoop Martin would plunge off dauntlessly into the white fragrant fog, that at once engulfed him and obscured him momentarily from view, till he reappeared further on calling to Simon to follow. And Simon, trusting him, would walk on confidently between the seething waters, to suddenly find himself there beside him, grateful and wondering.

At last they came to the end of the flats, and Martin ran ahead and flung himself down on a shaggy tussock of long straw-like grass, gazing up into the blue sky, going pale now as the sun grew low. Simon crouched down beside him, breathing in the cloying smell of sulphur.

"It's great to be home," said Martin. "This is where I grew up, and you always sort of feel you belong, eh?"

Simon looked at him stretched out there alone on the awkward hump of dry prickling grass, so completely relaxed and at ease. He seemed remote, like some wild animal. Simon did not know what to say. He shifted his feet to keep his balance in his precarious squat.

"Do you miss your home, Simon?"

A cold evening breeze was coming off the lake.

"Well, I don't know," said Simon quietly, "I'm never sure where my home is. Wherever I have been, I have always been a stranger. In Scotland I was so obviously English: but in England I felt – and sounded – Scots. Now, here I am, twelve thousand miles away from either place, at the other end of the world. But I don't feel any more or less of a stranger. I've always felt that I was looking for somewhere else to be. It's the same in a way with whatever type of people I mix with. In a working-class environment I feel – and sound – awkwardly middle-class; but in a middle-class environment, I want to repudiate it and run away. I don't feel at home with straight people: but I don't feel at home in a gay ghetto situation either. Perhaps my home is really just the sense of dissatisfaction, and of change."

"Well," said Martin, rolling over, his eyes closed, "I like coming home. It reminds me of being a child, eh? That was a good time. I didn't ever want to grow up. I don't think I really have."

"Perhaps not," said Simon, smiling fondly. "Yes, everything seems so simple in childhood when you look back on it, so straightforward. That's another thing – when I'm not wanting to be somewhere else, I'm wanting to be back somewhere where I was. Even if it's only the day before yesterday, life always seems to have been so much easier then than now. The future seems so demanding."

Martin was silent, his eyes closed. "I love the future," he said. "And I just can't have too much of the present to use for making it."

Simon nodded, and gently stroked Martin's arm within his bulky coat.

Martin's stomach rumbled noisily. He sat up.

"Tea-time," he said. "Come on, let's go and see what my sister's got to eat."

By the time they reached his sister's house, which was further round the shore of the lake, it was twilight. The inland cold was setting in. Martin knocked on the door in a flippant rhythm. From inside there came the sound of children. Martin's sister, Teresa, a person carefully dressed to look casual, opened the door.

"Oh! Well I never! Look who it is!" she cried, rather unconvincingly gushing. "Tom darling, it's Martin! Come in . . . and, oh, you've brought a friend."

Martin quietly introduced Simon. At once it was painfully apparent that he humoured his sister. Her husband Tom, someone who looked harassed by the effort of trying to look complacent and successful, emerged into the narrow hall with two boys of about six and four on his heels.

"A pleasant surprise, Martin," he said, genuinely, but not changing the look on his face of a fixed wince. Martin greeted him warmly.

He and Simon were fussed into the pretentiously furnished main room, and found two cups of coffee before them as if by magic, watery and instant, but in expensive pottery mugs. Looking up, Simon noticed that the source of the coffee was in fact a cowed and silent elder daughter.

"Well, how are you, Martin?" crowed Teresa, nervously tidying up a pile of children's books scattered over the coffee-table. "You're still . . . er, driving buses?" She handled the words almost as if they were a family shame.

"Yes, still sticking to it," said Martin, looking down.

"Oh well, sticking to it. Yes, that's something for you. Be quiet, children!" The boys were romping on a large cushion.

"Are you enjoying it?" asked Tom, who had sat down a little apart.

"Yes, it's already, eh? More fun than most jobs I've had."

"Well, what brings you to Rotorua, Martin?" said Teresa, trying to hide suspiciousness behind a laugh.

Martin said quietly, "We came up for a Gay Liberation picket of the National Party Conference."

"Oh. Oh. Oh well, did you really? How enterprising of you! All this way. I wonder what mummy and daddy would have thought. Yes, the conference is on this weekend, isn't it? Your cousin Bernard will have been there. Did you see your cousin Bernard? No, well, I suppose it would have been rather awkward if you had. Oh well, we must watch the news on television. You might be on the television, mightn't you? Do be quiet, Michael and Francis."

Tom said calmly, "And what kind of response did you get? Not too good, I would have thought."

"We got a few names on our petition, eh?" said Martin, "and a lot of abuse."

"Will you stay for tea?" said Teresa. "It won't be long."

"Yes, thanks. We're hungry."

"Oh well, that's – that's good. Mary dear, will you go and lay the table, and clear away these coffee mugs."

The elder daughter quickly and silently gathered up the mugs and slipped out of the room.

"Her speech impediment's getting a bit better," said Teresa. "Thank goodness. Well, I'll just go and have a look at the casserole. It's – it's nothing much, I'm afraid."

She rose, hovered awkwardly for a moment as if there were something more she should say, and then went out.

Tom struck up a conversation with Martin about other members of the family whom Simon did not know. The two boys had stopped playing on the cushion, and the six-year-old had begun to read a book. The four-year-old was toying rather half-heartedly with a boat made of Lego. Suddenly he got up and came and sat by Simon, beaming at him.

"Hallo," said Simon.

"Hallo," he said. "What's your name?"

"Simon. What's yours?"

"Francis. Look." He picked up a large brightly-coloured story book of Maori legends. "Read it to me," he said, putting it into Simon's hands and snuggling up beside him, with a look of rapt expectation.

Touched, flattered in a way, Simon opened it at random and began: "Once upon a time there were two friends called Ruru and Kareawa. They lived together by the side of the lake, and every morning they went fishing for eels together, and no one was more happy than they." Simon saw Francis gazing at him as he read with a look of committed absorption in dreams only a child could have. As if in mechanical imitation, Simon found himself casting a wistful glance at Martin, whose face looked solemnly beautiful in attention to his brother-in-law. Simon read on: "But Ruru was too beautiful for a mortal and Kareawa too happy. So one day, the fairy people who live in the forest, the Patupaiarehe, came and stole him away from Kareawa . . ."

At that moment Teresa returned. "Oh Francis, do leave, er, Martin's friend alone," she said at once, and as Francis showed the first tremulous signs of pouting, she added, "Go through and sit at the table. Tea's ready."

They all sat down rather tensely around the large family table in the next room, and over the unexceptional casserole Teresa tried nervously to guide what she seemed to feel the obligatory conversation with Martin along safe routes, but kept bumping into things like socialism and abandoned university courses and homosexuality. Spooning out the home-bottled peaches, she ventured to address Simon.

"And are you – are you a socialist, too, Simon?"

"Well, yes, not a very good one, I'm afraid, but I try to be a committed one."

"Oh well, I suppose it's the commitment that counts really, isn't it? And – and you'll be in this Gay Liberation too?" Since she knew the answer, it seemed she only sought to show she did not mind hearing it.

"Yes, that's right."

Tom interrupted, "Where are you staying tonight, Martin?"

Martin said, "Well, last night we stayed at the motor-camp, but we wondered if we could stay here tonight. We were thinking of flying back tomorrow."

"Oh yes, you must stay," said Teresa, rather over-eagerly. "Tom darling, they can have the double bed and we can sleep in the single ones in the spare room." She sat back with a look on her face as if she had just sent a large donation to famine relief.

Just at that moment Francis pushed his pudding plate petulantly away half-eaten, and climbed down from the table. He ran round towards the main room, but stopped instead at Simon's chair, and smiling broadly, he put both arms round Simon's neck and kissed him vigorously on the mouth, drawing back with a beam of achievement.

Teresa struggled valiantly to hide a blush, and said at once, her voice faltering a little at the world's unfairness in the face of her efforts, "Francis, it's time for you to go to bed. Mary dear, will you go and give him a wash."

There followed a distractingly noisy combat of wills. Somewhere underneath it Martin said quietly, "We don't mind where we sleep," resenting, Simon suspected, the assumption of coupleness. Hearing him, Simon felt the familiar stab of regret, so familiar it could scarcely be said to hurt, that things did not have that reassuring simplicity. And he thought of the straightforwardness of Francis's open kiss with a certain wistful envy.

Tom said, cutting through the situation again with the blandest practicality, "You want to fly back, you say? There aren't many planes on Sunday. I think there's one at half-nine in the morning. I'll go and find the timetable."

The table was disrupted, and Simon and Martin drifted back into the main room. A little later, Teresa appeared, dressed for outdoors, and explained that on Saturday nights she did some part-time nursing at a nearby geriatric home, and she would not be back until the small hours; but, she added with a strained breeziness, she would see them in the morning before they left, she hoped. And then, looking once round the room as if for something important she might have forgotten, she left quickly.

Simon expected Tom to ostentatiously relax once she had gone, like some bad stand-up comic's joke, but he remained uncertain of himself; only later, after producing some indifferent port, politely rather than ostentatiously it seemed, only then did he allow his eyes to stop screening themselves as if from a bright light, and to open into a little warmth. Simon only half-listened to the conversation, which was about people and situations he knew nothing of; but after the port, he could not help hearing an increasing note of caring in Tom's voice, and at one point he heard him say, "You're the only person I have conversations like this with, Martin. Teresa's fond of you, too, it's just that she . . ." He paused, with a look not of searching for a word, but of shocked realisation at coming triteness which was shocking because it struck him as unjustly inadequate. "It's just she – she finds it – difficult, to express it."

Increasing patches of boredom and the lack of sleep began to tell on Simon, and he was soon nodding and yawning. Exhaustion struggled with restlessness. He heard Martin say, also in the middle of a yawn, "Tom, I think it's time Simon and I went to dreamland."

Dreamland, thought Simon, bruised unexpectedly by the word, dreamland! Perhaps that's the only place one could ever be at home, the only place one could find all fulfilled.

Tom got up at once, explaining apologetically he hadn't meant to keep them up, he was only waiting up himself to watch the match between the All-Blacks and the Springboks on television.

"I know I shouldn't really be watching it, because I support the anti-apartheid movement," he said awkwardly, "but, well, I like to see a good game. Life's full of contradictions, isn't it? And anyway, it keeps me awake for a few hours. I don't like sleeping alone."

He showed them to the spare room with its two beds.

Simon undressed slowly and thoughtfully. Martin stood already naked, seemingly undisturbed by the night chill, watching him, and said softly, "Come into bed with me for a little while, eh?"

But Simon found himself lying diffidently beside him, haunted by a sense of regret, of unfulfilled longings that he must force into perspective. Staring at the ceiling, he said, "Couples are always very ready to place other people in the same relationship, aren't they?"

"I guess it was kind of her," said Martin. "They have their problems,

Tom and Teresa, eh, they have their problems. But they're both very generous at times."

"Yes. Sometimes I feel I've really no idea what it feels like to be a couple," said Simon. He felt like punishing himself for wanting the impossible. "And I'm sure I'll never know. Perhaps I'm not really any use to anyone!"

Martin gave him a patient head-shaking squeeze. "You're a good friend, Simon. And who motivated the picket?" he said gently, tolerantly. "Let's get some shut-eye now, eh?"

Simon climbed out and turned off the light and got into the other bed. The sheets were cold. The smell of Martin's body came with him on his own skin and filled his nostrils disturbingly as he shut his eyes for sleep. He could just hear the lapping of the lake on the shore a few yards away, the water reaching out and then retreating, reaching out and then retreating, over and over.

CHAPTER TWENTY-THREE

Two or three weeks later it was Martin's birthday. Simon had made him a card with two stuck-on pictures – an El Greco saint and Thumper from *Bambi*, a combination which seemed to Simon to epitomise Martin's physical appearance – and bought him a blue denim cap like one he had himself which Martin envied. But when he phoned, the phone was answered by Suzie, who was surprised that Simon did not know that Martin was not there. He had taken time off work and left the day before, she told him, for a high-hiking holiday in South Island. Perhaps he had tried to contact Simon and failed to get him?

"Perhaps," said Simon. "Why did he go?"

"Oh, you know him," said Suzie casually, "he's always got itchy feet, eh? He said something about being a year older, about wanting to look round Christchurch, because it had associations for him."

"Oh," said Simon, understanding.

He felt hurt and lonely. Even resentful.

But now there was the gay liberation conference to prepare for, only the second of its kind in the country. It had seemed an impossible feat to pull off when the idea was raised, just before the Rotorua picket, but now everything was already under way, the premises were being booked, posters were being printed, a programme was being drawn up. Several people from other cities had already indicated their interest. With Nick's encouragement, Simon struggled to sink himself in the elated purposeful activity of the group: but his success was partial.

Gradually, however, he found himself settling into the meagre comfort of routine. The strangest places, he thought, can come to feel like home.

He spent a lot of time with Nick. "Ah, lovers, lovers! You have to take Martin for what he is," Nick said rallyingly. It was late one night, the flagon of wine they had shared was almost empty. Peter was at a party after work, and Nick had been feeling lonely and anxious, though loth to admit it. His speech was solemnly slurred. "Martin's like a wild bird, eh? We've lost enough of our birds – through collectors collecting and farmers settling down. Would you rather see a bird in the museum or the bush?"

As usual it was hard for Simon to tell whether Nick was being playful or serious. It seemed often that for Nick this was not a meaningful distinction. Simon's mind was blurred and he groped for an answer. "I just want a stable relationship," he said inadequately. "Surely it's not too much to ask. Like yours with Peter."

"Stable!" said Nick, gesturing with his eyebrows. "There's nothing stable about our relationship. There's nothing stable about relationships."

"I know," said Simon, nodding sagely in wine-sheltered acceptance. "I just hoped you'd tell me I was wrong. One goes on hoping."

"There's nothing wrong with hoping, I suppose," said Nick, "but planning is better, Simon. And you know that." He reached out waveringly and seized the flagon by the neck. "Let's finish it off," he said, splashing some of it rather haphazardly into both their glasses. "You know, some of the happiest moments of my life were spent completely on my own. On my little bit of land in Coromandel. With its pumpkin-bed and its puriri tree. The noise of the waves all night long. I was terribly ascetic. No wine! Once a month or so I'd go on a fruit-juice fast. If you keep it up long enough, you go into this divine daze, and I'd wander along the beach for hours, watching the surf. Deliriously happy!"

"Almost literally, I suppose," said Simon, playfully nuzzling Nick's foot with his own.

"Where the creek went into the sea you could dig for pipis on the beach. I'd dig up my quota and go home for a solitary blow-out of pipi fritters. Have you ever tasted pipis? Delicious! Just like jellied sperm. One day you must come with me and we'll make a pilgrimage to my hermit's cell, eh?"

"I'd love to," said Simon dreamily. The last of the wine was proving a little overwhelming. Without really knowing why they both found themselves laughing.

Peter came home at that point, quietly sober as usual. Simon stayed the night on the divan, trying not to listen to the sound of their love-making in the next room.

A few days later, as unexpectedly as ever, there came a gentle intimate unmistakeable knock at Simon's door.

Simon froze in his chair, throwing an uncorrected essay impatiently back on the pile it had come from, making to bound to the door with a start of excitement; which changed, even as he rose to his feet, into resignation.

He opened the door slowly. Spring was on its way. A little light and mildness still lingered in the early evening air, and the smell of moist vegetation came on the restless wind. There he stood, his eyes searching, wanting, pleading, as unashamed as a dog's.

Looking down, Simon said, "Aren't you coming in?"

Gratitude and warmth welled up in Martin's eyes, they seemed to open like dark flowers. "I didn't know if you'd be in, Simon," he said softly, bowing his head as he came through the door, although there was no need to, looking at once clumsy and waiflike in his overlarge cycling-jacket, his crash-helmet jammed into a protesting bag in his hand. "I'm glad you were, eh? It's been a while."

Dusk filled the room. The edges of objects were blurred, as though becoming unreal. The scent of wet grass came in with Martin and lingered in the air.

He sat down without taking his jacket off, and talked quietly in the half-light of his travels in South Island, the rain, the mountains, the beech-forests, and how he had ended up at last in Christchurch; how he had sat down in the street within sight of Joe's house, just looking at it, for an hour. As he talked it became almost dark, his voice came out of nowhere, but Simon did not get up to put the light on. "Here, I brought you this, Simon," said Martin, and there was the sound of him taking something out of his pocket, and his hand reached out of the gloom. "I picked it up by a glacier." It was a stone, just a whorled stone, but in the last light from the window, Simon could see the glint of minerals as if trapped somewhere inside.

"Let's turn on the light," said Martin, "I've got something to show you."

Simon rose slowly and switched on the light. The moment stood revealed as harsh reality. Martin was bent over his bag, pulling the crash-helmet out by main force as it seemed unlikely to come any other way. He put it on the carpet, where it rolled over onto its side, and drew open the mouth of the bag so that Simon could see inside. There was a bag of flour, a couple of rags, a plastic bowl, and a wad of posters for the gay liberation conference. It was remarkable the bag had been able to hold so much.

"I thought we could hop on the bike and do some postering," Martin said after a moment, since Simon had said nothing but only stared vacantly at the obvious contents of the bag, pondering to himself the strange dogged resilience with which Martin stepped back from the precariousness of dreams and plunged into old friendships and interests as if nothing had changed.

"Yes," said Simon absently. "Ok. Good idea."

"We'll have to mix the paste first." Martin got up with the bowl and the flour and went into the kitchen, and Simon followed, but only stood in the doorway, watching.

Up to his wrists in a mess of flour and water, with caking white patches already splashed over his clothing, an absorbed expression on his face, Martin looked more like a child at play than ever. Simon thought, once not long ago he would have been watching him admiringly, almost enviously, flattered to be allowed to be present, as a timid well-behaved child watches the activities of a more adventurous playmate they would like to be able to imitate: but instead, as it was, he began to feel like an amused adult, privileged to watch the secret play of a child, but belonging to another world, and above all, another sense of time.

"There!" said Martin, shaking off the excess paste from his plastered fingers in a fine shower over the floor. "Shall we go, eh? Have you got something to carry water in? This bottle'll do." He snatched a not completely empty vinegar bottle from the shelf, emptied the remains down the sink, filled it with water, and lifting the bowl of paste in the other hand, turned to Simon with a purposeful look.

"Ok," said Simon, "I'm ready."

They went up the path silently in single file. Simon clambered awkwardly onto the bike behind Martin.

And they swooped off, they were racing along, speed absorbed them both. Far, far, as far as one of the suburbs on the other side of town, zigzagging up the main thoroughfare that snaked its way up through it to its highest point, where the houses and gardens suddenly ended and the bush began, and the harbour lay spread out below them like a map ringed with the dotted lights of the city.

There they stopped, leaning against one another, expectant. And turned, and slid back down the steep road in easy stages, stopping at every bus shelter and every parade of shops, to leap off the bike and into the shadows, lunging quickly and stealthily at the nearest flat surface with a wet poster, which would flap awkwardly in the wind dogging them like a pack of hounds. All this had the tension of a series of raids, though at that time of night there was no one about at all, let alone any sign of the police. It was tacitly stirring to think of the prim inhabitants of these family-sized houses rising the next morning to find gay propaganda, isolated but bold, at their local bus stop. It seemed no less than a vindication of some part of one's own reality, and in this case a reality which linked them.

After about an hour, they reached the foot of the hill. "Where now?" shouted Simon breathlessly over Martin's shoulder, as they paused, engine purring, before a red traffic-light.

"Let's put up a few round the university," Martin shouted back, his voice blurred by the visor, "and then call it a day." The lights changed, and beneath them the bike reared and swept off like a dashing charger.

From this direction they approached the university along an empty road that led under the rails of the cable-car. As they passed under the bridge, Martin slowed the bike down, and a few yards further on pulled into the side of the road.

"Let's put some up there," he said, climbing off.

Swinging his legs deftly over the seat, smiling at their complicity, Simon said, "Yes, I thought that, too."

Martin gave a laugh of excitement; his light stuttering bray of laughter, like a child swinging on a creaking gate.

They scampered to the bridge with the bag swinging between them, dropped it loudly to the pavement, and squatting on all fours began both vigorously to smear posters with the increasingly sticky paste. A car's engine could be heard in the distance. It drew nearer, and suddenly had driven past them. Martin glanced over his shoulder as it went on its way.

'It's the cops,'' he said in an alarmed whisper.

Simon looked up. They crouched, silent, unmoving, watching the car. It slowed down and stopped a little beyond the parked bike.

"Shit!" said Martin. "They're coming back. Let's beat it."

Beyond the bridge on one side of the road was a steep impenetrably wooded bluff, on the other a children's playground, at the end of which was a cable-car station. Without saying anything they hoisted themselves over the low railings and entered the unlit children's playground. Swings and seesaws loomed around them like strange mechanical monsters.

"Let's make for the station and pretend we just happen to be waiting for a cable-car," Simon whispered anxiously.

"Look at me!" said Martin.

Simon looked. He was covered from head to foot in flour-and-water paste.

Between the station at ground level and the bridge over the road the gradient of the cable-car track rose up steadily over a series of hollow scaffolding arches. At the far end nearest the station, where the track was at its lowest, the patch of ground beneath was lost in shadow.

"There!" said Martin, pointing.

They ran past a rocking-horse, its metallic head still and unseeing in the darkness, and in under the tracks, first bending and then crawling on all fours until they could squeeze themselves in no further. There they squatted, the grass cold and damp against their legs, trying to pant quietly, waiting. Simon saw one of the policemen enter the playground and switch on his torch. Beyond the ray of light, he was scarcely visible, a shadowy non-entity. Slowly the torch began to move towards them, swinging this way and that. Any moment now he must see them.

But incredibly the torch came to a standstill a yard or so away, and then turned and moved in a direct line back towards the road. Halfway across the playground it went out, and all that could be seen was the vague black shape of the policeman moving stealthily towards the fence, and then over it and under the bridge. In a few seconds Simon heard the car drive away.

He thought, How would one have asserted one's just cause with dignity caught squirming on all fours on the ground?

"They still might be keeping an eye on the bike," whispered Martin.

"We'll leave it. I'll pick it up tomorrow. Let's run for it. I can't afford to get fined."

"Ok," said Simon. "I'm following you."

They climbed over the playground fence where it bordered the path to the station, and found themselves in a patch of uncleared bush sprawling over a steep uneven slope. Somewhere a morepork called anxiously. They were surrounded by motionless black trees draped with creeper-like dustcovers. How long was it since a human being had set foot just here? Martin went first, cautiously, occasionally slipping and having to reach out for a branch to steady himself, but gradually becoming more confident, and scrambling out of sight into the treacherous darkness. Simon came after slowly, at once frightened and awestruck, listening for the sound of Martin moving ahead, inching his way down, and only at last, when street-lights could be glimpsed strangely through the foliage, catching his foot in a creeper and nearly falling.

They emerged just above the city, and when a car swept past, it felt to Simon for a moment as if they had not seen one for days. He looked at Martin, and gave a nervous laugh like a shrug. Martin beamed broadly, as if he had just won a race.

They made their way to a hotel and had a drink, and then went to the *Casbah* for something to eat. Martin asked Simon to come back to his place. And he went. Of course.

It was already late by the time they got there, and yet they were still too high and too shocked to go straight to bed. Both seemed to feel at once very vulnerable and very determined, at once threatened by isolation and reassured by solidarity. They sat talking over coffee in the front-room for a good two hours, the very air about them slowly seeming to become electric with dreams drawn like spirits to a seance.

At last, far into the morning, they went upstairs.

But as Simon undressed and climbed into bed beside Martin, he thought to himself, How many times will I go to bed with him only hoping and fearing? How many times? He felt so restless, and Martin's arm slipping gently about his tense shoulders felt for a moment only like a weight he wanted to throw off. "I can't rest," he said, turning his head away, looking at the wall. "I can't rest, Martin."

"Neither can I," whispered Martin, his breath warm against Simon's ear, but in his voice was the relishing of restlessness as the prelude to adventure.

Simon found himself smiling after all, and he turned towards Martin with admiring affection, stroked his face in gratitude for his very existence, brushing with a finger the hairs of his little beard, tiny but resilient.

"Read me a bedtime story," said Martin, with a voice that made fun of its pleading.

"Alright," said Simon, at once flooded with tenderness, "but you'll have to put the light on."

Martin slipped out of bed. If only we could always be so close, thought Simon, shutting his eyes, feeling the thought grating like a scratched record, if only we could always be so close! The light came on, and Martin scrambled back between the sheets with a battered book of fairy-tales. "Here, you choose," he said, snuggling down. "I've had this book since I was five."

Simon took the book, and it fell open in his hands at a story called "The Golden Fish", which he did not at first remember. There was a picture of a poor fisherman and his wife, holding between them a gleaming golden fish in front of a storm-tossed sea. He began to read quietly, carefully. It told how a fisherman, going out on a stormy day, caught a fish with scales all of gold, which he brought back to his wife to show her. He wanted to let it go again, but his wife said they were poor and hungry and they should eat it. And then the fish spoke, and said that if they let it return to the sea, it would grant them three wishes. First the wife wished that in their garden there might grow corn and fruit and vegetables that were never exhausted, so that they might never go hungry again. When this was done, they let the fish go. But the next day the wife went to the sea and called the fish, and wished that their home might become a fine palace, with courtyards and servants. Then she went to the sea again and called for the fish, and she wished that the sun might shine on their palace and their garden forever. But she was still discontented, and she went to the sea yet again and called for the fish, and she wished that she and her husband might be young together for the rest of time. "You have wished for too much," said the fish, " and now everything will be as it was before." The palace and the gardens and the sunshine disappeared, and the wife was poor and hungry again.

The half-light of dawn was beginning to slide under the curtains when Simon finished, swallowing up the light from the globe in the ceiling falling on Martin's rapt eyes. "I hope at least the fisherman didn't leave her," said Martin softly, turning to look at Simon. "Then at least they might have gone on living together happily in their hovel. Thank you for the story, Simon. I'm tired now. I'll put the light out, and we can get some sleep, eh?"

Gently they hugged one another, and Simon turned over and began to drowse at once. Beside him he could hear Martin's breathing rising and falling, rising and falling, calm and determined like the rocking of a boat. A canoe, he thought dreamily, slipping into sleep: a canoe that was carrying him over the vast spaces of the ocean in trusting search of a homeland, its whereabouts unknown, only legendary. In dream colours around him were Martin, Nick, and many others, each in their own canoe, eyes turned towards the horizon where a different place, another place, the Long-Bright-World the Maoris had told of, would surely loom up, some time. It was the perilous voyaging that was the achievement: and the joy.

It was Friday afternoon and suddenly as ever a cold wet southerly was rampaging through the city, sending its inhabitants scuttling to shelter behind closed doors. Simon had braved it home at lunch-time, and his sodden jeans and socks were drying off in the bathroom. A long awaited letter from Glasgow had been perched in the little wooden coop of the letter-box, looking a little worse for its great journey, forlornly wet and battered round the edges. But as he sat down expectantly to read it on this dingy afternoon, despite Annie's confidently racy style, something of a remembered anxiety and claustrophobia threatened to waft over him. Besides, behind the wit lurked ill-concealed tensions seemingly coming and going in Philip and Annie's relationship.

He pushed the finished letter aside and gazed out at the wind lashing the neighbouring tree-ferns and white wooden walls with rain. But how different this was from the rain of Glasgow. Most likely tomorrow, perhaps even this evening, the storm would have blown past as usual, giving way to a dazzling sunshine that bounced off the refreshed glossy leaves of gum-trees and taupata hedges. Everything was change, an exhilarating uncertainty. Quite unlike the steady lingering dampness that seemed to characterise Glasgow weather.

Not to mention the lingering tension that characterised the relationships that must persist amidst the dampness and the solid sandstone dourness and the poverty and aimlessness. Simon felt suddenly a sense of his tremendous good fortune. Not least in his companionship with Martin. No, it was not the absolute closeness he had once seen imaged in Philip and Annie. But this endless succession of passing moments of growing fondness, this feeling there was still something to work towards, to hope after – it was not just that it was more closeness than he had ever had, he was beginning to realise how much it really was by any standard. He was beginning to find solace in its very incompleteness, to trust in it.

In fact, the company of Martin was just what could be relied upon to brighten a wet day like this. He decided to phone him. He lifted the receiver with an immediate lightness of heart, only as he dialled remembering he had rung twice earlier in the week and no one had been in. But there was Martin's voice. Simon smiled into the unseeing plastic. "Hallo, it's me – Simon."

He sounded caught by surprise, as if Simon was the last person he would have been expecting to hear from. "Oh – oh, Simon! Hi! What are you doing these days?"

With a strange intuition, like a dog barking at an earthquake, Simon felt his hand begin to shake. Suddenly everything seemed to hang in a balance, and with the weight of every single word that either of them said Simon felt it swinging like a rope-ladder over a chasm. "Well," he said lightly, "nothing much. Going to work. Been to the movies once. I – I rang once or twice before, but you were out."

"Yeah, yeah, yeah." Martin's voice had the amused weariness of one who has been enjoying having their time unexpectedly filled to the limit. "Joe's here, eh? You remember him?"

A rope snapped. He was hanging over the abyss. "Oh yes, of course," he said, as if the memory was a distant and indifferent one. But he was slipping, he was about to fall. It's not fair, he thought, it's more than I can bear. I can't do it. He reached out desperately. "I wondered – I wondered if I could see you, tonight, or tomorrow, or – or sometime soon."

"Yes, but I'm not too sure when, eh, my friend." Martin's voice invited Simon to appreciate his delightful busyness.

At least, at least, Simon was telling himself, he didn't say No.

Martin went on, "I want to keep lots of time free for Joe right at the moment, seeing as I haven't seen him for quite a while, and – I don't know how long he's staying."

He's going away again, he's going away again, thought Simon. "Well, ok – shall I – shall I give you a ring the day after tomorrow?" He felt pleased with his own calm generosity.

"Sunday? I don't know about that, Simon, really. Look, I'll ring you soon, eh, and we can fix something up for next week, maybe."

"Well, alright. You could ring me at work on Monday. Perhaps."

"Maybe. Yeah. You know, my friend, I'm doing a lot of thinking, a lot of feeling, at the moment. Sort of feel my life's changed a bit, you know – the way it does when you're with someone you think you love. Anyway, I'd better go now, Simon, eh?

"Well, ok. See you then."

"Oh yeah, I expect so. Thanks for ringing, eh?" The phone went dead.

Simon put the receiver down slowly, almost reluctantly, as if for a moment he hoped it would somehow come back to life. While he held it the vibrations of Martin's presence still seemed to cling to it: once he put it down, he was quite alone. It was three o'clock. He had no need to go into work that afternoon, and the day stretched endlessly ahead with no way out. He felt completely cut off.

Outside the rain fell steadily, seeming to come from the side rather than from above, as if the world were being doused with cold hoses. Grey and sticky, the clouds oozed down over the tops of the dark mountains, slid into people's very back-gardens.

In a momentary panic, Simon turned on the radio. A cheerful voice was announcing that landslips had already blocked several suburban roads, and more were expected. "Well, the earth's certainly slipping away from beneath us today," it said breezily, "and if you're thinking of heading out of town, remember that the Rimutaka road is still closed by snow."

But the sound of another human voice was comforting. Then a song began: seeming to hold time in abeyance, to replace it with the past transformed into music. A wave of relief from the pressure of the moment flooded through Simon. "Well, how's that!" a voice sang. "I've found you out, I've caught you out, how's that! Now that I know what you're at – it's goodbye!"

Suddenly, out of the blankness within him, quite unexpectedly, anger began to grow. The traitor! he thought. The traitor!

He went into the kitchen to make a cup of tea, seizing hold of the electric jug, the pot, the mug, as if they were the hands of true friends that he could wring in his torment. He sat down to wait for the water to boil. A drip landed loudly on the table beside him. He looked up and saw that the lean-to roof had chosen to start leaking again.

Sorrow came, worse than anger. I want to see his face, I want to hear his laugh, I want to touch him, he thought, half-shutting his eyes, twisting his head on his neck till it nuzzled against his own shoulder. The closeness of his own flesh tantalised him. He could not bear that the warmth he felt, the skin he smelt was his own and not Martin's.

He got up and put the boiling water slowly onto the tea, and stood motionless, staring emptily out of the window. But what would he do with his time now? It was as simple as that. Day after day stretched remorselessly before him like a prison-sentence. He would be so endlessly lonely, so endlessly desperate. He felt as if he already knew every stain on the rough carpet, every mark on the dowdy walls of this cell-like basement flat.

He poured the tea, and took the cup through into the other room, casting a reproachful glance at the damp patch on the ceiling. He sat down, cradling the warm cup to him like a teddy-bear.

The phone rang. His heart began to leap, straining against the sense of realistic disappointment he tried at once to impose, like a dog that sees a garden from indoors straining on its leash. It would be the secretary from work, perhaps, or some acquaintance with an enquiry about the next gay liberation meeting. His hand trembling, and a voice still saying, But it might be him, it might be him, he lifted the receiver and spoke into it suspiciously, already hating its treachery.

Nick's voice spoke to him. "Hallo, it's me. We've been given the afternoon off because the weather's so – hopeless! It's hopeless! And I'm just sitting languishing at home, waiting for you to come round and brighten my day."

Simon's initial annoyance at Nick for being only himself changed as Nick spoke, into an at first grudging and then full-hearted gratitude for his existence. He wanted comforting company beyond anything else, and yet a certain shame at his grief, and even more at the reason for his grief as Nick might see it, made him unsure of his response. "Oh, were you really?" he said, playing for time, tightly clutching the receiver like the edge of a cliff.

"I didn't think you'd be in," said Nick. "No, I felt sure that if you weren't working, you wouldn't have spared a thought for poor little me, you'd be off and away with Martin."

Well, that didn't hurt too much, thought Simon. Nick's tone gave him the cue for his own immediate defences. "No such luck," he said, and paused at the daring of his own flippancy. "So, I could see you actually, if you like. Where's Peter?"

"Well, he'll be back from work soon. But we see each other all the time. Every day. I want to see you."

"All right. I'll come round. Actually, my place is leaking. If the rain goes on, I'll be flooded out anyway."

"Oh well, you'll just have to stay here. There's a spare bed, after all."

"Maybe. Thanks."

"There, there. Don't be long. I'll have all systems ready to go for tea and hot buttered toast in your honour."

He was moved. He could not hold out any longer. "I'm feeling a bit low, actually."

"Well, we'll cheer each other up. See you very shortly."

"Ok. Bye-bye."

He put the phone down, and relief spread up from his stomach to his head, making him smile. It was like water to a wilting plant.

And then all at once he hated Martin, hated the way he had betrayed him, the way he had led him on and then dumped him here, to linger on half-alive, having to console himself with moments like this. He wanted to ring him up again and shout abuse at him down the phone. You selfish treacherous prick-teaser, he wanted to shout, I hope you get nothing but misery from this sentimental adolescent infatuation of yours. It's all you deserve.

But no, that was not what he wanted to do. The thought of hurting Martin was at once intolerable.

He began to clothe himself for the journey to Nick's, which would be quite a struggle, although it was not far. He knew it was the kind of weather when one needed mountaineering gear to get as far as the gate unscathed. Quickly he put a few things in a shoulder-bag, so that he could stay the night if he wanted to.

As a last thought, he pulled out all the plugs, so that the house should not betray him by burning down while his back was turned, and with a final reproachful glance at the leak, which seemed to have stopped, he opened the door and edged into the icy barrage beyond, where at once every step demanded a certain obstinacy.

Later, after they had eaten, Nick had suggested they buy a bottle of wine. The storm was moving away, and it was easier to walk about outside. The activity of making the meal, the warmth of Nick's open fire, the cheerful profusion of thriving house-plants: all had cheered Simon with a familiar momentary sense of calm growth, like entering a walled garden in the middle of some teeming mouldering city. He made the journey down the steps to the nearest hotel in thoughtful silence, only speaking to acknowledge Nick's occasional comments on Wellington's weather and geography, that never-ceasing fund half of amusement and half of outrage for the non-native, which paradoxically gave Simon at this moment a reassuring sense of being at home. They agonised for a while over which wine to buy, and daringly plumped for a change from the usual, at Nick's insistence that this moment of their closeness be treated not as routine, but as an occasion.

"So," said Nick, as they made their way slowly back up the slope to the steps, heads bowed against the still swaggering wind, "you have love problems. A broken heart. Or cracked a bit, at least. Why don't you tell me about it? It'll make you feel better. Of course, I won't have a thing to say. Or even if I do, it won't stop it hurting."

"Martin's gone off with this guy he met at the sauna," said Simon offhandly. Even as he spoke, this trivialisation seemed alternately to function as dismissive contempt for Martin's action, and a consoling simplification of the complexity of the problems of their relationship.

"Oh, yes, Joe," said Nick, to Simon's surprise. "I remember he was coming back. Ah, love's so random, isn't it? You love Martin, and Martin loves Joe. And nobody loves you, who deserve it most of all, that's what you're thinking."

To be perceived brought a moment of comfort to Simon, but he spurned it petulantly. He said, "This thing with Joe seems so stupidly romantic."

"But one never appreciates the silliness of romance from the inside, eh?" Nick patted Simon's shoulder.

They reached the top of a flight of steps, and Simon stopped, catching his breath, panting hard. The wind flicked his hair annoyingly into his eyes, again and again, and bursts of cold air kept driving through his coat as though it were paper-thin. Nick came to a stop beside him, leaning against a concrete post, and clutching the wine to him as though it too needed protection from the weather.

Ostentatiously, Simon sighed and shook his head. "But Martin and I have been so close," he said, with the weariness of an over-repeated truth, "like brothers, in a way."

"Like brothers!" said Nick, pulling a face and standing upright. "You're not like one another in the least. Come on, rest over!" He began to walk towards the next flight of steps.

Simon followed in silence. Nick's observation had disturbed him, because it suddenly seemed perfectly true, or at least perfectly arguable; and yet, he told himself, it stood in stark contradiction to what he had felt for the last nine months or so. Or had told himself he felt. Could the observation really be said never to have crossed his own mind? "Well," he said at last, defensively, "we're similar in some ways." It seemed a weak and vague statement, so inadequate to the experience.

"You love him," said Nick between pants, climbing more slowly as he neared the top, "because he shows you strengths you don't have yourself. And vice versa probably. And a good reason for love too!"

They reached the top of the steps. Simon realised he was smiling despite himself, touched by the warm rays of Nick's clarity. He paused for breath, shaking his head at the confusion of it all.

"And he'll come back to you," Nick went on, stopping beside him. "Or you'll go back to him."

"I know," said Simon starkly, "I know." Loves are like stars scattered in the darkness, he thought; never burning out, only always growing fainter or stronger.

Nick said, "The very worst that could happen is that one period of growth makes way for another to take its place."

He touched Simon's arm and beckoned with his eyes. Simon walked on with him along the empty street, keeping his gaze ahead of them, where in the twilight the rainclouds still shifted about the ridges, now slowly revealing, now slowly hiding the windswept pine-trees.

CHAPTER TWENTY-FOUR

Another Saturday night had come round already. Once more the rain-clouds were drifting in over the mountains as evening fell. All day long, despite himself, Simon had waited for Martin to phone. But he had not. Looking at the thickening sky, Simon struggled to tell himself it was time to give Martin up. Let him go free. He phoned Nick and suggested they go drinking, and then to the party they knew about at Tony Hunter's.

But he did not enjoy getting drunk. It felt at first like a second best, then rapidly like the resort of despair, and he became haunted by the memories of other Saturdays, all happier it seemed, even the sad ones. Nick was tired, he was forcing energy from himself only for Simon's benefit, even his habitual flirtatiousness seemed mechanical. There were nights when their drinking made them feel the wise laughing controllers of their fates and other people's, and they longed for parties that were never there: but tonight when there was a party, it seemed each was going to it only out of a sense of duty to what is appropriate for a weekend.

By the time they left the pub it was raining. Drunken gangs with nowhere to go stood snapping at one another under the dripping hotel awning, a temporary island of light and dryness in the wet dark. Feeling got at, Simon curtly demanded that they take a taxi, and Nick simply followed after in silent indifference. They stood incommunicative in the long queue, huddled and shivering, Simon clutching the habitual flagon of red wine, whose sour hangover aftertaste he already expected, watching the drips tumbling from the awning through the lamplight in flashing strings.

It was a long uncomfortable wait, and they arrived to find the party in full swing. Normally that was what Simon would have preferred. But instead he just felt overcrowded. Catching a glimpse of some pretty gilded youth, Nick made a routine growl of sexual approval. Suddenly sickened, not even looking to see if Nick followed, Simon jostled his way in, glancing askance at the strange faces, all bland and trendy, towards none of which he felt any warmth; till he reached a wall, where he stopped and turned as though at bay. Now he saw Tony Hunter, the aspiring film-maker, coming towards him, looking gaunt and forlorn as usual, in a dusky pink embroidered velvet number, brought back no doubt from the Portobello Road. He began speaking to Simon anxiously, rapidly, his speech slurred, wheedling for sympathy Simon scorned to give him, complaining about how drunk and stoned he felt, about how worried he was the party should give the right impression, and vice versa, for the Black Power boys who were coming to honour it; they had performed under his direction their account of the Grey Street murders as a late-night show at the Hope Theatre, which had played to unfairly poor houses. Nick sidled up, perhaps to the rescue, and asked Simon for the flagon which he said he would look after, as he had found a seat whose comfort he did not intend to leave, in his condition, for the rest of the evening. "Come and join us," he added, with a rather tired twinkle, that was nevertheless meant to imply that there was more than just the comfort of the seat to keep him there. Meanwhile Tony had already latched onto someone else, and quickly leaving him with his new victim, Simon strode off into the party, challenging it to free him of his desperation, as if it could. He found, unexpectedly, two of the old gay liberationists whom he had made the acquaintance of when he first arrived, posed silently together in uncompromising blatancy, with the air of the knowing veterans of many struggles. He joined them, apparently just as they wanted, as conversation sprang up and at once assumed a subtext that was fondly nostalgic and keenly worldlywise. Soon the three of them stood staring at the rest of the party, like imprisoned revolutionary leaders looking down from a high window at the masses who have left them for some path they alone know leads to inevitable disaster.

But now the feel of the party began to change. The Black Power boys had arrived. Huge, heavy-shouldered, with straggling yards of frizzy hair and unkempt beards, their broad backs draped with leather and studs, their feet awkward in gumboots, here and there they towered above the trendy gays and the arty people like rocks rising out of the sea. And the trendy people fell away from them like foam from rocks, or a flock of little penguins taking to the water in fright, but looked back curiously, over their shoulders as it were and almost wishfully; then turned back to flatter each other with exchanged glances that they were at so socially diverse a party. The Black Power boys glowed darkly and childishly with the knowledge that they were, as they tried to be, the centre of attraction and awe, especially here in this unlikely preserve of wealthy white ineffectuality. And "their" women laughed together, touching one another in drunken fondness, cheeking the gays and trendies and scattering the smiling dazzle of their teeth, secretively sharing the enjoyed knowledge that somewhere beneath the naive folk-hero facade of their men lay a clumsy longing to seem bravely responsible and a fear of incompetence, which could indeed be seen flicking in and out like a tongue in the men's black eyes.

Almost at once the old gay liberationists seemed to feel free to leave, to relinquish their role. One who was half-Polynesian, smiling now perhaps in triumph, pushed an unlikely raffish cap onto his tight frizzy hair, while the other pulled on a pair of long red evening-gloves; and they left, saying goodbye affectionately to Simon, not inviting him to join them, knowing he would stay. He hovered only for a minute, before pushing out into the midst of it. Where he met Nick, who puckered his nose of course, and smiled conspiratorially; and for a few minutes they stood together, both floating on the excitement around them, catching the tang of the possibility of social adventure as on a breeze.

One Black Power boy, smaller and younger than the rest, pushing his way somewhere brushed against Simon, knocking some of the wine from his glass. "Hey, how are you going?" he said, and paused, swaying drunkenly, to stare at Simon, screwing up his face in uncharacteristic puzzlement. "Are you a girl?" he asked.

"No," said Simon. And caught Nick's eye looking at him half-enviously and sympathetically, as if to say, You almost said that reluctantly.

"I'm sorry, I'm sorry, eh," said the Maori, in confusion at himself.

"That's alright, I don't mind," said Simon, not routinely, but indeed venturing on flirtatiously, reassured by the presence of Nick as potential playmate.

But the Maori clouded his face with a smoulder of impatient and sincere aggression, and lurched quickly out of sight.

At once an atmosphere of jaded wistfulness descended on both Simon and Nick, though Simon had no idea what on earth, if anything, he could have expected, let alone wanted, from such an encounter.

He suddenly felt the recent sense of failure edging him into absurd unrealisable longings, into despairing oversimplifications.

Nick spoke, breaking what was left of the momentary spell, resourceful. "Come over here and meet this Canadian I've been introduced to."

Simon followed docilely, his eyes lowered, in shock at himself. He dropped onto the floor with his back to the wall and within arm's reach of the flagon where Nick had stashed it. Nick decided to leave him to himself, and joined in showy but monotonous conversation with the rather bemused-looking Canadian, about some mutual friends in Auckland. Simon sat unspeaking, routinely pouring the rough dark red liquid down his gullet recklessly, waiting only to be chastened by the moment of having drunk too much; waiting till it seemed every cell felt drowned and waterlogged, till when he closed his eyes there would run from his skull to the pit of his stomach an iron bar, a mast, pitching and rolling on a sea of nausea.

Nick spoke to him. "The wine's run out," he said.

Simon stared at the lurid purple residue round the bottom of the flagon. "I think I'll go home now," he said, and rose without further explanation, momentarily panicking that he had not even drunk enough to be assured of sleep; and at once as he went to walk, caught out by his unsteadiness. He moved slowly and deliberately towards the door, regarding the remains of the party with a look of studied reproach.

"Hey, are you a queer?"

It was the young Maori. He was leaning spraddled against a wall, a cardboard wine-cask of rosé hanging from one lolling hand, his head dropping heavily from shoulder to shoulder. For a moment Simon wondered whether to stop, uncertain as to how to react, fighting a qualm of physical fear.

"Are you a queer?" he said again. His glazedly ingenuous eyes floated up and hovered over Simon, shining out of his dark face like rising moons.

"Yes," said Simon quickly, brightly, trying to fend off the possibility of aggression.

But as if with the only gesture he could think to make, the Maori reached out the wine-cask to him. "Here, have a drink," he said. Simon raised the bulky cardboard box awkwardly to his mouth, feeling the sticky liquid spilling down his chin. It was sickly sweet.

"Good, eh?" said the Maori, encouragingly. "Sweet. You have some more. You have some more, eh?"

Feeling quite guilty that he did not enjoy it, Simon pretended to go on drinking gratefully. "Yes, thanks, it's good. Here, you have it back now."

The Maori took it back loosely in his hand, apparently suddenly lethargic. His tousled head nodding on his wide chest, he began to say over and over again, half puzzled, half pleading, 'People are always afraid of us, eh? Why are they always afraid of us?" He looked up at Simon, in drunken unhappiness, his awareness of the ineffectuality of his struggle to be acknowledged, not to be beaten down, as plain in his eyes as an open wound. "I don't know why people are afraid of us. We're alright. We're alright, eh?"

Simon felt almost intolerably painful, as if he were giving sixpence to a beggar for a cup of tea. He wanted to look away. The Maori's face roused reluctantly from his memory the faces of two others he had seen once, while he was on holiday, on a bus somewhere up the country, drifting to relatives somewhere, looking for work. They were not wearing proud leather and boots, but faded tee-shirts, torn jeans, sandals almost worn away. While the bus was stopped in a small town, they had got off to buy something to drink; and in the meantime a formidable local white matron, complaining loudly and needlessly about the crowdedness of the bus, had got on and sat in one of their seats. When they came back, laughing together, Simon saw them stop

304

and go silent before her in shock and bewilderment; while she, fussily gathering up the bags she seemed to carry as symbols of how much life weighed her down – as it must have – said to them sharply, "Oh, you're sitting here, I suppose. And don't tell me there's two of you." But it was not the words, it was their tone. Their soft faces were already going old and hard with dreariness and hopelessness, but she spoke to them not as she would have spoken to a white person of their age, but as if to some annoying small children she had found doing something she disapproved of, and was only stopped from beating by her respect for them as someone else's property. And the Maoris' spirit flickered and went out like a small flame in a draught, and they were cowed and silently apologetic. Simon felt the helplessness of a spectator out of reach.

And now the Black Power boy went back a step in his struggle with intoxication, slipping down the wall a little. As if with the farewell gesture of an unrescued survivor leaving his hold on a spar, he stretched out his open hand to Simon but it swayed about uncertainly in the air till Simon took it and dared to clasp it, amazed and touched, staring at their hands together. Then the Maori took his hand back, and it fell limply by his side. He turned away and stared into vacancy, an angry frustrated stare.

Simon went. As he left, a woman came up and stood by the Maori, and grinned at Simon.

In the hall the front-door was open: outside the rain had stopped, there were glimpses of the stars through the clouds; but the wind had sprung up, a chill damp southerly, with gusts that would halt the walker in his steps at every corner he rounded between here and home.

In Simon's mind the little glowing moment of closeness stood threatened by a great pointlessness, in a tangled place where feeling, however true and sweet, moved nothing forward, where only under-standing and planning would ever slowly whittle away the path ahead.

And at that moment, so strange it was like a dream, he recognised coming towards him the unexpected but familiar face: Martin. He was approaching through the moonlit frame of the door, his eyes baleful and huge; wide and eloquent as cinema-screens, like the Platonic form of James Dean. He made the little reticent indrawing of breath before he spoke.

"Peter told me you might be here," he said, tabling at once the fact that he had made a special effort to find Simon out.

"I – I was just going home, it's late," said Simon; feeling at once as drawn towards Martin as ever, drawn again to dive with him into the warm deep pools of his eyes; thinking at the same time of his cold bitterness, of the long-term pointlessness which this moment, no more than any other, would not solve; pulled this way and that.

"Can I come back with you and have a rave for a little while?" asked Martin openly, humbly. His gaze called, as an injured child in a storm calls out, and the passing stranger, anxious only to find shelter himself, is drawn to his own kind, come what may. It happened as it had happened before.

And would happen again, and again. I shall never be free, Simon thought.

"Yes," he said, as if it were a mystic acceptance of the world.

He put on his coat and stepped out into the cold, and Martin came after silently. Before Simon the long leaves of a cabbage-tree, a still felt symbol of a foreign land, flickered in the wind as if beckoning all at once in a myriad possible directions.

They walked, heads down against the wind. Now Martin quietly, solicitously asked after Simon's evening, and Simon in reply gave the surface details, in short phrases, keeping secret all the turbulence beneath. And in his turn Martin gave the surface details of his evening similarly, a visit alone to the pictures, a meal out alone, a return home at first to sleep, but then instead the restless search for Simon. Each knew the other was hiding a sense of things in collapse.

The moon edged out from beneath a rain-cloud, flashlighting the choppy waters of the harbour lifted in racing ridges. The cold wind gave little sighs and murmurs in the pohutukawas, turning up their silvery undersides till they looked as if they were already covered with the silvery new growth of the spring about to come.

When they reached Simon's place, they went down the long dark path in silence, anxious, Simon thought, not to wake the people upstairs' dog. But when they had passed the front of the house, he thought again it was because they were afraid to speak to one another. Inside his place it was cold, he had not left the heater on. He switched it on now, and the little red bar began to glow pathetically in the huge chill damp. Martin sat down in the chair above it without taking his cap off, on the edge of the chair at first, but then leaning over, so that the red glow caught his face from beneath as he warmed his hands.

"That's good," he said. "It's cold outside tonight, eh?"

"I'll make coffee," said Simon. He switched on the table-lamp, whose warm yellow circles of light dispelled the flat pale glare of the bare globe in the ceiling. He went busily into the kitchen, spooned ground coffee into the pot, and switched on the electric jug. While he did this, he heard Martin putting on a record, *Planet Waves*. As he came back into the bedroom, he heard Dylan's voice swooping up like a cry of joyful appreciation over warm soup. "On a night like this, I'm so glad you came around . . ." Martin was already sitting bent over the heater again, which was beginning to have some effect now, and Simon too went close to it and curled himself up fetally on the floor, so that it seemed to him this corner of the room became an island made up of him and Martin and a source of warmth. Into which both were staring, avoiding each other's eyes, as if waiting for something to be stirred spontaneously into growth.

With a great bang the table-lamp suddenly went out, the record-player fell into silence, the heater bar died into greyness, the jug stopped singing. Only the cold colour-draining glare of the globe in the ceiling.

"Ooh," said Martin, "a fuse has gone."

"There was too much of a strain on it, I suppose." The returning cold and dullness threatened Simon with terror and misery as he got up to go and look at the fuse-box. "I'll see if I can do anything about it."

"It doesn't matter anyway," said Martin softly, soothingly. "You'll be able to fix it, though, eh?"

Simon unplugged the jug, took a chair from the kitchen, and climbed on it to look at the fuse-box. One of the main switches had flicked itself off. Tentatively, unconvincedly, he pushed it back into the "on" position. To his amazement things came back on, Dylan began to sing again. A glow of surprise at unexpected achievement went through him. He finished making coffee, and took it through. Martin laughed at him and he laughed back. They both stretched out into the relaxation of a danger passed.

Martin said, "Joe's gone back to stay in Christchurch, you knew, eh?"

With one breath Simon's heart was sinking at the topic of Joe, ready to drown; with the next it was bobbing to the surface, to the light of hope despite itself, with the knowledge he was gone. He glanced at Martin's eyes. They were hooded, veiled, trying to hide, to let nothing through. "I thought he might have," he said, trying to sound con-doling, trying not to suggest anything but a consultant's disinterest on his part; but thinking, Now we can be together again, now we can be together again.

"Yeah, I think I might leave Wellington. Go to Auckland perhaps."

Again the sinking and the bobbing back, though this time not quite breaking the surface. At least not Christchurch, he grabbed at. He said flatly, trying to give a sense of balanced judgment, "Oh yes, well, Auckland would be an interesting place for you to live." He was looking away. He forced himself to look at Martin, partly for the sake of the performance as adviser, partly to play to himself the role of looking what was happening in the face. The eyes stirring now, like the quiet gathering of a symphony's slow movement after the silence that follows the already forgotten climax of the first.

As if trying to pull himself out of the water to see if it was worth it, Simon said, "Yes, I like Auckland. I'd like to live there."

Nothing in reply but a quick grateful smile, lost at once in reverie, registering no hostility to the idea, but denying its possibility. Simon retreated back below the surface.

Martin went on, looking into distance, the eyes like a far sun that was lifting itself slowly above the sea where Simon was. "You're like me, Simon, eh? It's a relationship that's what you're really looking for when you go to different places."

Yes, thought Simon, it is, that's all. But he said, "But I don't think we should think of couple-type relationships as being so central to our lives."

Martin looked at him, a gently knowing look, not believing him, but not reprimanding him for the dishonesty, accepting it rather as well-meant encouragement to keep calm. It's me that must keep calm, that must keep going, thought Simon.

"My relationship with Joe," said Martin, and a cloud passed across his eyes, putting them out for a moment, "I've expected a lot from it, eh? I feel very close to him, but in a lot of ways he's very different. I've been thinking the past few days, it doesn't work out like I want, I expect something he doesn't want to give, eh? So I sort of think maybe the best thing to do is" – he put a little exaggerated tautness into his voice – "move on. Hit the road."

Simon stared into the ground, struggling to hide his triumph, almost gloating inside. Then it let him down, of course, I knew it must.

"It's hard though, eh?.When you're in love." Martin said the phrase with an unaffected certainty Simon could never have done.

There was an expectant pause. "I don't know that being in love is really all that special," Simon said: thinking, You are the only person I ever dared to say I was in love with, but I never said it to you; because if you didn't know it, then what difference would saying it make, anyway? He was listening to himself speaking as if to a third person. He knew that everything he was about to say had crystallised for him through being with Martin, and yet he was speaking as if the wisdom he knew he was about to relay had dropped out of the air, was not born of any actual experience at all. "You know, when I was younger, friendship and being in love and sex used to seem to be three completely separate things. They were all quite different ways of relating to people, there wasn't any common ground between them. There were people who were your friends, there were people you had sex with, and then there were the people you were going to be in love with. And they were the special ones, the ones you weren't going to have to get to know, but who were going to drop one day out of the sky just for you, holding out to you the realisation of all your hopes and dreams like a new washing-powder that would make your wash whiter than anyone else's.

"But now it doesn't seem like that at all. Now it's actually beginning to make sense, I'm beginning to think of friendship and love and sex not as three separate things any more, but as one thing: a spectrum of communication, a spectrum of affection, along which all relationships between human beings take place, and move up or down. You know, casual acquaintances become close friends, close friends become lovers; and for that matter, lovers can sometimes become again only casual acquaintances. But you have to be *friends* with someone before you can be in love with them, you have to be friends with someone before you can have a sexual *relationship* with them. There has to be fondness and communication. They're all the same thing. Like, you know how in seventeenth century English they can use the same word 'love' – lucky people! – not just with lovers, but with friends, even of people they don't know well but respect and feel fond towards.

"Oh yeah, I know you *can* have sex like you have a bath. But when you've pulled the plug out, and got out of the bath, in a little while you're going to feel just as cold or as hot again, just as tense again as you did before you had it, however good it was at the time.

"You can say to yourself you're 'in love' with someone you hardly know, with whom there's no communication. Unattainability is meant to constitute its own thrill. But then you're really only playing out a role to yourself, because you expect it of yourself. There's no way forward because if you get a response, you get no response to you as a whole, only to the role.

"Being in love doesn't drop on us ready made, it's not a matter of destiny. It's just like making friends: we choose our friends, we create opportunities for friendship to develop, we work at it. Relationships are like the revolution: they don't happen overnight, and we've got to work to build them with the people and the level of consciousness that happen to be available."

He stopped in some surprise at how much he was talking, and saw Martin gazing at him with a doglike receptive earnestness, as if to be lectured to was what he had wanted. But I'm lecturing myself, I'm telling myself what I have learnt, thought Simon, it's I who need the wisdom to be able to cope.

Now Martin spoke softly, with his eyes deferentially downcast, like a respectful schoolboy bringing himself to dare to correct a teacher in an error of fact: "But being in love feels something different from all the other things in your life, eh?"

For a moment Simon felt an undertow swirl up and drag at his struggling mental limbs. But he said, pushing out, "Well, yes, but it's not surprising it feels like that when you look at the way we're always being shown how to think about it. Every cultural institution around us seems designed to make us feel we have no validity as human beings except as members of a couple. If you're single, you're oppressed for it. You're made to feel ashamed of what you are, afraid of what you are, and that you should struggle to rise into the class of couples."

Suddenly the memory of his past self, unreachable now, filled him with pity. He felt himself splashing about wildly, but not going anywhere, and he looked up at Martin to find his bearings. But Martin's eyes were looking away, far away, as far as the sun rising into mid-morning above the swimmer alone in all the ocean, the swimmer struggling forlornly to conquer something too vast to be comprehended as a whole.

Martin said, "I was just thinking about all the good talks we've had together, eh? It's good to hear *you* talk, Simon. It's usually me that does all the raving. Remember that time we were in bed, and I couldn't stop talking about when I was a kid and the things I used to do. I remember that, eh? It's good talking to you – you know, eh? My best friend. It's really good. Isn't it?"

"Yes," said Simon, feeling his words to Martin and his inner thoughts come together, fuse in a warm glow, "sometimes we're very close."

"So you think it's a good idea I leave Wellington?"

And he fell apart again, his thoughts into the cold of desertion, his words into the sternness of long-term advice and planning, so stern it had a cutting edge like a weapon. Don't go away from me, don't go away from me, though it's what I deserve, I'm no use to anyone, he thought. "Yes, I think it would be good for you," he said, trying to push concern for the other into his way of thought like a sword into the hand of a christian who would rather be publicly eaten by the lions.

"I'll go on thinking about it then, eh? But I don't want to go. In a way I'd rather stay on here, because – well, there's you here, and things. Who else would talk to me like you do, or bother to listen to my raves?"

The moment of his saying he is going to leave is the moment of our becoming as fond and close as we have ever reached, Simon realised.

There was a silence. Only the wind in the trees. Martin yawned, a sound that surprised them both. "It must be late, eh," he said.

"Yes," said Simon, dreaming.

Martin yawned again, quietly slipping in the question "Can I stay here tonight?" under cover of the yawn, a soft characteristic brush of humility. And as Simon said yes, it felt as if he had known all along he would ask, as if that was what he had been waiting for despite himself.

They stood up. Simon went and drew back the cover from the bed and wound his watch. Martin went to clean his teeth. Every action seemed to have a familiar ordinariness about it. They took off their clothes without looking at one another, without tension or expectation, as if they had done it too often to notice. And Martin climbed first into the bed and snuggled into it as if it were his own.

Simon put out the light, and as he groped his way back through the sudden darkness, a light patter of rain brushed against the window, and the wind nuzzled the pane like a sad caress.

When Simon took Martin in his arms, he felt the wants and fears and disappointments of another human being tangibly beneath his hands; he could touch them with his fingers, and feel them soothed and fulfilled by a stroke or a pressure. There was no remembering of the time before that was otherwise, no interest in what might come after, only all consciousness given up entirely to taking itself through the now. When he let his hand run down and up the slopes from Martin's waist to thigh, which seemed so long to travel, it ran not over flesh, but over expectation and joy in their reality; and when he put his arm about his shoulders and drew them to him, his arm was the actuality of consolation. There was such sureness here, which words in their defensive slipping and sliding could never have; such a sudden certainty of communication. And as it were in confirmation of this realisation, Martin scattered light words over him: "Simon, you have very talkative hands." And the silky sole of the foot and the toes that stroked Simon's leg were gratitude, or rather not just gratitude, because gratitude is only words, but this gratitude went straight through the brushed hairs of the skin to the very marrow.

Now, thought Simon, for the first time I have come within sight of what I was looking for. It is a communication that is *knowing* and *doing*, not speaking with all its vague inaccuracy. Here our wants and hopes and fears are answered and assuaged, they are quenched as if they had been only thirst. We are set free from the consciousness of pain behind and pain beyond. I understand sex for the first time.

And because the knowledge came from Martin, was his gift, he wanted to tell him as much, throw his loose ribbon of speech around their common experience.

And Martin spoke, stopping him, and laughing: "You know, other people are stupid sometimes, eh? I bet everyone else thinks we're having it off all the time!"

The words went through Simon like a knife into the heart. We should be, or we could be; but Martin wiped away the pain for ever with a stroking hand.

"Thank you for talking to me tonight," he said.

"No," said Simon, "it is you who make me able to talk. You make me understand things I have never understood."

Outside the light rain fell insistently.

They held each other in one another's arms all night, and when one turned in his sleep, the other woke and turned after him and held him again firmly: each fearful lest the other might break.

Simon woke slowly, consciousness breaking through sleep like shafts of sun through heavy cloud, illuminating awareness of his body still reaching out to clasp Martin's close to him, and vice versa; both reluctant to break apart, then all swathed again at once in sleep. At last he opened his eyes and looked at the clock. It was nearly midday. A cold grey light slanted in under the curtain, and the rain could be heard falling heavily now.

Martin stirred. "Is it late?" he said.

"Nearly twelve."

"Ooh. That's quite late, eh? Are you going to the socialist meeting?"

"Yes, I have to tell them about preparations for the conference. Are you?

"Yes. We'd better get up then."

Again as they got up and dressed an old familiarity descended on every action, defusing all emotional possibilities. Simon drew the curtains. A squally southerly was flapping solid sheets of rain.

"I'll go and have a bath," said Martin.

"I'll make coffee while you're there."

Everything was washed out by a kind of routine sameness, like the colourlessness of the day. Somewhere deep inside Simon, quite muffled up, was the thought: We have been as close as we will ever be. But even if it rose above the misty surface of routine, it surfaced as something quite different, as a sense of amazed gladness at just how close they *had* been, in spite of everything.

They were silent over the coffee. The rain hissed in the wind and smashed against the window-pane, which was beginning to steam up everything from view. And then Martin wanted to go home for a while before the meeting.

"You'll get wet."

"I'll phone a taxi."

"Yeah, you'd better. But you'll get soaked just going up to wait for it."

"I know."

"I'll give you my cap, it'll keep your hair dry."

"Won't you want it?"

"I've bought a new one."

Martin phoned. Simon said nothing about the story of the new cap, intended as a birthday-present for Martin, kept back in resentment when Joe loomed up. He took his old denim cap, to which he had become attached, which had protected him through two long wet alien winters, and smoothed it out caressingly; then put it not into Martin's hands, but on to his head, tilted slightly. "For you," he said.

The cap seemed to complete Martin's appearance, perched raffishly above the dark roaming eyes, sealing a sort of boyish wanderlust, confirming his utter unattainability.

312

"I'll go up and wait, eh? The taxi said it would be here in a minute."

"Ok. See you at the meeting then."

Simon watched at the door as he ran off quickly through the tossing downpour, brushing a shimmer of drips from the broad leaves of the rangiora bush, and out of sight.

The moment he closed the door the flat took on the very opposite of familiarity, assuming a strange unwelcome emptiness. He had a bath, made himself some lunch, grasping at the actions for normality. But it did not convince, and for a while he wandered about in his own room, feeling dazed by the sense of togetherness that had already passed away, as if alone in a wide open unfamiliar space.

Then it was time to walk to the meeting. He put on his coat and the new cap, and made his sodden embattled way down to the city.

Martin came in late and sat down beside him, giving him a quick smiling glance, eyebrows raised in mock depreciation of his own unpunctuality. The cold air in the room was heavy with the smell of damp clothes and shoes. The wind rattled the window-panes. Simon sat head down, only half-attending. Apparently that morning the police had launched a series of dawn raids on the houses of islanders, ostensibly looking for those who had overstayed their work-permits, and the news cast a general shadow of depression. The previous night already seemed not hours, but ages away. He rose reluctantly to give his own report.

When the meeting finished, Simon and Martin descended the muddied stairs together in silence, and stood hovering in the doorway. The rain had stopped now, but it was still grey and chill and damp, with a powerful southerly driving up the empty Sunday streets.

"Shall we go and have a coffee somewhere?" said Simon, with no conviction.

"Mmm . . . Oh yeah, if you like."

They began to walk with the slow pace of comparative aimlessness. All along Herbert Street the buildings were being demolished to make way for a new thoroughfare.

"Let's have a look in here," said Martin, pointing to one of the buildings, with an air of playground conspiracy.

They went through a doorway and found themselves in only the shell of a building, open to the pale sky. Here and there flaps of sodden washed-out wallpaper were still peeling from the exposed walls. Among the rubble and glass on the floor was a broken photograph-frame still holding a faded old photograph, rapidly being eaten away by the damp, of two smiling young men standing nervously in front of the building, which was bright with the freshly painted signs of a newly opened business.

"Come on, let's go up here," said Martin, leading the way to a staircase which disappeared enticingly from view. They climbed up slowly, and rounded a corner into nothingness. There was no upper floor, only a gaping hole into which they stared down at the clutter below.

Martin said, "We'd better be careful not to fall."

When they got to the bottom again, Martin suddenly ducked down and picked up something from among the rubble. It was an old-fashioned soft felt hat of the kind still worn by older New Zealand working men.

"Oh, I must keep this hat," he said. "This is the kind of hat islanders might wear too, eh?" He pulled it down onto his head, and the broad brim almost shaded his face from view. "Now I can give you your faithful old cap back."

"Yes, ok," Simon said. He took the cap, which Martin was holding out to him, and screwed it up uncaringly into his pocket.

"Listen Simon, I don't think I'll come and have coffee, eh? I'll just go home and listen to some records. I've got a few letters to write too."

"Yes, you do that," said Simon, almost relieved at not having to struggle with the wet curtain of incommunicativeness that was clinging to him. "I'll go and have tea with Nick and watch television, and talk about the conference, no doubt."

"Ok then. See you soon, eh, my friend?"

"I expect so. Give me a ring if you like. Well, see you later then."

The dark lean figure in the alien hat stepped over the rubble and through the doorway and turned unflinchingly into the wild weather. Simon followed, and turned the other way, and walked slowly and circuitously through the deserted city streets, hunched against corners round which the sprung-up wind came like a whiplash, under the awnings from which a few drips of last night's rain were still falling.

CHAPTER TWENTY-FIVE

Strangely, at heart he felt quite calm.

He was sitting apart with Nick at a table in a dark corner furthest from the loudspeakers. The hall was crowded, and already misty with smoke. Only half of the people there could actually have been at the conference. The Maori band was breaking into yet another turbulently nostalgic version of some hit that had haunted the radio recently. Simon's eyes turned to survey the dancers, as if from a great height. But at once winced away. Every time he turned, like brushing someone's lighted cigarette, his eyes caught Martin in a gesture of affection to the tall bearded stranger from Auckland.

Nick said gently, "There, there, I know! Even though you know it's not the end of the world, now and again you'd almost as soon it was."

Simon glanced him fondly, and at once looked down with a self-disparaging smile. It was strange. Just as it had seemed to make no difference how long Martin was out of touch, the moment he saw him again all the old intimacy returned; so now it made no difference he had taken him for gone more than once already.

If this time was final – whatever that could mean – it could only be because he decided it was.

"No, the world goes on," he said, shrugging his eyebrows. "And that's the trouble. The world goes on. And all I can do, it seems, is choose to stop seeing it in one way, and start seeing it in another."

He lay back in his chair, experimenting with this new strange freedom. He was holding the future at bay, refusing to let it crowd in on him. And at the same time he seemed to have rushed away from the past, as if he had been shot from it in a rocket, so that he could see its vast spaces spread out like a map.

For a moment even yesterday seemed distant, a different place. The sun had shone then, it had been a spring day. He arrived at the conference with a sense of excitement and involvement. Coming into the wide sunlit spaces of the hall, the harbour laid out beyond the big windows, he saw the size of the crowd and knew it was a success. All that effort had paid off.

He was told there were something over a dozen people from out of town there, even two from Australia. They stood out from the rest at once with the glamour of strangers, and people swirled towards them as they gathered in the hall, drawn by possibility like moths to a light.

One face only had stuck in Simon's mind, the tall bearded man, from Auckland, he thought, whose deep-set eyes had shown so grim a

315

struggle, born of such dark desperation. Somehow troubled, Simon had wondered again and again, what could ever bring peace and hope to such justified grimness?

He should have guessed the answer. And now he had only to turn his head to see. What, after all, had once brought himself peace and hope?

This morning the sky had been grey, a jostle of clouds was buffeted by a cold bullying wind. The hall had seemed full of an unwelcoming emptiness as he entered it, a little late – like everyone else, it seemed. There had been a long Wellington caucus at Nick's place the night before. But Simon could see Martin's coat already hanging up. He had not come to the caucus, drifting off with the people from Auckland for some reason, probably to show off his favourite haunts. Coming in now behind Simon as he stood hesitating in the doorway, Martin had greeted him warmly; but then strangely walked on by. Simon had hung up his jacket, collecting himself, and looked round once again: and suddenly glimpsed them silhouetted against the grey expanse of the window, the landscape beyond swallowed up in cloud. They touched one another with such a fond certainty; and the obviousness of it struck Simon with all the completeness and immediacy with which it must have struck them.

For a moment, in spite of himself, he had thought: They are saved.

Yes, he reflected now, his mind sinking back to the present once again, how I long to be able to make the world simple! Like a bird that must use one song to cover so many experiences, I want to pin the world down beneath defining labels.

"You know, I want the world to be simple," he said aloud.

Nick stirred from some open-mouthed reverie of his own, staring out at the dancers, and clasped his glass. "You, of all people, get bored by simple things!" he said, with a playful outrage, raising his eyebrows high. He took a sip of his rum and coke, and his look flooded with thoughtfulness. "But yes, when it comes to it, I don't think we can get very far without simplifications. We need to try out simplified versions of what to do to learn from their failings how to do it better. In private life just as much as politics. If there's any distinction between the two, which I don't think there is."

"I suppose I want my revolution now," said Simon, trying hard to smile at himself, looking wistfully ahead. "But is that such a wrong thing?"

"It's not wrong!" said Nick with theatrical emphasis, his face contorting into a look of wonder that Simon could ever suppose such a thing. "But it won't get you very far, eh," he added quietly, "simple Simon? And anyway, after a revolution, there's a long struggle to make things work."

Simon stretched his arms across the table and slumped over, leaning his head on them, staring away from the dancers at the wall. It was like stretching himself on the earth: waiting for it to cover him. He said softly, "I feel I've struggled enough already. I feel I deserve a bit of easiness."

"We all feel that," said Nick.

Reluctantly, Simon pulled himself back up again, and took a determined drink of his beer: a stirrup-cup for the long journey onward.

A bearded man of forty-five or so suddenly lurched off the wall, glass in hand, and came and leant unsteadily over their table. He had been standing timorously pressed against the back wall for an hour or so, often glancing over at Simon and Nick. He had a clumsy helpless look, the air of someone from the country who was still ill at ease in the city. "Good on you," he said quietly, in a slurred voice, raising his glass waveringly, "good on you." He paused, nodding as if with the satisfaction of having said something momentous he had been brooding on for a long time.

Nick smiled, with a delicate combination of amused warmth and admonitory politeness. "Well, the same to you," he said.

"Yeah, I've been watching you two," the man said solemnly, as if revealing a secret. "You don't know how lucky you are, you know. It wasn't like this in my – in my young day."

"It's a neat dance, eh?" said Nick, with a nervous laugh, shouldering the burden of the intrusion uncertainly. "Were you at the conference?"

The man looked puzzled, as no doubt Nick meant him to. "No, I'm not one for – for conferences. That's a bit beyond me, that. Don't want to get too involved, eh? Got my job to think of, too. They're neat people I work with, though, eh? I wouldn't say anything against them. I'm on the ferries, you know, on the ferries." His eyes roved forlornly, his train of thought lost. He took a contemplative sip from the little that was left in his glass, hanging there as if his business was unfinished. Then he looked down seriously, and laid a hand on Nick's shoulder. "And you, you know, you're a very lucky man, in particular. The moment I saw this young fellow here come in the door" – and his thickly eyebrowed eyes gestured coyly towards Simon – "I fell in love with him. Fair dinkum. Well, I wanted to say, good on you both. That's all. Good on you both." His hand slipped limply from Nick's shoulder and dangled in the air like a severed cable.

"I shouldn't fall in love with him!" said Nick vigorously, his eyes playful now that the man seemed on the point of leaving. "He's not just a pretty face, you know. He's a closet intellectual. And a secret rebel. Wishful and full of righteous anger!"

Behind glazed eyes the man good-naturedly smiled off the confusion that Nick was trying to foist on him, and turned and walked back slowly and diffidently to his place against the wall.

317

"You know, you might have helped me out with him," said Nick, "instead of sitting there saying nothing. It's not good enough, eh? Still shutting yourself off in self-disparagement or something when other people need something you've got to give. It doesn't do!" His voice and mannerisms played their usual games with his seriousness.

"Yeah, I know, I'm sorry," said Simon, grateful at the chastisement for confronting him with the demands of reality. "I know I should have helped." His eyes went to the man, propped back against the wall, with confused pity and a tug of outrage.

"Helplessly in love with you! I can't think why," Nick said. "Poor weaponless old queen! You see, the gay movement does struggle through to a bit more freedom, a bit more ease. Well, I know you see. Maybe not much freedom, and not much ease, yet. But still more than we had. And if things have become easier for you, if you've become stronger, it's through your struggles, eh?"

Simon nodded slowly. "Yes, yes, Nick, you're right, you're right. You know, even a couple of years ago I had no hope of having a relationship with anybody. I suppose I had to struggle – to find an identity. I had to struggle to be treated as an equal. Even as a human being. By anyone." And suddenly a pain reached up inside him and drew his eyes shut, stranding him in the stifling darkness of himself like a cupboard.

"And still I didn't get the love I wanted," he said.

"You still have to struggle with your expectations," said Nick tenderly. "That struggle goes on." In his blindness Simon felt Nick's hand brush his own, gentle and yet firm, reassuring and yet warning. "And so do all the others," he said.

Simon opened his eyes. For a moment the dingy hall seemed brightly lit.

From the Maori band came a shrug of yearning chords, and then a distant voice began, "All alone at the end of the evening . . ."

"Let's have a dance," said Nick, getting to his feet at once wearily and purposefully. "I'm not as young as I was, and I know you don't particularly want to, but there's nothing like a little dance to help you fight back. Come on, doctor's orders!"

Simon rose diffidently. Trying to give himself up to the dance was strange, he had to coax the music into his limbs like blood into frozen toes. The life hurt as it returned. Despite himself, his eyes slipped away from watching Nick's heavy determined movements, and glimpsed Martin there, a few feet away, abandoned to the dance, head thrown back a little like a flower opening to the sun. Martin's eyes bobbed over and saw Simon, and he smiled affectionately, and then again at the tall bearded man opposite him, whose features seemed now soft and yielding, as if the grimness had been melted quite away.

318

"You know I've always been a dreamer," came the singer's voice, with a sharp edge of self-appraisal. "But the dreams I've had lately . . ."

Simon felt his movements becoming more eloquent. He felt his balance becoming more certain. Again and again his lifted feet, his bending back, would carry his body into unknown empty space and return it safely to equilibrium.

"So put me on the highway," sang the singer longingly, "and show me a sign, and take it to the limit, one more time . . ."

Then the music died slowly away, like a summer sunset, and there came an expectant hush.

"Oh," said Nick disappointedly, "have they finished?"

Simon shrugged wistfully. Voices rustled around them like cicadas.

The small and previously unnoticed lead-singer of the band stepped tentatively forward, nervously fingering the microphone. The sound of his soft speaking voice came strangely over the hall, which seemed to be still quivering with musical exuberance. "Well, that's it, brothers and sisters. We'd just like to say how pleased we were to play for you tonight, and that we hope some day you'll show us your support in return. Maybe some of you came out to meet the Land March not so long ago, and perhaps some of you from Auckland have been to the sit-in on Bastion Point. And we hope that perhaps we'll see some of you joining in the protests about the dawn raids on the islanders. Brown people like us, eh? You know, well – the islanders are here now, they're a part of our past, a part of our lives." He had seemed shy and clumsy at first, but as he warmed to his topic, his voice became as convincing as music. He was like a speck in the bush that had suddenly become a rare bird, thought Simon, drawing all eyes to watch, all ears to listen. "And – we have to accept our past, and grow from it, whatever it is, eh? We can't cut ourselves off from it, because away from it – you know, how will we grow? We'll be without roots. We have to fight, like you have to, to make a good future out of a hard past. And you know, we have a saying, eh – *Tama tu, tama ora. Tama noho, tama mate.* It's the one who stands up and fights who lives, who is healthy: the one who just sits down is sick and dies."

He paused, glowing now in the gathered silence, his whole body shimmering with purposefulness. He is strong, thought Simon. He is beautiful. He has mana.

Nick touched Simon's hand. "You see," he said to him quietly, "it's struggle that gives us dignity too."

The speech was over with a call to a meeting. The lights went up on the stage, and the band began to pack up. Voices surged up again at once; and all around one could see eyes flaring with the need to be reassured that they had found someone for the night after all, or with the desperation of trying to find someone now. Nick touched Simon's arm and gestured questioningly with his brows, and Simon turned and moved with him through the jostling excited crowd towards the exit.

Out of the corner of his eye he saw Martin, just a few feet behind him, arm in arm with the tall bearded man. They were talking and laughing quietly into one another's ears; their faces seeming as softly radiant as the Maori orator's.

Their purpose and their dignity came from affection and compassion.

And they too, Simon thought, were a wonderful sight. As Martin's eyes met his, he smiled tentatively. And waved goodbye.

Outside the wind was raging. Nick paused just ahead of Simon, waiting for him to catch up, his eyes sweeping the storm-tossed street. A newspaper placard had been tumbled over and was drifting along the pavement, squealing noisily. The leaves of the flax in the road-island were bowed over, one after another bobbing up a little only to be pushed forcefully back down. In a pool of light over the crossing, little figures from the dance could be seen staggering heads down into the giant gust that guarded the corner.

"Sometimes I love the wind!" said Nick with relish, turning to look encouragingly at Simon, his words carried off even before he finished them. He buried his hands determinedly in his pockets and sauntered out, the wind at once trying to tug him its way.

Simon trudged beside, his chin digging into his chest. For the moment there was no need to decide if their paths should branch. They walked on, pushing into the wall of air, passing through the middle of town, which looked besieged and deserted.

Nick suddenly ducked inside a shop doorway and leant against a window where there was some shelter. "I'm going to have a cigarette," he called out to Simon, still hovering on the windswept pavement. "Come in and have chat for a moment."

Simon went into the doorway, and propped himself beside Nick, his head pressed back against the glass. The wind bayed at the mouth of the doorway, struggling to reach them.

"I don't know about you," said Nick softly, breathing smoke out leisuredly beneath dreamy eyes, "but I've decided I'm heading for the library bogs. I feel it's a night full of wildness. You never know who you might find! Why don't you come with me? It might do you good."

In the trackless waste the idea beckoned Simon like a mirage. And yet his answer came with the cool lack of compromise of one who has learnt just how hard it is to find water in the desert. "No, I won't come," he said. "All I remember now of trying to be promiscuous is problems. The problems of delusion. Of disappointment. The problem of responsibility. The fear of exploiting, the fear of being exploited. Just the same set of problems, in fact, I find in trying to be monogamous.

Neither is a solution to the other, nor a solution in itself."

There was a pause. "Well, you're right, of course," said Nick, unexpectedly sadly, and suddenly his arm came round Simon's shoulders and briefly hugged him. "I'm trying to have both, so I should know. No, I'm not protected against anything, I'm not escaping or solving anything."

We all remain so fragile, thought Simon, we all remain so precarious. But at least, at least we can touch one another. His arm went awkwardly round Nick's big back, padded with his heavy coat. Outside the doorway the wind yelped and snarled. The touch may be so little, thought Simon, and our bodies are so vast and empty; the touch may be so short, and our lives are so long and empty. But, look, feel, it is there. For a moment he sensed they both knew together this strength of gentle touching for what it was: real, however fleeting, however vulnerable.

"But what alternatives do we have?" said Nick softly. "Should we give up trying to have sexual relationships at all?"

Simon smiled. "No, we can't do that, can we?" he said. "We can't give up having an involvement with other human beings. We don't even have a meaning except in the context of other human beings."

Smoke was curling about Nick's face. His brows were solemn and furrowed in thought, his eyes surrounded by little cracks like an old painting. "And so often," he said, "our compassion seems to speak better through our bodies than our words."

"Yes," said Simon dreamily, "sex is so direct. And so – so intense. It's as if it were an intensified version of the way we want to relate to people in general."

Nick's hand round Simon's shoulders pulled them closer to him, and his voice, soft but just loud enough to be heard above the wind, seemed to gather the restrained elation of some scientist checking discoveries with a colleague. "Yes, exactly. People who have possessive and exploitative personal relationships believe in a world run for possession, eh? By means of exploitation. But we – we believe in a world run for everyone's fulfilment. Through sharing. Don't we?"

There was a silence. "That's not going to happen tomorrow," Simon said quietly.

"It's not going to happen without a long hard struggle. Perhaps it's not going to happen in our lifetimes. And the same with our relationships."

"What do you mean?"

"We both – in our ways – want to have relationships between equals. Relationships that fulfil needs mutually. Through sharing resources. But – we live in a world that doesn't work that way. Doesn't think, doesn't feel that way. And so – trying to achieve the relationships we want is this constant struggle, against enormous odds. Hundreds of years of thinking of relationships in terms of possessing and using. Of one who enjoys and one who services."

"Of putting something in only to get something out," added Simon slowly. "Those ideas don't just motivate other people. They lie in ambush in ourselves."

"For us, Simon, it will always be a struggle, always. But that doesn't make it any the less worthwhile, eh?"

The wind could be heard still grumbling, but it sounded to Simon as if for a moment it knew it was shut out.

"I like to imagine," he said dreamily, his head leaning back against the glass, "the world when the resources of affection and communication are shared equally."

"How do you imagine it?" Nick said.

"People won't be discriminated against just because of what they look like. Or how old they are. There won't be any such things as monogamy or promiscuity. There will be so much closeness to go round that no one will ever need to be afraid that they won't get their share. No one will need to hoard it. Nor demand it with menaces, nor take it by violence. Love – love itself will be available to everyone, including the old and the ugly."

"But that world, Simon, you and I will never live in. We've just got to be content with being among the ones who laboured to build it. And with coping with reality as best we can."

Simon nodded slowly. "I'm not going to stop trying," he said.

"Well, now I'm going to cope by going to the bogs."

Simon laughed, and slipped his hand from Nick's shoulders. "And I'm going home," he said.

He pulled himself up and began to move towards the doorway, but turned, and grasped Nick's hand fondly, holding tight the warmth and softness contained in its solidity. "Thank you Nick for offering me ways to understand," he said.

Nick said, "Thank *you*, for helping me to understand." He squeezed Simon's hand and gave a shrug of a smile. "Come and see me tomorrow morning," he said, "and we'll go to the islanders' defence meeting together." And then their grasp fell apart, their fingers slid from one another back into emptiness.

As for affection, thought Simon, one must give what one has, and take what there is.

He stepped out of the doorway into the wind, and turned to Nick as he followed after. They waved briefly to one another, their goodbyes snapped up and swallowed by the wind; and swung away quickly in their opposite directions.

Simon breasted the wind, pleased with his own strength. He climbed the endless steps to the Terrace, he wound up the steep hill past the university, breathing easily. The climb became gentler, and soon he turned down the sheltered path to his basement.

He switched on the light and the heater, and drew the curtains. The room was not too cold. He sank into his armchair.

The future opened out before him, its uncertainty no longer a threat but a challenge. Perhaps he would take these years of experience back home, or to somewhere new. He would take them to the gay liberation group with him, and to others like it. He would share them with old friends, and new friends; and new lovers.

He paused, his eyes going round the room.

So it all had not turned out as he wanted? No, it certainly had not. But it made up a life. In a time.

Tired, he laid his hands on the arms of the chair, preparing to get up to go to bed. There were clean sheets to go to. He had changed them that morning – in case Martin came back.

He was crying. From somewhere far away and long ago within him, sobs whirled up and took him by the shoulders and shook him, like a lifeless doll. Tears carried him away like the waters of a broken dam. A voice wept inside him, like an uncomprehending child, again and again. I want the world to be other, I cannot bear the world like this, even if you tell me it must be like it. I cannot bear it. I want it to be as a dream. Let the world be as I dream.

The tears flowed down, over his face, over his whole body, as if some part of himself were melting away.

After a while, he seemed to come suddenly upon himself sitting there. Pulling himself to his feet, he hunted about for a tissue. Now a gentle pain was stroking him soothingly along the chestbone. He went into the bathroom, and caught sight of his tear-stained face in the mirror. Stopping, he touched the glass tenderly. He reached for his comb and attentively combed his hair. Then he gave his nose a final blow and wiped it, and cleaned his teeth.

He put himself carefully into bed. And closed his eyes. Slowly, steadily, the tide of sleep surged up to where he lay beached, and carried him away.

He woke early, at once unable to retrieve unconsciousness. Yet getting up, drawing the curtains on weather still grey, he felt mysteriously relaxed: strangely free of a little weight, strangely clear of vision.

He dressed with care, singing a little to himself, and made some breakfast. He wondered how Martin was greeting the day. It wasn't fair – but he pushed that thought away. He had a wash, and put on a jacket, and set off for Nick's place.

It was a little milder, the wind had dropped a bit, the clouds were higher.

Well, he thought, as he walked, so he was still learning, still coming to understand. And from understanding came strength. And a strength to be shared.

A sudden gust knocked him off balance, as he turned the corner to begin the descent to Nick's place. And the view opened out before him. The weathered old houses balanced surefootedly on the precarious slopes plunging all around, the bush trickling down between them. The wind bounded up the spreading valley, tugging at Simon's hair. Beyond the valley's mouth, the mountains slid or leapt into the shadowy water on either side; and past the wave-lashed heads, the Pacific glinted silvery, vanishing somewhere unimaginably distant into the sky. For a second, a split second, the sun broke through the clouds at last, spotlit the brown and leaden landscape here and there with pools of light and detail, and then was gone again; and was more precious in that half-glimpse than if it had been shining all day.

ALSO ON OUR FICTION LIST

Tom Wakefield
Mates

Cyril and Len meet up doing National Service in the 1950s. They begin a life together which reflects the ups and downs, changes and continuities in the position of gay men over a quarter of a century. Comic and sad by turns, *Mates* shows just how extraordinary the lives of ordinary gays can be, sensitively portrayed by a novelist with a well established reputation.

'It's refreshing to come across a writer who knows exactly what he's doing and does it resoundingly well' (Peter Ackroyd, *Spectator*).

'Tom Wakefield is one of our most engaging of novelists' (Valentine Cunningham, *Times Literary Supplement*).

'He manages to construct a character, ordinary and everyday on the outside, with a rich and individual interior . . . weaving a complex structure out of the simplest, most direct observations and intuitions' (*Sunday Times*).

'A writer with the gift of leaving things raw' (Edward Blishen, *Guardian*).

Ian Everton
Alienation

A highly emotive novel from the gay movement, set in the context of a gay group struggling for survival in a homophobic North of England city. Like their new-found friends, lovers Peter and Jon try to make a better life for themselves; but the real and ideal worlds rarely coincide.

'Ian Everton is to be congratulated on having the courage to write a book that asks uncomfortable questions about gay identities' (*Voices*).

'Will probably appeal to fewer readers than some other recent gay fiction, but it seems to me much closer to our real situation, much truer . . . I recommend it to any reader' (Ian Young, *Body Politic*).

'Powerful . . . fascinating . . . complex yet stimulating. *Alienation* draws you up short: you can't dismiss it with a few syrupy words of praise. The skein of romanticism which was wrapped round the core of Gay Liberation's ideals has been torn to shreds in this book' (*Gay Scotland*).

David Rees
The Estuary

A further novel from the author of *The Milkman's On His Way*, centring on Luke, young, attractive, but totally selfish, who surprises himself and those around him when he gets involved with an older gay man after breaking up with his girlfriend Cheryl.

'Highly readable, and once begun is difficult to put down. It examines sympathetically and realistically the complexities of homo, hetero and bisexual relationships, and the irrationalities, uncertainties, doubts and suspicions which surround love and sex . . . Highly recommended' (Michael Griffiths, *Time Out*).

The Milkman's On His Way

Teenager Ewan Macrae's struggle for a positive gay identity is charted with sensitive frankness in this bestselling novel.

'A better account of gay coming–of–age is not to be had' (*Mister*).

Giovanni Vitacolonna
A Sweet and Sour Romance

Through a series of letters and diary entries spanning the last decade, we follow Sal's quest for personal, cultural and sexual identity as he plunges from the Midwest into the sexual whirlpool of San Francisco and then off in search of a new life in Italy.

'Races along, funny and stylishly written . . . try it for fun' (*Night Out*).

FICTION ANTHOLOGIES

Richard Dipple (ed)
Cracks in the Image

'A superb collection of short stories by gay men from both sides of the Atlantic' (*City Limits*).

Stephen Airey
Messer Rondo and other stories by gay men

Twelve short stories and one novella make up this collection of fiction by both new and established gay male writers.

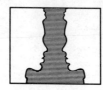 Gay Men's Press is an
independent publishing project
set up to produce books relevant
to the male gay movement and to
promote the ideas of gay liberation.

Our full catalogue is available from:

Gay Men's Press
P O Box 247
London N15 6RW
England